JONATHAN JANZ

THE DARK GAME

This is a **FLAME TREE PRESS** book

Text copyright © 2019 Jonathan Janz

FLAME TREE PRESS
6 Melbray Mews, London, SW6 3NS, UK
flametreepress.com

Distribution and warehouse:
Baker & Taylor Publisher Services (BTPS)
30 Amberwood Parkway, Ashland, OH 44805
btpubservices.com

Publisher's Note: This is a work of fiction. Names, characters, places, and
incidents are a product of the author's imagination. Locales and public names
are sometimes used for atmospheric purposes. Any resemblance to actual
people, living or dead, or to businesses, companies, events, institutions, or
locales is completely coincidental.

Thanks to the Flame Tree Press team, including:
Taylor Bentley, Frances Bodiam, Federica Ciaravella, Don D'Auria,
Chris Herbert, Matteo Middlemiss, Josie Mitchell, Mike Spender,
Cat Taylor, Maria Tissot, Nick Wells, Gillian Whitaker.

The cover is created by Flame Tree Studio with
thanks to Nik Keevil and Shutterstock.com.
The font families used are Avenir and Bembo.

Flame Tree Press is an imprint of Flame Tree Publishing Ltd
flametreepublishing.com

A copy of the CIP data for this book is available from the British Library
and the Library of Congress.

HB ISBN: 978-1-78758-187-6
PB ISBN: 978-1-78758-185-2
ebook ISBN: 978-1-78758-188-3
Also available in FLAME TREE AUDIO

Printed in the US at Bookmasters, Ashland, Ohio

JONATHAN JANZ

THE DARK GAME

FLAME TREE PRESS
London & New York

'The wizard stirs, opens his eyes, and looks at the reluctant boy. "Oh, you'll get your heart broken," he says. "Is that what you're waiting to hear? It'll be broken, all right. But you'll never get anything done if you walk around with an unchipped heart. That's the way of it, boy."'
Peter Straub
Shadowland

'"Fancy thinking the Beast was something you could hunt and kill!" said the head. For a moment or two the forest and all the other dimly appreciated places echoed with the parody of laughter. "You knew, didn't you? I'm part of you?"'
William Golding
Lord of the Flies

'The muses are ghosts, and sometimes they come uninvited.'
Stephen King
Bag of Bones

#1 Internationally Bestselling Author

Mr. Roderick Wells

Requests the honor of your presence at his estate on
May 26th for a six-week writing retreat.

From the multitude of applicants, you and nine others have
been selected for the opportunity of a lifetime.
One of you will become
the next Legendary Author.

Please find enclosed:
One airline ticket
A contract outlining Mr. Wells's expectations

★ Contract must be returned by mail no later than May 1st.
Any mention of the retreat will automatically void the contract.
Absolute secrecy is required.

PART ONE
MAGIC

CHAPTER ONE

Lucy reached up, fingered the sweaty fabric of the blindfold. "Mind if I take this off?"

No answer from her driver. Around her the limo juddered like a malfunctioning carnival ride.

Relax, Lucy told herself. *You'd have been a fool to pass up this opportunity.*

She laced her fingers in her lap, the limo shuddering harder. She imagined a barren landscape out there, the trees stunted, the ground scorched. Like her future, if this didn't work out.

Lucy balled her hands into fists.

It occurred to her she hadn't even asked the driver for identification. No one knew she was here, and she wasn't allowed a phone. She chewed a thumbnail, a hundred horror movies flashing through her head. Why was it always a woman who got hacked to pieces?

The limo rumbled over a rougher surface. Branches thwacked the roof with appalling violence, the antenna twanging. Lucy's stomach performed a somersault as the limo jounced over a pothole and slewed sickly.

Hands trembling, she thumbed the window control, but he'd evidently engaged the child lock.

"At least let me have some air," she said through her teeth.

An endless pause. Then her window lowered and a muggy breeze flooded the car. Her heartbeat had begun to decelerate when something – a fingerlike branch, she assumed – harrowed her shoulder. She gasped and a grisly scene flickered through her mind: the forest closing in around her, eager to spill her blood, the trees groping for her like a shambling horde of ghouls.

Dry-mouthed, Lucy asked him to raise the window.

"Sure," he answered. "And you can take the blindfold off if you want."

She burrowed her fingers under the slick fabric and worked it upward until, with a final tug, it came loose. She flung it aside, the dreary May afternoon a punishing contrast to the darkness of the blindfold.

When her eyes adjusted, she realized they were rolling through a murky forest, the swirled trunks and gnarled, low-hanging branches reminiscent of the Brothers Grimm. At their approach a screeching blackbird tumbled from its perch, veered toward the windshield, and swooped over the limo's roof. Heart pounding, she peered through the rear window after it, but all she could make out were massed shadows and ancient trees. She half expected to glimpse a witch leering at her through the undergrowth.

After a time, the corridor of trees widened into a grassy clearing. Across it, she spotted a lone figure leaning against a tree. As they drew closer, she noted the scarlet tank top, the khaki cargo shorts, the faded leather Birkenstocks. The man was perhaps thirty, very handsome, skin smooth and tan, his curly brown hair not quite shoulder length.

The limo stopped. Lucy flung open her door, sucked in a great heave of cedar-tinged air, climbed out, and stretched luxuriously. The driver opened the trunk, hefted out her suitcase, and without making eye contact returned to the car. A moment later, the limo described a gradual loop and disappeared the way they'd come.

Lucy studied the fantastical forest. No sign of a house. Or a path, for that matter. Was this whole event a practical joke? The worry had plagued her since she received the invitation. Her first thought upon being invited was that they'd made a mistake, that she was too successful for a contest like this. Her second, more upsetting, reaction was the old fear, the suspicion her early success was dumb luck, that she'd be eaten alive by the other contestants, who were no doubt younger and more talented.

But Lucy couldn't be a has-been at age thirty-three. Could she?

The stranger approached. There were reddish indentations on his temples where a blindfold had been. He raised his arms, stretched, the movement clearly intended to show off his lean but sculpted biceps. He sighed and halted, his bare toes only a foot from hers.

"Tommy Marston," he said, hand out.

She shook. "Lucy Still."

He narrowed his eyes, appraising her. "You look like a YA writer. Am I right?"

She considered telling him of her early success, transforming his arrogant expression into a look of awe. She could boast of the advance she'd received at age nineteen, the starred reviews in *Every Important Writing Publication*, her instant literary fame.

But then he'd ask The Question: *What have you written lately?*

"She's forty minutes late," a deep voice called.

Tommy scowled at the man emerging from the woods. "How do you know that?"

The man waggled his wrist.

"I thought we couldn't have technology," Tommy said.

"That's not what the contract stipulated," the man answered. "Anyway, this watch is analog." He was taller than Tommy, the white t-shirt and dark blue jeans stretched taut by bulging muscles. He reminded Lucy of a college football player, one who's been kicked off the team after too many arrests. He had a crew cut the color of weak coffee, wintry blue eyes. His mouth was fixed in a permanent smirk.

He nodded at Lucy. "Bryan Clayton. You are?"

She told him.

Bryan studied her a moment, then gestured toward the woods. "It's majestic in there. Poplars, willows, tamarack, hickory. Even a grove of Fraser firs. Extremely rare for Indiana."

Tommy frowned. "How do you know where we are?"

"Innate sense of direction."

Tommy looked at her. "Innate sense of bullshit."

"We're southeast of Chicago," Bryan said. "That puts us in Indiana, right?" He reached into his hip pocket, brought out a folded sheet of paper. "My driver told me to follow these directions once you guys arrived." He favored her with an indulgent look. "That is, if the princess is ready."

Asshole, she thought.

"Time to get my hands dirty," Bryan said, shouldering a hunter-green backpack. "I'm ready to show Wells I came here to win."

Tommy glanced at her. "So did we."

Bryan eyed him. "You'll be gone in a week."

"At least I'm not some fake man's man."

Bryan's smirk faded. "I write fact-based survival stories."

A corner of Tommy's mouth rose. "Personality like yours, I bet you know a lot about being alone."

One moment they were nose-to-nose, the next Tommy was spinning and crumpling to the grass with Bryan atop him. Tommy's forearm was pinned behind his back, Bryan levering the wrist higher until Lucy was sure the arm would burst its socket.

"*Okay okay!*" Tommy yelled.

Bryan straddled Tommy's back, his big arms flexing as he drove Tommy's wrist higher, nearly to his shoulder blades now. Bryan leaned down. His square jaw strained a few inches over Tommy's reddened face, which was mashed sideways in the grass. "Gonna talk shit now?"

A high-pitched keening issued from Tommy's throat.

"Get off him," Lucy said.

Tommy moaned. Any moment she expected to hear a sickening crunch.

"Call me fake again," Bryan said.

"I said get *off*," Lucy said, stepping toward them.

Bryan shot her a glance, something feral in his eyes. His face spread in a slow grin. Then he released Tommy and rocked back on his heels with a look of almost euphoric satisfaction.

Tommy groaned, his arm limp in the grass.

Bryan pushed to his feet. "Next time you mouth off, make sure you don't insult a collegiate wrestler."

"Prick," Tommy muttered, rising. His overstressed arm hung limply at his side. Lucy didn't think it was broken, but he'd be sore for days.

"Can we go to Wells's house now?" she asked.

"Sure," Bryan said. He started toward the forest but paused and looked at her. "I hope you remember what happens when people cross me."

CHAPTER TWO

Rick Forrester gazed up at a twist of ivy, vines, and slender green branches.

WELLS FOREST, the sign read. A PLACE OF MAGIC.

His driver had told him to wait here for the next writer, but now that he was alone in this primordial forest, a discordant note sounded over and over at a volume his ears couldn't detect but his bones could.

He winced, slapped the back of his neck, and examined his palm. The dead mosquito resembled a smudge of mascara streaked with red greasepaint.

Maybe coming here hadn't been such a brilliant idea.

A white limousine rolled down the lane and stopped beside him. The window descended and the driver, a young guy with a close-cropped ginger beard, leaned toward him. "I presume you're one of the authors?"

"What gave me away, my profound gaze?"

The driver got out and opened the door for a young woman with punkish blond hair and a couple dozen bracelets. Nice figure, but it was toward her clothes that Rick's eyes were drawn. Her frilly top was purple and white, her beige skirt adorned with colorful buttons. One said MARK DARCY'S LOVE SLAVE; another read IF YOU'RE NOT CAREFUL, I'LL KILL YOU IN MY NOVEL. She donned a pair of tortoiseshell glasses and gazed dubiously about the forest. "This is Roderick Wells's estate?"

"You're Elaine Kovalchyk, aren't you?" the driver asked.

She grunted. "I wouldn't have gotten in your car if I wasn't."

The driver wrestled an immense suitcase from the trunk. "Then I'll leave you here."

"Wait, where is 'here'?" She glanced at Rick.

He nodded at the vine-twisted archway. Elaine lowered her

glasses to the tip of her nose, gazed at the sign. "What kind of magic we talking about?"

The driver executed a U-turn and motored away.

Her bracelets clinking, Elaine rolled her suitcase toward Rick. "You're not a serial killer, are you?"

"Gave that up years ago."

A hint of a smile. "Since you've been appointed my guardian, I think I should know your identity."

"Rick Forrester."

"Where have I seen your work?" she asked.

"You ever read *Gruesome Unsolved Murders*?"

Her pink lips formed an impish smile. "Are you always this evasive?"

"I'm unpublished."

She flicked her hair off her forehead. "My profs at NYU said I was born to write dialogue."

"I'm sure it's better on the page."

She looked him up and down. "Unpublished, huh?"

"Guess the world isn't ready for my work."

"Shame. You'd look good in an author photo." She nodded at the archway. "Shall we?"

He waited for her and her refrigerator-sized suitcase to pass, then followed her down the trail.

"You're awfully coy, Mr. Forrester. A man your age, you've surely got *some* writing credits."

"I could make some up."

She stopped, peered at him over her glasses. "What other problems do you have?"

He moved past her. "Aside from being interrogated?"

"How old are you?"

"Thirty-five."

"Married?"

He adjusted his backpack. "Not at present."

"Which means you were."

Rick didn't bother explaining. He glanced up at the trees, but they were so dense, he could only make out the merest slivers of heather-colored sky. It hadn't rained today, but the clouds kept threatening.

"Want to hear about me?" she asked.

"Doubt I could stop you."

"I'm twenty-seven. Single, so far. I've been featured in the *Goose Neck Review* and the *Maryland Quarterly*."

"Those hunting magazines?"

"They're two of the most prestigious literary publications in America."

"Huh."

"You're sort of handsome for your age."

He cringed. "You make me feel like a creepy old man."

"Eight years isn't much," she said. "Too bad I'm not here to hook up."

If you knew what followed me, he thought, *I'd be the last man in the world you'd want to date.*

She moved ahead but kept talking. "I'm going to prove my parents wrong. Oh, they paid for my schooling, helped me that way. But they always assumed *this writing thing* was a phase. On holidays they'd ask me, thinking they were being subtle, if I'd contemplated changing over to some less starry-eyed pursuit."

"But they put you through college."

She glared at him over her shoulder. "They *tolerate* my lifestyle."

He let that hang. Hoped she wouldn't elaborate on her lifestyle, whatever that meant.

She halted. "When I win this competition, they'll stop acting like this is a lark."

"You didn't tell them you were coming?"

She gave him a sly smile. "You *are* cagey, Rick." Punching him lightly on the shoulder. "Looking for ways to get me disqualified?"

He opened his mouth to answer, thought better of it, then sidled around her.

"You agree with my parents?" she called after him.

"I don't know your parents."

"You're probably just like them. A political conservative."

He wasn't, but he'd rather catheterize himself with a lit sparkler than discuss politics.

To his relief, she ceased talking for several minutes. The trail threaded through blue-green groves of spruce, hulking stands of pine. At about the time Elaine began to complain of her acute thirst and her throbbing feet, the forest opened a little and revealed a dull glint of glass.

"Oh thank Christ," Elaine moaned.

They emerged into a vast, rising meadow of foxtail and wildflowers. Rick stopped and stared at the mansion situated at the summit.

For reasons he couldn't explain, he'd expected Roderick Wells to live in a contemporary house, something sleek and shimmering with windows. The mansion looming before him was much older and larger than he'd envisioned. Rick would never have said such a thing aloud for fear of sounding foolish, but there it was – the place looked *sinister*. Three stories tall, its many dormers and gables jutted forth in challenge, daring him to scale the hill and do his best to endure whatever tricks it had in store. The predominant façade was brick, though there were stretches of discolored stone. The mansion was in dire need of repairs. The covered porch leaned to the left, the faded ivory pillars splotched and peeling. One pane of a first-floor window was spiderwebbed; a couple shutters hung askew. The slate roof was short several shingles, though the pitch was so steep Rick couldn't imagine anyone replacing them. A soaring tower rose from the mansion's far side.

Rick peered at the tower and felt a chill breeze whisper over his skin.

"Think this is it?" Elaine asked.

He tried to smile. "What's wrong?"

She shivered, scratched her forearm. "I don't know. It's just so…"

"Imposing?"

"…*haunted housey*. I didn't expect it to be *this* secluded. If something goes wrong, how will anyone know?"

What's going to happen? he almost asked. But for some reason, faced with this towering, eldritch structure, it felt like tempting fate.

He began the long climb.

"Rick?"

He glanced backward, saw she hadn't moved. "Want me to lug that suitcase for you?"

She smiled, hunched her shoulders in a way he found endearing. If she expended less energy competing, she'd be a tick north of tolerable.

He grabbed the suitcase handle, and side by side, they began the hike through the knee-high grass. He caught a glimpse of a purple butterfly tattooed between her breasts but didn't comment on it. Instead he directed his gaze at the late-afternoon clouds, which were churning and muddy. He smelled rain in the air.

"Thanks," she said. "You're a gentleman."

"But not talented enough for the *Goose Egg Review*."

She gave him a shove. "*Goose* Neck."

As they trudged up the incline, he studied the mansion, estimated it was more than twenty thousand square feet.

She asked, "Why did you get divorced?"

"I never said I was married."

"Be enigmatic then." A pause. "Why are you single?"

Because anyone I love will die? Because something is following me, and half the reason I'm here is to escape it?

"Doesn't look like a place of magic to me," Elaine muttered.

It did to him, but of the wrong variety.

Wells's mansion looked like every ghost story he'd ever read.

CHAPTER THREE

At dusk there was a knock on Lucy's door. She opened it and beheld a scarlet-haired woman with a tiny, upturned nose and lime-colored eyes. She was younger than the writers Lucy had met, her green tank top and tattered jean shorts very snug.

"Anna Holloway," the young woman said. "I love your work."

A blush crept up Lucy's neck.

"*The Girl Who Died* got me into reading," Anna said.

Lucy glanced back at her bedroom. "Look, Anna, I'm not done unpacking and—"

"I highlighted all the naughty parts," Anna said. "Mom was furious when she caught me reading it. She called the librarian and ripped her a new asshole."

Lucy smiled despite herself.

"But it wasn't just the sex I liked, it was the writing. The *voice*." Anna took Lucy's hands, gave them a squeeze. "You're so *good*."

The present tense wasn't lost on Lucy.

"And when I heard you were here, I couldn't believe it. It'll be like having two teachers instead of one."

Lucy scoured the younger woman's face for traces of irony, but if Anna was acting, her performance was seamless.

Lucy forced a smile. "It's nice to know I still have a fan."

Anna gestured down the hallway. "We're supposed to gather on the front porch."

"Did Wells tell you that?"

Anna shook her head. "The maid – this miniature woman named Miss Lafitte – she told me to collect everyone."

Lucy nodded. "Okay, you tell the rest while I—"

"You're the last one." Anna gave an embarrassed little shrug. "I wanted to meet you alone, before the others monopolized you."

"Why, so they can ask me what went wrong?"

Anna sobered. "Your critics can fuck themselves."

Lucy laughed.

"My folks figured they were purifying me by sending me to Catholic school," Anna explained. "I got corrupted instead."

"I was homeschooled," Lucy said.

"I know. That's how you started writing. All that time on your hands."

Lucy frowned. Something about Anna's tone....

"Come on," Anna said. "You can unpack later."

Lucy fidgeted with the doorknob. She'd already done what she could with her makeup – not much – and brushed her teeth to rid her mouth of the dank travel taste. There was no reason to delay. Plus, if Wells was waiting....

She closed her door and followed Anna down the stairs. They stepped onto the covered porch, and with a cursory scan she noted they were still two shy of ten. Tommy leaned against a pillar talking with Elaine Kovalchyk. She'd struck Lucy as a bit of a smartass, the kind who tried too hard to be edgy. Bryan Clayton hunkered on the bottom porch step surveying the meadow. He would gaze for a while, then scribble in a notebook. No doubt cataloguing some piece of minutiae with which to annoy future readers. A black woman stood apart from the others. She was about five-ten and attractive. Her hair was drawn back in a simple bun, she wore a bold shade of magenta lipstick, and her sleeveless multicolored dress hung all the way to her open-toed sandals.

The man closest to the door turned and regarded Lucy. He was dour looking, with a scraggly growth of beard and large, mournful eyes. He reminded her of a refugee from some war-torn country.

Finally, someone older than she was.

A pack of cigarettes drooped from the pocket of his pale green shirt. He was about to light up when he caught Lucy watching him. "Smoke?"

She shook her head. His smile was kind, if a trifle nicotine-stained. He cupped his hands to light the cigarette.

Lucy introduced herself. He squinted at her, took her hand in both of his.

"I'm Marek," he said in a Russian accent.

"*Marek*," she repeated, trying to roll the *r* the way he had.

His smile widened. "That's good. You say it better than my friends."

He took a drag from his cigarette, expelled smoke from the side of his mouth. "I'm forty-one, in case you're wondering. People are always mistaking me for an older man." He tapped the cigarettes in his pocket. "Must be these."

They turned as a pudgy newcomer emerged from the mansion. Black hair, parted on one side, sloping shoulders. His short-sleeved dress shirt was pitted out, the pinstriped fabric clinging to pale, hairless arms. His pleated beige trousers looked expensive. Worsted wool, maybe. He surveyed the group through wire-framed spectacles.

"Who're you?" Tommy asked.

"Evan Laydon," the newcomer said. He took out a handkerchief and dabbed sweat from his brow. "It's a sauna out here."

"You need to get in shape," Bryan called over his shoulder.

Evan glanced at Lucy. "Have you met the resident survivalist?"

"Classic candidate for heart disease," Bryan said.

"I didn't know I was going to have a personal trainer," Evan muttered. His eyes shifted to something behind Lucy.

She turned and felt her stomach lurch. The man smiled at her. "Rick Forrester."

He had light brown eyes, a nice smile. He reminded her a bit of a young Harrison Ford, about whom she'd been fantasizing since adolescence.

"How long are we supposed to roast out here?" Evan demanded. He pinched his shirt, flapped it for ventilation.

Lucy crossed to the tall black woman and introduced herself.

"Sherilyn Jackson," the woman said, her accent Deep South. "I can't believe I'm actually here. Roderick Wells's estate. Where Corrina Bowen's career was born."

"I *love* her work," Anna said. "She's a national treasure."

Sherilyn put a hand to her chest, donned a dreamy expression. "I met her at a signing in Mobile. She was even more charming than her stories."

Lucy kept quiet. She enjoyed Bowen's work, but evidently not as much as Sherilyn and Anna did. After winning a contest like this fifty years ago, Corrina Bowen had skyrocketed to fame. Since then, she hadn't written many novels, but the few she had were hailed as classics of Southern Gothic literature. Years ago, *Variety* had deemed her William Faulkner's heir.

Anna glanced at Lucy. "You think the winner this time will be as famous as Bowen is?" She glanced up at the house. "God, what I wouldn't give to live in a place like this."

Evan mopped sweat from his brow. "I wonder what happened to the other nine in that contest," he said. "Anyone ever hear of them?"

"Who cares?" Anna said. "They faded into obscurity, like most writers do."

Lucy kept quiet. It was the exact question that had been plaguing her.

"I wrote Ms. Bowen a fan letter once," Rick said.

Sherilyn's eyebrows rose. "Did she respond?"

He nodded. "The most eloquent form letter I've ever read."

They all laughed.

"Am I the only one who's nervous?" Anna whispered.

"We all are," Sherilyn said. "No one knows what Roderick Wells is like."

"Sure we do," Evan said. "He's a throwback. Like Hemingway, without the bullfighting."

"But the same sexism," Elaine called as she and Tommy approached.

Evan waved a dismissive hand. "Nonsense. He's the reason I became an author."

"Is that right?" Tommy said, eyeing him. "What have you written?"

Evan raised his chin. "I edited the Columbia literary magazine for three semesters."

"That doesn't mean you can write," Elaine said.

Evan laughed incredulously.

Bryan mounted the steps, called to Evan, "Your boobs are jiggling."

Evan looked stricken.

Rick turned to Bryan. "There some reason why you're so nasty?"

Bryan returned Rick's stare. "It's people like you who do the most harm. I bet Evan surrounds himself with enablers."

"You're the one with issues," Lucy said.

"Oh yeah?" Bryan asked. "What's my issue, sweetheart?"

"You're a jackass."

Several of them laughed. Rick grinned at her. Bryan opened his mouth to answer, but a female voice interrupted, "I see you're already at each other's throats."

They turned and beheld a woman in a low-necked sable evening gown. She had long black hair and looked like a partygoer who'd just stepped onto the veranda for some air. Furthering the impression was the long-stemmed glass she carried, some clear drink undulating within.

"You the tenth writer?" Tommy asked.

"My husband is the artist in the family."

Anna's voice was wondering. "You're Mrs. Wells?"

"Amanda," she said.

They all supplied their names.

Marek looked around. "I thought there were going to be ten."

"The last man will arrive later," Mrs. Wells said.

"Car trouble?" Tommy asked.

"I doubt it," Mrs. Wells said.

Sherilyn asked, "Are you saying your husband deliberately delayed him?"

Choosing her words carefully, Mrs. Wells said, "One thing you must know about Roderick is that everything he does is for a reason." She eyed them each in turn. "Will you abide by the rules of our agreement, or would you prefer to go home?"

Bryan stepped forward. "I think I speak for everyone when I say we're grateful for the opportunity."

"You should be," a voice answered.

Lucy turned and discovered a figure peering at them through the doorway, just a shadow really, tucked in the dimness of the entryway. Lucy had been standing nearest the doorway, and now the other writers crowded nearer to better see Roderick Wells. Lucy squinted into the semidarkness but could only make out a pair of unblinking eyes, the hint of a pitiless smile.

Lucy realized she was holding her breath. Despite the fact that the man in the shadows was slightly stooped and ravaged by age, she sensed a power emanating from him, an indefinable thrum. Judging by the others' expressions, they felt it too.

Evan was the first to speak. "It's an honor to meet you, Mr. Wells."

Wells ignored that. "Before we proceed," he said, his voice cultured but slightly reedy, as if speaking cost him a great effort, "you must submit yourselves to me. You must prepare to withstand extreme conditions, both physical and emotional."

Sherilyn half grinned. "No one said there'd be a physical component."

"My dear," Mr. Wells said, "this experience will require *everything* from you. I give my blood, my tears…my very soul to my writing. I demand no less from my pupils."

There was a silence as that sank in.

Mr. Wells went on. "For the next six weeks, you will have no technology, save a laptop with word processing capabilities. You'll each have a printer. I have amassed an extensive library that is more than adequate for your research needs. We will, of course, provide food, lodging, whatever you require. However, if you leave the grounds, you will be banished from the property, never to return."

"Mr. Wells," Bryan said, his voice uncharacteristically shaky, "the contract made reference to an award – the Best in Show prize, so to speak – but the details were nebulous."

"Is that why you're here, Mr. Clayton? For prizes?"

Bryan opened his mouth, raised a placating hand, but Mr. Wells overrode him. "The winner will receive three million dollars."

Marek whistled softly. Tommy muttered, ".Hell, yeah."

Mr. Wells peered at them from his nest of shadows. "The money is merely a safety net, should your novels not prove lucrative.

"Which brings me," Mr. Wells went on in a stronger voice, "to the publishing contract. Two or three books with one of the major New York houses."

"I knew it!" Elaine said. Anna squeezed Lucy's arm.

Wells continued: "I have assurances from several editors that the publicity surrounding the retreat will warrant a sizable advance, with potential for a film tie-in, foreign rights, et cetera. The point is, you will have my involvement, instant fame, access to the best editors and marketing minds in the business. You all remember how Corrina Bowen got her start?"

The name elicited a smattering of enthusiastic comments.

Mr. Wells's voice washed over them: "For the first time in half a century, I'm opening my home to ten aspiring writers. You will receive the education of a lifetime. And for one lucky author, the chance to become immortal." He glanced at Lucy. "The next Corrina Bowen." His eyes shifted to Bryan. "Or the next Roderick Wells."

Bryan's grin was smug enough to turn Lucy's stomach.

"When you leave here," Mr. Wells went on, "you will tell no one what transpired. I want my secrets to remain my own and have no wish to see the market flooded with tell-all memoirs."

"No one would do that, Mr. Wells," Evan said.

"You're right," he answered, his voice taking on a raw, guttural edge. "Unless you want to face my wrath."

With that, Mr. Wells turned and, moving gingerly, receded into the house. They watched after him, speechless.

After a time, Mrs. Wells clapped her hands together. "If you're certain you'd like to spend the summer with us, despite the risks, let's get you out of this heat."

Lucy spoke up. "Risks?"

Mrs. Wells surveyed her with mild astonishment. "Yes, darling. Aren't there always risks?" She smiled, but the smile didn't go near her eyes.

Wordlessly, Mrs. Wells entered the house.

The others followed, but Rick lingered on the porch. Lucy studied his face, said, "What?"

He shook his head. "Just what the hell *did* happen to the other nine writers in the first contest?"

CHAPTER FOUR

When Lucy's career had been thriving, she'd been invited to read in dozens of public libraries. And though many had contained more books than Wells's private collection, none of them surpassed Wells's in elegance. Rectangular, illumined by wall sconces and table lamps, the high-ceilinged room was comprised of built-in bookcases, cozy leather chairs with matching ottomans, and rich oriental rugs. Yet despite the opulent furnishings, there hung a caul of dreariness over the room and subtle hints of disrepair. The tables and lamps were dusty, the colors of the book spines faded. A window along the eastern wall was marred by a lightning-jagged crack.

She shifted her gaze to study the immediate area. There were ten burnished mahogany chairs ranged in a semicircle, one of them empty. Facing them was a wine-colored wingback Lucy assumed was reserved for Wells. The writers had been arranged near a fireplace broad enough to accommodate a mid-sized car. Beneath the acrid odor of burning wood, Lucy detected the pleasing mildew of old books. She inhaled deeply of the scent, her tension ebbing.

She was about to ask Sherilyn if she'd met the tenth writer yet, when a man jogged into the room, his balding head peppered with sweat.

"I swear I was on time," he said, bracing himself on the back of the vacant chair. He gestured, out of breath. "My driver claimed he wasn't delaying me, but...I know he was going in circles. We passed the same...damned...farmhouse—"

"Save it," Bryan muttered. "Wells is about to address the group."

Lucy glanced at Rick, who looked like he'd tasted something sour. She recalled what Mrs. Wells had said: *One thing you must know about Roderick is that everything he does is for a reason.*

Lucy rose, introduced herself to the newcomer, whose name was Will Church. Rick, Sherilyn, and Marek also shook his hand. Will examined his sodden gray Chicago Cubs t-shirt. "I'm a mess. Do I have time to clean up?"

"I doubt it," Sherilyn said, not unkindly.

Lucy returned to her seat, studied Will from the corners of her eyes. His brown goatee was a shade darker than his curly hair; a small potbelly tented his shirt. He sat, folded one leg over the other, then decided against it and sat up straighter.

All ten of them in their chairs, the group lapsed into silence. In the flickering firelight, Lucy stole glances at the others and reminded herself she belonged. The problem was, they all looked so damned *together*. Sure, they were a motley bunch physically, but their faces exuded confidence. They hadn't been battered by the industry the way Lucy had.

If you lose, there are always the pills, her agent's voice reminded her. *Sometimes it's easier just to give up. Isn't that right, Lucy Goosy?*

Her stomach muscles clenched at the mocking voice, which belonged to Fred Morehouse, founder of the Morehouse Literary Agency. The man who brokered seven-figure deals in his sleep. The man who emotionally destroyed you when the whim struck.

It wasn't the industry, Fred Morehouse told her. *It was you. I gave you your shot, and you blew it. You let us all down, little lady.*

She closed her eyes, her toes curling inside her shoes.

Focus, she reminded herself. *Focus.*

As they'd been instructed, she'd brought her work-in-progress. She'd even rehearsed in the mirror as though this were a televised reality show.

Question: *Why do you write?*

Answer: *Because in real life, everyone lies. Only in fiction do people tell the truth.*

Question: *What makes you think you can win this competition?*

Answer: *Because I wrote a great book once, and I know I can do it again.*

She assumed the dreaded question would come eventually. Wells had done his homework, after all.

Question: *If your book was so wonderful, why did your career crash and burn?*

Answer: *Because I experienced success too early, received too big an advance. Then I realized I wasn't as skilled as I thought, and I crumbled under the pressure.*

Yes, Lucy thought. Painful, raw, humiliating. But true. And truth was everything.

Roderick Wells entered the room and her thoughts scattered.

Now that she saw Wells in better light, he resembled an old-time Hollywood movie star. He was tall, his silver hair slicked back and a trifle wavy, just like the characters in those classic films from the thirties and forties. He wore charcoal trousers and a pale blue shirt open at the collar. It was obvious he'd once been exceptionally handsome, but his age showed around his eyes and the loose folds of his neck. His forehead was deeply furrowed. There were liver spots on his cheeks, white whiskers along his jaw that his razor had somehow missed. His hair, too, she realized upon closer inspection, needed a good trim. It stuck up in stray tufts around his ears. His eyes were a trifle bloodshot and underscored by discolored pouches of skin.

Wells eased into the wingback chair and took in their scrutiny. "Are you dismayed by my appearance?"

"You're exactly the way I pictured," Anna said.

Wells looked pleased. "Truly?"

"Not me," Tommy said. "I expected someone a lot older."

Wells laughed softly. "Any other surprises?" he asked.

"Your house is so far off the grid, I feel like we're on another planet," Sherilyn said.

"Removing myself from society," Wells said, "was the only way to quarantine my madness."

They laughed, and a good deal of the tension dissipated.

"Ah," Wells said. "It's nice to see your real faces."

They laughed again, but not as heartily this time. Lucy caught a few of her peers casting furtive glances at each other.

"Now that you've seen I do in fact exist, I'd like you to bring me your works-in-progress." He patted an end table. "Place them right here."

As one, they complied. Anna got there first, Tommy and Elaine trailing after. Marek placed his atop the pile and was followed by Will, Sherilyn, and Evan. Lucy went next with Rick following.

As Lucy returned to her seat, she noticed Bryan had been waiting with his neatly bound manuscript clutched before him. Jaw set, he placed his novel on top of Rick's.

Wells stood. "That's an efficient beginning, and as we all know, openings are vital to a great story."

Murmured assent from the group. Something tickled at Lucy's mind, a nameless stir of misgiving. She thrust it away, told herself she had to focus. Wells might pick her novel first.

"Therefore," Wells said, bending to scoop up the manuscripts, "from the flames of this sacrifice may you rise anew."

And with that, Wells hurled the manuscripts into the blazing fire.

CHAPTER FIVE

Tommy leaped to his feet. Several of them gasped, and Elaine said something Lucy couldn't make out. Then came a pregnant, unbelieving silence. Though fifteen feet away, Lucy felt a blast of heat as the thick reams ignited. Loose sheets of paper curled and blackened, sending charred scraps with glowing red edges floating out of the fireplace. Wells regarded the group, his expression serene.

"What the hell?" Tommy said hoarsely.

"Mr. Wells," Elaine said, "I'm sure everyone backed up their work. Destroying one copy is hardly ensuring a new start."

For the first time, Marek's affable demeanor slipped. "But it's the only copy we have *here*."

Lucy's lips formed a grim line.

Wells stared steadily back at her. "You disapprove, Miss Still?"

"It was cruel," Lucy heard herself saying.

"Perhaps so," he allowed. "But it was necessary."

"But sir," Evan broke in, "the gesture was symbolic at best. Even if the others didn't back up their work – a possibility I find difficult to fathom—"

Tommy shot him a fierce glare.

Evan went on uneasily, "—I'm sure we all remember what we'd written in our novels."

Tommy muttered something under his breath.

Wells interlaced his fingers. "Do you have a comment, Mr. Marston?"

Tommy glowered at him, licked his lips.

"Nothing?" Wells asked.

Tommy stood there mutely, seeming to shrink before Wells's withering stare.

"Then sit down."

Looking ill, Tommy did.

Wells surveyed the group. "I did you all the greatest favor anyone can do for a new writer."

He caught the way Elaine shifted in her chair. "And before you claim to be anything but a novice, remember that I've read your work and know your limitations."

Elaine folded her arms, her bracelets clinking together.

Wells sat and sighed contentedly. "An effective teacher goes to extremes to assist his pupils. Before I can make you better writers, I must make you stronger people." He studied them as he spoke, and when his dark eyes lingered on one of their party for longer than the others, Lucy scooted forward to see who it was.

Rick. Oddly enough, given her earlier reaction to him, she'd forgotten all about him during the manuscript burning. He looked like a man who was being punished for some unexpiated crime, who was both anguished by his punishment yet darkly pleased by it. The result was an expression both ghastly and ancient, as though Rick were an elderly man masquerading as a young one.

Wells said, "Don't mourn your novel, Mr. Forrester. You're about to see the world as it really is."

Wells stared at Rick.

Whose expression transformed into horror.

CHAPTER SIX

Rick was drowning in Wells's eyes, those obsidian pools sucking him into their icy depths.

Yessss, Wells cooed in a voice Rick was certain only he could hear. *Yes, Mr. Forrester, you see what I am, don't you?*

Rick tried to look away but couldn't. Wells had him in his grasp, and he knew it. Knew how powerless Rick was against this mental onslaught.

Look at me, Rick. Look…at my…face.

Wells changed.

Wells's cheekbones protruded and pulsed, his chin elongated. The teeth tapered into bestial points, the lips stretching in a joker's leer. But the eyes…those coal-black eyes…they pinned Rick to the chair, crucified him, and reveled in his torment.

Rick realized why no one could find a recent image of Roderick Wells, why he never showed up to accept awards. Because if someone did gaze at the man too long

(*he's not a man*)

it would drive you insane, you'd get lost forever in those murky black tarns, those *wells* – the aptness of the name slammed into him – and once you sank into those stygian waters, you'd be lost, irretrievable. Jesus God, couldn't the others see what was happening?

He's a demon, Rick thought. *A beast.*

Wells's eyes began to glow. *I am infinitely more than that, Mr. Forrester. I am your eternal fate. Now drown in my eyes. Suffocate in my embrace.*

Rick fought for control, strained to move his arms, his feet, to utter a whimper, for Christ's sake. But he couldn't, could only watch in impotent dread as the black eyes grew lambent, the hellfire within raging. The leer broadened, the teeth like dripping pikes. Wells's face became a lunatic death mask, and when he spoke, his lips never moved.

I know what haunts you, Wells gloated. *I can summon it here to claim you.*

Rick's vision grayed, his breathing reed thin. But unconsciousness would be a haven now. Just when he believed Wells would lunge at him and rip out his throat, the demon released him. As if no time had passed, Wells once again addressed the group. Rick sank in his seat, enervated.

"For you to become what you most desire," Wells said, "you must devote yourselves to this experience entirely. You must open yourselves to *me* entirely. I must receive your unmitigated trust." He gestured toward the fireplace; the heat rolling out of it shimmered like a desert road at noonday. "This is your past. *I* am your future."

Rick's pulse began to decelerate. By degrees, the terror of the psychic attack — how else could he explain what had happened? — dissipated. He armed sweat off his brow, took a deep breath, and concentrated on Wells.

"What I did with your trifles felt to you like an act of viciousness, a bullying liberty taken by a man who has won every major writing award."

Rick's heart rate was normal now, the grasp of terror slipping away. He glanced about the group, decided the others hadn't seen the demonic Wells. It hardly seemed possible. My God, had he nodded off and dreamed the whole thing?

"But awards don't make me a writer," Wells said.

"I couldn't agree more, Mr. Wells," Elaine said. "Critics only champion what other critics praise."

Wells tilted his head. "Go on."

"If you bow at the altar of the right person, you're accorded privileges." She glanced at Lucy. "Like big advances and glowing reviews."

Tommy was nodding, the horror at witnessing his work reduced to ashes apparently having subsided. "That's damn straight. It's why some of the best writers never make a penny."

Wells was smiling.

"What?" Elaine asked.

"You know what, Miss Kovalchyk."

"You think I'm wrong?"

"You and Mr. Marston are repeating the mantra of the unsuccessful writer."

Tommy frowned. "You said awards didn't matter."

"That's not what I said."

Elaine brushed a lock of blond hair off her temple. "I don't see the difference."

"Clearly. If you did, your illusion would be shattered, and you'd be faced with the stark truth."

"And what's that?"

"Your writing is shit."

Elaine gaped at him. She glanced from face to face, searching for an ally. She turned back to Wells, her chin drawn in with rage. "If my writing is so horrendous, how did I graduate with honors? Hell, why did *you* choose me?"

"You have potential, Ms. Kovalchyk, but your voice is tinged with a thousand toxins."

Elaine stood. "I don't have to listen to this."

"No one's making you," Anna said.

Rick turned to Anna, noticed how the firelight had dyed her hair Halloween orange. Her gaze was utterly bloodless.

Elaine put her hands on her hips. "And what the hell do you know? You're not even old enough to buy booze."

"I'm twenty-three."

"See? You're a child."

Wells smiled. "Miss Kovalchyk is seething because we've diverged from her mental script."

Elaine rounded on him. "My mental *script*?"

"You imagined reading your work to us."

"You have no—"

"You imagined dazzling your peers, very much the way you dazzled in your farcical classes—"

"*Farcical?*"

"—and like your smug professors, you assumed I would nod knowingly in recognition of your talent and gaze into the fire as you transported me with your sublime prose."

"You don't know anything about me," she said, but her voice was small.

"I know *everything* about you, my dear. Your solipsistic tendencies and your revolting pretentiousness."

Tears brimmed in Elaine's eyes. "Tell me what else is wrong with me. Right here in front of the others."

"'In front of the others'," Wells repeated in a musing voice. "Yes, those are the key words, aren't they? What we do and say in front of others prevents us from becoming what we might become. Our social masks merge with our flesh to alter, for the worse, our true selves. Take Will," he said, turning in his chair to face Will Church.

Will's eyes widened. The poor guy looked like a dozing audience member who has awakened to find himself onstage in some magician's perilous trick.

"Mr. Church suspected his driver of sabotaging his arrival."

Will hesitated, said, "It crossed my mind."

"You were correct."

"I knew it!"

"You were delayed because you lack confidence, Mr. Church. You also suspect yourself of being lazy. That's because you *are* lazy. You are constantly tardy, and due to this unfortunate habit, you repeatedly expose yourself to situations that prey on another flaw – your debilitating self-doubt."

Will looked like he might be sick.

"You were made to enter last, after the others had become passingly acquainted. You dreaded this scenario, you lay awake fretting about it." Wells rested his cheek on a fist. "Tell me, Mr. Church. How did it feel?"

"Awful. Like being the new kid in school."

"And how do you feel now?"

"I'm not sure what you want me to say."

Wells's expression hardened. "It's not what I want you to *say*. It's what I want you to do."

"What's that?"

"Stop being a coward."

Will flinched.

Wells turned to Elaine. "Will has flaws, but he's more than he thinks he is. You, however, are considerably less. Like Tommy, you have sought shelter in the last refuge of the stunted artist: the belief that those who are successful got there by clever subterfuge."

Rick heard himself asking, "What was the point in humiliating Will?"

Wells smiled. "I'm giving Mr. Church what he needs – a verbal cuffing and a dose of confidence. I'm also providing Miss Kovalchyk and Mr. Marston with what they require – a proper humbling."

Tommy turned his sullen face toward the fire. Elaine slouched in her chair, arms crossed.

"How are we supposed to finish our novels now?" Bryan asked. "My files are in Minnesota. There's no way I can go on without referring back."

"You're to create a new story."

"A short story?" Marek ventured.

"A new novel."

Evan smiled. "With all due respect, sir, we're only here for six weeks."

"And you," Wells said, his grin reptilian, "have forgotten whom you're addressing."

Evan's eyes widened. "I'm sorry, Mr. Wells," he said in a small voice.

"You will listen for inspiration," Wells said, his voice slightly hoarse. The effort of speaking so much, Lucy decided, was a strain for him. "That isn't to say you will riffle through your mental notebook of stale ideas. You will *listen* to your subconscious, and when you hear its voice, you will write."

"Write *what*?" Bryan said, eyebrows knitting together. "That pile of pages you just incinerated represents the last four years of my life."

"Then you've wasted four years."

Bryan looked pleadingly at the others, but no one came to his defense.

Wells glanced at Marek. "You, Mr. Sokolov, will be our first reader. Tomorrow night."

Marek's mouth twitched. "If you'd like."

Wells's grin didn't waver. "I'd like."

Marek seemed to sink in his chair.

Wells surveyed them. "What you will write will be true to yourselves. But the novels will have one commonality."

"And that is?" Sherilyn asked.

"Horror," Wells said. "Everything begins with horror."

Sherilyn's eyebrows went up. "Horror? As in, vampires and werewolves and big-breasted starlets being terrorized?"

"What's wrong with that?" Tommy asked, grinning.

Evan sat up primly. "I'm a playwright. Not some lurid scaremonger like Stephen King."

"I'd kill to write like Stephen King," Rick said.

Evan threw up his hands. "I've never read a horror novel in my life. How do you expect me to write one?"

"The only thing I *expect* of you," Wells said, "is to stop mewling."

Evan stiffened.

Wells rose. "Search for inspiration. If you cannibalize your past work, I'll send you home. We'll meet at six tomorrow evening. I expect five thousand words."

Elaine gaped at him. "What?"

"I'm not your mother, Miss Kovalchyk. I'm not here to hold your hand. If you don't possess the toughness or the will to produce, you can return to the sea of failure in which you were adrift. Remember," he added, his bloodshot eyes widening, "only one of you can win."

Elaine fell silent and fiddled with her bracelets.

Wells eyed them all grimly. "Get to work. If you fail to produce," he went on, "there will be severe consequences." He moved toward the door.

"What," Sherilyn said, "you restrict our diet to bread and water?"

Wells stopped at the threshold of the library, the shadows darkening his face. "I don't believe in half measures, Miss Jackson. You'd be wise not to test me."

CHAPTER SEVEN

Rick lay in bed and gazed at the ceiling. He'd studied under demanding teachers, played for tough coaches. Unless they weren't very bright — a few had been dumber than dishrags — he never minded being pushed, could endure a verbal lashing, or in the case of his high school football coach, a four-hour practice with full pads in a hundred-degree heat.

But Wells....

He rolled over and listened to the grandfather clock tick. He discerned its antique ivory face, the shapes of a moon and sun limned by the starlight. Was everyone, like him, lying awake?

I doubt it, he thought. *Not everyone has a reason to fear the dark.*

Rick ground his teeth, struggled against the thought, but now that it was there, it wouldn't go away.

Just like Raymond Eddy.

No! He thrashed onto his other side. *Don't think of him. If you don't know where you are, he can't know either.*

But Raymond had found him everywhere else. Why should this be any different?

Because I can't take it anymore, this life of constant dread.

A vicious voice spoke up: *It's the life you deserve.*

Scowling, Rick pushed up against the headboard. He willed his chest to stop heaving, his heart to stop jittering around like an errant firework.

Raymond *hadn't* followed him here. He was safe.

But are you safe from Wells? the voice whispered.

"Hell," Rick muttered.

He recalled how Wells's features had transformed in the library, how the man became a leering demon before Rick's eyes. Yet none of the others had seen it. Nor had they heard Wells's voice when he spoke to Rick.

There was only one explanation: it hadn't happened.

Maybe he was insane. If he was the only one who saw Wells change into a monster, who was to say the other horrible things he'd seen weren't visions also?

Dammit. Maybe what he needed wasn't a writing teacher, what he needed was a team of mental health specialists. If he could—

There was a familiar whine in the distance. He cocked his head, the sound growing more distinct.

He threw off the sheet, climbed out of bed and padded over to the window. It took him a moment to operate the casement crank in the dark, but once he remembered to unlatch it, the tall pane swung outward without fuss.

The noise came again, more insistent now. The sound reminded him of his grandpa, who'd owned a farm. Grandpa's land was mostly cleared, rice fields dominating for miles, but there were scatterings of trees, and it was these his grandpa culled for their wood-burning stove during the frigid Iowa winters.

Rick leaned forward, the midnight air whispering over his bare shoulders. It was still May, but the night was sultry, more like July. He surveyed the meadow, the hillside sweeping gradually down to the forest. The noise clarified.

Someone was working a chainsaw out there. In the middle of the night.

The vision slammed Rick like a blast of freezing air: a gigantic, uniformed man and a younger man standing in the meadow. The enormous man — it was a police uniform he wore, and a cowboy hat — was pumping the chainsaw's trigger, the bestial drone buzzing higher and higher, the younger man — a cop too, but in plainclothes, his youthful face handsome but frozen in a look of purest terror — standing transfixed.

The meadow was barren of life, but in Rick's mind he watched it all with disturbing clarity: the big cop lowering the chainsaw between his legs, clamping something over the trigger to keep the machine buzzing even if the big cop let go of it. And let go he did, heaving the droning saw high into the air, the steel teeth never stopping. The big cop bellowed laughter as the young cop cowered, unable to track the chainsaw as it rose into the sky. It was a form of Russian roulette, Rick realized. If the chainsaw came down on either man it would reduce him to crimson gruel, but the big cop didn't mind at all, appeared to welcome the agony the whirring teeth would bring. The younger cop turned to run. Rick glimpsed the chainsaw falling, falling, the smoking arm tumbling almost gracefully, and the young man was screaming, the buzzing arm tossing silvery glints as it fell....

Rick inhaled sharply.

He stood there, fingers digging into the windowsill, heard the plummeting chainsaw, the young man's screams.

The psychotic cop's laughter.

John Anderson, he thought. *John Anderson is the deranged cop's name.*

Rick rushed over to the desk, clicked on the lamp, and began to scribble out the scene.

CHAPTER EIGHT

Dear Justine,

As I suspected, I'm the youngest here. I figured Lucy and I would be the only agented writers, but it turns out Evan and Elaine are too.

Lucy looks very different than she did on the inside cover of *The Girl Who Died*. Even less like the girl in the author photo for *The Girl Who Wept*. As an aside, have you ever heard a more wretched title in your life? I know it was a sequel, but Jesus Christ. I feared they'd follow it up with *The Girl Who Sucked. The Girl Who Fisted. The Girl Who Never Had Any Talent in the First Place but Managed to Write One Decent Novel Before Revealing What a Raging Shitstorm She Was.*

Anyway.

In the picture from *The Girl Who Died*, Lucy has that shyness, the hope that she'll make it big. The naiveté. The photo is amusing in a fateful sort of way. The lamb before the slaughter. The bug before the windshield.

The throat before the blade.

The author photo from *The Girl Who Wept* is high comedy. On the stairs of some brownstone. I'm part of the canon now, that setting tells the reader. *I've made it, and you're lucky enough to read my new book!*

Lucy's not looking at the camera; that would be too much to ask of our princess. Instead, she's in profile, laughing and reclining on her skinny little butt, her blue jeans tastefully tattered, sporting Louis Vuitton sandals (like she didn't give them a thought that morning – ah, the life of a critical darling!), and my favorite part, the detail that makes me want to reach into the picture and throttle that lily-white neck of hers: the exposed bra strap. Like that subtle touch of sensuality wasn't strategic.

The photograph from *The Girl Who Wept* is what motivates me whenever I miss my daily word count. I pull out that wretched sequel and study that laughing face. I want to smack the smile right off it.

Then I remember: this is the *Hindenburg*. This is what brought it all crashing down. The stupid little bitch. Did she really think she'd remain the flavor of the month forever?

My God, Justine, do I sound bitter?

I am. I can tell you that now, but after this retreat (I still chuckle at the word 'retreat'. Retreat from what? Civility? Why not call it what it is — a literary war) I won't be bitter anymore.

I'll be famous.

I'll be bigger than Lucy ever was.

Poor, poor Lucy. Her third novel was a disaster of such epic proportions that it defies metaphor. Something biblical maybe. A flood or a pestilence.

And now look at precious little Lucy. A cautionary tale for writers, a blond-haired boogeyman to scare every talentless hack?

I'm going to crush her first.

And the others?

I'll gut them.

Oh, relax. I don't mean literally gut them (though I would deeply, achingly love to shove that Elaine bitch's face into an unguarded fan and watch it cleaved into bloody ribbons). I simply mean I'm going to beat their sorry asses with my words.

Tommy? A joke. He'll be gone before the week is over.

Bryan? A witless misogynist with the empathy of a hatchet. Wells will eat him alive.

Sherilyn? Don't like her. She could be trouble because unlike her idol, the gardening, tea-drinking Corrina Bowen, Sherilyn seems willing to, you know, work.

Rick might be an issue too. Other than wanting to jump his bones, I find myself disliking him. He appears to have some depth, and depth, Justine, we don't need.

I'll still beat him.

Evan, Will, and Marek?

They'd kill for the chance to lick my toes.
It's time to start the eradication process.
Talk to you soon, Justine.

Hugs and Kisses,

Anna Holloway

CHAPTER NINE

Rick strode through the meadow, the witchgrass and goldenrod so thick he longed for a scythe to hack his way through. Fat, furry bees lit on violet thistles, their subtle *burr* flaring as he passed. He wiped sweat from his temple, gazed up at the sky. He'd written until three in the morning and while he knew what he'd written was rough, gruesome, bizarre even, he also suspected it was good.

Ahead, a forest path waited. He pitched a sigh as the shade drowsed over him, the sun sweat cooling on the instant. The fragrant aroma of honeysuckle reached his nostrils. As he meandered through the woods, which reminded him of a state park, he recalled breakfast and the wearying attempts of the others to one-up each other:

Elaine Kovalchyk spoke surreptitiously of her idea. Her manner and hushed tones suggested she was embarking on the next American classic.

Evan Laydon sniffed and told them his story idea was *upmarket* and *high-concept*, whatever the hell that meant.

Bryan Clayton declared that his idea would obliterate them all.

Moving leisurely, Rick followed the trail until it opened onto a glittering lake.

It was enchanting. Blue-brown water, maybe a hundred yards across, ringed with fine white sand. He nudged off his sandals, approached the water. He was reminded of the time he and Sarah had vacationed in Cancun, the night he'd proposed to her.

The night she'd nearly been strangled to death.

"Stop it," he muttered aloud. No more bad thoughts. The nightmares that besieged him while he slept were ghastly enough.

Rick tightened, the hair at the base of his skull prickling.

He was being watched.

He swallowed, performed a slow scan of the coastline. Nothing to his right, nothing on the lake, though there was an island out there populated by several trees and more white sand. He glanced to his left and spotted it, tucked within a bay: a wooden gazebo.

A figure reclining within its shadows.

Terror gripped him. Rick tottered on nerveless legs. *No,* he told himself. *It's not what you think. It's just one of the writers. Or Wells. Or his wife.*

It's too big to be his wife, a voice answered. *Look at the shoulders.*

Wells then. Or Bryan or Tommy.

Or Raymond Eddy, the cruel voice whispered.

Rick shook his head, heart pounding. He set off toward the gazebo.

Marching to your death, the voice insisted. *He's found you again, and this time he'll make you pay for what you did.*

No!

As Rick neared, the shadowy figure rose. Stretched.

Yawned.

Rick's shoulders slumped, the tension dissipating.

Will Church gave a little wave.

"What are you doing here?" Rick asked, conscious of the edge in his voice.

Will arched an eyebrow. "Well, I'm not bird-watching."

Rick nodded at the notebook held loosely at Will's side. "Pretty different writing without a computer, isn't it."

Will emerged from the gazebo. "You have any idea how illegible my handwriting is?"

"Use your laptop."

"I was afraid the battery would run out."

Will's goatee and receding hairline were dotted with perspiration. Rick noted the dark bib of sweat around the neck of Will's t-shirt, which featured the book cover for Hunter S. Thompson's *Fear and Loathing in Las Vegas.*

Will shook his head. "My hand's already cramping up, and I've hardly written anything."

They moved toward the bay. Rick peered out at the water. "Sometimes the words are shy."

"You ever get writer's block?"

Rick bent, picked up an umber-hued stone. "Sometimes what I write is lousy, but I keep going until it's less lousy."

"If that answer was meant to make me feel worse, mission accomplished."

Rick smiled. "What's your story about?"

Will crossed his hairy forearms. "What if you steal my idea?"

Rick reared back, side-armed the rock. It skipped five times before sinking with a muted plop. "Then I'd be a real bastard."

Will selected a rock of his own. A poor one for skipping, Rick judged.

"Why do you think Wells delayed me?" Will asked.

"Maybe he doesn't like you."

"Asshole," Will muttered, but he was grinning. He hurled his stone. It promptly sank, the lake swallowing it like a hungry leviathan.

They got moving again, headed toward a place where the shore abutted a sheer rock wall. Will asked, "You ever been to the Rappahannock River?"

Rick nodded toward the cliff. "Let's hug that. The sand's so wet my feet keep getting sucked in. No, I've never heard of it."

"It's beautiful," Will said, "but it's old. I know every river is old, but this one…it's got this aura of antiquity. Dark as root beer…slow and wide. But shallow. You can walk across it even though it would take you half a day."

"Your story's about the river?"

"It's set there," Will said. "But…well, I have a title."

Ahead, the shore hooked left, the bay ending and the lake opening up again. "It's called *The Siren and the Specter*," Will said. "It's a ghost story."

"That's a good title."

Will looked at him. Probably wondering if he was being mocked. People frequently thought that of Rick. He couldn't imagine why.

"What's yours called?" Will asked.

"*Garden of Snakes*."

"Wow," Will said. "You written anything yet?"

"Some."

Will stopped walking. "Don't tell me you've gotten your five thousand already?"

When Rick didn't answer, Will hurried up beside him. "How? We just started last night."

Rick shrugged. "I couldn't sleep."

"I hate that."

Rick raised his eyebrows in question.

"False modesty," Will explained.

Rick chuckled. "Okay, I wrote something incredible last night. That better?"

"At least it's honest. I'd rather...." Will halted, mouth agape. "Holy God."

"What?" Rick followed Will's gaze toward the island, which was maybe forty yards from them.

Then he spotted it. A figure, sunbathing.

In the nude.

"That who I think it is?" Rick asked.

"She's like a painting."

Rick couldn't contradict him. Anna Holloway lay on her back, completely naked, her breasts round and pallid in the sunglare. A reddish tuft of pubic hair was outlined by the backdrop of chalk-white sand.

"Holy God," Will repeated.

Rick scratched the back of his neck. "We should go."

Will nodded faintly. "Yes, we should."

Instead of moving, Will visored his eyes.

Rick cleared the thickness in his throat. "I'm enjoying the view as much as you, but if she catches us spying—"

"I know, I know. Just a few more seconds."

With an effort, Rick tore his gaze from Anna's nude form and started back toward the gazebo.

Several seconds later, Will hustled up beside him. "That was a religious experience."

"It was an experience."

Will favored him with a wondering glance. "You believe it?"

"She's a nice-looking woman."

"I've heard of nude beaches in Europe, but it's different when you know the person."

"You think we know her?"

Will was quiet a moment. "Guess not. But from that perspective, I don't know you either." He frowned. "I'm not going to discover you sunbathing naked, am I?"

"I favor a two-piece."

They proceeded down the shoreline. When the gazebo came into view, Will murmured, "Son of a bitch."

"Something wrong?"

"The opposite of wrong." Will's eyes were shining. "I think I've got a start for my novel."

"This have something to do with what we just saw?"

"The Siren," Will said. "My protagonist will find her on an island in the Rappahannock."

"She going to look like Anna?"

Will nodded. "Exactly like Anna."

CHAPTER TEN

Tommy slogged through the forest and brooded about Bryan Clayton. The fuckstick. It was early afternoon, and though Tommy had gotten off to a decent start on *Flesh Diary*, his progress had stalled.

All he could think about was the way Clayton had humiliated him.

Tommy leaned against a tree but jerked his hand away when he felt the sap. He endeavored to wipe it off his fingers but only succeeded in staining his white t-shirt.

Tommy surveyed the pine grove, nose scrunching at the odor. Clayton would get a hard-on over a place like this, would go on about its seclusion and unspoiled beauty. Like Thoreau, that wanker Tommy had been forced to read in English 201. He remembered little from that class except a bunch of enraged Puritans railing against sex and alcohol, and others like Thoreau who found the meaning of the universe in an acorn.

Tommy stepped through the burnt-orange carpet of pine needles, remembered how Clayton had pinned him to the grass…. God*dammit*, that made him mad. He bet Lucy was impressed at how effortlessly Clayton had manhandled him.

He realized his face had twisted into a jealous sneer, and he immediately slackened his features. That kind of expression wouldn't do at all. Any of the girls caught him looking that way, they'd know Clayton had gotten to him. He'd have to remember that tendency – getting tight when he thought of Clayton – and suppress it in the future.

He took a deep breath, exhaled.

Clayton hadn't impressed the girls yet or Tommy would've noticed. And no way did Clayton possess the versatility that Tommy did, Tommy who could play guitar, could sing a little. Tommy who could write poetry and make the ladies swoon. No way had Clayton bedded as many girls as Tommy had.

Unbidden, he recalled the first time he had sex. As an eighth grader, no less. Hell, Clayton probably didn't even know how to use his hand in eighth grade, much less where to stick his thing.

That's because he didn't have Sloppy Suzy around.

Tommy's limbs went rigid, his good spirits draining away.

Your first lover, the slithery voice whispered.

She doesn't count and you know it, he thought. He strode through the pine grove, hell-bent on escaping this shaded oven.

Your first time—

No—

Sweet, slack-jawed Suzy.

Stop.

Suzy, who used to ride the short bus to school with the other special needs kids. Suzy, who was seventeen but had the mental capacity of a four-year-old.

The world began to cartwheel. He sank back on his rear end. Still the grove was spinning, so he lay down. He threw an arm over his eyes to deflect the sunlight knifing through the pine boughs.

Better. Much better. He didn't think he was going to puke, but memories of that scorching June day were arising more adamantly now, images of him and his friends Jason and Ty on bikes whizzing down a hill in the country, an area inhabited by farmers, most of them Amish. He and Jason and Ty always got a kick out of the Amish, the women with their bonnets, the men with their long goat beards.

Suzy Powlen was one of the Amish kids, though Tommy seldom saw her. She'd stopped going to their school at some point, but none of them noticed. What they did notice that searing June afternoon was the basket sitting beside the baking macadam road. Tommy remembered that basket vividly. It had a thick weave, a hinged wooden lid, and a fake blue carnation strung to the handle. Jason and Ty hurtled right by, but Tommy braked hard, the ten-speed skidding to an ungainly halt. He walked his bike to the shoulder, rested it on the kickstand, and hunkered down to examine the basket. It was a pretty thing, in pristine condition, which told him it hadn't been chucked out a car window.

Ty and Jason circled back to him. "Think the person's still here?" Ty asked.

Jason nodded. "There's a path down to the creek. She might've gone down there."

Something about those words still echoed in Tommy's memory. That magical, talismanic pronoun. *She might've gone down there.*

She.

It was the pronoun that started Tommy down the path. A minute or two and they were there, the brown water gurgling and frothing like a giant soda machine, the creek shaded by trees with exposed roots. Tommy glanced upstream, didn't see anything but a trout line somebody had rigged and forgotten about, the fishing wire snagged on a rotten log.

Jason whispered, "*Look.*"

Tommy glanced stupidly at his friend, then discovered what Jason was staring at. Downstream, maybe forty feet away, a girl stood hip deep in the water.

Naked to the waist.

She had her back to them. Tommy watched, heart sledgehammering in his chest, as the girl turned, her boobs large and droopy, her shoulders snowy and round.

The first day, they'd merely watched Suzy bathe.

They returned to the country road the next few days, but the pretty weaved basket wasn't there. Tommy began to fantasize about how it might feel to take one of those plump, saggy breasts and plop it in his mouth, to suck on it and revel in the grunting noises Suzy would make.

Jason and Ty had protested the ride to the country that fourth day, but when they discovered the basket, they shut right up. They discovered her in the same place, shirtless again. Tommy spoke boldly to her – his friends would later tell him they couldn't believe he'd done it – and splashed right over to where she stood, the dark water eddying around her thick legs. He'd asked her simple questions about the creek. Did she like it? And about the heat, wasn't it fierce? After gaining her trust, he surprised himself by peeling off his damp t-shirt and slipping his arms around Suzy's waist.

She let him kiss her, and that was nice. Kissing her made him forget how she was and how he would have never said one word to her at school, unless that word was a teasing one.

But summer was different than school.

He tugged down her sodden undergarments and pressed himself against her, keenly aware of his friends watching him from across the creek. He was aware of the hotness in his athletic shorts, his white briefs, so he jerked them down. He commenced kissing her, pushing up into her until he felt a greater heat, a slippery wetness, and it didn't take him long, twenty seconds at most.

For two weeks they journeyed there on their bikes, looking for the basket.

Jason and Ty took their turns. Soon they had sex with Suzy every day, now bringing along a blanket and some towels so they could swim and then do it on the shore.

It was June twenty-fourth – Tommy remembered because his fifteenth birthday was the following day – when they rode out to the countryside expecting to find the basket by the roadside.

A man waited there instead.

He was alone, but he was enough to turn Tommy's blood to ice. He had a long white beard, a gaunt, dour face. His eyes were a ghostly blue, so pale that Tommy was reminded of a husky dog they once owned. The man wore a black hat, a light blue shirt, and navy trousers.

The man waited for them, hands dangling at his sides. Tommy wanted to ride past, *would* have ridden past, but the man stepped into the road to bar their passage. Tommy clenched his hand brakes too hard, bounced to a nerveless stop.

"Suzy told us about you," the man said in a low, trembling voice. "What do you have to say for yourself?"

Tommy's mouth was open, and he was breathing hard. He wanted to say something to impress his friends, something they could joke about later, but he was so frightened of this gaunt man with the ice-chip eyes that it was all he could do to avoid shitting himself. He realized he was close to tears.

"You've done a wicked thing," the man said. "All three of you. You're bad boys."

Tommy nodded, the molten tears beginning to spill down his cheeks. He stumbled turning his bike around. They pumped back to town in silence and didn't address the incident until that night, when

Ty asked in a hesitant voice, "You think it was her dad?"

In his parents' basement, Tommy said, "He was too old to be Sloppy Suzy's dad. Her great-grandpa maybe. Or the family goat," and they all three laughed, a cathartic fit of laughter that simultaneously erased Tommy's shame and opened the spillgates of a new river of conversation, a way of talking about girls that made them feel stronger and older than they were. After that, when they'd see a woman on TV with big breasts, one would say, "Not as big as Sloppy Suzy's." If they watched a sex video, someone would joke, "Bet she can't suck dick like Suzy," and they'd laugh some more.

They stopped laughing that October when they encountered Suzy at the fall festival.

Old Settlers it was called, a seedy traveling carnival that rolled into town just before Halloween. They were playing games and burning through their money when Tommy happened to glance over at the village green and spot her, the Amish girl who might have been pretty if not for her mental defects. Suzy's hair was contained by a gauzy net of some kind, her plain green dress covering her throat, her arms, her thick white legs.

But the dress couldn't conceal the bump in her belly.

A week later, the white-bearded man showed up at Tommy's house.

He was upstairs when the doorbell rang, and he knew who it was, knew even without getting out of bed to peer through the window. But he got up anyway, wishing he hadn't slept in so late. His dad would be at work, but his mom might still be home if she hadn't gone shopping. *Oh hell*, Tommy thought, tiptoeing to the window. If his mom was home and that pale-eyed spook with the white beard told her what he knew, Tommy's life would be over. He listened for his mom downstairs, but the house was cloaked in silence.

Tommy reached the window, his fingertips brushing the sheer curtain, and the man looked up at him. Tommy gasped and backed away, and God help him he scuttled *under* the bed and lay there sweating for the better part of an hour, the dust and hair sticking to him in that sweltering, lightless place. Tommy waited for the doorbell to ring again, and though he didn't hear it, he knew the man was still down there.

That night Tommy dreamed of the man. And the next night. And the worst of it was, the man never harmed him, never laid hands on him, never trampled him with his fucking horse-and-buggy. Only accused him with those chilling eyes, and in his nightmares the man did speak to him, repeating the same words he'd uttered that terrible June afternoon.

You've done a wicked thing.

Tommy glimpsed the child for the first time the following summer when he and his buddies were playing baseball. A group of Amish were ambling along the sidewalk bordering the field, the shade trees obscuring their faces. But Tommy could make out a slatternly girl pushing a stroller, and the words echoed in his head: *You've done a wicked thing, Tommy. You've done a wicked thing.*

"No!" he wailed, returning to the present. He sobbed into the forest dirt, mashed his face into his forearm, his legs writhing in the pine needles, the odor suffocating him, but the memories far, far worse.

When he raised his head, the loam mingling with his sweat, he distinguished something across the clearing that made the terror evanesce. He didn't think it was real at first, so he pushed to his knees, used the front of his shirt to dab at his eyes.

Anna Holloway stood with her back to him. He'd know that scarlet hair anywhere.

And that killer body.

She had on a white, pleated shirt that hung loose, so that her neck and the tops of her shoulders were bare. Tommy pushed to his feet and dusted himself off. He fingercombed his curly hair, did his best to pick the pine needles out of it.

He started across the clearing. He didn't look his best, but that obviously didn't matter to Anna. Why else would she have come all the way out here? He knew this forest was vast, so it could only be intentional that she had ended up with him in this silent, secret place. Tommy crept closer.

Her hands were busy with something, her shoulders hunching slightly.

The shirt slithered down her back.

Tommy grinned to himself, already erect. Now *this* was how things should be. A romp with the lovely Anna would restore his confidence, would establish him as the Alpha dog. Would even help his writing.

He wondered if Anna knew he was right behind her. An arm's length away, he hesitated, debating which would scare her more, speaking aloud or touching her bare shoulder. And man, *look* at it. Supple skin. He bet she massaged lotion into those shoulders. He reached out.

His fingers were an inch from her flesh when he paused, frowning. He'd been wrong about her skin being flawless. There were pimples speckling her back, a paleness he hadn't noticed.

His fingers hovered over her shoulder.

She swiveled her head toward him.

Tommy's breath clotted.

The blocky shoulders rotated, the sly, downturned face peering up at him with mock coyness. The blubbery lips spread wider in a dreadful grin. The bare torso moved into focus. Tommy clapped a hand over his mouth, his paralysis breaking, and when he beheld the misshapen newborn suckling at the girl's breast, Tommy was already backing away. Suzy opened her leering mouth wider, her lips stretching in a hideous jack-o'-lantern grin, and before Tommy turned to run he watched in horror as a furry black spider crawled over the girl's bottom lip.

CHAPTER ELEVEN

From *Flesh Diary*, by Tommy Marston:

This is how you die.

Not from cancer, not from heart disease. You don't die choking on a hunk of gristly steak.

You perish from desire.

You die from *I want*.

When you see her for the first time, you're not looking for the one who'll destroy you. The one who'll eat you from the inside out.

The one you'll choke on.

When you see her, you're striding through a bookstore and she's working the information desk, hair dyed blue, black wool sweater concealing enough to make you turn, and the force of your stare swivels her head around. She looks at you. One part coquette, six parts curiosity. Gazes at you over her shoulder, head tilted, almost like she's upside down.

You're upside down.

You're sick in your stomach. Good sick. Dangerous sick. You consider saying something, but what you'd say can't be said, and anyway, there's someone standing across the counter from her. So you stare at her, blushing, and she holds your gaze a moment longer and you know to wait. She'll be with you in a second. Would already be with you if not for this fucking job.

...the new James Patterson book, the customer is saying. The customer female, bespectacled, somewhere between forty or sixty. Toadlike.

It's in fiction, under P, your blue-haired murderess says, showing more patience than you would.

Is it thirty percent off of hardcovers? Toad asks, as if there aren't stickers on every hardcover in the store.

Yes, your murderess says, and only you can sense her impatience.

Her smile is serene, but she's as eager to get rid of this squat lump of cluelessness as you are. You stand waiting until the patron is gone, and the woman with the blue hair turns and rests her forearms on the hunter-green laminate surface. You tell her your name. She looks you straight in the eyes and says, *I won't sleep with you until I'm comfortable in your presence.*

You tell her that's fine. You're about to leave when she says your name.

Yeah? you ask.

And she says, *I'm already comfortable in your presence.*

CHAPTER TWELVE

The wall sconces and lamps scattered throughout the library did little to mitigate the shadows that clung to everything. To the chairs, the bookcases. To Marek, who clutched his papers and stood before the seething hearth.

He looked to Lucy like a schoolboy made to recite his essay in front of the class.

He glanced at the door. "Should we wait for Tommy?"

Elaine smiled mysteriously. "Tommy is indisposed."

"What does that mean?" Anna asked.

"Still nursing that arm of his," Bryan said and winked at Lucy. *Dick.*

"I don't know what's wrong with him," Elaine said. "I knocked on his door maybe five times, then he told me to go away."

"Too scared of being picked," Bryan said. "I bet he didn't make his word count."

Marek shuffled his papers. He opened his mouth, then devolved into a coughing fit.

"You okay?" Sherilyn asked.

Marek straightened, smiled an apology, and went on in a steadier voice. He sounded self-conscious at first, but soon the rhythms of his narrative flowed more smoothly. Wells reclined in his chair and gazed into the fire. Marek was halfway through a sentence when Wells said, "Garbage."

Marek smiled uncertainly. "I'm sorry, sir?"

Wells folded his legs. "You're a sycophantic fraud."

Marek uttered a disbelieving laugh. "I'm not a fraud, Mr. Wells. If you don't like the piece, tell me how to make it better."

"It's unsalvageable, Mr. Sokolov."

The first real flickers of anger banked in Marek's eyes. "Then tell us why we're here. To be belittled? To be mocked?"

"You're guilty of a writer's greatest sin," Wells said.

"What are you talking about?"

"The bottom drawer of your dresser."

Marek's smile faded. Lucy realized her hands had balled into nervous fists.

"Yes," Wells said, nodding. "You know what's there, Mr. Sokolov. And you know why you must leave."

Lucy said, "What's he talking about, Marek?"

"Wilson," Wells called.

A man with square-framed glasses and a brown ponytail appeared at the door. Though Wilson's ivory chambray shirt and faded blue jeans looked vaguely professorial, Lucy felt her flesh tightening. There was something disquieting about him....

"Yes?" Wilson asked.

"Please have Mr. Sokolov escorted off the premises."

"Then what?" Marek demanded. "I don't even know where we are."

"The police chief will."

"*Police* chief?" Marek said, glancing at the door, but Wilson had already disappeared.

Sherilyn went to Marek's side, but it was to Wells she spoke. "You weren't very tactful, Mr. Wells. I don't blame Marek for being hurt."

"Marek deserves to be hurt," Wells said. "His duplicity dishonors all of us."

"Sherilyn's right," Rick said. "We're here to learn from you. There's no need to be vicious."

Wells fixed Rick with a wondering gaze. "You think I'm being vicious, Mr. Forrester? My handling of this traitorous behavior has been singularly *humane*. Have you no competitive spirit, Mr. Forrester? This...*dissembler* attempted to cheat his way to the crown. He attempted to gain advantages none of you would have."

"What'd he do that was so awful?" Sherilyn asked.

"Never mind," Marek muttered. "I knew last night this was wrong for me."

Wells appeared interested. "And how did you know that?"

Marek made a square with his hands. "Your insistence on putting us in the same box. Making us write *this* much in *this* amount of time. Ordering us to write in the same genre."

"He has a point," Elaine said.

"Be careful, Miss Kovalchyk," Wells said. "I have a long memory."

Elaine opened her mouth, closed it.

Wells glanced at Marek. "My words are wasted on you, Mr. Sokolov, but for the others' benefit, I'll tell you one more thing."

"This should be good," Marek muttered.

"It is," Wells agreed. He gazed about the room. "Mark my words well, everyone. They might save your life."

"Save our lives how?" Sherilyn said.

Wells ignored her. "Storytellers have existed since the beginning of time. Even though society regards them as mere entertainers, their role is a sacred one. An *essential* one. And though they deal in fantasy, in fabrication, the essence of their power resides in truth. No one is more honest than the storyteller. No one has greater power. They have the ability to create life." He looked at Marek. "Or to bring death."

There was a loud thump from the foyer. Then another.

Wells rose. "Your escort is here."

"That's not possible," Will said. "It's only been, what? A minute?"

"I contacted the chief earlier," Wells said. "After I discovered Mr. Sokolov's deception."

Wells exited the library.

Lucy glanced at the others. "Shouldn't we fight this? Or at least ask for proof?"

"There's no need," Marek said.

Bryan leaned back in his chair. "I guess we're down to nine."

Voices approached from the hallway.

"I'll get my things," Marek said, going out.

Lucy glanced at Rick, but there was no help there. He was staring at the door as though it would explode inward at any moment and immolate them in a sheet of flame.

The door opened. The policeman who entered was at least six and a half feet tall. His head was proportionate to his vast frame, but the square jaw and protruding features made him look like a caricature – a college mascot made flesh. He was handsome in a brutish way. His legs were Doric columns, his feet great black slabs. He had a gut, but even this looked granite hard. He wore a brown cowboy hat.

The chief grinned at Lucy, doffed his hat. "Ma'am."

She gave him a half-hearted wave.

The chief glanced at Evan. "What about you, young man? You enjoyin' it out here?"

Evan's smile was almost a grimace. "Sure I am. What writer wouldn't?"

The chief nodded. "I've never read Mr. Wells's work myself, but my wife loves him."

Evan's smile brightened. "Your wife has excellent taste."

"Does she?" the chief answered.

Evan's smile faded.

"I'm ready," a voice said.

Marek stood in the doorway, a faded brown knapsack slung over his shoulder.

The chief turned. "You have anything to say?"

Marek raised his chin defiantly. "I have nothing to apologize for."

A corner of the chief's mouth twitched. "Just as well. Come on then." Marek exited, and the chief was halfway through the door when he paused and turned.

To Rick he said, "Much obliged." And he went out.

Lucy exhaled, unaware she'd been holding her breath. She said to Rick, "What did he mean by that?"

Rick's face was bleached of color.

"Rick?" she asked. "What's wrong?"

"That's him," Rick said in a small voice.

"What do you—"

"John Anderson," Rick said. "He's the villain from my novel."

CHAPTER THIRTEEN

The police chief said nothing on the way through the forest, nor did he speak after they'd climbed into the cruiser. That was fine with Marek. He didn't feel like talking anyway.

He imagined the other writers celebrating his departure. Marek had considered himself the favorite to win. For one, he was the oldest. Maybe that didn't count for much in the minds of the youth-obsessed, the fad-chasers perpetually on the lookout for the newest, *youngest* thing. But Marek could write, goddammit. He could *write*. And that should have counted for something.

He glanced out the window, watched the black forest whir by. It was so damned unfair, being ousted this way. It was inexplicable how little the others had stuck up for him. Marek thought of his favorite novel, *Lord of the Flies*, of the innocent child hacked to pieces by his peers.

"You're nothing like Simon," the big cop murmured.

Marek turned. "What did you say?"

The cop's expression was bland. "You heard me."

Marek gazed at the huge man. He remembered a night in Belarus, caged in the back of a police car.

You're nothing like Simon.

Marek shifted in his seat. Just coincidence. Nothing more. The big cop was a corn-fed hick. There was no conceivable way he could know what Marek had been thinking. No way he could have referenced the first character to be killed in *Lord of the Flies*.

He could stand the silence no longer. "How long have you been an officer?"

"We gonna be friends now?"

Great, Marek thought. *An asshole.*

Why should he be surprised? Weren't all cops assholes? In Marek's experience they were.

Try a different tack. "You know Wells a long time?"

Instead of answering, the cop glanced at him. "You know, you don't look so good," he said. "You shouldn't steal so many damned cigarettes."

Marek's belly dropped through the seat. He couldn't feel his limbs.

Because the cop hadn't said *smoke* so many damned cigarettes, he'd said *steal* so many damned cigarettes. But that was impossible. Beyond impossible. It was paranoid and deranged. *Please*, Marek thought. *Just get me out of this forest.*

The cop's expression was neutral, like he'd commented on the weather. But Marek knew what the man had said, and what he'd said had frozen his fucking marrow.

You shouldn't steal so many damned cigarettes.

He can't know about that! Marek thought.

But he did. Marek was sure of it.

The cop eased to a stop, slid the cruiser into park.

"Go sit in the back," the chief said.

Oh God. Was this an elaborate setup? To undo the plea bargain? Or, Jesus Christ, to extradite him to Belarus?

"Don't have a conniption fit," the policeman said. "I just want everything to look kosher."

"Kosher?" Marek asked.

"Folks around here, they like things done traditionally. If I'm to take you through Shadeland to the bus station – which is what I assume you want…?" His boulderlike head tipped forward, eyes wide, awaiting Marek's confirmation.

Marek nodded.

The cop nodded too. "Then it would appear awful strange if you were sitting next to me as we rode through town. Don't you think?"

"I don't know why." Marek tried a laugh, but it came out tinny. "I'm not your prisoner after all."

The cop didn't say anything to that. The chill in Marek's bones deepened.

"You ready?" the cop asked.

Marek tapped his fingers on his knees. "It just seems…excessive."

Genuine mirth in the cop's eyes. "Why don't you let me decide that?"

Marek sighed. The chief was on his home turf, there were no witnesses nearby. And even if the man weren't a giant, he carried at least two guns – what looked like a Magnum .44 on his hip and a .38 Smith & Wesson on his ankle. Marek had gotten a good look at both, since the cop wore the .44 on his right side, and the man's pant leg rode up when he sat down. Maybe, Marek reflected, that was by design. Maybe the cop wanted him to see the guns.

But why?

Because he likes the power, a voice in Marek's head explained. *Have you ever met a cop who didn't? Just let him have his fun, and it'll be over soon.*

Marek opened his door and climbed out. The cop did too. Briefly, Marek considered making a run for it, just bolting blindly into the forest. But that was unwise, he knew. If the cop did mean him harm, the man would have no trouble gunning him down. Marek was in horrid shape. He drank too much, smoked even more, only exercised when there was no other alternative.

"It's unlocked."

Marek turned, discovered the cop's monolithic form watching him over the cruiser's roof.

Marek got into the back and shut his door.

The cop climbed in beside him, the whole car dipping with the man's weight.

Marek frowned. "Why did you sit here?"

Leaving his door ajar, the cop leaned back in the seat. "That's better."

Marek's heart boomed in his chest. "Please take me to the bus station."

"There's no bus station."

"*What?*"

The cop laughed. "Hell, I'm just kiddin'. I figured we'd take a few minutes, get things out in the open."

"I don't know what you mean."

"Why did you bring a phone?"

Marek sagged. So that's what this was about. "I don't know. I guess I hated the idea of being cut off completely."

"How does it feel to sell out your best friend?" the cop asked.

Marek tried to swallow, but it was as though someone had lined his throat with straw. "Did Wells...."

"I like to know something about the people who come under my jurisdiction. I checked out every one of you little shits."

Marek's thoughts raced. So the cop knew about the smuggling. That was bad – maybe extremely bad.

Marek swallowed. "What do you want to hear?"

"All of it."

He hesitated. "What if you're recording this?"

The cop gave him an easy smile. "How about we trust each other?"

Looking into the chief's black eyes, Marek felt hypnotized. And a little disarmed. The man was a giant, but he seemed a gentle one. So he wanted to talk about Marek's indiscretions, so what? Maybe the cop had his reasons.

Marek nodded. "Can we maybe roll down the windows? It's a bit close in here."

Had the cop tightened, his smile growing strained? "I can only control them from the front seat."

That made sense, Marek supposed. But he still didn't like it. The big cop took up over half the back seat by himself. His right knee was touching Marek's, and Marek was huddled against the door.

Tell him what he wants to hear.

"My father left when I was young. I began stealing so we could—"

"Skip the *Oliver Twist* bullshit," the cop snapped. "Tell me about the plea bargain."

Marek's throat constricted. "That was later. That was—"

"—when you were twenty-five, I know. You were scared shitless of going to prison because you knew you'd become someone's bitch, so you sold out your best friend."

Marek began to tremble. "Why ask if you know it already?"

"I know the facts of the case," the cop said patiently. "What I'm asking you for is the personal stuff. The details. I'm asking you to explain how it felt to betray your friend to save your own lily-white ass."

A tear slipped down Marek's cheek. He wiped it away, the wet stubble rasping against his palm. "You know how it felt."

Something swooped toward him, and then his head was snapping back, his ears ringing. Liquid pumped from his nose, and as he pawed at his mouth, the pain flooded in, like a torch blowing its blue jet of flame at the center of his face.

"You can't hit me," Marek said, his voice querulous. "You were supposed to—"

"To fuck you?" the cop interrupted.

Marek stared at him in horror.

The chief roared laughter. "Jeee-zus Chrrrr-*ist*, you're a pussy. You know that, Suckalot?"

"It's *Sokolov*," Marek protested. "My name is Sokolov!"

"'*My name is Sokolov!*'" the cop crooned in a ghastly falsetto, his voice like Count Dracula on helium.

"You can't assault me," Marek persisted. "You can't flash those guns and do whatever you want."

The cop drew back, his black pupils wreathed by huge white coronas. "You think the guns matter? Well, shit." He threw open the door, and in two brisk movements discarded first the .44, then the .38.

Marek clambered over him, thinking to tumble into the grass and squirm his way into the concealing underbrush.

But the cop caught him and hoisted him bodily into the air. The back of Marek's head cracked against the open doorway, his shoulders bashing the ceiling. The pain was extraordinary. Marek was wrenched sideways, his left eyebrow crashing into the cop's battering ram of a forehead. Blood drizzled over Marek's eyes. He was too dumbfounded to fight back, so when the cop thrust him toward where he'd been sitting, Marek crumpled to the floor and grasped his bleeding face.

The chief's tone was so jocular he might have been recollecting a fond childhood memory. "One of my favorites was a pretty blond girl. Just a kid, really. She'd gone home with a trainee of mine – he was married, mind you – and they were gonna get busy." The chief tittered. "But I followed them inside – they didn't lock the door, too horny for that – and I told the girl to pick up a pillow and hold it to her face." The chief slapped his knees. "And can you believe it? She did what I asked! Jesus H. Christ, I never can figure why folks'll go along with whatever you tell them. 'Put the pillow to your head.'

'Get in the back of the cruiser.' 'I promise I won't hurt you.'" He whistled. "Bunch of ignoramuses."

"What else was I supposed to do?" Marek wailed.

The cop went on as though Marek hadn't spoken. "I figured the pillow would dampen the sound, but it was still plenty loud. Her face sprayed like a bowl of pink soup."

"I'm sorry for what I did to Aleksei," Marek said.

"You sent him to *prison*, Suckalot. Let's not mince words here. Not at this late hour."

"I'm sorry! Doesn't that count for something?"

"You think I care about your friend?"

"So why are you doing this? If you don't care, then why—"

"Because I like killing people."

Marek began to weep.

The cop gusted laughter. "Shit, buddy, don't get so bent out of shape. I ain't really gonna hurt you. How about you sit by me again?"

Facedown, Marek began the job of pushing himself off the floor, but his hips became wedged between the seatback and the seat.

"Here," the cop said. "Lemme help you."

The cop jerked back on his arm. Pain slammed Marek's shoulder, unspeakable, reddish-black pain that writhed like vipers. Marek was sobbing, but he didn't care.

"Whoops!" the cop said. "Damn thing just snapped like a defective toy. Here...." And he pushed Marek face first onto the floor. Before Marek knew what was happening, the cop placed a boot on his rear end and hauled back on his shoulders. Marek realized distantly that he was being bent backward, *bent in half*. Something in his innards popped. He wanted to go numb, but he didn't. He could feel *everything*. And the policeman was folding him over backward, bearing down on him until his shoulder blades rested on his calves. Marek could feel himself ripping open somewhere in the vicinity of his abdomen.

Then, mercifully, he didn't feel anything.

PART TWO
SHADOWS

CHAPTER ONE

Rick knocked on Wells's door again, and again there was no answer. He hesitated, heard sounds from within. Rick hammered on the door, waited.

Nothing.

He tested the knob, found it locked. He cocked his fist, about to pound the door so hard he'd rattle the frame, when he heard it. Grunting. Feverish grunting. And moaning. Roderick and Amanda Wells.

For God's sakes, Rick thought.

He'd anticipated an argument, telling Wells off and stalking away into the night. What he hadn't anticipated was intruding on a violent lovemaking session.

Rick lowered his fist, stood a moment. Turned and descended the stairs.

Behind him, a voice called, "Mr. Forrester?" Wells emerged from his room. "I was preoccupied."

Rick stared sourly at Wells's sweaty hair, the man's chest glistening out of his burgundy robe. Despite Wells's disheveled appearance, the man looked younger than he had in the library. Had Wells shaved since then? His eyes were certainly clearer, less bloodshot.

"You celebrating?" Rick asked.

"You came to ask me a question," Wells said.

Rick opened his mouth, hesitated.

Wells watched him. "Yes?"

Yes, Rick? he asked himself. *What exactly do you want to talk about? That the man who showed up to take Marek away is a character you created?*

Madness.

Wells placed a hand on Rick's back and led him down the staircase. "Let's walk together. There's something you need to see."

They moved down the stairs in silence. Wells led him to a hallway behind the kitchen. At the end, Wells opened a door and flicked on a switch, revealing a flight of wooden steps that burrowed into darkness. A puff of musty air assaulted Rick's nostrils.

"The basement?" Rick asked.

"My dungeon," Wells said with a broad smile.

Rick discerned the challenge in Wells's eyes. "What's down there? A menagerie of your former students?"

Wells moved past him into the murk. Rick followed. A moment later a naked bulb spilled light over a spacious circular room ringed with steel doors.

Wells said, "Police Chief John Anderson."

Rick felt the bulge of his heart as it strained within his chest.

Wells smiled. "You honestly believe you wrote the gentleman who escorted Mr. Sokolov off my property?"

Rick said nothing.

"You believe you…what? Conjured him with your imagination and, God-like, made him flesh?"

Rick could feel his Adam's apple bobbing. "How do you explain it? The voice, the face, even the sense of humor, they all—"

"—come from your memories, Mr. Forrester."

"I've never met anyone like that sheriff."

"Police chief," Wells corrected. "We're all products of our experiences. So is our fiction."

Rick's mind raced. Was it possible Wells was telling the truth? Could the seeds of the character have been planted without his knowing it?

It didn't seem likely. "Mr. Wells, there are too many similarities…I don't see how—"

"I do," Wells said and reached inside his robe.

Wells was gripping a sheaf of pages.

Rick eyed them. "That what I think it is?"

"*Garden of Snakes.*"

Rick's jaws tightened. "How did you get them?"

"While you were out, my wife made copies of your new manuscripts."

"How...." Rick started. "That's a violation."

"Of what?" Wells said, laughing. "Your privacy? You agreed to put yourselves in my hands."

Rick reached for the pages.

Wells snatched them away. "Don't, Mr. Forrester, or you'll be the next to go."

Rick dropped his hand, but a new thought arose. "If your wife made copies...you already read Marek's sample."

Wells didn't reply, but his self-satisfied smile was answer enough.

"If you didn't like it," Rick asked, "why have him read in front of us?"

Wells spread his hands as if it were self-evident. "To demonstrate there are consequences for bad writing." Wells stepped closer, his head bumping the low-hanging bulb, so that it began to swing, the light swimming up and down the cinderblock walls. "Think of how much better the world would be if every inept writer were muzzled."

Rick was sweating, the swirling yellow light making him dizzy. "You could have just said, 'Here's where you're going wrong, here's how you make it better.'"

"Don't you *see?* You're softening the blow for him."

The room performed a slow sideways roll. Rick extended his arms to steady himself.

"Would you like to lie down, Mr. Forrester?"

The bulb continued to pendulum.

He's hypnotizing you.

Ridiculous.

Fight it!

Rick brought a hand to his brow, massaged it, as if he could manually stimulate his sluggish brain.

"Anderson," Rick muttered. "In my book he's a killer."

"He does have a penchant for bloodshed. What's your point?"

"I want to see Marek."

"Marek is gone."

"Did Anderson hurt him?"

Wells's muddy eyes widened. "Do you realize what you're saying, Mr. Forrester? The preposterousness of it?"

The bulb continued to swing. One moment Wells was bright yellow and glitter-eyed, the next he was a shadow.

"It's worse than I thought," Wells whispered.

"Let's go upstairs."

"I knew you had issues with reality, but I never guessed they were this severe. You truly believe you're living in a fairy tale."

In the strobing light, Wells seemed to be growing. Rick took a backward step. "I don't feel so good...."

The tarry eyes gleamed. "You're reverting, Mr. Forrester, becoming infantile. I expected much of you, yet you're afraid..."

Rick couldn't feel his legs.

"...like a child huddled beneath the covers, quailing at monsters."

Rick took another backward step, cast a glance behind him. He needed to lean against a wall to keep from falling, but the walls were nowhere in sight, as if the basement were expanding. The smell of dirt filled his nostrils. A dull, distant roaring battered his ears. Wells was encroaching, but Rick had nowhere to retreat to.

"Please," Rick murmured, staggering.

"Good night, child," Wells said.

The concrete rushed to meet him.

CHAPTER TWO

The atmosphere in Lucy's room was smothering. The unused laptop stared back at her in reproach.

"To hell with it," she muttered. She stalked to the door, opened it, and gasped at the faces staring back at her.

Will and Sherilyn.

"We didn't mean to startle you," Sherilyn said.

Lucy clutched her pounding chest. "Did you time that for maximum terror?"

Will ventured a smile. "Sherilyn thinks we've all gotten off on the wrong foot. She thinks—"

"—our energy is bad," Sherilyn finished. "Come upstairs with us."

Lucy followed them to the third floor, where they entered a massive room that reminded her of a church. The floor was rough-hewn stone, the walls comprised of the same. There were a dozen pews flanking a broad central aisle. On the far side, perhaps forty feet distant, was a raised area, not unlike a stage. Beyond that, the outer wall was composed almost entirely of stained glass.

"What the hell is this place?" Lucy asked.

Sherilyn looked at her. "A chapel."

"Why would Wells have a chapel?"

Sherilyn's tone was thoughtful. "His books do have a metaphysical vibe."

"An indignant one," Lucy said. "Characters denouncing God, attacking organized religion...."

"*Martin's Oath*," Will said, and they both looked at him.

He shrugged as if it were obvious. "The scene where Martin desecrates the cathedral? Tell me you guys remember that."

"Sorry," Lucy said.

"How can you not remember that? The shouting and the knocking things over and the—" he gestured, "—the urinating...."

"Glad I never read it," Sherilyn said and made her way down the center aisle.

"You're religious?" Lucy asked after her.

Sherilyn eased down onto her side. "Let's eat."

As Lucy neared the front of the chapel, she discovered the two had laid out a picnic. Atop several cloth napkins she found crackers, a cheese wheel, a foot-long cylinder of salami, and several bottles of water.

Will sat opposite Sherilyn, gestured to the food. "We raided the pantry. Go crazy."

Lucy realized she'd skipped supper. Her mouth flooded with saliva. "I didn't think about it until now, but...."

"You're ravenous," Will finished. "We were too. I get hungry when I travel anyway – something about it drains me, you know? – and add to it that fucking driver—"

Sherilyn gave him a look.

"Sorry. That prick of a driver—"

Lucy laughed.

"—when you put it all together...I guess I was too stressed to eat."

Lucy sawed a hunk of cheese from the wheel, inclined her head. The vaulted ceiling was populated by multiple painted images, but the sconces' illumination didn't reach far enough to reveal what they portrayed. Screwing up her eyes, Lucy made out what might have been a capering demon chasing a small child through the forest. Or maybe it was an amorphous blotch and she was just wound up too tight.

"You asked me if I was religious," Sherilyn said.

Lucy stopped mid-chew. "I retract the question."

"Good," Will said. "Nothing makes me less comfortable than God talk. Well, that and cancer."

Sherilyn squinted at him. "You won't talk about cancer?"

"What can I say? It freaks me out."

"Did someone you know die of it?" Lucy asked.

"Not yet."

"Then why—"

"Because it *scares* me, okay? You're fine one day, going along with your life, and then you find a lump. You tell yourself it's no big deal, but deep down alarms are going off and this creepy organ music is playing in your head, because you know – I mean deep down in your gut – you *know* that if it's malignant, you might be well and truly fucked."

"Could we abstain from the f-word while we're in here?" Sherilyn asked.

Lucy glanced at her. "Why *are* we in here?"

"Communion," Sherilyn said.

"You mean, 'This is my blood,' and, 'Do this in remembrance of me'?"

"Communion with other *people*. The three of us are forming a positive bond. Not one of Wells's twisted dynamics."

Will grunted. "Like making sure I arrived last?"

"That was unkind," Lucy said.

"It was," Sherilyn agreed. "And having you enter with Tommy and Bryan. What 'dynamic' was he trying to create there?"

"I hadn't thought about it."

"Well, think about it."

Lucy took in the woman's intensity. "Evidently you have a theory."

"I do."

"I'd like to hear it," Will said, standing and stretching. The bottom of his belly showed below his gray Cubs shirt, his paunch hairy and white.

Sherilyn went on. "Grouping you with two dudes – two attractive dudes – spawned a rivalry between them. It also—" Sherilyn broke off, gazed up at Will. "You mind not looming over me like that? I feel like I'm about to be paddled by the principal."

"Sorry," Will said and sat down.

She turned to Lucy. "Wells made you an object."

"I hardly qualify as an object."

"Did the guys compete for your attention?"

Lucy made a face. "I wouldn't say they *competed*. They… you know…."

"Got into a fight?" Will supplied.

"Of course they competed," Sherilyn said. "You're young and pretty—"

"Debatable."

"—and they went all Alpha male on each other, and Bryan showed what an utter twat he is, and Tommy tried to get in your pants."

Lucy took a bite of salami, chewed. "Sounds like you were there with us."

"I didn't have to be, dear. I know men."

"Now hold on," Will said. "If you want us to *commune*, stereotyping is a lousy way to do it."

Sherilyn raised her eyebrows. "Am I wrong?"

"About Bryan and Tommy?" Will asked. "Probably not. About *all* men...."

Lucy sipped her water. "What does being together accomplish? We're still fighting for the same thing."

Will's face clouded. "You don't think Wells is really like that, do you? He's just setting a tone."

"You don't believe that," Sherilyn said.

"I *have* to believe it. Did you feel the tension in there? It was worse than the company I work for."

Lucy carved off a chunk of salami. "So this is like a support group?"

Sherilyn got to her feet. "Stop being so cynical." She moved toward the stained-glass windows. "We all know what's at stake. Anyone who claims three million dollars isn't a serious incentive is lying."

Lucy chewed. "Why didn't you invite Rick?"

"We tried," Will said. "He wasn't in his room."

"Sturdy guy like him, he's out in the forest chopping wood or something," Sherilyn said.

Lucy laughed but couldn't help imagining him with an axe. Shirtless.

Sherilyn turned to face them. "There's something none of us have mentioned. Some*one*."

"Marek," Lucy said.

Sherilyn gave a curt nod. "Marek." She leaned on a lectern, which featured numerous unfamiliar runes. "Marek was exiled before our eyes, and none of us lifted a finger to save him."

"He broke the rules," Will said.

"Then why not just tell him to leave?" Sherilyn challenged. "Why put him through the charade of reading his work and having Wells trash it in front of the group?"

"Power," Lucy said. When they both looked at her, she said, "That's what it comes down to, right? Power? Control?" She glanced at Will. "I'm sorry, but the Wells we've seen isn't a show. This is how he really is."

"Agreed," Sherilyn said.

"The way he dealt with Marek proves it," Lucy went on. "He not only wanted Marek humiliated, he wanted the rest of us to witness it."

Will gestured vaguely. "If Marek broke the rules...."

"He didn't deserve that," Sherilyn said. "He didn't deserve to be bullied by that mountain of a cop."

Lucy remembered what Rick had said about the policeman and fled from the thought.

Will was frowning at his knees. "I suppose you're right. It was out of bounds, heartless, all that. But if I think too much about it, I get neurotic."

"You're already neurotic," Sherilyn pointed out.

"No, really," Will said. "And seeing how Marek was dispatched—"

"Could we use a different word?" Lucy said.

"—shown the door, I can't help thinking that's going to be me soon."

"Maybe it is," Sherilyn said.

Will glared at her. "Thanks a lot."

"Maybe it'll be you," she said to Lucy. "Or me."

Will's expression was strained. "Your point?"

Sherilyn smiled. "What I'm proposing is simple. The three of us – and anybody else who chooses to join our little cabal – make a pledge to retain our humanity, in spite of the incentives to do otherwise."

Lucy got to her feet, stretched. "But it's so much more fun to destroy each other."

Sherilyn's face went grave. "Oh, there'll be plenty of that, dear. Rest assured."

"Especially with Bryan around," Will muttered.

Lucy said, "I think it's worse than you realize."

Sherilyn frowned. "Why do you say that?"

"Just a feeling," Lucy said, moving over to gaze at the stained glass. "When he gets angry—"

"Which is often," Will said.

"—I feel this...psychic chill. Like he wants to maim people."

"I know what you mean," Sherilyn said. "When Wells contradicted him, his expression was scary."

"He's all bluster," Will said. "There're tons of guys like him in my office. They have to establish their dominance over you, show you what badasses they are. It's why I stopped going to the gym. All that posturing."

Sherilyn gave him a look.

He shrugged. "Okay, that and the fact that I hate working out."

Lucy started to laugh but stopped when she saw the look on Sherilyn's face. "What is it?"

Will followed Sherilyn's gaze to the stained-glass window. "What's that man doing?"

But there was no need to explain. It was perfectly clear to Lucy, and judging from their silence, it was clear to the others as well. The figure depicted in the stained glass appeared to be a medieval knight bedecked in full battle regalia: red-plated armor, a cruciform sword forged of antique gold, silver helmet with the visor open.

Lucy wished the visor had been left shut.

Because the face resembled a younger Roderick Wells, Wells as he must have looked in his forties, a bit careworn, yet stunningly attractive. His rugged features were a mask of determination as he wielded his sword in the company of numerous serpents and human onlookers.

"Jesus Christ," Will breathed.

The serpents were baring their fangs, but rather than fending them off with his sword, the medieval Wells was exhorting them to attack the onlookers, who were garbed in peasants' clothes.

Clothes soaked in blood.

The vipers teemed over the shrieking stained-glass figures, their fangs either buried in the rent flesh of their victims or moments from killing them. A nightmarish inversion of the St. Patrick legend, the knightly Wells showed his teeth and brandished his sword at a helpless young woman, who could only wail as mad-eyed snakes swarmed over her.

"Now why," Sherilyn said, "do you suppose Wells would commission an image like that?"

Will ventured a smile. "Maybe he posed for it."

Sherilyn looked at him flatly. "Now there's a cheerful thought."

CHAPTER THREE

At the first milky light of dawn, Rick shivered and thought, *I'm dying.*

Then, *Wells knows. Somehow, impossibly, he knows the truth about me.*

His teeth chattered, his bed soaked with icy perspiration. He scarcely remembered how he crawled out of that godforsaken dungeon, but that didn't matter now. What mattered were the shadows he spied in the basement. What mattered was what happened when he was twelve.

The undertow sucked him lower, plunged him into the maelstrom of nightmarish memories:

His stepfather, Phil, getting worse, and Rick taking the brunt of it. His mom mistreated too, Rick blanching at Phil's cutting words, his relentless bitching.

Linda, why don't you make yourself more attractive?

Despite Phil's sloppy untucked shirt and tousled hair.

Linda, stop letting the bugs in. Shut the door, for God's sakes!

When Phil went out twice as often and never closed the door behind him.

To Rick: *You're not going to play video games all summer.*

Rick at twelve, already mowing lawns, doing the dishes, lugging out the trash, a slew of other menial tasks. Indentured servitude and he hardly ever complained.

You don't finish what you start! Phil would roar. When Phil would start a dozen tasks and leave them unfinished. Tools all over the house. Electric drill on the kitchen floor. Hammer and nails on the dining room table. The garage a riot of sawhorses and neglect.

Phil getting worse:

Linda, haven't you heard about the break-ins? Who's going to pay for our things if they get stolen?

Rick's mom meekly suggesting they get their valuables insured.

So violent was Phil's reaction you'd have thought she'd piled their money in the yard and made a bonfire out of it.

One night, Rick awakens to voices.

What do you mean you forgot? Jesus Christ, we have three fucking doors. Three! And you forgot to lock one? And what about Rick? I told him to double-check.

It's my fault, Phil. I'll have everything replaced.

Rick comes out of his room not the slightest bit drowsy. Terror does that to you.

In the dining room, his stepdad towers over his mom, gesticulating wildly, his bloodshot eyes bugging. *Oh you will, will you? How will you replace a twenty-thousand-dollar musket, Linda?*

His mom takes a shuddering breath, her bony shoulders tense under the shabby brown robe. *I'm sorry. I'll make it right.*

You won't make anything *right. I can't believe you were stupid enough—*

When he discovers Rick, Phil's face takes on an even deeper shade of red.

I thought you did your chores.

Rick finds his voice. *It was my fault the door was unlocked.*

Phil's face hardens, not giving an inch despite Rick's contrition. *You're right it's your fault. You and your mother both. And if you think you're going to get away with it, you really do have shit for brains.*

Looming closer. Face approaching purple, index finger jabbing at him.

You're going to work every day until you pay me back. And your mom's not going to protect you anymore. The kid gloves are off.

Okay, Phil, he says, and he realizes he's not supposed to say *Phil,* is supposed to call him *Sir,* and then Phil is shouldering Rick's mom out of the way, stalking toward him with his fist raised. He's slapped Rick more than once, but he still can't believe Phil is going to coldcock him right in front of his mother.

Rick's feet get tangled, and he lands gracelessly on his elbow. He stares up at Phil, who roars, *Get up, you lazy little bastard!*

Rick starts to rise, but he isn't fast enough. Phil is hauling him upward by the t-shirt, lifting him and shaking him and bellowing spit-flecked profanity into his face. He's always known his stepfather is strong, but this is like being buffeted by a tornado.

There comes a whistling sound and a crunch.

Rick stumbles back. Phil crumples to the floor at Rick's feet. Rick gapes down at him, looks past Phil's unmoving form, sees his mom grasping the hammer.

Her head droops dejectedly. She weeps silent tears.

After a time, Rick's eyes meet his mother's.

You had nothing to do with this, she says.

Okay, he answers, though he's distracted by his stepfather's body lying prostrate between them.

Do you love me? she asks.

He opens his mouth to tell her of course he does, but she stays him with a hand, aggravated with herself. *Sorry, honey. Stupid question. I know you love me.* A shuddering breath. *And because you love me, I need you to do something for me.*

He feels small now. Six years old. Maybe four. He can't even communicate in grunts, he's so distraught.

I need you to turn around, his mom says.

Rick begins to turn and as he does he makes the mistake of looking down at Phil's head, the ridge at the base of the skull. There's a dark red circle there, not a perfect circle but definitely hammer-shaped. Queasy, Rick completes his turn.

His mom's voice, closer now. *Promise you won't turn around.*

Okay.

Say it. Her voice hoarse.

I won't turn around.

At all. Not once. Not until I'm completely done and I tell you it's all right. There's not much time. Promise?

Okay.

A pause, something swishing behind him, like a blanket slithering to the floor.

She says, *Scoot forward.*

He does.

More, she instructs.

He keeps going, about eight feet from Phil's head now.

The thud is enough to make him jump. Another. Then the hammer strikes become rhythmic and...*slushy*. On some level he knows what's occurring behind him, but he flees from it, tells himself it isn't happening, gropes for anything that springs to mind. The Cubs game that day. The new gas station three blocks over. Maybe it has a slushy machine.

Shit. Slush. Red slush. Red brains. Red blood.

Rick turns and knows it's all real.

His mom is panting, her bare feet straddling the corpse, which is convulsing now, the smell of shit filling the dining room but not yet connected to the quivering, convulsing lump on the floor. His mom is naked and quite bloody. Holy shit. She looks like a cannibal from some South American tribe or that vengeful woman from the movie he watched at a friend's house, the one who got raped and left for dead and is paying back the guys who did it.

That draws his gaze back to Phil, whose arms and legs aren't flopping anymore.

Phil isn't a rapist, not that Rick is aware of, but he's sort of like those guys in the female-revenge movie. Rick realizes he wanted Phil to die, but he's never considered the event a likelihood, had actually doubted Phil could die. He was too much an asshole for that.

I'm sorry you had to see me this way, his mom says.

Suddenly embarrassed by his mom's black thatch of pubic hair, which is splashed with red, he averts his eyes and finds himself staring straight at the pile of tomato pasta that had been his stepfather's head. Rick feels his gorge rise and his mom's voice is loud and commanding: *Get to the bathroom, Rick! Now!*

He does as he is bidden and makes it with maybe a second to spare. He vomits luxuriously, for once in his life happy to be puking his guts out. At least it's gotten him away from the murder scene.

His mom steps past him, draws the shower curtain back, twists on the water. Rick reaches down and automatically begins taking off his shirt, but she puts a hand on his back. *It's for me, Ricky. You're going to wait here while I clean up.*

He does, though the room keeps carouseling. His mom takes a long time. He realizes she is rinsing off every atom of blood that might have splattered. She must be scrubbing under her fingernails and scrubbing the shower for good measure.

Climbing out, she says, *Now you get in. Your story is, you heard me scream. You came out of your bedroom. You saw me crying over Phil's body, and you threw up. Then you took a shower on my orders. That'll explain the wet towel. Can you remember all that?*

Rick scarcely listens. The sight of his naked mom climbing out of the shower has frankly freaked him the hell out. He's seen her nude more tonight than he has since he was a little kid and could've gone the rest of his life without seeing her this way.

Rick?

He blinks at her. *What?*

Can you remember?

Sure.

She nods. *Shower. By the time you come out, the police will be here.*

His stomach lurches. *Police?*

She gives him a pleading look. *Ricky, I need you to do this. I didn't want to kill your stepfather, but he was a horrible person and he was hurting both of us. Wasn't he?*

Uh-huh.

If I divorced him he would've kept everything. I don't know how, but he would've. He would've gotten me fired and spread rumors about me.

Rick nods, though he has no idea what his mom is talking about.

The police come and ask Rick about it. Rick does well. So does his mom. No one imagines anyone but the thief killing Phil with the hammer.

The night ends.

The horror begins a month later.

CHAPTER FOUR

The eggs and bacon only made Lucy's shriveled stomach pucker up tighter. Nauseated, she picked up her pen, tapped it on the notebook, thought to herself, *You traveled halfway across the country to outrun your troubles, and guess what? They traveled right along with you. You still can't write. You're still a one-hit wonder. Fred Morehouse was right:* The Girl Who Died *is you.*

To escape the thought, she studied the dining room around her, the faded crimson-and-gold art deco wallpaper, the antique lace curtains yellowed with age. The entire room needed rehabilitation, including the discolored brass door handles.

"Wells is a man with style," Bryan said. He popped a purple grape into his mouth, chewed. "Bet this room cost more than most houses."

"Could use a little love, though," Sherilyn said.

Lucy glanced at the coffered ceiling, noticed the subtle warping of the wood, and decided Sherilyn had a point.

"Hey," a voice beside her said.

Tommy.

"What?" she snapped.

He held up his hands in truce. "Take it easy."

Sighing, she dropped the pen, scooted her chair from the table.

"Hold on," Tommy said. "You don't have to go."

"I don't want to be next."

"Have you met your word count?"

Her stomach tightened. She hadn't written *anything*.

"Something's wrong, isn't it?" Tommy asked.

Lucy blew out a quavering breath, told herself to take it easy on him. It wasn't his fault she had issues. Other people had writer's block; Lucy had a goddamned mountain range.

She made to stand, but Tommy said, *"Please.* I need to talk to someone."

She hesitated. His tanned face had gone a sickly hue, and there were bags under his eyes, the skin there bruised-looking, as though he'd been in a car accident.

"What's wrong?"

"Quieter," he muttered. A nod across the table. "I don't want them to hear."

"I need to get something on paper, Tommy. If this isn't life or death—"

"It is."

She read the anguish in his eyes. "Is it to do with Marek?"

"Indirectly." He leaned forward, elbows on knees, his curly hair hovering an inch from his untouched plate.

"I'm listening," she said.

"Do you ever have the feeling your past is following you?"

Every minute of my life, she thought.

He brought his clasped hands to his forehead, like a praying child. She was alarmed to note he was crying.

"Tommy?"

"I'm in trouble," he whispered.

She put a hand on his shoulder, for once not worried he'd misinterpret the gesture. "Did something happen?"

"Not here. Not…oh *God*."

"I can't help you if you don't—"

He cleared his throat, stared at the floor. "I'm sorry for how I looked at you before."

Lucy hesitated. "I don't know—"

"Yes you do. You're really pretty, but that's no excuse. I…." Tommy swallowed, shook his head. "I know it's wrong, but I keep doing it anyway. Thinking with my libido…."

"Hey, Tommy," she started.

He stood, drifted toward the door. "I shouldn't have said anything."

Bryan smirked, called across the table, "Cracking under the pressure, Marston?"

Sherilyn glanced at him. "How can a writer have so little empathy?"

Bryan ignored her. "He lacks discipline."

Tommy was gone.

Lucy considered going after him. She felt no particular warmth toward Tommy, but what she'd seen in his eyes went well beyond normal stress. He was haunted by something, teetering on the brink. Maybe, she decided, it would be better if he did decide to leave. She told herself she wasn't being like Bryan, wasn't celebrating the demise of another competitor, and she was fairly certain this was true.

Go after him then, she told herself.

But she didn't. Only sat there and told herself the empty feeling in her gut wasn't guilt.

She couldn't shake the feeling she'd never see him again.

CHAPTER FIVE

Time to go, Tommy thought. *Time to go.*

Moving away from the mansion, he fought the urge to run. If he broke into a sprint the way his nerves begged him to, he might step into a hole, snap an ankle. He'd left his stuff behind, but who gave a shit, it was all replaceable anyway. The clothes were nothing special, the only item of significance a letter a girl had once written him, one he'd kept because it was flattering, and when you got down to it Tommy liked to be flattered. He liked to be stared at and told how nice his eyes were, how dazzling his smile.

He neared the base of the hill and the shadowed forest lurking there.

He grinned, sweating now, and decided he liked the idea of the woods lurking. He'd use it in a story someday. Not a horror story – to hell with that creepy shit – but something dark. Something about a woman who strides naked into a clearing with a fake baby, a woman who leers at him and lets a spider crawl out of her mouth—

"Jesus Christ," he said, shivering despite the heat.

Tommy experienced a moment of perplexed terror, thinking the trail he sought had been swallowed by the forest. But no, thank God, there was a trail, the same one he followed here less than two days ago.

Hasn't taken you long to come unraveled, has it?

Tommy scampered down the trail, fleeing the question, fleeing its implications.

It wasn't the same trail. He saw that plainly. For one, the plant life was different, more like the trees he remembered from his childhood.

(like the trees you saw yesterday, the ones surrounding you and Suzy and the furry spider oozing out of her mouth)

"Shit," he muttered. Whatever was happening, he could outrun it. If he followed this trail long enough, he could find his way back to the clearing, and then who cared. He'd walk, he'd hitch a ride, he'd even let that big cop drive him…

…no he wouldn't, scratch that, he'd hide in a ditch if he encountered the cop who took Marek away. The big cop gave him the willies.

Focus, he told himself. He kept his eyes on the trail ahead, which wasn't at all the way he remembered it. The one they took to the mansion was a deep, rich brown, almost like walking on a chocolate sponge cake. This trail was pebbled and sandy, the kind you'd find by a river. Tommy even fancied he could smell the river now, the slow-moving water and the fish…

…and in his mind's eye he saw the rope swing, saw his own body sweeping out over the water, his friends hooting and clapping, and Tommy flipped and splashed and surfaced and saw them all with beer cans raised, and there was Lexi, one of the girls he dated in his late teens, the years he was drinking and screwing and doing what drugs he could get his hands on and claiming he was discovering himself. What he discovered beside the river was Lexi's naked body, and it was so natural and good that he talked her out of the condom, and a few months later one of his buddies said, *Hey, you hear about Lexi?* And Tommy, not very interested, answered, *What about her?*

She got an abortion.

Huh, Tommy answered, feigning a lack of interest.

That's all? his buddy asked. *Huh?*

What am I supposed to say? Tommy demanded.

His buddy hadn't answered, nor had anyone verbalized it in Tommy's presence, but he'd thought about it obsessively for weeks afterward. And a year later, he'd definitely impregnated a girl because she told him so, and when she asked him what he was going to do about it, he said, *I'll drive you to the clinic.*

She said, *I'm keeping it.*

He said, *Fine, it's probably not even mine anyway.*

She said, *It has to be. You're the only guy I've been with. I'm only sixteen.*

God. Reminding him of it. Tommy not even knowing the laws. Was it illegal when he was only twenty? He didn't know, but he'd stayed awake sweating and imagining a judge asking for evidence in the statutory rape case, the girl placing the baby on the judge's desk, saying, *Here's my goddamned evidence.*

The trail curved in front of Tommy, and he tripped, going way too fast to fall gracefully, and laid out at full speed, a real header, and skidded on his belly, his palms chewed up by the trail, and…

…was that laughter he heard?

It was. Kid's laughter.

He knew where he'd heard it before, back when he dated that Megan chick. What was her last name? She had a nice body for having spat out a kid, and the kid was cute when he wasn't squalling.

Tommy pushed to his knees, dusted off his shirt, his cargo shorts.

He rose, heard the kid's laughter, and shot a look toward where the trees were sparser. The sound was definitely issuing from there. Uncanny how much it sounded like Megan's kid…what was his name? Justin maybe? Jacob or Justin?

Jacob or Justin had only been three but the kid had really taken a shine to Tommy, which made it easier with Megan, who had an ulterior motive but acted like it was all about their relationship. *Sure, Megan,* he would think, sitting beside her on the couch pretending to enjoy some crappy romantic comedy, *it's all about us, isn't it? It isn't about you wanting a provider for your boy. The guy who knocked you up wants nothing to do with Justin/Jacob, so you figure if you treat me nicely enough I'll be the new daddy.*

Except I won't. Because I've been that guy, the one who ditched you. And I totally relate to him, totally get why he fled. Who wouldn't? Diapers and runny noses and no sleep and getting scolded by the wife. Who'd willingly agree to that?

Laughter, clearer this time.

Tommy gazed into the forest and thought, *Justin/Jacob, is that you?*

The trees were hung with Spanish moss, which made not a bit of sense because that was how trees were in Georgia, not Indiana. Tommy took care, stepping gingerly. When he found the kid, the kid would tell him how to get out of here. Maybe the boy would even have a dad with him, and the dad would give Tommy a ride to town.

A chipmunk skittered across the trail before him.

He screwed up his eyes, and when he spotted the immense cypress tree, the Spanish moss draping its stout branches like skeins of molted skin, he couldn't believe it. It was the exact tree he remembered from the vacation house next to theirs, the one where he spent the summer of his twenty-second year. The English teacher had come to write a novel on her time off. She'd been thirty-nine, attractive, and completely mysterious to Tommy, who'd never slept with an older woman. It hadn't taken long for her to give in. She'd wanted to, after all, and he'd been nice to her, snipping roses from his parents' garden – thank God they'd skipped the summer home that year – and presenting them to her, along with some of his poetry. She'd loved the flowers and the words, had told him he had real talent, and Tommy said, not meaning it, that they should work on a book together, and Tammi – *With an i*, she'd reminded him – had positively swooned at the prospect.

Late-night walks along the ocean, making love on the shore or in her big cozy bed. She never wrote her novel, nor did the infatuation last long. Not for him anyway. But before she went away in August, his fall term not beginning until early September so he could at least enjoy the last few weeks of break without her constant presence, she informed him she was 'with child', saying it exactly like that.

Tommy scowling, asked her what she was going to do about it. She'd looked at him sadly and said, *I'm going to name him Thomas*, and it had taken all he had not to puke. *Won't you go with us?* she'd asked. *You can write during the evenings and watch Thomas during the day while I teach.*

And Tommy had laughed at her, laughed so fucking hard that tears had streamed from his eyes. He refrained from slamming the door in her face, but she saw how it was, just looked at him with her sad doe's eyes, and wished him well, which was the worst part of it, the part that returned to him now.

This was the tree in front of Tammi's vacation house, the place she'd rented in order to write her novel, the place she'd been impregnated. The child would now be...what? Seven years old? Almost eight?

Hard to believe.

Almost as hard to believe as the sight that awaited him on the other side of the oak tree.

The creek. The exact creek that serpentined around the countryside near his hometown. His heartbeat whamming in his chest, he halted before he tumbled down a ridge, certain he would find Suzy Powlen awaiting him on the shore below, the mentally challenged girl, pimple-backed and drooling.

He was ready to bolt in the other direction the moment he glimpsed Suzy or any other spooky shit, but peering through the dappled leaves that swayed gently over the creek bank, he saw nothing but wet stones, gritty black sand, and gently lapping water, dark and soothing as dreams.

Tommy was sweating like crazy, his clothes pasted to him, so he peeled off his tank top, chucked it onto the path. He wasn't listening for it, so when he heard it, it caught him off guard.

The laughter.

Tommy walked along the gritty sand and breathed in the river smells. He heard the laugh again, and though it was faint, he thought he'd pinpointed it now, from just around the rock wall to his right, the bank very steep there.

Finally, the shore broadened, the bank becoming a sandy beach, gorgeous, and mottled with sunlight. Tommy smiled, taking it in. He couldn't believe his luck. He couldn't believe—

A sloshing sound to his right.

He turned that way and beheld the blue-black object in the water. A small boulder, poking through the surface. Tommy frowned, stepped from the thick sand to the stone-littered verge. Saw the object was rising, discerned a paleness, someone's forehead, and before he could comprehend what he was seeing, there was a face, shut lids and...

...it was Tammi, her face as it had been that summer long ago, the neck, the breasts, the nude body rising out of the water.

Her belly distended in pregnancy.

He took a step backward, unwilling to believe it. How had she found him here?

Tommy retreated, and though the sight of her pregnant belly shocked him, his eyes shifted to her flanks, where another pair of heads began to breach the surface. The first head rose, a blond one. His former girlfriend Megan, nude, strode out of the water, a shaft of sunlight passing over her closed lids and her large breasts. Under that, the enlarged stomach, the belly button pushed outward like a grotesque flesh dome.

On Tammi's other side he spied Lexi, the girl he'd boned by the river, and Lexi hadn't aged a day. Except she must have aged about nine months from the time he impregnated her, her gut was so swollen. His eyes tracked lower, and he gagged when he saw the tiny foot dangling from her vagina. Her labia spread wider, and he glimpsed the child's lower half, another leg, a tiny penis, and it was too much. He moaned, reeled backward, and discovered two more heads emerging from the water.

One of them was Suzy Powlen's.

Like the other women's, Sloppy Suzy's eyes were closed. But her belly was enormous. Tommy sank to the sand, but he couldn't look away. The women's eyes were opening, the naked, pregnant women, and their eyes were stark white, their mouths stretching in leers, their teeth blackened and mud-caked, and grime was squeezing from between their teeth.

Tommy marshaled the strength to crawl away from the creek, but he heard laughter. He realized there were several children on the beach, five or six of them. The children were perhaps kindergarten age, they were naked and staring at him, and somehow this was worse than anything else, worse even than the mothers, because the eyes of these children were normal, they were *his* eyes, because they were *his* children. Little boys and girls, their arms out, their feet padding toward him.

Tommy screamed at the sky, wailed, and the kids were surrounding him, and Tommy screamed, *"I'm sorry! I'm so sorry!"* but his words died in a choking rattle. The children forced him backward to the sand, they held him down, preparing him, and he looked up, saw the white-eyed mothers, and squealed in horror, because their babies had plopped to the sand, were crawling sightlessly toward him, their tiny teeth like razors. The mothers leered at him, supervising the kill, the afterbirth trailing from the hideous newborns, which reached Tommy and began tearing at his flesh.

CHAPTER SIX

From the Diary of Sherilyn Jackson:

My partner Alicia has been pestering me to keep a diary. I argue that a record of my life would be worthless. Who reads that shit anyway? Biographies are always of presidents or rock stars. Who the hell am I?

But since we have to start somewhere, let's begin with this:

It sucks to be poor.

Oh, my family wasn't so poor that my brothers and sisters and I sat around in a dusty dooryard like you see in all the pictures. But we definitely qualified for food stamps and plenty of disdain from the folks in town. Then our daddy got gangrene because of poor circulation, which was brought on by diabetes, which was caused by a shitty diet because he couldn't afford a better one. At any rate, it all comes down to money, doesn't it?

I just re-read this and want to slap myself. It sounds so goddamned lachrymose. I just wanted to get it out there that money has always been an issue for me and as a result, I'll admit it, I started looking for a man to marry when I came of age. My number one criterion, even before a good sense of humor and a smile that made me moist down below, was the dude had to have money. The more the better. Because by the time I was seventeen I was seriously tired of wearing hand-me-downs from my older sisters. I'm talking about clothes that had been cycled, recycled, and finally flung at me, holes in knees, busted zippers, faded colors. Even streak marks in panties. And when you're forced to wear your sister's shit-stained underwear, you really start to crave something better.

That something better was David Zendejas.

Let's get the name out of the way first. It sounds Hispanic, and somewhere along the line one of David's relatives might have lived in Mexico. I don't know. What I know is he looks black, and my mom lit up whenever he called on me. Daddy by that time had lost both legs and spent a couple years stinking up the back bedroom and finally died looking nothing like the strong cheerful man who used to toss me up in the air when I was a little girl.

Sad. And unfortunate. I think if Daddy had been healthy when Zendie began sniffing around, he would've seen right through him and either kicked his smiling ass or at least sent him away.

No one sent him away, least of all my mother. Zendie would bring her flowers (not me, mind you, her) and smile his brilliant smile, and his hugeness and good looks and deep voice would charm the shit out of my mom. He could've fucked me right on the front porch if he'd wanted to. Hell, Mom would've pulled up a chair and complimented him on his technique.

But like I said, I was only seventeen, and if seventeen sounds old enough to you, please note that Zendie was already twenty-eight and the father of three illegitimate children (from three different women).

I look back and wonder why he chose me. He was already head pastor at a Tuscaloosa church and had a score of attractive young women to choose from. He bedded half of them after we got hitched, and when we'd been married two years he got an offer from a slightly larger church, and he took it, but that one didn't have as many sets of pert breasts and tight asses, so in short order we moved to another church, and for eighteen months we were happy. I was happy because he was finally talking about having a baby. I was still a kid, barely over twenty, but my sisters were having babies, and every lady in the congregation seemed to have a child on each teat and I caught the fever and began to assert myself, which was probably why he put an end to that talk pronto (one of his favorite words) by garnishing my allowance and using the hard flat palm of his hand.

Allowance was what he called it, but it was really my spending money. I used to be ashamed of this, but I've realized over time that everyone is an asshole sometimes.

So I was being an asshole and letting the money go to my head. It wasn't much money in the vast scheme of things but it was more than I'd ever had in my life. I became a fixture at the outlet malls and started buying organic food even though I didn't give a shit that it was healthier. I just liked the sound of it. So maybe to support his wife's organic carrot addiction, Zendie took an offer to shepherd a flock of eight thousand parishioners in one of the biggest Baptist churches in Tuscaloosa.

Now why, when his congregation had never been larger and his pickings more plentiful, Zendie had to prey on a married woman – the wife of the youth pastor, for fuck's sakes – I'll never know. (Oh, Zendie never stopped cheating. If it was pretty and willing he'd hump it. Only once if the girl just lay back and let him rut out his passion, multiple times if the girl wanted to get more adventurous. Of course, he never wanted me to be adventurous. If I ever made a comment he judged too lewd he'd show me his hard flat palm. So forget any adventures in the bedroom for Sherilyn Jackson, who was then called Sherilyn Zendejas, whose initials were SIZ, for Sherilyn Irene Zendejas, which always sounded to me like some sexually transmitted disease or maybe some syndrome infants got in the hospital, but anyway....)

Zendie got caught with his pants down. Literally. And I abhor tired clichés and the adverb literally but both descriptions fit. My husband was banging the youth pastor's wife in the church toddler playroom, the young woman draped over one of those Fisher-Price kitchen sets, her bare ass in the air and my husband ramming her from behind like he was punishing her for burning an imaginary cake.

Unlike other administrators, the ones in the First Baptist Church of Tuscaloosa weren't willing to overlook my husband's habit of sticking his dong in every willing lady he encountered, and he was promptly sacked. I was pissed about my allowance being cut in half (a result of my husband's firing and subsequent return to his previous church, which apparently took no umbrage to Zendie's never-ending search for sexual gratification), and I wanted a child. Zendie argued it was a bad idea to conceive when we had less money coming in. I pointed out that he'd by that time fathered four illegitimate children and didn't seem to mind sending payments to them, so why would he demur to impregnate his own wife?

I'd seen people choked in movies. But let me tell you, feeling those big viselike fingers on your throat and looking into those bulging mad eyes is some seriously scary shit. You think to yourself, Whoa, this is real. And then, Damn, this really hurts. Then, Holy shit, I just might die here. And finally, Son of a bitch, I am dying here.

Okay, it's time for me to work on my novel. I aim to win this contest.

And not for the reasons you think.

I said I was writing this diary because of Alicia's pestering, and Alicia, if you ever read this, that's true. You do deserve some of the credit.

But here's the thing (and if this is me being an asshole again, so be it):

I'm afraid of Roderick Wells.

I've tried not to let it show, but there it is. I'm afraid of him. If anything happens, I want there to be a record of what occurred here. Wherever here is.

Which reminds me of one more thing. The strangling. Or near-strangling. The first of many.

I lay on the kitchen floor and wheezed into the tile and dirty grout. I thought about my twenties and thirties going by without having a baby. I thought of growing older while Zendie kept preying on the same young sluts who fell for his charm and his looks (which only seemed to be growing better). I cried thinking about it and began to feel hopeless.

And angry.

It was when I was being strangled that I first entertained the notion of killing my husband.

CHAPTER SEVEN

Blocked, frustrated, Lucy climbed the staircase, but rather than stopping at the chapel she continued down the third-floor corridor. She was halfway down the hallway when she paused, one door in particular calling to her, and for no reason at all she thought of Belle in *Beauty and the Beast*, and where she'd been forbidden to go. The West Wing?

With a delicious tremor, Lucy reached out, twisted the knob. Nudged the door inward and stepped inside.

She stood openmouthed at the ballroom unspooling before her. It was breathtaking. Perhaps sixty by eighty feet, the ceiling domed and hung with numerous chandeliers, a mammoth one in the center of the dance floor, which was comprised of black-and-white tile and wreathed with circular tables, and all thoughts of *Beauty and the Beast* scattered, replaced now by thoughts of *The Great Gatsby*, a grander time. Lucy strode onto the dance floor and imagined the tables peopled by women in flowing gowns, their men shiny-haired and black-tuxed, everyone smoking, every face full of knowing good humor, watching her. Feeling slightly foolish, Lucy executed a pirouette, stumbled a little, dancing never really being her thing.

She regained her balance, heaved a sigh, and beamed at her surroundings. Though it was gloomy in here, there were skylights that threw enough illumination for her to see. If she were to turn on the chandeliers, she'd feel exposed, ostentatious. As though she believed she deserved this sort of grandeur. And…

…and did she hear the faintest musical notes sounding from the recesses of the ballroom? As if some elegant orchestra were tucked in the shadows, urging her to dance?

No, she realized, not to dance – to *write*.

Oh my God, she thought, aware of the thrum in her head. At first she didn't credit the vibration for what it was, but now she realized…

yes, this was the vibration she'd experienced before writing *The Girl Who Died*, all those years ago. It had felt like this, a psychic thrum, a spiritual thrill. She was starting to see the figures materialize from the darkness, to hear the music from the orchestra. She could almost identify the tune. Then the voice spoke from behind her, making her shriek, flail her hands, and she whirled and stared at the figure seated beside the door, her heart jackhammering.

"Aren't you going to answer my question?" the figure asked.

She knew who it was, and the knowledge did nothing to soothe her jangling nerves. Wilson, Wells's handyman, was watching her, waiting for a response. Worse, he was amused. She knew this as surely as she knew she was in trouble. No one had any idea she was up here.

No one but Wilson.

She knew it would come out unconvincingly, but she drew herself up anyway. "You always sit in shadowy rooms waiting to scare the hell out of people?"

"I was here first."

"I would have seen you."

"Seeing isn't your specialty. Nor, evidently, is overcoming your demons."

Lucy frowned. Though it was gloomy near the door, she couldn't help but notice the way his hair gleamed. Slicked back. And what was he wearing?

A tuxedo.

Lucy's chest tightened.

She fought it off, said, "I'm gathering details for my novel."

"Am I supposed to report that to Mr. Wells? Make you sound dutiful?" His drawl was affected, honey-sweet. Overlaid with a scornfulness so thick she couldn't help but think of Fred Morehouse.

"I don't care what you do," she said.

Her feet itched for the door, which was open, thank God. But escaping not only required moving within arm's reach of Wilson, it was a bald admission that he was scaring her.

"You and one other are the stragglers," Wilson commented. "And I suspect he'll be writing by night's end." A nod. "That leaves you."

Her voice came out shaky. "I'm going downstairs."

"And leave this place?" Wilson asked. "You gonna tell me you weren't imagining what it'd be like to own this ballroom? To throw fancy galas here?"

"I'm not a fan of crowds."

"There's another spot you should see."

She hated the way he'd invited the obvious question, also a Fred Morehouse tactic. She refused to play along. "I wish I could say I've enjoyed talking to you—"

"A farmhouse. There's an upstairs room that'd be particularly fascinating to you."

She moved toward the door. "I'm not interested."

Wilson sat sideways in his chair, half-blocking the doorway. "Isn't it funny how we're shaped by our experiences? How things just... *dog us*, no matter how we try to run?"

"Look, Wilson...." She stopped when she saw him chuckling.

"Wilson?" he said, passed a hand over his mouth. "No *Mister*, huh? Just Wilson?"

"I didn't mean—"

"'Get me my dinner, Wilson!'" he called, his voice deepening in mock authority. "'Carry my bags for me, Wilson!'"

She swallowed. "If you've—"

Wilson popped to his feet, swung a fist past his stomach. "'Get a fire going, Wilson. Dust those shelves!'"

He was taller than she remembered, broader. His ponytail pendulumed as his gesticulations grew wilder.

She edged toward the door. "I'm going to my room."

He brayed laughter, hands on knees. "Going to your *room*? What are you, a child?"

Her teeth ground together. "I don't think Mr. Wells would appreciate his help being rude."

"Oh, we're going there, are we? 'The *help*'?"

She made to move past him, but he stepped with her. "Is that anger I see?" He bent toward her. "My goodness, so it is!" He threw back his head, arms spread. "Hallelujah! Lucy has a backbone!"

"Shut up," she growled, elbowing past him.

"My Lawd yes," he crooned, "there's life in her yet! And here I thought I made a mistake."

Her hesitation was infinitesimal, but she knew he'd marked it. Lucy hurried out the door and veered toward the staircase. She was starting down when Wilson called after her, "Best embrace it, Miss Lucy! Best get it down on paper before the fear creeps back!"

She descended the stairs in a wild clatter, reached the second floor, and halfway between the landing and her room there was Rick, whose smile died when he saw the ferocity of her expression.

"Everything okay?" he asked.

"What do you think?" she answered, knowing she'd hate herself later for being rude. But writing was like a sieve, she knew, the magic sifting out if you carried it around too long. She couldn't let this idea slip away.

She entered her room, knowing Rick was where she left him, watching after her. Firing up the laptop would take too long. Teeth bared, she hastened to the desk, fetched a pencil, but the lead was broken. Heart sinking, she cast about for something else, found a pen, but the ink wouldn't come, and though it helped nothing, she flung the pen aside, ripped open the middle drawer, more pens and pencils rattling around in there. She grabbed a pencil, found an unblemished page, scrawled out a word or two and realized she was too distraught to write, had nothing to say anyway. There was nothing, only a formless idea she'd smothered with rage and desperation, and she clenched a fist around the pencil, pounded it into the desk, stabbing the wood, aware she was growling, cursing, and the whole desk jumped with her blows.

"*Goddammit, Goddammit, GODDAMMIT!*" she roared, objects tumbling off the desk. She slammed her forehead on the wood, reveled in the pain, repeated it. She became aware of a knocking on her door, and she lunged over to it, whipped it open, and glowered at Rick, whose eyes flicked to her forehead.

"*What?*" she snapped.

A bemused smile. "Thought I'd check on you."

"Is that all?" She felt the blood trickling down the bridge of her nose.

He nodded at the cut in her forehead. "Want me to take care of that?"

Unaccountably, she found herself grinning. "I'll take care of me."

"Okay. If you need me, I'll be around."

She nodded, flung shut the door, turned and regarded herself in the mirror. Hair disheveled, rivulets of blood striping the middle of her face, she reminded herself of a savage, some demonically possessed woman in a movie.

She decided the look was an improvement.

CHAPTER EIGHT

Evan crept toward the forest. He loathed insects, had an atavistic fear of small creatures, snakes most of all, and any time his mother had taken him and his sisters on what she deemed a 'nature walk', he'd been gripped by a superstitious certainty one of the fork-tongued monsters would dart at him from the shadows. Snakes did that, he knew, slithered along branches and attacked unwary victims from above as well as below.

But his story involved a forest setting. He *had* to experience it firsthand.

Evan moved from trail to trail, dismissing each for one reason or another. Some veered suddenly into darkness, and Evan preferred to see where he was heading. Others he bypassed because of suspicious-looking weeds. His skin, his mother had informed him, was susceptible to rashes. She'd taken great pains to educate him about the number of leaves on poison ivy, the devastating effects of poison oak. The only lesson Evan's young mind had taken from these tutorials was that plants, in general, were to be feared.

After thirty minutes of scouring the meadow's perimeter for a suitable point of entry, Evan found one. The mouth of the trail was perhaps six feet wide, broad enough for even a person of Evan's girth to pass through. Further, the corridor seemed a straight shot – no sudden turnings or tumbles into an abyss. Likewise there were no weeds that threatened to inject his bare knees with their insidious poisons. Most importantly of all, he didn't spy a single hanging branch, which meant that any snakes would have to approach from the ground.

Glad he'd chosen the high-reaching tube socks to cover his calves, Evan entered the forest. A minute's walk reassured him he'd chosen the correct trail, for though he did glimpse the occasional bird, he'd heard no secretive rustlings among the dead leaves.

Something tickled at his shoulder.

Evan gasped and stumbled away, his arms thrown out in a warding-off gesture.

Just a branch, he now realized, broken but not snapped completely. How had he not seen it? What thoughts had possessed him so utterly that he'd failed to spot the very thing he was so vigilant about noticing? Like a spear, the branch tapered to a wicked point, almost as though someone had arranged it there, a snare meant to impale its victim.

The Sword of Damocles, he thought.

Evan smiled wryly. Now where had that come from? He'd heard the tale a long time ago and remembered liking it. Something about a servant named Damocles telling the king he wanted to switch places. The king told him yes, he would switch places with the servant. Only there was one stipulation: a deadly sword would hang by a single horsehair over the servant while he sat upon the throne.

It was, Evan remembered his teacher explaining, a lesson about the responsibilities of leadership and the constant shadow of fear a leader must endure.

Evan continued down the trail. It was Roderick Wells who occupied the throne in this strange kingdom. What was it like to be the most celebrated author on the planet? Did Wells feel pressure to—

A dull crack sounded behind him.

He spun, mouth open in a soundless scream, and saw the long branch pierce the path exactly where he had just stood. The branch remained upright for a moment, like a javelin. Then, it listed slowly to the side and came to rest on the soft humus.

If you'd been standing there... a voice whispered.

Enough! Evan's mind cried. *I came here to find my muse, not to frighten myself into a tizzy over a falling branch.*

Still...Evan found himself inclining his head, eyeing the overhanging trees with suspicion.

Time to go back, the voice told him.

No, he answered. *Time to stop being a coward.*

Resolutely, Evan continued into the forest.

CHAPTER NINE

Someone was following him.

Evan spun around, skin tingling. Maybe he should turn back. Though he could still pass untrammeled, the trail had narrowed markedly, so that several times he had to draw his arms in to prevent them from scraping some hoary-looking shrub. The vegetation had grown larger and denser, so that it now seemed to surround him like the forest in some macabre fairy tale.

Evan brushed off the thought, his mouth fixed in a grim line. He'd lived his life in fear, and at age twenty-seven it was long past time for him to mature, to *do something* rather than remaining cloistered in his room. Alone.

Exploring the woods wasn't the same as lying with a woman, he knew, but it was a start. If he could tap into his well of creativity, maybe he could write something salable. And if he did that, the professors at Columbia would reward him with offers of assistantships. Then he could teach part- time and write. Oh, the first book might not be a bestseller, but it would garner attention. With his second and third books his audience would swell, and he'd begin to make money, money that hadn't come from his parents, and then he could afford nice things, and with better clothes and a sleek new car, he would attract *women*.

Yes....

Evan trudged up a hill and ruminated. Men got good jobs and lifted weights and did things to make themselves handsome because they wanted to attract women. Why should women be any different? They exercised and picked out sultry dresses that displayed their breasts and hugged their buttocks so that the electrifying lines of their panties showed through...and they did this to attract men. And why hadn't Evan enjoyed, up close, the fairer sex? Very simply, because he hadn't done anything to make himself attractive. That's what it came down to, wasn't it?

The heat of the day permeated the forest. Evan's light blue shirt clung to his skin, so he unbuttoned it and peeled it off his shoulders. He endeavored to tie it around his midriff the way he thought men sometimes did, but no matter how he bundled it, the fabric wouldn't stretch far enough around his middle to tie a knot. Evan decided to stuff one end of the shirt into the front of his waistband.

He set off again, not liking the way the shirt dangled between his legs. He felt ridiculously like a little boy who's picked up some long object and pretended it's his penis.

He angled toward a dark valley and thought about women. They'd be amazed at his ability to use words – all his professors commented on his word choice – and ask him questions at book signings.

Evan chuckled, no longer bothered by the foliage. He imagined a cocktail party at an old house. It would be located in a venerable – Evan smiled at the adjective – neighborhood in the Hamptons, and would belong to his editor. There he'd meet the long-legged blond woman. Her skin would have that tawny glow, her hair that just-cut-and-styled look that made him ill with longing.

He would half turn to her – he'd be leaning over the rail of some balcony – and with the breeze attractively stirring his hair, he'd say hello.

She'd be giggly, and he'd put her at ease and permit her to ask questions:

What made you become a writer?

Oh, it's just in me, I suppose.

She'd smile. Pearly teeth. Full, pink lips. *Where do you get your ideas?*

Mostly – he'd tap his head – *they come from in here.*

That's amazing. Her tongue flicking out and playing over her teeth. *What do you do when you're not writing?*

A self-deprecating laugh. *Oh, I like to read, explore nature. I'm very much at peace in the forest.*

Her face becoming earnest, a coyness in her blue eyes. *Maybe you'll take me with you some time.*

Oh yeah? A sideways look from him. Cool. No trace of eagerness.

She'd nod, the offer plain in her sensual expression.

He'd say, *How about tonight? Take some wine, a blanket.*

She'd shiver, lean into him, grip the elbow patch of his tweed sports coat. Her sweet, citrus breath close to his lips. *I'd love that.*

And they'd go.

Evan was semi-erect. He imagined the spot in the forest to which he'd take her, the bluegrass still matted from the last woman. But the leggy blonde wouldn't know that. She'd think they had a future together and she would be a rich author's wife. But she'd be wrong. And they'd lie together in the starshine. He would lick at her round, ethereal breasts and bury his face between her splayed legs, make her moan, make her howl.

Evan was stroking himself through his shorts, but it was no good, too many layers of fabric. It made it better in a way, a filthy, itching unrequited heat, but he longed so badly for that sweet release that he tore open the zipper and yanked his shorts down.

He shed his boxers and staggered forward, the divine heat of the forest making his nudity seem natural rather than something vulgar. It occurred to him he'd never been naked outdoors before. He'd never gone skinny-dipping, never made love in a bluegrass dale, and despite his autoerotic addiction, he'd never masturbated in the forest.

But he was doing it now, by God. He diddled himself expertly, taking his time about it, and he discovered something that made him pause.

The trail had come to an abrupt end.

He stood there, breath coming in torrid waves, and studied the semicircle of shrubs, the density of the palmated leaves.

A corner of his mouth rose. Rather than disappointing him, this sudden terminus pleased him. He had followed the trail to its conclusion.

And that meant his fear hadn't vanquished him! The poison and the bugs and the prowling snakes hadn't done a thing to him, nor would they, he suspected, anymore. If he could master this forest, he could meet any challenge.

Exultant, Evan faced the bullet-shaped end of the path and took himself in hand. He would finish his fantasy here, would spurt his seed on the soil.

He detected a furtive rasp in the brush to his left, but that no longer mattered. No animal would bother him. He was Evan Laydon, future famous author, and the women would genuflect at his feet. His body trembled, the exquisite pain razoring higher, deeper, and his fist pistoned up and down his short length, which wouldn't matter to the women he bedded because of who he was. The gorgeous blonde arched her back and bucked her hips, and Evan let loose inside her, a white geyser lifting her body in a perfect bright explosion....

Evan opened his eyes. Turned.

Discovered Bryan Clayton watching him.

Bryan's olive-green shirt hugged his hard muscles, his camouflage pants stretched tight over powerful quadriceps. Something jutted behind Bryan's head, but Evan couldn't quite see what it was. Nor did it matter. What mattered was how naked Evan was and the bundle of clothing Bryan clutched at his side.

Evan tried to swallow but couldn't. He hadn't realized how thirsty he was until now. Upon spotting Bryan he'd cupped both hands over his privates, but he was painfully aware of his droopy breasts – *titties* the jerks in his P.E. class had called them – and the pitiful tufts of hair reefing his nipples.

Take it easy, he told himself. *Bryan's probably just as embarrassed as you are.*

"Hey," Evan said and tried a smile.

Bryan watched him impassively.

"I didn't hear you," Evan said.

"Spanking your monkey too hard," Bryan said.

Evan cleared his throat. "I don't know what came over me."

"Were you thinking of Anna?" Bryan asked. "Or Lucy?"

He recognized the hectoring note in Bryan's voice, but there was something else there that bothered him a good deal more.

"Elaine maybe?" Bryan persisted. When Evan shook his head, Bryan's eyebrows rose. "Me?"

It acted on Evan like a slap. "I'd like my clothes back."

"You have to earn them."

"Give me—"

"Tell me something juicy."

Evan heaved a sigh, looked around at the unbroken wall of foliage.

"No fine print, Evan. Just tell me a secret and I'll give you your clothes back. One secret for every article of clothing."

Disgusted, Evan started to turn away, but he didn't like the idea of exposing his bare buttocks. He glanced at his laced fingers and saw the milky semen dribbling over his knuckles.

"Maybe this'll jar your memory," Bryan said, reaching back and pulling something long and slender from his back. It was a branch Bryan had fashioned into a spear, Evan now saw. One end of it glittered. Dangling from its opposite tip was a length of coiled rope.

"You know what this is?" Bryan asked, untying the knot that encircled the coil.

"A spear," Evan said, his throat dry.

"A *rope* spear," Bryan corrected. "The ancient Chinese used it as a weapon. African and South American tribes have fished with rope spears for millennia. Back where I grew up, in Carlsbad, we used to fashion these out of birch. It's a good, flexible wood. Hard enough it won't crack if you hit a rock, but with enough give you can haul up anything you gig with it. A friend and I, we frequented this hidden enclave over in Loma Point." He fingered the barbed steel tip. "We made four of these spearheads. Only one of them got lost. My friend Barry, he spotted a tuna that had caught itself in a tide pool. Barry harpooned it and reared back. The force of the spear had stunned the tuna, but when it felt Barry tugging, it went wild. The next thing we know, the spear is jerked right out of Barry's hands, and the tuna's swishing its tail at us as it disappears into the Pacific."

Evan took a step forward.

"A secret," Bryan demanded.

"That's absurd."

"I just shared something. Spear fishing is outlawed in California. Barry and I could have gotten into a lot of trouble."

Just say something, a voice insisted. *Just make something up so you can get your clothes back.*

"I...." Evan licked his lips. "I...uh, one time I cheated on a math test."

"How old were you?"

"Fifteen."

"What class?"

"Algebra."

"Why didn't you say 'algebra test'?"

Evan stared at him.

"You don't call them math tests when you're in high school," Bryan explained. "You say algebra or geometry, not math."

Evan shook his head. "I'm—"

"—*lying*," Bryan finished for him. "But I'll play nice."

Bryan reached down and pulled Evan's boxers out of the bundle.

"Here you go," Bryan said and lobbed the boxers at Evan. The air caught them and made them fall. Still covering himself with one hand, Evan shuffled forward and stooped. He turned the boxers around and was about to step into them when Bryan said, "Not yet."

Bent at a ninety-degree angle, Evan peered up at Bryan. The sweat stung his eyes. The blur made it seem like there were two Bryans rather than one.

"You don't get to put them on yet," Bryan repeated.

Evan eyed him through the stinging sweat for a long moment, then decided to hell with it, he'd put the damn things on anyway.

A zinging sound rent the silence of the forest. The boxers were jerked from his hands and flying away from him. Evan's glasses flew off. He straightened in time to see Bryan snatch the spear deftly out of the air. He plucked the boxers off the barbed point.

Teeth clenched, Evan retrieved his glasses. "Why'd you do that?"

"You lied to me."

Evan regarded the glittering spear tip. "How personal does it have to be?"

"*Juicy*," Bryan answered.

Evan hung his head. "I used to spy on girls."

"Spy how?"

"Watch them when they didn't know it."

"Naked?"

Evan swallowed. "Yes."

Bryan's expression grew doubtful. "You're awfully vague about it. Weirdos have kinks they fixate on. But you just said 'girls'. Why is that?"

"What do you want from me?"

"Why'd you say 'girls'?"

Evan shook his head. "Fine. I used to watch my sisters take showers."

Bryan's face lit up. "Evan! That *is* juicy. Older or younger?"

"One older, one a couple years younger."

"Excellent." Bryan reached down, grabbed Evan's shirt, and tossed it backhand.

"What about the underwear?"

"How'd you watch them?"

"Please stop this."

"You peek at them around the shower curtain? Your sisters weren't in the shower together, were they?"

Evan rolled his eyes. "No, they weren't *together*."

"So how'd you—"

"With a drill, okay? I used my father's drill to make a tiny hole."

Bryan's face clouded. "Through the tile?"

"It wasn't tile all the way up. There were...there was drywall between the tile and the ceiling."

"Did you jack off?"

Evan pursed his lips, hot shame burning his cheeks. "Yes I did, okay? Can I have my clothes back now?"

"That's pretty good," Bryan said. "I'll give you the rest, but don't put them on yet."

Bryan balled up the clothes, but hesitated.

"What now?"

"There's something you're not telling me."

"For God's sakes," Evan said. "I already told you something I've never told anybody, now give me back my pants!"

"Who were you thinking about just now?"

Evan shook his head. "What's the matter with you?"

"You'll tell me about whacking off to your little sister, but you won't admit to what you were just thinking. It stands to reason the thing you aren't telling is worse than the one you told."

Evan shook his head in astonishment. "What in the *hell* is wrong with you? Why are you so insulting? What gives you the right to—"

"This," Bryan said, raising the spear.

And before Evan knew what was happening, Bryan was slinging it right at him, the gleaming point hardly wavering as it sliced down the path, whizzing toward his stomach. Evan jerked his hands together instinctively. White hot pain sizzled his palm. A shallow cut, but one that bled freely.

"Talk," Bryan said, catching the rope spear. "And if you leave anything out, I'll put this through your windpipe."

Evan looked up slowly from his wound.

And started to talk.

CHAPTER TEN

From *The Stars Have Left the Skies*, by Elaine Kovalchyk:

Kerri squirms in the passenger's seat and knows something has changed. Scott's teeth are chattering so violently she's reminded of those joke-store wind-up teeth, and though she's freezing too – she still can't get over the fact that Scott got the Hummer started despite the fact that it's hovering below negative forty degrees out here – a weird species of calm is beginning to sough over her, not unlike a sifting of powdery snow. The only parts of Scott that aren't mummified by scarves are his mouth, his nose, and his eyes, and what skin is visible is already bright pink from the chill. The Hummer, miraculously, hasn't gotten lodged in the grille-high drifts yet, but she suspects it's only a matter of time. They're approaching a ridge, and though it isn't steep, it's going to be enough to fold its bone-white fingers over their vehicle, the same way the other vehicles they've passed were claimed by the snow.

How many dead? she wonders again. *How many corpses per car?*

For the first time in days the sun is out and absolutely beaming over the hardpacked snow, yet it doesn't provide the merest suggestion of heat, only a brain-piercing sunglare. Scott's teeth are clicking so rapidly she's sure they'll chip, and that's when she sees it, the farmhouse to their left. Kerri remembers the psychologist – psychiatrist? She can never remember the difference – who lives there, recalls the stories about him, but frankly she doesn't care about any of that now because it isn't just the psychologist/psychiatrist she sees in the window of the farmhouse, it's a phalanx of faces, six or seven of them at least, the pink oval chins and the boiled-egg eyes goggling at the Hummer as it bulls its way up the ridge.

The Hummer begins to lurch.

"Stop at the farmhouse," she says in a voice so tight she doesn't recognize it.

"Fuck that," Scott says and rips off his gloves.

She shoots a glance at his knuckles, sees they are white, though not the bluish-white of the barren iceworld entombing them. She imagines the skin of his hands turning gray and sloughing off, revealing lusterless bone, and the thought unnerves her to such a degree that she glances at his face to make sure he still has a face. She's seen the denuded bodies, has no idea what is doing that to people, as if the worst cold spell in recorded history isn't enough, as if death wasn't already a certainty.

Kerri is thinking this when the Hummer slams into a drift.

The seatbelt whips her against her seat, and Scott says, "I guess you get your wish."

She stares at him uncomprehendingly and he grins a singularly terrible grin and explains, "The farmhouse. Hell, it was your idea to begin with."

That's right, she realizes. Her idea has never been to escape, has always been to find shelter in another house. Because Scott has begun to scare her. Seventeen days snowed in their home, and her husband no longer resembles the man she married. Or the man she thought she married.

"Come on," he says, and begins to open his door.

"*Wait*," she yells, but it is too late then, and she sees it happen with crystalline clarity:

The door crunching into the frozen drift, the gap between door and frame perhaps six inches.

The figures from the farmhouse, two men, evidently attempting to rescue them. They stumble through the snow, shouting, but something makes them stop, their eyes widening in terror, and then they beat a wild retreat back the way they came.

Scott is watching them too, and he grunts, in his cynical way, "No more Good Samaritans, huh? Well, screw it. Come on," and he grabs her hand too roughly, and when he turns and looks at her, she sees the first beetle crawl over his shoulder. It must have dropped inside from the roof, or perhaps it emerged from the drift itself, but now there are a dozen of them, gleaming obsidian beetles no larger than pencil erasers, teeming over Scott's exposed flesh. He begins to scream, but they're already feeding on his skin, peeling his lips back, his teeth and jawbone exposed like something on the desert sand.

CHAPTER ELEVEN

When they sat down for dinner that evening Lucy noticed the extra chair and figured it was for Wilson. She didn't like that at all, got goose bumps thinking about the stone-faced man. Rick sat catty-corner from her. As Miss Lafitte, the tiny maid, walked around filling their water glasses, Lucy mentally implored Rick to look at her, but he appeared too consumed with his thoughts to pay her any mind. *He's in the zone*, she thought, a little wistfully. What she wouldn't give to be there too.

Lucy's gaze was drawn to Evan. His skin appeared sallow, his shoulders slumped. Had Wells given him a stinging private critique?

He's next, she thought. Then wondered, *Where's Tommy?*

Servants bustled about the room, several Lucy hadn't seen before. They filled water glasses, brought in trays of bread and silver tureens of soup.

"I could get used to this," Bryan remarked.

Anna's eyes glittered as she studied the coffered ceiling. "To hell with getting used to it. I'd like to *live* here."

Lucy tracked Anna's gaze to the French doors that led to the courtyard and experienced a moment's vertigo. Not only were the curtains new – or at the very least, they'd been washed and bleached – but the brass door handles gleamed like they'd just been installed.

What's so extraordinary about that? she wondered. *The servants spent their day preparing the room. So what?*

So it feels like we've traveled back in time to when the dining room was first built.

She brushed away the thought with a shiver.

Wells entered with his wife. Lucy stared at the man, stunned at the change in his appearance. She supposed it was a matter of simple grooming: he'd shaved, and the hair around his ears had been trimmed. Yet there was something more at work, something subtler yet more profound. His eyes shone with a vitality that hadn't been there the first night. The deep grooves in his forehead were less pronounced.

It's the chandeliers, she told herself. *You saw him by firelight last night. The glow in here is more flattering.*

Still....

Mrs. Wells sat to her husband's right, the empty seat to Wells's left. Lucy waited with crawling flesh for Wilson to occupy the empty place.

Wells said, "Tommy Marston has left us."

"I knew it," Bryan said, sitting back.

Lucy glared at him. "You don't have to look so gleeful."

"He didn't say goodbye to anybody?" Elaine asked.

"Why," Bryan said, "you hurt he didn't share a moment with you before he left?"

But rather than taking the bait, Elaine frowned. "Neither of them did. Marek just went with that cop, and Tommy...he just disappeared?"

"Stop being sentimental," Anna said. "Eliminations are part of the contest."

"That doesn't mean we have to be heartless," Elaine countered.

Anna opened her mouth to respond, but stopped abruptly. Lucy followed her gaze and discovered Wells leaning on the table, his expression livid.

"Are you quite finished carping?" Wells said.

"I'm sorry, sir," Anna said.

He glanced at Elaine, who averted her eyes. "Sorry," she mumbled.

Wells looked at Bryan, who drew back a little, shrugged. "I didn't mean anything by it."

"Our words," Wells said, "have meaning. When one claims he didn't mean anything by what he said, he's lying through his teeth. Have you forgotten the importance of honesty?"

Bryan lowered his gaze. "I apologize."

"That's better," Wells said. He pushed away from the table and nodded. "Tonight marks the end of our third day together, and experience has taught me that the fourth day of any endeavor can be trying. At roughly four days, fatigue sets in. It's why many writers never finish their first novel, and if they do, it's the only one they ever write."

Wells swept the group with his keen eyes. "At four days, the initial burst of creative energy is all but spent. Enthusiasm is potent stuff, but like a magnesium flash, it is short lived. Writers cannot endure on a single blinding burst. They must continually search for means of renewal, of inspiration."

Wells smiled and said, "Please welcome our guest."

The dining room door opened.

Lucy's first thought upon beholding Corrina Bowen was that the woman was both shorter and scrawnier than she would have guessed. In a *Publishers Weekly* feature, the black-and-white photos depicted an elegant, sweet-natured woman with a knowing smile and a perceptive gaze.

In person, Bowen's gauntness was borderline disturbing. Her light brown skin and frizzy gray hair looked healthy enough, but the knobby appearance of her shoulders – bare in a navy blue sundress – and the manner in which her cheekbones protruded troubled Lucy. A quick mental estimate put the woman in her early seventies, but because of the haggard look in her eyes and the prominence of her bones, Bowen could pass for someone ten years older.

The group applauded, the others apparently not as shocked by Bowen's appearance as Lucy was, and as the sounds of adulation swelled, Bowen responded with a humble bow.

As she sat, her gaze lingered on Lucy. If Bowen noticed how forced Lucy's return smile was, she didn't let on.

At dinner they talked of Bowen's books, the successful film adaptations. Bowen confessed to an aversion to the films, arguing they routinely missed the point of her stories. Lucy listened but said little. Anna kept turning away from Bowen's gentle-voiced descriptions to whisper to Rick, who seemed uncomfortable.

Near the end of dinner, Wilson entered and said to Mr. Wells, "The woman from the *New York Times* is on the phone again. She wants a quote about being named Nobel Laureate."

"I gave her one last week," Wells said. He shook his head. "That's ten minutes I'll never get back."

"She claims she needs more. I wouldn't bother you, but her deadline is this evening."

Wells sniffed, placed his cloth napkin on the table. "Typical inefficiency," he muttered. He glanced at Corrina Bowen and said, "I know this reporter's type. If I don't provide some witty aphorism, she'll dream one up and make me look foolish."

With that, he left the dining room. Lucy noticed Anna watching after him with a starstruck gaze.

After dinner they had drinks in the courtyard and patiently awaited the chance to speak with Ms. Bowen. Lucy spoke to Sherilyn and Will a bit, but she spent much of the time by herself walking about the courtyard. It was a bit depressing out here, the landscaping overgrown in some places, the plants blighted in others. The walkways and pavers were cracked and moss-covered, the marble and granite benches weathered and sinking. Much of the ivy creeping up the brick and stone walls around them had withered and died, and damp catches of leaves choked the majority of the gardens. A characterless gray fountain, ten feet high, stood disused and forlorn in the center of the courtyard.

Bryan stood staring up at the fountain and scribbling in his notebook. As Lucy looked on, Wilson appeared from the other side of the fountain and approached Bryan.

Wilson's voice was just audible from where Lucy stood, twenty feet away. "You need to spend less time looking around and more time doing," Wilson said to Bryan.

Bryan didn't even look at the servant. "I'm writing, like Mr. Wells told us to."

Wilson reached out, seized Bryan's wrist.

"Hey," Bryan started, but Wilson cut him off.

"I'm not talking about writing, Mr. Clayton. I'm talking about *doing*."

Bryan stared incredulously at Wilson. "Let go of my— that hurts, dammit."

"Keep your voice down, Mr. Clayton," Wilson said, and as though Bryan were a child, the servant drew him closer.

Lucy strained to hear Wilson's words.

"This is a process of elimination, Mr. Clayton. I need you to be more *competitive.*" He squeezed Bryan's wrist; Bryan winced. "Do we understand each other?"

"I think so," Bryan said in a small voice.

Wilson released him, smiled broadly. "Enjoy the rest of your evening, Mr. Clayton. And get to work."

Watching after him, Bryan rubbed his wrist. Then, he moved toward the French doors and disappeared inside.

Lucy frowned, appraised the remaining dinner guests.

Rick had disappeared early on. Anna did as well, though they left at different times. Their dual absences cast a cloud over Lucy's mood, and when someone tapped her on the shoulder and she turned to find Corrina Bowen smiling at her, Lucy was utterly unprepared.

"I hear you've been through the circus already," Bowen said.

The woman stood about five feet tall, weighed no more than a hundred pounds.

Lucy managed a smile. "This is an unexpected thrill."

Bowen nodded as Lucy told her how much she enjoyed her work, how deeply she admired her skill.

Bowen said something Lucy couldn't make out.

Lucy leaned forward. "I'm sorry?"

The serene grin still fixed on her face, Bowen repeated, "Escape now."

Lucy drew back slightly. "I'm not sure I understand."

The grin was still there – just the merest hint of white teeth gleaming through pink lips – but the eyes had widened considerably.

"Get out while you still can."

Lucy glanced about and noticed the others were occupied. Evan and Elaine were squabbling. Sherilyn and Mrs. Wells were listening to Roderick Wells, and Will was standing by himself, looking out of place and miserable.

When Lucy glanced again at Corrina Bowen, the woman's grin had fled. Her eyes were huge and haunted, her mouth trembling. Bowen leaned closer, grasped her by the shoulders. "Can't you see I'm in hell, girl? Can't you see where all this is leading?"

The breath puffing out of the woman was fetid, a rank broth of coffee and halitosis. Lucy tried but could not look away. The fingers on her shoulders dug deeper.

"Don't you see it, you stupid little cunt?" Bowen demanded. The bony fingers squeezed. "Your dreams are *bullshit*. You think this isn't gonna come at a price? You think I can sleep at night knowing what went on here fifty years ago?"

Lucy tried to push away. "Miss Bowen, you're hurting me."

Bowen's grin was ghastly. "*I'm* hurting you? You don't know the meaning of hurt." Bowen shook her. "You're just stickin' that tight ass out hoping Roderick will pick you. I know it because I *lived* it."

"Stop it."

"Why do you think I came back here tonight? To get you fuckers out of here." A brutal shake. "You hear me? Tell the others—"

Bowen sucked in air and released her. She was staring at something to Lucy's right. Lucy turned, saw Wells glowering at Bowen, his face taut with rage. The others looked on with thunderstruck expressions.

"Have you forgotten what you did, Corrina?" Wells asked.

Bowen backed away. Wells didn't have to follow. His venomous stare even made Lucy tremble.

"I don't countenance treachery, Corrina," Wells said. "And I certainly won't forget."

Bowen was almost to the French doors, on her face an expression of purest terror. Tears streaked the woman's brown cheeks. Lucy experienced a moment's pity for her.

The last she saw of Corrina Bowen was the woman hurrying through the French doors, the curtains billowing behind her.

PART THREE
MONSTERS

CHAPTER ONE

That night Will sat at his desk and told himself he had to keep writing. But an ugly truth hovered over him like a cloud of gnats.

He had to return to the island.

Something told him he'd left the island too quickly, that there was more to see than just Anna Holloway and her killer body.

So go back.

Will considered.

What have you got to lose? the voice in his head asked.

Will drummed his fingers. He hadn't taken off his clothes for bed. All he'd have to do was slide on his tennis shoes and head outside.

You remember the way?

He thought he remembered the way, but he couldn't be sure.

He pushed away from the desk, went over and laced his sneakers. Then, taking care not to slam his bedroom door – the others were probably asleep by now – he hurried down the corridor.

It's very late, a voice reminded him. *And very dark.*

He frowned but kept going.

What if you trip and hurt yourself?

I'll be careful.

What about mosquitoes? You don't have bug spray.

They haven't bothered me yet.

If you're really lucky, you can get yourself lost in the forest.

He'd reached the first-floor landing when he stopped, a feeling of absurdity taking hold.

What the hell was he doing? It was going on one in the morning. If he was going to be worth anything tomorrow, he'd better get to bed now. Otherwise, he'd wake up around noon and drift through the day like a zombie.

Will was slinking up the stairs when he became aware of another figure on the second-story landing. Stopping, he looked up, and saw Roderick Wells.

Wells said, "Never avoid truth, Mr. Church."

Will experienced a fleeting, but very powerful memory of the way his big brother used to bar his way up the stairs after they ventured down to their basement. He'd laugh in Will's face and say, "How long you gonna be a crybaby, *Willy*?"

"Move, BJ." The cold sweats would start then, a harbinger of panic.

"Almost a third grader and still afraid of monsters."

"I'm not afraid of them." Telling himself not to glance into the pooled shadows behind him because if he did that, he would see something, and once he saw something – real or not – the wild fit would ensue, the pummeling of fists on BJ's chest and the sobbing and the pleading.

"It's that thing in the crate," BJ would tease. "The gorilla creature."

Will would sneak a glance between the open stair slats then, a movement brought on by the memory of a movie BJ rented with the sole intent of scaring the bejesus out of Will, a movie called *Creepshow*. It was really several movies in one, but the storyline that stuck with him involved a husband whose wife was a total shrew. The husband found a large crate that turned out to have something really bad in it. A monster. And the wife – an actress named Adrienne Barbeau; Will had memorized her name because he'd seen a lot of her cleavage in *Cannonball Run* and almost her entire naked body in *Swamp Thing* – ended up getting eaten by the monster. The crate had been stored under a stairwell, and though Will's family didn't have any crates and didn't store anything under their basement steps, at moments like these, when BJ was playing his cruel game, Will became convinced the very same creature would seize him by the ankles and drag him screaming through the stairs.

"The monster's gonna get you," BJ would say.

"No he's not," Will would answer, his bottom lip trembling.

"He's got sharp teeth, Willy. He's smiling at you now."

"Dammit, BJ, stop!"

Will would try to barge past his older brother, but he knew he had no chance.

"He's staring at you with those red eyes, Willy, he's *hungry* for you, he's...." And BJ's voice would blend with the white noise of panic shrilling in Will's ears, and Will knew the gorilla monster's eyes were not red, were a pale yellow, except for the crocodilian pupils that laughed at him and told him he was dead, but first he would suffer, and the mane of stark-white hair surrounding the ghastly face would loom closer, enshrouding him, and the teeth, my God the *teeth*, too numerous and sharp to belong to any living creature, were opening as the great laughing jaw unhinged.

"Brothers can be awful, can't they," Wells said.

Will swung his head up. He told himself it was impossible that Wells knew about BJ, because if he knew about those things, he could know *other* things.

Will gestured lamely behind him. "I was going downstairs for a snack."

"Be candid, Mr. Church."

"I was...." Will broke off, shook his head. "I had this crazy idea that if I went somewhere, I might...."

"You've been struggling."

Will looked at him. "That's right."

"You had it in mind to return to the place where inspiration struck."

Will clutched the banister tighter.

"It's a wise notion," Wells said.

"It is?"

"I learned as a young writer that a place can serve as a touchstone for a story. I've frequented carnivals, brothels. I once spent the night in a graveyard to better hear the voices of the dead."

Will stared at Wells, awed. "Do you still do that?"

"Mr. Church, why do you think I live here? For the convenience?" He spread his arms. "This place...*this place*...is a wonderland of hideous beauty. Of dreadful passion. The water that flows on this property is laced with the elixir of madness, the trees nourished by the blood of the damned."

Will swallowed. He found it impossible to look away from Wells's black eyes. Within them he saw colors swirling, luring him deeper, deeper....

"The night is your mistress," Wells said, his voice supplicating. "The forest is your gateway, the island an enchantment. Your muse awaits you there, Mr. Church. You must go to her. You must accept her macabre embrace."

"Her embrace," Will whispered.

"Now, Mr. Church." Wells gripped his shoulder. "*Now.*"

Will was seized by the sensation of rushing upward; the staircase around him reappeared. He blinked at Wells, realized the man's eyes were a dark brown, not black.

Released from whatever spell he'd been under, Will thought about Wells's words. After a moment, he finally found his voice. "So you think...if I revisit this spot...."

"It's your touchstone," Wells said. "Where your magic is contained."

"You think?"

"It only needs you to draw it out."

Will gestured behind him. "So I should go there now?"

"I wouldn't delay, Mr. Church. You are the story's sorcerer. You must conjure it into existence."

Will found a shy smile forming. "I'm the sorcerer?"

"You are," Wells said. "Now go. Create!"

Feeling better than he had since arriving, Will hustled down the stairs.

With the help of a flashlight he commandeered from the kitchen pantry, he made his way to the lake. He aimed the flashlight beam across the water. The island looked very different without Anna sunbathing on its beach. The woods beyond the pale strip of sand looked denser, the darkness deeper.

Quit stalling.

Will removed his socks and shoes. He stepped closer to the shore.

Okay, he thought. *Here I go.*

He waded into the water. A dozen aquatic horror films flickered through his mind. *Jaws*. A spine-tingling little affair called *Open Water*. He peered at the lake.

Remembered a scene in *Creepshow*, how the monster in the crate had sunk to the bottom of a quarry.

The water lapped gently against his bare shins. Another couple steps and his shorts would be soaked.

Did he really need to set foot on the island? Wasn't he close enough already?

Move your ass, he told himself. *You heard what Wells said.*

Wells isn't the one out here in the middle of the night with his testicles shriveling.

Will frowned. He steadied the flashlight, aimed the beam at a spot perhaps fifty feet distant. He'd been sure there'd been movement on the beach, a subtle shifting in the sand.

He spotted it then, a figure. Unmistakably female, unmistakably nude. But it wasn't Anna Holloway. The hair was too dark, the skin color all wrong. He played the flashlight beam along the woman's body.

Screamed when the hideous black eyes battened onto his.

He backpedaled through the shallow water. The woman

(*the Siren*)

was crawling toward him, a wormy black tongue slithering out of her mouth, the lips rippling in a hideous grin.

Will scrambled onto the shore. He didn't even pause to grab his shoes and socks, instead sprinted toward the gazebo, where he hooked a left and bolted for the forest. He had no idea whether the Siren was pursuing him, but he sure as hell wasn't going to tempt fate.

His lungs burning, a sharp pain stabbing his ribs, Will staggered into the woods. He'd shambled along for maybe a minute before he came to a rise. He clambered up the hillside, stood panting.

Something at the base of the hill drew his attention.

"Oh Jesus," Will whispered.

The remains of a house.

Before a face could appear in the hollowed-out foundation, Will took off running in the opposite direction.

CHAPTER TWO

From the Diary of Sherilyn Jackson:

Left you hanging, didn't I?

I thought I'd feel foolish spilling my guts to a flower-covered notebook (Where'd you get it, Alicia? Target? Barnes & Noble?) but I've gotta admit, after I shared my thoughts last time, I felt a hell of a lot better.

I was telling you how David Zendejas tried to strangle me. It became a frequent thing later on. I once read a book called The Joy of Sex, which contained detailed sketches and a lot of stuff that made me blush. There was a term in it called 'little death'. It's apparently a state of such intense passion that the woman faints, therefore dying a little death. I've also heard that people incorporate strangling into their bedroom routine. As in 'I'm fucking you and strangling you at the same time and this'll somehow make your orgasm more powerful.' To me that's a dumbass concept, but you look hard enough you'll find folks who get off on just about anything. Being peed on, getting abused with flyswatters, what have you.

For Zendie the choking wasn't a kink. He was authentically pissed off. But it wasn't the worst thing he did to me. Not even close.

I can't tell you about that. Not yet.

What I can tell you is how motherfucking poor we became in those three years. Not only had Zendie been demoted and emasculated (his word), but his church underwent hard times. Donations were down, the coffers ran low, and Zendie's paltry salary nosedived into poverty territory. Predictably, he became mad-dog mean and took it out on me.

I don't tell you all this to elicit pity. I hate pity. Nothing pisses me off more than someone pitying me.

Which is why it irks me to say I pitied myself during those three years of hell.

Everyone knew that Zendie was paying for dipping his wick in the wrong pot and deserved the humble pie he was eating. The head pastor, a white man with a great shock of blond hair and a smile almost as electric as Zendie's, made a habit of giving Zendie the jobs nobody else wanted. You know, driving all over God's creation to administer communion to shut-ins. Canvassing the neighborhoods for more members.

Then everything changed.

The first was a bombshell about the head pastor. Turns out, he and his shiny blond hair had been embezzling funds going on a decade.

The blond bastard went to jail, that was the first thing.

The second was my husband getting promoted.

If there's one thing David Zendejas likes more than pussy, it's playing the hero. Living out his messianic fantasies, accepting folks' tear-stained gratitude. And Lord, did the gratitude flow after Zendie saved the church. He still beat the hell out of me and returned home smelling of perfume and womansweat. But he saved the church from bankruptcy and in doing so caught the eyes of Montgomery First Baptist, the biggest and best-paying church in Alabama.

There was even happier news.

Though my mom had always been dirt poor, her parents had been smart enough to purchase land when prices were low. Suburban development encroached and what was once worth a few thousand bucks was now worth several hundred thousand. Bidding careened out of control and the price tag breached a million dollars. When the land sold, my grandparents did the most surprising thing of all. They gave it to my mom. Said they had no use for it and would be happy knowing their only daughter would have some security and a few nice things.

How did all this affect me? you might ask.

Lord in heaven....

I've told you Zendie is a charismatic son of a bitch. He'd always had a Svengali-like hold on my mother. Unbeknownst to me, he got her to invest in some projects. My mom figured this would ensure a sizable inheritance for each of her children, not just a million or so divided up nine ways.

Goddammit. Another thing I can barely talk about.

You ready for this, Diary? You ready for the coup de grace?

Zendie told me we could get pregnant.

And lying beneath him, his handsome face smiling beatifically down at me, I believed all my dreams were coming true. I orgasmed so hard our rafters rattled. Three weeks later I peed on the stick and did a double take. Zendie told me, Honey, this is marvelous news. Would you like some more marvelous news?

I told him sure, I was up for that. I really dug that word, marvelous, and was craving more of it.

I got the head pastor job at Montgomery First Baptist.

I damn near fainted.

When he informed me what his salary would be, I'm pretty sure I did faint. We celebrated by making love, and I told myself this was the end of all the badness. His abusiveness, I reasoned, was brought on by financial strain, his infidelity born of insecurity. He'd always felt unsettled about his profession, and now that he'd scored his dream job he wouldn't go around looking for validation under some woman's skirt.

I'd never been more wrong.

Okay, I just went downstairs to the bar of Wells's mansion and steeled myself for what I'm about to write. In case you're wondering, I didn't drink when I was pregnant with baby Vivien. I got the name from Gone with the Wind. My mom was proud of the actress who played the servant because she'd broken the race barrier at the Oscars, but I asked my mom, What's the big deal, she's playing a slave. Mom had gotten that cold stubborn look she got when she thought I was being disrespectful and told me I would do well to accomplish half as much as Hattie McDaniel did. Mom may have been right but I couldn't get over the slave thing. *To hell with that,* I thought. *I want to be the one who owns all that land, not the one stuck in the kitchen.* So I chose the name Vivien.

Then Zendie took the job at First Baptist and became a monster again, only now it was a hundred times worse.

Turns out, his philandering wasn't caused by professional unrest. Within a week of taking the post he began disappearing for long stretches, some nights not even bothering to come home. You'd think all that fucking would take its toll on a man, but Zendie never looked more robust than he looked then.

Also incorrect was my assumption he would stop beating me. Now he raged at me every time he saw me. He boxed my shoulders, punched my breasts. He choked me but I'd become used to that and could hold my breath for a long time.

The breaking point was when he targeted baby Vivien.

See, here's where we get into abortion. I've always been saddened by the whole goddamned thing. I guess if I have to come out on one side or the other I'd be pro-choice, but that might only be because I've been abused so fucking much and feel bad for women who have to carry the babies of monsters. But I understand the pro-life crowd (except for the ones who bomb abortion clinics, those fuckers are monsters too) and feel heartsick when I think of a fetus dying, and that's probably because I never look at a pregnant belly and think fetus, I think baby, and goddammit, I thought of Vivien as a baby from the moment Zendie squirted his spunk inside me. I can even tell you the time, day, month, and year because it was the best sex we'd ever had and Zendie had ejaculated like a fire hose, and because some primitive sense in me knew it had taken in that moment, I could almost hear a rabid soccer commentator screaming SCOOOOOOORE!

One night Zendie punched me in the gut.

He apologized afterward and told me it had been an accident. My breasts and my stomach had always been his favorite targets and I thought when he punched me in the gut it was just Zendie forgetting.

Okay, just returned from the bar again. I should probably just carry the goddamned bottle up here (we're drinking vodka tonight, Diary) but I'd like to believe I can escape when I want. These words judge me. They condemn me. And when I look at them, it all comes back, and I'm coming to the worst parts so I'll just let them out.

Zendie knows this doctor, a childhood friend named Terry Dove (like the bird or the soap, though nothing about Terry is peaceful or clean, least of all his conscience) who's a general practitioner but is willing to do jobs on the side. Terry Dove had performed three abortions on me and I hate myself for allowing Zendie to bully me into them but in my fucked-up twisted mind I thought it was my fault I got pregnant those times and I didn't deserve a baby yet. Zendie would always hold me afterward and tell me we could have a baby when we planned it and that somehow made it better.

I'm back. Didn't even know I was gone did you? More vodka.

Four months went by. Every time Zendie looked at me he was really looking at the baby. I avoided him when I could. Even put my hands over my belly in a protective gesture and if he noticed he didn't say anything, only stared at the growing bulge like it was an insect that needed killing.

The last time Zendie hit me I knew it was no accident because he did it again and again, and I staggered into the bathroom and tumbled into the tub and he was grasping the shower rod and stomping on my belly and I knew he was killing baby Vivien and as stupid as it sounds I kept repeating, *You said I could keep it if it was planned! You said I could keep it if it was planned!*

He didn't let me keep it. Terry Dove confirmed it that night in his office. Helped me deliver my dead baby and on the way home I told Zendie I was going to kill him. He was calm and said, yawning, that he was divorcing me. I said, *I'll get half of your possessions and still have all of my mom's money* and he said, *You won't have shit.* Said if I told anyone what he'd done he'd kill me. Said he'd give me a small amount to get me started and that my mom's money was gone, the investments had gone belly-up.

Do you know yet, Diary? Have you figured it out?

Most writers want a few things. Money (it always comes down to money). Fame (it often comes down to fame). Self-respect (not everyone gives a shit about self-respect, particularly if money and fame can offset their lack of it).

I don't want any of those.

Okay, maybe I want all of those, but I want something else.

Mom died a few months after learning what Zendie had done to her. Like he had with me, he threatened to have her killed if she said anything, and like me she shut up like a whipped dog. Mom died, and I was broken, but now I've got a decent business, a loving partner, and my writing.

I want more.

Zendie told me I was too chickenshit to kill him and in a way he was right. I don't want to go to jail. I don't want to lose the years ahead of me. I refuse to waste any more time on account of David Goddamned Zendejas. So I won't kill him.

Myself.

The most surprising part of hiring someone to murder your ex-husband is how expensive it is. In movies you can find someone to do the job for ten thousand bucks, but if anyone will do it for that sum I'd like to meet him. I must be frequenting the wrong hired-killer websites or something.

Alicia, she knows a woman who went through something similar. A woman who had her husband killed. Alicia asked the woman how much it cost and the woman told her a hundred grand.

I don't have a hundred grand but if I win this competition I will, and the first thing I'm going to do is pay the man I already hired to murder Zendie. I told him I'd pay him double if he'd videotape the killing and read a short script I prepared.

I don't want to go to jail, but I do want David Zendejas to die an ugly, nasty death. I want his secrets to come out so that the congregations he has led will see he's a monster. A dead monster who got castrated and tortured and raped with a machete.

Is it happening right now? Has it already happened? That was the deal: Five thousand bucks up front, the rest of the money after Zendie is dead.

The best part?

I have an alibi. I will have a publishing contract. I'll have what money I need.

Zendie, my man is coming for you.

You fucked with the wrong woman.

CHAPTER THREE

His body aching from his flight through the forest, Will lay in bed and remembered the summer of his tenth year.

Their house backed up to a dense forest, a place his brother avoided because it was infested with poison ivy. But a little poison ivy, Will reasoned, was better than being bullied by BJ. His parents would've killed him had they known where he was, but his parents weren't here, were they? And BJ was probably with his friends staring at *Playboys* and talking about which girls in their class had the biggest tits.

Will spotted a trail, a thin swath of weedless ground, full of crisscrossing roots and dried silt. He followed it for ten minutes. As he walked, the savage July heat descended on the forest. He was considering turning back when he noticed something that froze him where he stood.

An abandoned house.

Holy crap, he thought. He'd never spotted this derelict structure before, and he doubted any of his friends had either.

Which meant the discovery was entirely his.

Heart slamming, Will headed for the ruin.

One of the walls was missing, the others intact except for broken windows, which gaped at him like hollowed-out eye sockets. He eyed the dimpled roof warily. The door was gone, and it was this opening that afforded him a view of the missing floor and basement beneath.

He lingered outside the house, knowing he should turn back. That was the intelligent thing to do. The mature thing.

He climbed the steps and peered inside. His eyes swept the underside of the roof, which looked as if it had been riddled with shotgun blasts.

A strident caw made him cry out. He peered up, spotted the blackbird sheltering in a rafter and covered his thundering heart.

He didn't notice the man staring at him from below until a voice said, "Hey, champ."

Hissing, Will sprawled at the base of the porch and scrambled to his feet. He'd sprinted a goodly distance before the words the man was shouting registered.

"*Don't leave, champ! Aw, please don't leave!*"

Will cast a frightened glance backward, and the first seed of curiosity brought his mad dash to a halt. What kind of man, he wondered, lived in the foundation of an abandoned house?

A lunatic, that's who, a voice declared.

Will considered. The chances of encountering a lunatic in this sleepy town were remote. More likely it was a homeless person. Will licked his lips, keenly aware of his thirst. *And if* I'm *thirsty,* he thought, *how parched must the man in the house be?*

It's not just a man, the voice contended, *it's a bum. Homeless people can be dangerous. Unstable even.*

He still needs water, Will thought.

He mulled it over, rummaged for the word his father sometimes used.

Indigent.

The man was an indigent, and were Will's father here, he would have had the man arrested. Therefore, Will went home, packed a cooler, and returned to the shack.

Despite the basement shadows, he could clearly make out the man's figure. He lay in the ruins like a discarded mannequin, his clothes dusty and pale blue. The guy was older, fifty at least, and had a sunken face.

The man gazed up at him with woeful eyes and reclined awkwardly on a pile of boards. The pant leg covering the guy's calf glistened a dark red.

The man gave him a wan smile. "Doesn't look too good, does it, champ?"

Will slowly shook his head.

"I was trying to lower down here when a board gave way." The man glanced at his leg and winced. "Must've busted it when I fell. It hurts like a sonofabitch, apologies for my language."

Will relaxed a little. Something about the word *sonofabitch* made the man seem less like a fairy-tale troll trying to lure him under a bridge.

Shielding his eyes against a shaft of sunlight, the man said, "I was scared you wouldn't come back."

"My parents will wonder—"

"I'm not gonna hurt you."

When Will didn't answer, the man chuckled. "I guess that's what bad people always say, isn't it?" The man closed one eye and spoke in a crone's falsetto. "'*Don't be afraid of me, sonny. I ain't gonna hurt ya!*'"

Will grinned despite himself. The man made a decent witch.

Will gestured behind him. "I brought you some stuff."

"Don't tell me you've got some water with you. I'd just about kill for a drink of water." He grimaced. "Great choice of words, huh?"

Will got hold of the cooler. "How do I get it to you?"

"Looks like hard plastic. Should be okay if you drop it down."

Will nodded, was about to heave the cooler, when he paused. "You promise you'll give it back? My mom would kill me if she knew I was doing this."

"It'd probably be better if your mom didn't know about me."

Will took a step back and saw the man's eyes spring wide in fear.

"I didn't mean it like that," the man said hoarsely. "I'm not going to hurt you. I just…shit." He shook his head. "Everything I say sets off alarms in my head. I can't imagine how it sounds to you. I just— please don't leave, champ. I swear I'm not dangerous. I don't know how else to say it."

"Why don't you want me to tell my parents?"

"You know how people are. They hear of a homeless person around, they get worried. They get worried, they call the police."

"Is that what you are? Homeless?"

"Champ, I'm real thirsty. Could I have a drink? Then I'll tell you all about it."

Will heaved the cooler into the open foundation. It thumped down inches from the man, and without speaking, the man manipulated the cooler lid, came out with a bottle. With palsied hands, he tilted the bottle and chugged it in a few gulps. As he wolfed a ham sandwich, he hummed a tune Will recognized because his mother listened to the same kind of music: Glenn Miller's 'Moonlight Serenade'.

Soon the man was arranging the empty cooler on the tip of a board and raising it to where Will waited. He was about to leave when a thought hit him so hard that his fear returned in a black gush.

"A doctor," Will said.

The man stared at Will confusedly. "What's that, champ?"

"You didn't ask me to get a doctor."

The man shook his head, not getting it.

"You have a broken leg. You're bleeding. But you didn't ask me to get you a doctor. Why?"

The man's mouth worked a moment, then he made a vague gesture. "I can't afford one."

"That doesn't matter. He'd have to help you. He took the…." He flailed for the word, couldn't find it. "He took an oath."

The man gazed at him for a long moment. Then, perhaps realizing he wasn't going to fool Will so easily, he blew out a disgusted breath. "All right, champ. You want the story, I'll give it to you. But I warn you, it's a long one."

So the man told him how he got laid off, and his wife left him because he couldn't pay the bills. He lost his house, got sick, and because he didn't have health insurance, he nearly died. He'd thought this old shack might make a good shelter until winter.

The man rubbed his kneecap. "I could really use some Tylenol. You got any at your house?"

"You can't come there," Will said quickly.

The man held up a hand. "I didn't mean that. I was just hoping you'd fetch some painkillers."

So Will returned that day and twice the following day. He learned the man's name was Peter.

He brought Peter whatever he could scrounge from their medicine cabinet. He knew his mom would get wise to him eventually, but what was he supposed to do? Peter was badly injured. Will didn't need an oath to know you helped someone in need. Especially if he was poor.

In idle moments, Will found himself humming 'Moonlight Serenade'.

The third day he spent the better part of the afternoon hearing about Peter's two daughters. Peter teared up as he spoke about them and would rant about his wife. He called her The Bitch, and when the shock at hearing her referred to that way wore off, it made Will laugh because of how Peter would clap a hand to his mouth every time he said it, like it was always an accident. The Bitch, Will decided, deserved the things he said about her. Peter wasn't perfect – *What man is perfect, champ?* – but he tried to be a good dad, and for Will, whose father was about as involved as the guy who brought salt for their water softener every couple months, this was a highly admirable trait.

When his family went to town on Friday night, Will stole over to the drugstore and used the money he'd secreted to purchase more pain relievers.

He'd begun to worry about Peter. The man's complexion had grown sallow, and the dark circles under his eyes looked like more than the product of poor sleep.

Peter cried a great deal that evening and thanked Will over and over for his goodness. Not his kindness or his generosity, but his *goodness*. That word really stuck in Will's mind because it was so different to the way his family spoke about him.

Will does love his comic books, his mom would say.

He needs to screw his head on straight, his dad would answer, unoriginal even when he was demeaning.

BJ's verdict? *Will's a scared little pussy.*

They all regarded Will with a toxic mixture of bemusement and contempt.

But not Peter. With Peter it was always Will's goodness, his willingness to do the right thing.

They'd talk about other stuff too. Peter would say:

I love horror movies, champ. Which one's your favorite?

Or: *There's nothing wrong with using your imagination. It could take you places.*

Then: *I used to be afraid of the dark too. Don't you sweat it.*

So it didn't feel strange at all one evening to lower himself into the foundation to console Peter when he got emotional about his daughters. It didn't feel weird or wrong to hug Peter and let the man sob into his shoulder.

Those feelings would come later.

On the morning of the fifth day – it was Sunday, so his dad was home for breakfast – he heard his father saying something about a manhunt. Will looked up from his waffles and noticed how his mom shivered despite the equatorial heat in their cramped little kitchen.

"They think he headed to Indy," his dad was saying. "Figured he could blend in down there."

"Maybe he's nearby," his mom said.

"*Sharon*," his dad answered as though his mom had an IQ commensurate with the syrup bottle, "what would he want with Shadeland? He'd stick out like a sore thumb here."

Chastened, his mom returned to her toast and coffee. Will waited for someone to take up the conversation, but his mom had opted out and BJ was looking at a sports magazine.

"What did the man do?" Will asked.

His dad looked at him blankly.

Will felt his cheeks burn. "The man they're after. Why'd he go to jail?"

His mom tensed. "That's not something to discuss while we're eating, honey."

"Dad brought it up."

"He butchered his family," his dad said flatly. "That answer your question?"

Will's stomach dropped. "What's his name?"

"What's that got to do with it?"

Will looked at his dad's hostile face and thought, *Why can't you be more like Peter?*

Which was why it came as such a gut punch when his dad answered, "Peter Bates. The Morton Mangler."

That brought BJ out of his *Sports Illustrated*. "I thought you said he was from Peoria."

"Morton's just outside Peoria," his dad said.

"How did he kill them?" Will asked. He felt like he might puke up his waffles, but he had to know.

His dad set down his fork and folded his hands on the table. "I've kept quiet about your twisted fascination with blood and guts." When Will's mom started to intervene, he said, "And just because your mom is too gutless to put her foot down doesn't mean I have to let my son become a freak."

Will forced himself to meet his father's gaze. "How did he kill them?"

His dad's eyes widened, an ugly grin contorting his normally expressionless face. "You want to know how he killed them? I'll tell you how he killed them."

"Richard," his mom pleaded.

His dad ticked off facts on his fingers. "First Bates tied them up. His wife and his little girls. He raped his wife. He used tree loppers to cut off her hands at the wrists."

His dad counted off another finger. "He tied tourniquets around his wife's bleeding stumps so he could torture her longer. They speculate she was in and out of consciousness while Bates raped and lopped the hands off his little girls—"

"*Please,* Richard," his mom said.

"—and then staunched the blood from their stumps so they could witness their mother's decapitation."

"Stop it!" his mom yelled.

"Then he cut off *their* heads. Does that satisfy your morbid curiosity, Will?"

His mom left the room, ashen faced and sobbing.

A tear or two had spilled down Will's cheeks as well, but for a different reason. But he wasn't going to share that with his dad. He'd resolved to never share anything with his dad again.

BJ asked, "Why'd they think he was in Lafayette?"

"Bates escaped and stole a car. He strangled the driver and left the man's body in a ditch. He was spotted near Lafayette, and there was a chase."

Will's mind was racing. He didn't want to ask the question, but he had to. "Did he get shot in the leg?"

His dad's eyes narrowed. "How did you know that?"

Will swallowed. "It was on the news, wasn't it?"

"You said you didn't know about the manhunt."

Will gave a poorly contrived shake of the head. "I must've forgotten."

His dad's face went deadly serious. "I don't believe you."

Unable to meet that cold, penetrating stare, Will picked up his fork and studied what remained of his waffles. He could no more eat them than he could have eaten a tire iron, but if he moved them around long enough, he might get through breakfast unscathed.

Later that day, Will returned to the woods.

He'd been watching Peter for over a minute before the man opened his eyes, blinked up at him, then broke into a goofy grin. "Hey, champ. I must've been sawing logs. You bring me something to chow?"

Will didn't speak.

Peter's face clouded. He pushed into a sitting position. "Something wrong, champ? You're looking at me like I stole your favorite comic."

"Is your last name Bates?"

The man's goofy grin disappeared, something alert taking its place. "Before you make assumptions, I need to explain some things."

"You could've explained them the first time we met."

"They framed me, champ."

"What about the driver?" Will asked.

"Huh?"

"The one whose car you stole. The one you killed."

Peter shifted uncomfortably.

"Did someone else kill him too? Were you framed by the same person, or did someone different frame you this time?"

"You need to understand something, champ."

"Don't call me that."

"Fine," Peter snapped. "I'll just call you kid or something. What I'm trying to tell you, it wasn't my fault."

"It's never your fault."

"That's not what I mean."

"Someone made you cut off your wife's hands—"

"Don't say that."

"—and chop her head off—"

"I didn't—"

"—and kill your little girls—"

"*I didn't hurt them!*" Peter shouted.

Will turned. "I'm telling."

"Jesus Christ, stop!" Peter began to sob. "You're just like the others. The judge and that fucking lawyer. Those old bitches on the jury."

A question occurred to Will. He could ask his dad, but he knew where that would lead. He could ask his mom, but she'd end up taking him to a doctor. BJ wouldn't have the answer he needed since this didn't involve sports or the amount of hair on Miss February's crotch.

He peered down at the man he'd befriended, the monster who'd murdered four people.

"What was your sentence?"

Peter scowled. "What's that got to do with anything?"

"What did the jury give you?"

"I'm innocent."

Will clenched his jaw. "What did they give you?"

"A life term, what else?" He chuckled mirthlessly. "Three life terms, if you want to be specific."

"Why not death?"

"They don't have the death penalty in Illinois."

Will nodded. It's what he expected.

Peter's face hardened. "You gonna tell them? Get your name in the papers? The boy who caught Peter Bates, never mind that he aided and abetted him first."

Will was surprised to find himself grinning. "You'd tell them that?"

"Damned straight I would."

"You think that's going to stop me?"

Peter didn't answer.

The silence drew out.

Will said, "Peter?"

When Peter only stared obstinately ahead, Will repeated it in a louder voice.

Peter's lips twisted bitterly. "What?"

"I'm not going to tell on you."

Peter glanced at him. "You're not?"

Will shook his head. He walked away.

And never returned.

CHAPTER FOUR

You're certifiably insane, Lucy thought. *It's two in the morning. The last time you spoke to him, blood was sluicing from your forehead and you basically told him to get lost.*

She stopped outside his door.

You'll wake him up, the voice persisted. *He'll be livid.*

Lucy knocked. Waited.

He's lying in bed, wondering what kind of imbecile calls on people at two in the morning.

Rustling from within.

It's not too late to run, the voice urged.

Lucy stood her ground.

Muffled footsteps.

Okay then. Take your medicine. You deserve whatever you get.

The door opened. Rick stared blearily at her from the shadows.

She scanned his chiseled torso, his rippled stomach, like the cover of a romance novel. Hell. He wore black boxer shorts that drooped a bit at the waist, revealing muscles that were dizzyingly pronounced.

His eyes met hers, and though she was blushing, she didn't look away.

"How's the forehead?" he asked.

She touched the Band-Aid. "Not my proudest moment."

He grinned. "You want to come in or go somewhere else?"

Her mouth half-opened at the question.

A slight nod. "I'll get a shirt on. Shoes, if I can find them."

She stood in the hallway while he rattled around, muttered under his breath, finally switched on a lamp. Though she wasn't consciously spying on him, she couldn't help but notice him pause in the middle of the room, evidently scouring the floor for his clothes. She studied his back muscles, his defined shoulders.

She tore her eyes away before he caught her looking.

When he joined her in the hallway, she caught a whiff of something fresh. "Did you brush your teeth?"

"Had to," he said. "I can't do anything until I've showered and brushed my teeth. I feel gross if I don't."

They started down the hallway.

"You didn't shower," she said.

"Should have. But I didn't want to keep you waiting." He ran a hand through his hair. "I would've put on a hat, but I couldn't find it."

"You always this disorganized?"

"You always call on people in the middle of the night?"

"Ouch."

He chuckled softly. "I'm glad you did. We haven't had much chance to talk."

"I figured you were avoiding me."

He looked away, but before he did she glimpsed what might have been frustration. They reached the staircase, started down.

"I began my story," she said.

She braced herself for a caustic response – *It's about damned time* – but instead he smiled broadly. "Hey, that's outstanding! What's it about?"

When she hesitated, he put his palms up. "No pressure. If you don't want—"

"It's a mystery," she said. "*The Fred Astaire Murders.*"

"That's a hell of a title."

"Yeah?"

"Truth."

"I mean, *I* like the title, but I would, right?"

"I can see it on the spine. All caps, big white letters, black background."

"You think?"

"Uh-huh. It'll be suspenseful but classy. Bloody when it needs to be—"

"How do you know?"

He shrugged. "The title."

They reached the bottom of the staircase. "I'm not sure if mine qualifies as horror."

They stepped around a corner, into an area she'd never explored before. The corridor was handsome – chestnut wainscoting, a few paintings – but there was a disused quality to it, like it needed a good airing out.

There was a door to their left. Rick paused, opened the door, and poked his head inside.

"What's in there?" she asked.

He moved aside. "See for yourself."

She stepped beside him, beheld a cramped room not much larger than a closet. In it there was a workbench, tools, a fire extinguisher, and an axe. "Looks like a torture chamber," she said.

Rick closed the door and they continued on. "Speaking of that, what's your antagonist like?" Rick asked. "That's where the horror could come from."

"He scares me."

"Good."

"No, really," she said. "He's totally amoral, but I've known people like that."

Rick slowed as they came to a door at the end of the hall. "You've already gotten to the bad guy?"

"I wrote the last scene first. Is that weird?"

He shrugged. "I've heard of it happening. Writers know the ending, then they go back and do the rest."

"You ever work that way?"

"Uh-uh," he said. "I'm not that weird."

She punched him on the arm. "Where are you taking me?"

He seemed to debate. "That's the thing. I don't know if I should."

"Well, now we have to go inside."

"Curious, huh?"

"Aren't all writers?"

"Not necessarily," he answered. "Some think they know everything."

"Like Bryan?"

"There's one."

"And Elaine."

"She's pretty set in her ways," he agreed.

"Open the door."

He favored her with an appreciative glance. "Well, okay."

When he drew open the door, she scrunched her nose at the odor of damp earth. She reached through the doorway, switched on the light.

"You said you had an ending," he said as they started down the steps.

"I can't tell you that."

"Tease."

Halfway down, the bare yellow bulb only revealed a small oval of concrete at the base of the steps. The rest of the basement remained shrouded.

She glanced at him. "Do you tell people about your stories?"

"No one asks."

"Okay, but *would* you tell them?"

"Probably not," he conceded.

"The scene I wrote is at the *very* end," she said at the bottom of the stairs. "The denouement."

Wordlessly, he sidled past her, reached out, and tugged a string. A yellow bulb spilled jaundiced light around the basement. The space was circular, broad, with multiple doors off the main room, reminding her of bicycle spokes. She had no idea how large the adjoining rooms were, but the feeling that they stood in the hub of an enormous wheel was strong.

"I fainted down here," Rick said. When she raised her eyebrows in question, he explained, "Last night. With Wells."

She thought the doors were metal or steel. It was difficult to tell in the gloom. "I can see how this place might make someone ill."

"I felt pretty foolish today. Told myself I was being skittish. But now that I'm here again I feel the same thing."

Lucy studied his face, took in the beads of sweat peppering his forehead. "What you said about the policeman...."

His skin reddened. "Ah. That."

"You said he was a character from your novel."

He grunted laughter, but there was no humor in the sound. "Deranged, right? I don't know what was wrong with me."

"Maybe—"

"Could you do me a favor and pretend I didn't say it?"

She opened her mouth to push the matter but saw the appeal in his eyes. She nodded to her left. "Should we try one of the doors?"

"I wasn't going to suggest it."

"Why'd you bring me here?"

"Did I come to your room at two in the morning?"

"Yikes."

Rick smiled. "I'm glad you did."

She glanced at a door that was slightly more illuminated than the others. Started in that direction

Moving abreast of her, Rick said, "Tell me about the denouement."

"My hero is at a banquet hall," she said. "The killer shows up, but he's not there for her."

"The hero and villain both make it through the story alive?"

"It surprised me too."

They reached a steel door. It was bowed in places. As if something had tried to batter its way out.

"That seems like a bad sign," Rick said.

"Let's check a different one."

The next door was comprised of the same aged steel but featured no bulging dents. She experienced a tremor of alarm as Rick reached out, twisted the knob. The door creaked inward, and a flood of fetid air rolled over them.

"Smells like an open grave," he said.

"Rick...."

"No, really. I took a job one summer as a gravedigger—" At her dubious expression, he said, "Okay, graveyard *worker*. Even back in college I wanted to be a horror novelist. So I approached the local cemeteries, asking if they needed help."

"Do they call that a sexton?"

"Nobody there called it that. I think that's someone at a church graveyard in the eighteen hundreds. Anyway—" He took a step forward, reached into the dark doorway, felt along the wall. "Damn...no switch."

"You sure?"

He shrugged. "Maybe there's a pull string inside, but I'm not going in there."

"Can we close the door?"

He did, moving with poorly concealed haste. "Glad I'm not the only one with the jitters," he said, starting back toward the stairs.

"How was the graveyard?"

"Most of it was mowing, weed-whipping, tidying up the cemetery." They reached the steps, where he paused, letting her go up first. He extinguished the main bulb, started after her. "But when there was a death, I helped dig the grave."

"Aren't graves dug with a machine?"

"Partially. But the backhoe only does the main excavation. It's imprecise at the corners."

They emerged from the basement. "You had to climb inside the grave?" she asked.

"The other guys couldn't believe I wanted the job. They usually drew straws."

"Probably thought you were a ghoul."

They ambled down the hall.

"You gonna tell me how you cut your forehead?" he asked.

Her smile dwindled. "I think you already know."

"Frustration."

She nodded.

"I'd like to read your books."

It stopped her. "How'd you hear about them?"

He didn't bother playing dumb. "I heard Elaine mention it. Anna too."

She glanced at him. "You like Anna?"

"You're the only one I've taken to the basement."

She smiled despite herself.

He said, "You know…that's in your past."

When her eyes narrowed, he rushed on. "I'm not saying your books are bad – I haven't read them. I just mean, whatever disappointment, frustration—" a nod at her forehead, "—it's over. It can't hurt you if you don't let it."

"You live by the same advice?"

He looked stricken. With a weary sigh, he stared down at his feet. "I'm the last person who should be giving advice."

She wanted to take it back, to restore the vibe. But before she could find the words, he said, "It's late. We should get some sleep."

Fuck, she thought.

She followed him up the staircase, and with barely another word, he returned to his room.

She was on the way to her door when a voice said, "No goodnight kiss, huh?"

She discovered Bryan watching her from his doorway.

He shook his head. "Some guys move too slowly."

"Hey, Bryan?" she said. "Go to hell."

She slammed her door on his laughter.

CHAPTER FIVE

Anna heard a knock on her door. On the way out of the bathroom, she thought, *Evan*, probably hoping to catch a glimpse of her in her terrycloth robe.

She wondered, *Rick?*

It was seven a.m., a horny time for her. Perhaps Rick was horny too.

At the door, Anna paused, spread the green folds of her robe to reveal the tops of her breasts. They were tanner than usual, her sunbathing paying dividends.

She opened the door and took an unconscious step backward.

Bryan grinned at her.

Anna's fingers twitched toward her chest, but she forced her hand downward. "Come in. I was just getting dressed."

Bryan entered, closed the door. Stood awkwardly in the middle of the room as she went to the makeup table. She never wore much, but what she did apply required good light.

Her back was to Bryan as she sat, but that was okay, she could see him in the mirror. Before she realized what he was doing, he was striding over to her bed, reaching down to awaken her laptop.

She turned instinctively but kept quiet.

He gazed at the screen. "You have a lot written."

Thirteen thousand, five hundred and twenty-six words, she thought.

"Is it good?" he asked.

She stifled a snort. *Is it good? Of course it's good, you hemorrhoid.*

"Rothenburg," he murmured. "That's in Germany, right?"

So he knew his geography. Was that surprising? She bet he'd memorized the world capitals, the periodic table, ready for his debut on *Jeopardy*.

"'The sexton's wife moved to the window,'" he read, "'and with slender white fingers, brushed aside the curtain.'"

Anna's toes curled into knots, the skin of her chest burning.

Bryan continued, insensitive to her annoyance. "'She screwed up her eyes and peered over the hill. The cemetery gates were fastened tight, as always.'"

Anna stood, moved beside him. The fact that he was the first person to speak these words aloud was an outrage. He was sullying her story, his inflectionless voice leeching it of passion.

"Cemetery," Bryan said, eyes crawling down the screen. "The moon." He turned to her, one eyebrow cocked. "This a vampire story?"

"Of a kind."

"Title?"

She folded her arms. "*The Nachzehrer.*"

"Ah, the German vampire legend. I've always enjoyed that one. Very quaint."

Her lips thinned.

"How have you worked in suicide?" At her silence, Bryan grimaced. "Tell me you know the legend?"

She couldn't face that incredulous grin. She turned away and stepped purposefully toward the window.

"You *didn't* research it, did you? Christ, you're like every other writer. You go joyriding and the reader is forced to ride along, and, my God, suicide is the most important aspect of the legend!"

And this time the word *suicide* clanged in her head like the tolling of sinister church bells, and Bryan was raving now:

"...and here I thought you were different. I told myself, here's someone who's not afraid of a little elbow grease, who understands that...."

Bryan's words died as, her back to him, Anna untied the robe. Spread it open.

"What are you—" he started and fell silent when the robe piled at her feet.

She felt his stupefied gaze on her naked backside. Sensed his churning conflict.

Anna turned and riveted him with her eyes.

Bryan's gaze roved over her bare sex. He looked like he might be sick.

"Something wrong?" she teased.

He didn't speak. She let the morning sunshine drowse over her, augmenting the brown of her flesh. The russet curls of her pubic hair.

"You don't have to compensate with me, Bryan."

His eyes were unfocused. "I'm getting breakfast."

"I'm going to win."

His smirk returned. "The hell you are. My story is gonna blow the doors off—"

"You're going to help me," she said. Her nipples were hardening. She could feel his gaze descending, tearing away, descending. "If your book is as good as you claim, you'll be helping yourself win."

He barked out a harsh laugh, dragged a hand through his hair. "I have no idea what we're talking about."

"Pressure," she said.

"What—"

"Everyone feels it," she explained, stepping toward him. "We need to intensify the pressure."

"How?"

She kept coming. "You liked it when Marek got kicked out."

He glared at her. "You liked it too."

She stopped a foot from where he stood. If he turned, his arm would brush her jutting nipples. On some level, she longed for this. His body was heavily muscled, hardened by cardiovascular work. He was a physical specimen. His mind, though, was a hornet's nest of self-loathing.

"I liked it too," she agreed. "I liked it when Tommy ran away."

This brought a chuckle. "Couldn't take it."

"I'll enjoy it when Elaine runs."

"You think?"

"Or Evan."

A hungry look flitted over his face. She stored it away for later. "Or Lucy. She was frail to begin with."

"Had her shot and blew it," he muttered. His eyes lowered to her pubic region, flicked to her face. "I assume you have ideas about how to get rid of them?"

"I do. But first we have to trust each other."

He snorted, began to turn away.

"*Bryan.*"

At her tone, he froze.

"When it's down to two, we can hate each other again. Until then, let's cooperate."

He didn't speak.

"Will you do that?" she asked. "Knowing, in the end, one of us will destroy the other?"

He stared at her for a long moment. Then his face spread into a wicked grin. It simultaneously chilled her and made her ache below.

"Let the bloodletting commence," he said.

CHAPTER SIX

Dear Justine,

The Nachzehrer is my masterwork. And you know what else, Justine? You're an insolent bitch. And tricky. Oh, so tricky. I thought I knew myself, but it turns out self-knowledge is as elusive for me as it is for everyone else.

But you know what?

It doesn't matter.

Doesn't matter that you're in my story, doesn't matter that I'm writing *you*.

You know why it doesn't matter?

Because it's good, Justine.

Fuck that. It's *fabulous*.

More fabulous than you were when we roomed together our sophomore year at Syracuse.

Yes, Justine, I'm admitting it. You were fabulous then. *Quiet grace* is the phrase my mother used after I brought you home, and I think it might have been then that the idea began to form.

You see, my mother never used that phrase with me. Hell, she never used anything approximating that phrase with me. *Lively*, sure. *Prima donna* was another. Or my favorite, the damning cliché that made me want to claw her eyes out: *Her head is in the clouds.*

Do you see, Justine? The words imply I'm a flake, some hippy-dippy lovechild who glides about uttering gibberish about tolerance and acceptance and living in harmony.

Fuck tolerance.

Fuck acceptance.

Fuck harmony in the ass.

And fuck you, Justine. You had the unattainable quality I could never match. Oh, sure, when it came to sex appeal, I blew you away, and to most men, that was enough.

But not to Jake. And because Jake was the one who ignored me, he became the only one that mattered. We're simple creatures, really. Wanting what we can't have. A guy could be a leper, but if he showed no interest in me, I'd fixate on him until he did, at which time I'd dump him and move on.

Yet Jake wanted you.

You might have been happy together, built a life, all that crap. Four children, I'm thinking, a brick house in a gated community. Him working some prestigious job, you shuttling the brats around in your SUV, sipping Starbucks and rocking your tennis skirts. Everyone would look at you and think, *There goes Justine. My, she has quiet grace.*

But we fixed that, didn't we?

Jake was the best-looking guy in his frat. Cocky, but able to feign tenderness. That was your first mistake, overlooking the lusty gleam in his eyes. He hid it well, but if you peered closely enough, you could distinguish glimmers, the wolf beneath the lamb. When he drank, his eyes would become freer, bolder, and that's when he'd stare at you, and that was torturous for me.

I saw where things were headed, and I had two choices. I could cut and run, for the first time admitting defeat. Bested by my roommate, the girl I called my dearest friend, the one my parents wanted to adopt.

Or I could do what I've always done.

I once witnessed something I'll never forget. In high school a group of us visited a friend whose parents were dog breeders. They had kennels crammed with yipping dogs. One kennel was compartmentalized, a father Dalmatian on one side, the mommy and her puppies on the other. Separated by wire mesh.

My friend Alec commented that it was cruel to keep the father away from his puppies. Alec decided he'd give the father visitation rights. He raised the dividing panel between the daddy and the puppies.

At first nothing happened. The father Dalmatian paused to eye his brood. One puppy approached. I remember thinking how sweet a moment it was, how unjust the breeders were for keeping the family separated. I was thinking this when our friend exited her house, realized what Alec had done, and raced forward, shouting, "No, no, no!"

It happened so quickly I could scarcely believe it. One moment the puppy was inching toward its father. The next the father gripped the puppy in his teeth, whipped it in a mad frenzy, and spiked it on the ground with appalling force. The puppy squealed in pain, and even in the flurry of teeth and claws between the mother and father, I could see the puppy's broken foreleg, the bone piercing the skin and dribbling blood in the kennel dust.

I've thought a lot about that horrid incident. I've turned it over and over in my head. What made the father attack his own child? I think there was something in the father's nature that made him do it. He couldn't help inflicting violence.

Could I have stopped what happened to you?

You began dating Jake in October. Every time you two started to kiss, you'd pull away from him, a hand on his chest, an embarrassed smile on your face, and murmur an apology, as though you'd just inflicted irreparable damage on me.

I'd return your smile. Toes curled into ballerina knots, neck tendons straining, I'd assure you it was okay, I'd seen people making out before.

The thing was....

I lied.

Never had I been so thoroughly humiliated. Never had I wanted a boy the way I wanted Jake Bryant. Jake with his blue eyes and black hair and his close-cropped beard before the look came into vogue.

Jake, however, wanted you.

There was only one problem.

You wouldn't put out.

Your reason? One November night, the two of us drinking wine coolers in our sorority, the windowpanes frosty and the comforter warm, you told me your darkest secret.

Freshman year, you'd shared the precious gift between your legs with four different boys. Nothing abnormal about that, nothing to be ashamed of.

What doomed you was one boy's possessiveness and his rage at being cast aside. The boy had gone to your high school, knew all your old friends. When you stopped returning his calls, he vented his rage online, shared details about your sexual appetites. He *named names*. All of a sudden, sweet little Justine was the girl who banged anything with a pulse. Even your parents found out! You were mortified, you confessed over your fourth wine cooler, and you even, *gulp*, considered suicide. The evils of social media, you claimed, had almost ended your life.

My God, Justine, don't you see it now? Don't you realize what you did?

You forged the axe. You whetted the blade.

You handed it to your executioner.

The week before Valentine's Day, you were on your period. By that time Jake was confiding in me. *Venting* to me might be a more appropriate description. Quiet grace only goes so far, and after a while, a man needs to fuck. No matter how sweet a guy is, no matter how chivalrous, when you get down to it, his urge to stick his thing in something hot and wet trumps all.

Which is why Jake fucked me first.

It was all unplanned. I was sitting in the back seat of his Mustang and listening sympathetically to his complaints about you. Great girl. Might be the one. But so *frigid*. So insensitive to his needs.

I nodded, knowing all of it already. I knew that while you were devastated by what happened your freshman year, there was a part of you that enjoyed your little sex spree. Yes, you enjoyed it, Justine, and I think that was the true reason you held out on Jake for so long. You associated pleasure with humiliation, and a connection like that can be a thorny one. Your waking mind despised what happened, grew terrified of being shamed again.

But your subconscious yearned for that wanton release. I watched you in your sleep, read the conflict in your furrowed brow, your sweaty sheets. You longed to lose control, dreamed of being naughty.

When I informed Jake, he was eager to test my theory. We agreed it should seem last-minute, my tagging along on your romantic Valentine's Day excursion. Jake booked a hotel, one of those sybaritic establishments with a mirror over the bed.

You were cool to the idea of my coming along at first – after all, you wanted Jake to yourself. But he drew you aside in the sorority lobby, explained how poor Anna was going to be alone, and did you really want that? On Valentine's Day?

Of course you did, Justine, but you pretended it was okay. You pouted on the ride to the restaurant, but a few Long Island iced teas thawed you. At the bars you continued to drink, and more importantly, to dance. Sandwiched between me and Jake, bodies grinding, you ceased caring about whose hands were caressing your ass, whose tongue was in your mouth.

By the time we arrived at the gaudy hotel with the rose-red bathtub and the black satin bedspread, you were up for anything, and Jake was more than game. The three of us writhed like vipers, though the next morning you claimed not to remember any of it.

Good thing I brought the camcorder.

Filming the festivities had been my idea, but Jake offered no resistance. He was too happy to be living out his most cherished fantasy. The only time he frowned was when I refused to hand him the camera.

But that wouldn't have worked, would it? Because had Jake become the cameraman, he might have caught my face. As it was, I was able to focus on *you*, Justine, you bent over, perfect buttocks in the air as Jake rammed you. You, Justine, with your face between my legs, your tongue lapping at my clit like a dutiful submissive. You, Justine, deep-throating your boyfriend and guzzling his load.

The quiet grace of a hardcore porn star.

I still remember your shock when I told you, tears in my eyes, that I couldn't find the camera. It had been in my purse when I'd gone to the coffee shop, but when I got home, it was gone.

The horror on your face was so satisfying I almost let it go at that.

Almost.

But I hated you, Justine. In the end, it was a matter of hatred. Everyone doted on you. Treated you with more dignity. More respect. And I had the proof you were no better than anyone else.

The hardest part was waiting until Spring Break to upload the footage. I didn't do it, of course. That might have been traced to me.

It's amazing how many unscrupulous people there are. How easy it is to find a guy who'll post a sex tape to social media, to porn sites, for a hundred bucks.

I'll never forget the silence, Justine. How after I texted you the link to the video – OMG THIS IS TERRIBLE WHAT R YOU GOING TO DO??? – you never responded. You were getting ready to go on a mission trip for your church (the irony!), but you never made it. I often wonder what your final hours were like. Did you pace your bedroom? Did your mom knock on your door? Offer you peanut butter and jelly sandwiches? How long did it take you to decide on pills?

Here's the part that kills me. My goal was to devastate you. To humiliate you. To ruin your reputation. I wanted you out of our sorority, out of Syracuse. Out of New York State, if possible.

I didn't mean to kill you.

Regretfully yours,

Anna Holloway

CHAPTER SEVEN

Evan sat fidgeting with his pages.

Nine chairs lined the edge of the dance floor, eight of them arranged in a semicircle, the other a folding black-and-white director's chair. Their circle was illuminated by a ring of candles in holders of various heights. The rest of the ballroom was steeped in shadow.

Footsteps sounded. Wearing a dapper black suit, Wells strode onto the dance floor.

He must be sleeping better, Evan thought. *His clothes are pressed. New shoes too.*

As Wells neared, Evan noticed how healthy Wells's skin now appeared. Gone were the liver spots on his cheeks, the saggy skin near his ears.

No way he's eighty, Evan thought. *Sixty-five at most, and even that's a stretch.*

Wells said, "Mr. Clayton."

"Yes, sir?"

"The floor is yours."

Bryan swallowed. "You want me to read?"

Wells eased into the director's chair and smiled a self-satisfied smile. "Yes, Mr. Clayton. I want you to read."

Bryan looked around. "Should I sit?"

"Stand in the center. Show me why I should make you famous."

Bryan nodded, attempted to maneuver between the candleholders without knocking them over.

I hope you burn, Evan thought.

Bryan began to read.

The story chronicled an invasion of Taipan snakes, evidently a deadly breed. Though Evan's skin crawled at the snakes' descriptions, Wells didn't appear impressed. No one in the ballroom spoke, but the disapproval oozed out of the audience, several writers shifting in their chairs or scribbling notes. Bryan looked like he was about to faint.

Evan remembered the way the son of a bitch had abused him; Evan had yearned for revenge. But this…this was better than anything he could have imagined.

He realized he was leaning forward, fists clenched and teeth bared like a member of a lynch mob. He caught himself and relaxed. When he was sure no one had noticed his feral expression, he pulled out his notebook and began to write:

THE SHAMING OF A LOUT
A One-Scene Play by Evan Laydon

BRYAN (sweating): …and then the fierce snake wriggled closer. The man tried to push away, but the dripping fangs—

WELLS: Please God, no more.

BRYAN (looking up from his crumpled pages): Sorry?

WELLS: Cease. Before I grow too nauseated to stop you.

BRYAN: I'm not even done with the first scene.

WELLS: Then thank God I stopped you when I did.

BRYAN (gesturing to the pages): This is only a rough draft.

WELLS (massaging the bridge of his nose): Let's, um…let's get into specifics with this…manuscript. I scarcely know where to begin….

BRYAN: (Silence)

WELLS: Firstly, your dialogue is wretched. Your characters all sound alike, which wouldn't be as exasperating if they were interesting. Unfortunately, they display the same robotic soullessness that you do. Furthermore, the monologue on page three is atrocious.

BRYAN (flushed and sweating): You use monologues. In *Overtree*, when Joe confronts Maria—

WELLS: I'm allowed to.

BRYAN: Why are—

WELLS: Because I'm better than you. For a master craftsman, every tool represents an opportunity. For the hack, the same tools present nothing but danger.

BRYAN: That's so damned…elitist.

WELLS: Do you doubt it?

ELAINE (quietly): Mr. Wells is right.

BRYAN: You can fuck yourself.

WELLS: More ingenuity.

(Laughter from a few group members.)

BRYAN: You use profanity in your books.

WELLS: I repeat – I'm better than you.

BRYAN (throwing up his arms): Of course you're better than me. Your books have won everything. But you're also older than God.

(Wells smiles a furtive smile, but Bryan doesn't notice, ranting now.)

And where will I be in fifty years? I guarantee I'll be more prolific than you. Three books in the past twenty years?

WELLS: Drivel takes no time to create. Any artist can scribble the human form, yet few can capture the subtle delicacy of a nose or the lissome curve of the throat.

BRYAN (strained): You're one hell of a teacher. Browbeat your students, kill the creative impulse—

WELLS: Assuming there is one. Your soul is impoverished, Mr. Clayton, your arrogance a brittle shell. We're watching it crumble before us.

(Scattered laughter.)

BRYAN (looks around challengingly): You think he's gonna be any easier on you?
ELAINE (quiet but firm): You have to know the rules to know how to break them.

BRYAN: Don't give me that crap. I know how to show instead of tell. I know how—

WELLS: Paint-by-the-numbers chicanery. 'Read this book and write a bestseller!'

BRYAN (thinly): I just mean—

WELLS: Sit down, Mr. Clayton. I almost feel sorry for you.

BRYAN: Mr. Wells, I didn't mean—

WELLS: Sit down, Mr. Clayton. Before you embarrass yourself further.

Bryan sat. It took all the self-control Evan possessed not to cheer.
"Bad fiction is an affront to the soul," Wells said. "After enduring that torment, I need something to cleanse my palate. May I have a volunteer?"

Evan's pulse accelerated. When better to unveil his work than when his adversary was at his weakest? It was too delicious. Bryan dismantled before their eyes, Evan recognized as the preeminent talent of the group....

"Anyone?" Wells prompted. "You'll not reach the mountaintop by cowering among the masses."

Do it, Evan thought.

Wells surveyed the group with an amazed grin. "My God, people, can't you endure a little honesty? Don't you want a house like this? Don't you want universities begging to bestow upon you honorary degrees? Award juries pleading with you to attend their ceremonies? Actors and directors cutting each other's throats to adapt your novels?"

Yes, Evan thought. *I want all those things. By God, I need them!*

He began to raise his hand, but a stir of movement made him pause.

Bryan was scowling at him and shaking his head.

Hand half-raised, Evan stared back at Bryan, and it was as if every worry that had been nagging at him since that day in the woods was now crystalizing before his eyes. He'd told himself Bryan had just been threatening him for sport. That the rope spear was a harmless prop.

Yet even if that were true, Evan had told Bryan some of his darkest secrets. Not only the humiliating business about watching his sisters shower, but his literary fantasies, the ones featuring leggy blondes and posh publishing parties. Evan had been sensible enough to withhold the most damning revelation, but Bryan still knew enough to ruin him.

Evan jerked down his hand, but he was too late. Wells had seen him. Was watching him with merry good humor.

"Don't be shy, Mr. Laydon. I have high hopes for your work."

Evan suppressed a moan. He glanced at Bryan, whose forbidding glance made plain how severe the ramifications would be should Evan read.

"Go ahead," Sherilyn said. "I've been wanting to hear your stuff."

"Me too," Lucy said. She gave him an encouraging smile, and Evan thought, *Dammit. Don't you know how much I'd like to read?*

Wells's smile was fading. "Come, Mr. Laydon. I have no time for stage fright. A creature cannot evolve by huddling in the swamp."

Evan grimaced. "It isn't…Mr. Wells, I, uh…." A glance at Bryan, who reminded him of a bull shark who's just scented blood. "I can't."

Wells's look was steely. "Fear is corrosive, Mr. Laydon. You mustn't let it overmaster you."

Runnels of sweat streaked down Evan's sides. "I'm sorry, sir. I'm not feeling my best."

"You do look a little pale," Will said.

Lucy's hand was on his arm. "You want me to walk you to your room?"

"Mr. Laydon will remain with the group," Wells said in cold, measured tones, "or he will go home."

Sherilyn made a face. "Come on, Mr. Wells. If a guy's sick—"

"I need someone with guts," Wells said. A scan of their faces. "Don't any of you want to sit where I sit? Are you that frightened of success?"

Evan lowered his head and tried not to weep.

Wells smiled without pity. "Yes, Mr. Laydon, cry over your weakness. We predators drink your tears." Wells's voice rose to a shout. "By God, isn't there anyone in here with *teeth*?"

To Evan's left, he sensed someone rising. And when he looked up and saw who it was, his mouth fell open.

CHAPTER EIGHT

Her gaze unwavering, Anna faced Roderick Wells.

Will stared at her, amazed. She'd never looked more frightened. Or more attractive.

"Ah," Wells said. "Are you a predator, Miss Holloway? Or merely toothsome?"

She returned his smile, glanced down at her pages.

Man, I hope it's good, Will thought. *For her sake.*

Anna asked, "Anyone know the legend of the Nachzehrer?"

Wells frowned. "Don't give us context, Miss Holloway. Your work should speak for itself."

"Just one little bit," Anna said. "With your permission?"

Wells looked irritated, but fluttered a hand as if to say, *If you must.* "Anyone?"

Rick said, "A vampire myth, right? Something to do with a belfry?"

"A combination vampire and ghoul," Anna said. "It can feast on itself as well as others. Or bring death by ringing church bells."

Sherilyn chuckled. "Versatile creature."

Anna smiled, her white teeth showing. Will's stomach fluttered.

"Now that you've provided tonight's lesson on German mythology," Wells said, his words clipped, "perhaps you'll be kind enough to read your passage."

"Yes, sir," she said and strode to the center of the circle.

Holy Mary Mother of God, Will thought, noticing her dress for the first time. It conformed to the contours of her body as though it had grown on her, an emerald membrane that clung to her curves, accentuated the delirious musculature of her buttocks.

Anna took a deep breath and read, "'Karl mounted Ragna, who spread her pallid legs farther.'"

"What the hell?" Elaine said.

"'Over her husband's shoulder floated the black square of window, beyond which no stars shone. Since her latest miscarriage, they'd not been able to beget a child, and though she tried to relax, she couldn't help wondering whether Karl would leave her for a woman whose womb wasn't fallow.'

"'Ragna's body responded to her husband's. The woven black hair of his chest tickled her breasts, tantalizing her, starting a fire in her belly, which joined with the greater heat between her legs.'"

Will made sure to keep his expression dispassionate. *Regard the excerpt the way you would a painting*, he told himself. *Focus on the brush strokes, the craftsmanship.*

"'After a time, a pleasing drowsiness spread through her. His thrusts intensified, her thighs undulating…'"

You're at the Chicago Art Institute, Will reminded himself. *You're studying Monet…Manet…Mannheim Steamroller….*

"'…she hears a rustle from the window, but all that matters is their lovemaking. Karl's mouth is on her throat. A delicious thrill scurries down her shoulder. She squeezes his member with her sex, and he is moaning into her ear now, his whiskers scraping her lobe….'"

Monet, Will reminded himself, his cargo shorts becoming uncomfortably snug. *It's art. It has nothing at all to do with hot sex or Anna's increasingly husky voice.*

"'The rustling sounds again, so Ragna opens her eyes to see if a large moth is fluttering outside their window. But Karl's brawny shoulders blot out the pane, and she is glad of this. Because a molten heat is spreading through her—'"

"Seriously?" Elaine said.

"Don't interrupt," Bryan snapped.

That's right! Don't interrupt the reading!

"No, really," Elaine persisted. "What the hell is this?"

Anna lowered the pages. "Something wrong?"

"It's porn," Elaine said.

Anna watched her evenly. "You dislike erotic scenes?"

Elaine removed her glasses, began to clean them with the stomach of her shirt. "A scene doesn't need explicit sex to be steamy."

"Is the piece disturbing you, Ms. Kovalchyk?" Wells asked.

"It's grossing me out."

"You don't look grossed out," Bryan said.

Anna smiled at Bryan who tipped her a wink.

What's this? Will wondered.

Elaine shot Bryan a disdainful look. "I'm not *disturbed*. And you only like it because it's whacking material."

"Got *me* hot," Sherilyn said.

Elaine threw up her hands. "Oh for God's sakes."

Lucy was frowning at Anna. "I thought you wrote urban fantasy."

"The one my agent just sold is. But we're supposed to do something horror-related, right? I'm writing about a woman who was driven to suicide by a rival. The dead woman becomes the Nachzehrer and preys on those who are most alive." She glanced at Elaine. "Like people who are making love."

Elaine rolled her eyes.

"Where will you take it from here?" Wells asked. His hands were tented, the index fingers touching his lips.

"The vampire kills Karl and Ragna," Anna said.

"Come again?" Sherilyn asked.

"It's like those horror movies where we meet a character in the first scene, get attached to her, and then—"

"—she gets hacked to pieces," Will finished.

Elaine grunted. "Real subtle."

"It's all about the execution," Will said. When Rick laughed softly, he added, "You know what I mean."

Wells stilled them with a hand. "I agree with Ms. Kovalchyk. This is titillation."

Anna gaped at him. "What?"

"You hoped the subject matter would conceal your lack of skill."

She uttered a brittle laugh. "Lack of skill?"

"It was a wretched sample, Miss Holloway. It didn't even work as pornography."

Elaine tilted back her head and laughed.

"Shut up," Bryan growled.

Anna had tears in her eyes. "If I'm so horrible, why did you choose me?"

"I didn't initially. You and Mr. Clayton were the nineteenth and twenty-seventh selections, respectively. Only Mr. Laydon and Miss Jackson were members of the original ten."

There was a thunderstruck silence. *That explains a lot,* Will's inner critic remarked. *What number were you, six thousand and eight?*

Bryan's voice was thin. "What happened to the others? They realize how outrageous your methods were?"

Wells looked amused. "They violated the confidentiality clause."

Elaine glanced around. "Wait a minute. That was real?"

"Once you were chosen, you were all tempted to share the news."

"How could you know that?" Lucy demanded.

"Do you deny it?"

Will certainly couldn't deny it. The moment he'd been selected, he'd snatched up his phone, opened his contacts, and dialed his parents' number. He imagined his father, Mr. Disapproval himself, gasping with shock.

But in the end he didn't tell, not because of the secrecy clause, but because he knew what would happen if he didn't win.

Condescension, more than ever before. His mom patting his hand. *I know you did your best, honey. How are things at the insurance company?*

Anna crossed her arms. "You're trying to humble me."

"If I wanted to humble you, I'd share the truth about your debut."

Anna stiffened.

Wells's dark eyes gleamed. "Don't want that getting out, do you? How the editor who acquired your drivel was forced into retirement—"

"Mr. Wells," Anna started.

"—because he'd developed a habit of meeting buxom young writers and touting them as the next big thing—"

"That's not—"

"—despite the fact that you had no talents beside the ones crammed into that little dress."

"Stop it!"

"Am I lying, Miss Holloway?"

"*Yes,*" she almost wailed. "Ed loved my writing. He got it from my agent, not from me."

"And did he acquire the book before or after meeting you?"

"That had nothing to do with it."

"Once his successor got a look at your manuscript, he halted the editorial process. It will remain in limbo until their legal department discovers a means of breaking the contract."

There was a gravid silence. Anna kept her eyes on Wells, her bottom lip quivering.

"Well, well, well," Elaine said.

Anna stood a moment longer. Then she dropped her gaze, and clasping her pages, she departed the circle of candles and returned to her seat.

Will watched her, wishing he could say something consoling. She could be abrasive at times, but this?

No one deserved this.

Wells watched Anna without pity. "Put away your feminine wiles and earn your place at the table, Miss Holloway." He faced the group. "Who's my next victim?"

CHAPTER NINE

Rick worried he'd be chosen, but Elaine said, "Sherilyn should read."

Wells looked pleased. "Ah, yes. Miss Jackson. I've been looking forward to this."

She regarded him dourly. "I'm sure you have." She glanced at Elaine. "Want to see me beaten up?"

Elaine's eyebrows rose. "I genuinely want to hear your story."

Sherilyn's eyes narrowed for a moment, but apparently what she saw in Elaine's face satisfied her. "Okay."

Wells gestured. "The stage belongs to you, Miss Jackson. Don't fail me."

Sherilyn remained next to her chair. Rick didn't notice she was holding two sets of papers until she raised them for Wells to see. "Before I begin, I need to know whether you're going to eviscerate my work the way you did the others."

"A writer mustn't fear criticism," Wells said. "If you desired sugarcoated praise, you should never have accepted my invitation."

Sherilyn nodded, handed one sheaf of pages to Lucy. "I figured as much. That's why I brought two samples." She ambled into the center of the circle.

"What if I require Miss Still to read the one you handed her?" Wells asked.

Lucy looked alarmed.

Sherilyn lowered her chin, regarded Wells with lifted eyebrows. "'Require' her, Mr. Wells? Just how would you do that?"

Wells smiled, unabashed. "Offer a reward or punishment."

Lucy looked ill.

Sherilyn's mouth went thin. "You'd punish Lucy for holding my pages?"

"For holding your pages?" Wells asked. "Of course not. For listening to a middling writer rather than a master storyteller?

Yes, I would certainly punish her for that." He turned to Lucy. "Please proceed."

Rick saw Lucy's face tighten with panic and felt a sudden urge to slug Wells in the teeth.

Lucy bit her bottom lip. "I don't think it's my place to read it."

Wells's expression darkened. "Miss Still, I asked you to read the pages."

"Mr. Wells...they're not mine."

"They are in your hands. Once a reader holds a book, the story belongs to her."

"They're not my *words*."

"Miss Still, you signed an agreement, and now you deign to flout that agreement the first time I ask something of you?"

Lucy glanced down at the pages. "I'm not flouting anything, Mr. Wells."

"If Miss Jackson didn't want that excerpt read, she shouldn't have brought it. She is deliberately trying to undermine my authority."

"Authority?" Sherilyn asked. "You're our host, not our warden."

"You're mistaken, Miss Jackson. In this realm, I am everything." He glowered at Lucy. "Read it."

Lucy shook her head. "Mr. Wells, I—"

"I said *read* it!"

"Leave her alone," Rick heard himself saying.

Slowly, Wells rounded on him. "That sounded like an order, Mr. Forrester. Are you developing a spine?"

"You're bullying her."

"Feeling mutinous, eh?" Wells's mouth twisted into a sneer. "Would you like to share your theory about the police chief, Mr. Forrester? Or the hallucination you suffered your first night here? Why don't you tell the others what I truly look like? The monster beneath this flesh?"

And for the briefest instant, the demonic Wells flickered before his eyes. The coal-black gaze, the joker's leer. The teeth sharpened to razor-fine points.

Rick blinked, his vision swimming. He closed his eyes against it, his hands knotting into fists.

"Tell them, Mr. Forrester," Wells urged.

Rick opened his eyes, and Wells's face was normal again. Yet the afterimage of what he'd seen still hovered in his mind's eye.

Rick licked his lips, which had gone dry. "You're abusing your power," he murmured.

Wells tilted his head. "I can't hear you, Mr. Forrester."

"I said you're abusing your power," Rick said in a stronger voice.

Wells showed his teeth. "What do you know of power?"

"I know that a truly strong person doesn't use it to intimidate."

Sherilyn nodded at Rick. "Finally."

Rick said nothing but didn't look away.

Sherilyn faced Wells. "Truth is, both sets of papers are the same. I just wanted to see how you'd react to this situation." A nod. "I'm happy to say you behaved exactly as I thought you would."

Wells's face might as well have turned to stone.

Sherilyn rustled the pages, smiled pleasantly. "I know some of you turn your noses up at children's books, but this is something I plan to illustrate and, if I can find an agent for it, sell one of these days."

Bryan muttered something sarcastic, Rick couldn't hear what, but Sherilyn ignored him. "'*The Magic King. A Dark Fairy Tale* by Sherilyn Jackson. Illustrated by Sherilyn Jackson and Alicia Templeton.'"

Seeing their quizzical looks, she explained, "My partner. She draws faces better than I do."

Rick felt himself relax a little. Not completely, not with Wells fuming. But Sherilyn's voice was clear and confident, and he wanted to hear her story.

"'Once upon a time there lived a mighty king. Folks believed he was a caring leader. He regaled his subjects with tales of love and adventure such as they had never heard. They traveled from the far reaches of the country to hear him weave his spells, and none would miss the solstice marking each new season, for on these nights, the king would lead a procession to the village square, where he would weave a new tale of enchantment.'"

Anna raised her hand.

Sherilyn raised her eyebrows. "Yes?"

"Is the entire book like this?"

"There a problem?"

"It's all telling," Anna explained. She faced Wells. "You just ripped my manuscript apart. I want to make sure Sherilyn is held to the same standards."

Lucy glared at Anna. "Why wouldn't she be?"

"Her race," Bryan said.

Sherilyn lowered her chin. "Come again?"

He shrugged. "You're the only minority writer here. Wells might go easier on you."

Wells's voice was dangerously soft. "Miss Jackson's skin color has nothing to do with my opinion of her work."

Elaine chuckled. "Exactly. It's not like we're a diverse group anyway."

Sherilyn smiled. "Oh, I don't know. I'm the token black. Marek was an immigrant. As far as my sexuality—"

"Enough of that crap," Bryan interrupted.

Sherilyn glanced at him. "I suppose you like things the way they've always been."

Bryan raised his chin. "You're damned right."

"Where guys like you have every advantage."

Bryan flicked a hand at her. "What a crock."

"He's scared," Lucy said. "He knows he can't win on a level playing field."

"Let me tell you something," Bryan began, but Wells cut him off.

"Continue with your reading," Wells said through his teeth.

Sherilyn nodded, unruffled. "As you command."

Wells's expression went tighter.

"'Decades passed, and generations lived and worked under the king's watchful leadership.'"

"Will this have pictures?" Bryan blurted.

Will glowered at him. "She already explained that."

"It's okay," Sherilyn said. She turned to Bryan. "Alicia and I like to include one for every chapter. Mind if I continue?"

Bryan shrugged. "Do what you want."

Rick resisted an urge to knock the dickhead off his chair.

"Thank you," Sherilyn said with freezing politeness. "'The king's servants were loyal to a fault. Rumors began that they were spying on the commoners, and some began to gaze upon the castle with a mistrustful eye. One of those was a peasant girl named Anna.'"

At Anna's smile, Sherilyn said, "I'm changing the name."

Anna's smile disappeared.

"'Anna was capricious, taken to long rambles in the forest. But she had a loving heart. She recognized the king's talent, but she never trusted their ruler. In quiet moments, mostly while the preliminary skits took place during the solstice feasts, she noticed the king speaking curtly to his underlings when he thought no one was watching. Anna was convinced that the king's smiling face was a mask that concealed something darker, something cruel.'"

Rick glanced at Wells, took in the man's avid gaze. Then he turned back to Sherilyn, a chill coursing down his back.

"'Whenever she spoke of her misgivings, those few who agreed were too frightened of the king's wrath to voice their objections publicly. They were too meek to see the king for what he truly was: a bullying monster.'"

As Sherilyn continued, the muscles in Wells's jaw and throat went taut.

"'Meanwhile, the king grew colder. No longer content with being the ruler of his realm, he believed he could increase his renown by selecting a protégé. Not only would this protégé become the king's heir – he and the queen were childless – but by choosing a humble commoner, the king would restore his reputation as a just ruler.'"

The ballroom was so noiseless Rick hardly dared breathe. Wells wore a look Rick had never seen before: nostrils flared, big hands grasping the arms of his chair, mouth drawn in a fierce line. If Rick didn't know better, he'd guess Wells had entered some sort of trance.

"'Fleetingly, Anna wondered if the king might choose her. After all, she was smart. She was fair minded. She was strong enough to lead a kingdom.'" Sherilyn paused, drew in a shuddering breath. "'Yet she knew she was too temperamental, too rash to lead effectively.

"'So Anna set about combing the countryside for a suitable protégé.'" Sherilyn glanced at Rick, who returned her gaze despite the urge to look away. "'Anna knew if she could find a suitable heir before the king did, she might yet save the kingdom, which she feared was heading toward dark days, bloody days such as no one had seen.

"'So it was that she ventured into the forest one bright summer morning. When she first spied the young man, his back was to her, and he was approaching some animal with gentleness and caution. A foal, Anna saw, its hide a light brown with ivory patches. The little horse's foreleg was bleeding, and the young man was whispering soothing words as he inched nearer....'"

The scene continued for several minutes, during which time Anna and the young man, whose name was Richard, began to speak, first about the injured foal, then about the king, for whom Richard had no use either. And through it all, Wells's expression grew increasingly murderous.

When Sherilyn finished, they applauded. At least, most of them did. Anna and Bryan remained conspicuously stoic.

Wells waited until the applause died down and said, "Amusing piece, Miss Jackson. Your peers enjoyed it. I'd like to hear what you think."

"That's an odd question," Sherilyn said.

"You wrote it, did you not?"

"'Course I wrote it. I've done little else since arriving."

Wells nodded curtly, his teeth showing. "Since you're clearly fond of allegory, perhaps you'll enlighten us as to the piece's meaning."

Sherilyn's good humor faded.

Bryan sat forward. "Allegory implies a one-to-one relationship—"

"I know what allegory is," Sherilyn interrupted, her eyes never leaving Wells's. "You told Anna our work should speak for itself. Don't you think mine does?"

Wells smiled, but there was frost in it. "No need to be evasive, Miss Jackson."

"That's the last thing I'd be, Mr. Wells."

"Then explain," Wells commanded. "Unless you're unable to speak intelligently about your own work."

Sherilyn glanced at her papers, for the first time appearing uncertain.

Wells's gaze was predatory. "We're waiting, Miss Jackson."

Sherilyn shook her head.

Lucy asked, "Do you know where the story is going?"

"I know how I *want* it to end," Sherilyn answered, "but I don't know if it's going to happen that way."

Bryan made a scoffing sound. "I hate that crap." He put his hands in the air, spoke in a childish voice. "'*The story is the boss.*' '*The characters drive the story.*' '*I'm just along for the ride.*'"

"It's true," Evan said.

"Bull. Shit." Bryan jabbed a finger in Evan's direction. "You're the one putting the words down on paper. You're the one in control."

Elaine gave Bryan a baleful look. "You're articulating why your stories have no soul."

"Fuck soul," Bryan said. "How about plot? How about *logic*, for Christ's sakes? All you guys with your hidden meanings…. Why not just tell a coherent story?"

"They're not mutually exclusive," Lucy said.

"*Enough*," Wells said, with enough heat they all turned and regarded him uneasily. He stood. "Miss Jackson, since you're unable to discuss your narrative, I think it would be prudent to end the session."

Wells strode away. Sherilyn stood, head down, in the center of the circle.

Just as Wells was about to exit the ballroom, Sherilyn called, "Mr. Wells."

Wells paused at the door. "Something to say, Miss Jackson?"

She nodded. "You're the king."

Wells's face spread into a cunning smile. "That's the first intelligent thing you've said tonight."

CHAPTER TEN

From *The Magic King: A Dark Fairy Tale*, by Sherilyn Jackson:

The king's coach drew nearer.

Anna told herself to get moving. The day was growing long, and though her folks expected her home within the hour, she hadn't even visited the three shops from which she was supposed to purchase supplies for the week. At best, she'd return home by nightfall, and even that seemed optimistic.

But the king's coach, its burnished black surface giving it the aspect of a rolling coffin, held her gaze.

Go! she thought.

Too late. The coach rumbled to a stop a few feet from where she stood. The driver climbed down, opened the coach door, where the king and queen sat, the queen peering straight ahead, a study in regality.

The king was peering at Anna.

She forced herself to stand up straighter.

Make him speak first.

But she heard herself blurting, "I was going to the grocer's."

The king regarded her with good humor. "Your family doesn't grow its own? The valley is fertile enough."

So he knew where they lived. Which meant he knew who she was. She suspected it, but to hear it confirmed set her hands to tremble. She shoved them in her pockets, lifted her chin. "We grow everything but spinach. For some reason it doesn't take."

The king nodded. "Yes, there's a blight on. You're lucky your other crops yet grow."

She frowned. "You said the valley was fertile."

He went on as though she hadn't spoken. "The cycle is reaching an end. The kingdom must endure these times in order to rejuvenate."

"Rejuvenate," she repeated, mesmerized by the king's rich voice. Passersby had stopped to listen to the exchange, but Anna was scarcely aware of them. The queen, too, had taken notice, though the only alteration in her bearing was a slight tilting of the head.

The king's expression darkened. He fixed her with a grim look. "That boy you've been speaking to."

Her throat closed. She contrived to appear guiltless, though she knew she made a poor job of it. Deception never came easily to her. "What boy?"

"The hostler's son has wicked ideas, young one. Best steer clear of him."

Anna yearned to shout at the king, to remind him that Richard was the same age as she and that no one had the ability to lead her astray. She refused to be led by *anyone*, least of all this deceitful egomaniac garbed in king's robes.

But all that came out was, "I only met him last week."

"Aye," said the king, his grin widening. "Met him last week and been stealing into the woods with him ever since. Bet your father would like to know why you're just now making it to the grocer."

The driver, about whom she'd completely forgotten, chuckled haughtily and said, "A mite young for meetings in the glade, aren't you, dear?"

She gaped at the man, who despite his pressed white suit was grinning like the lowest alley scum. "He's never laid a finger on me!"

"It's not your body he's alluding to," the king said. "It's your mind the boy is sullying."

She turned to the king, but before she could answer, he nodded significantly and said, "Meddling with the cycle is an affront to the kingdom, young lady. You two keep plotting, and you'll come to ruin. Both of you."

CHAPTER ELEVEN

Evan paced his room, fists clenched, molars grinding like unoiled gears.

He had to do something about Bryan. But what?

The son of a bitch was everything Evan wasn't. Muscular. Tall. Skilled with weaponry. That Evan was a far superior writer didn't matter. What good would that do him? He couldn't very well bludgeon Bryan with figurative language.

Evan glanced about him, the bedroom like a tomb. Impulsively, he snapped shut his computer and lugged it toward the door.

Outside the bedroom, he already felt better.

Down the corridor, the stairs, through the back hallway, into the night. Evan inhaled deeply of the summer air, caught hints of lilac, jasmine, cedar, dogwood, aspen, and birch. My God, a riot of fragrances he could include in his play.

Would he get a chance to share it with Wells?

He'd have to do so on the sly, he realized. Otherwise, Bryan would stop him.

Thank God Evan didn't tell Bryan everything.

He frowned, shoved the thought away.

He'd never explored this part of the yard. Behind the mansion, the trees encroached nearer than they did in the front, the area wilder.

It emboldened him. Evan puffed out his chest. He imagined himself in a film. The budding writer striding into the forest with his laptop clutched to his side. He ached to share *The Death of the Prince*. It was far superior to anything the others had done so far.

Evan paused at the forest's edge, realizing he had no flashlight. Damn. He bit his lip, considering. He could return to the mansion, hunt for one, or...

...or just use the illumination from the laptop screen.

Evan opened the computer, delighted at his ingenuity. The pale glow didn't reach far, but it was enough to illumine the immediate area.

He plunged into the forest, holding the open laptop before him like a talisman.

What, he wondered, had he to fear? Bryan was back in the house, either tapping away at his inane story or stewing in the anguish of his defeat.

God, it had been amazing. To see the filthy cretin belittled had been the highlight of the retreat. The evening would have been the best of Evan's life had he only been able to—

Oh, how he wished he could read his work to the others!

He imagined the women reacting to his prose. Sherilyn. Elaine. Lucy.

Anna.

The laptop dimmed, so Evan swiped a finger over the mouse pad. The screen once again tossed its lucent glow over the trail.

He wished Anna could see him now. Bold. Intrepid. Yes, he was still out of shape, but now that he'd learned to conquer his fear of the outdoors, might he perhaps take control of his physical fitness as well?

Yes, he thought. He believed he could. Over the next month, he'd work out when he wasn't writing, and by that time, Bryan would be eliminated, would no longer be here to prevent Evan from sharing his brilliance.

And rounding a bend in the trail, Evan realized something else. Connecting with nature was cleansing him, dispelling the rank atmosphere of his room.

His expression darkening, he thought of his apartment back in New York. It was unhealthy, being alone. Too much time for the skulking, infernal demons in his head to take over, too much opportunity to act on his basest urges…

…to click on ruinous websites.

With an icy shiver, Evan brushed away the thought. No need for that now. He'd made mistakes. Who hadn't? As long as he was able to erase the history of sites visited, no one would know how low he'd sunk, how deeply into those depraved places he'd wriggled.

But the images flashed through his head:

People urinating into each other's mouths. Defecating on each other.

Stop.

Women tied up, the videos never making it entirely clear if they were playacting or being raped.

No.

Adults doing things to children.

"*Enough,*" he moaned, fingers grasping the sides of his head.

He had to stop thinking about it. It terrified him, how close he'd come to spilling these transgressions to Bryan. He'd been frightened, certain the man would kill him; he'd come perilously close to revealing his addictions.

The laptop dimmed again, and with an angry swipe, Evan restored the screen to full brightness.

He was panting, aware he'd ventured a goodly distance into the forest. His throat was itching, the sweat trickling down his back. He shivered, nudged a spiderweb with his elbow. Gasped and jerked his arm away, aware again of the laptop light dimming. Goddammit, he'd just brightened it again. He swept a finger over the mouse pad, but this time the screen didn't flare. Teeth bared, he spun the machine around to identify the problem, and when he saw what was there he cried out and dropped the computer.

His little sister was nineteen now, but back then, when he'd begun to spy on her....

"*Jesus Christ,*" Evan whimpered, retreating from the computer.

For on its illuminated screen was his sister at age six with Evan as he was now, both of them naked, both of them in the shower, and it wasn't possible, that had never happened, and he realized he was screaming, flailing at the branches and cobwebs, and he'd somehow left the trail, but the glow of the screen condemned him as he turned to flee.

Evan tripped, landed face first, the ground beneath him marshy. His glasses tumbled off. His fingers sank into the muck, the foul-smelling liquid squirting over his knuckles. He strained to push away, but the suction of the mud kept him pinned, and beneath his screams, he heard the noises issuing from the laptop, the vile, horrible sounds, and felt something slithering up his pant leg.

Evan froze, eyes widening.

He flopped onto his back and slapped at his leg, but the snake had already slithered under his knee, was squirming its way toward his groin. He fumbled with his belt, a high-pitched keening in the back of his throat, and another snake, moist and wriggling, slithered over his face. He batted at it, but it clamped down on the side of his open mouth, its fangs puncturing his cheek, and below, the snake bit his scrotum. Evan bellowed in horror, grappled with the snakes, but more teemed over him, squirming against his armpits, his lower back. Rather than injecting him with poison, he could feel them sucking, sucking, the blood streaming out of him, and somewhere, below the agony and the revulsion, he wondered if anyone would find the laptop....

CHAPTER TWELVE

At the exact moment Evan was being exsanguinated, Elaine rose from her bed, drifted to her window, and peered into the cloudless night. Her sleep had been fitful, a delirium really, the way it often was when she was shitfaced. The last three nights, she had smuggled a bottle upstairs – tonight it was Grey Goose vodka – and swigged from it until her writing devolved into incoherence. She told herself that the sound she heard was her imagination. An agonized voice. Someone's death throes.

Elaine squinted into the night, teetered, and thought, *Yes. Shrieking.*

Abruptly, it stopped.

She was about to open her window when something else arrested her gaze, a shadow beneath her. She stared, spellbound, as a figure emerged from the mansion and waded into the lush grass of the backyard.

It was a nude man, she could see that instantly, despite the way her vision tried to double. He was sinuous, well formed, if a bit older. She realized it was Roderick Wells.

Unexpectedly, she felt a wave of arousal, the man incredibly well preserved. She disregarded her estimates of his age. He couldn't be in his seventies, or even his sixties.

He had the body of a man in his early fifties, and even that was a stretch. Wells's buttocks were smooth and round, his hamstrings striated. In the moonglow the calves looked like polished apples, ripe ones that cried out to be tasted, to be licked.

He's old enough to be your grandfather. Get ahold of yourself.

Wryly, she thought, *I'm about to get ahold of myself.*

Wells stopped, faced the forest.

Elaine noticed the yard was illuminated not only by the moon but by a series of accent lights as well. Funny she never noticed before. Strung around the trees, spangling the yard like rhinestones, they lit up the deep blue night like a carnival.

But Wells alone absorbed her. He was motionless, godlike, his arms hanging loose at his sides. Though she couldn't see his eyes, she knew he'd heard the screams from the forest, was staring raptly toward them.

Wells knelt, placed a hand on the ground. Head bowed, he remained like that, some anomalous lovechild of a sprinter and a parishioner, and Elaine couldn't help but notice the bulge of his triceps as he waited, waited....

She became aware of the new sound not with her ears, but with her skin, which tightened in dread. Shivering, Elaine tried to back away from the window but couldn't. Frigid perspiration trickled between her breasts. The sound was a slow, metronomic pulse, a bruising thump. Her eardrums stung, her head throbbed, the sound like iron calipers squeezing her brain, and somehow the lights in the trees had begun to blaze up in time with the throb, and Elaine saw something that stole her breath, that made the wet mass in her chest threaten to burst in terror.

A ghostly skein of luminescence was advancing toward Roderick Wells, was serpentining from the forest, brightening and darkening in the same relentless pulse that illumined the rest of the night. It was all around, she realized, not just in the meadow, but flashing in the woods deeper in, coruscating from the treetops in the hazy distance. The whole. Fucking. Forest. It was gathering, pulsing straight to Wells. It glowed, darkened, glowed, darkened, advancing toward Wells, and when it touched the grass at his fingertips, he too caught the pulse, his entire body lighting up with the brilliant glow. Elaine wanted to scream but couldn't. The vodka simmered in her belly. For over the bunched muscles of Wells's shoulders she discovered swarming black rivers on the ground, knew they were blood, and as she watched, the blood seemed to bead, to sparkle in the pulsing light, and then it was swallowed by his pores, by the kneeling man's ravenous skin.

Slowly, the throb abated. Leaving the meadow in darkness. Leaving Wells alone in the tall grass.

He rose, turned, and though the clouds had eaten the moon,

Elaine could see his glowing white eyes fixed on her, discerned his jack-o'-lantern grin. Elaine stumbled back from the window, collapsed on her bed with a sob.

She struggled for breath, wondered, *Who's dead now?*

A minute passed before footsteps sounded at the end of the hallway.

Elaine glanced at the closed door, couldn't remember if she'd locked it.

Footsteps.

She shoved a knuckle between her teeth, bit down, scarcely registered the salt sting on her tongue. The footfalls ventured nearer, and as they approached she remembered the difference in Wells when he stood, after the pulsing lights had done their work. The back muscles had stood out a bit more, the flesh nowhere near as loose. The pectoral muscles bulging, the abdominals like chiseled stone.

The figure outside her door was...what? Replenished?

Breathing. She heard it through the door.

A floorboard creaked. Elaine trembled on the bed, praying for Wells to move on. Her eyes crawled down the door, examined the gap beneath it. Was there the slightest deepening of shadow there? Was the rasp she heard Wells's fingertips on the wood grain?

He wants in.

Elaine held her breath, her mind like an animal in an oven, flailing about wildly, the panic blazing in a white-hot cage.

Soft laughter, taunting her, the tone sadistic, demonic.

She shivered, fought the urge to let loose with the shriek that was rising in her throat.

When she thought she could stand it no longer, the footsteps sounded again, retreating.

Elaine couldn't react. Could only watch the door and hope Wells wouldn't return.

CHAPTER THIRTEEN

At a quarter past midnight, Will was hunched over his laptop when a knock on his door made him jump. He opened the door and felt himself relax. "Hey, man."

Rick nodded. "Got a few minutes?"

"Sure," Will said, returning to his chair.

"You recovered from the ballroom?" Rick asked.

"Seriously, man. What the hell was that?"

"He would've killed Sherilyn if he'd had a gun."

"Sit anywhere," Will said.

Rick hesitated and Will saw the room through Rick's eyes. A total wreck. Clothes strewn on the bed, some on the floor. The only chair the one Will was sitting on.

"Sorry about—"

"You think I care?" Rick asked, tossing aside a shirt and slouching on the bed. "I need to tell you something."

"You want to get a drink?" Will asked.

Rick said something Will couldn't make out.

"Sorry?"

"I said I'm haunted."

Will smiled. "That a joke?"

Rick looked up at him.

"There's gotta be more." Will's smile faded. "Right?"

"Do you believe in ghosts?"

Will thought of what he'd seen on the island, and resisted an urge to bolt from the room.

Rick shook his head. "I've never told anybody about this."

Then don't start now, Will thought. "Hey, man, if you're not up to sharing, it's totally—"

"It's got to be you."

"Why?"

Rick hesitated. "I thought about Sherilyn, but then, tonight… did you get the impression…"

"You're the one who's supposed to challenge the king?" Will finished.

"I did."

"Shit. I was hoping I was just imagining things."

"Did you see the look on Wells's face?"

"Wish I could forget it," Rick muttered. "If Sherilyn thinks I need to somehow overthrow Wells.…" He smiled, but there was fear in it. "I mean, that's crazy, isn't it?"

You know better.

"Do you feel any different?" Will asked.

Rick looked quickly at him. "I felt…something. Even though it's madness, I can't totally dismiss it. It was like Sherilyn's words were changing me."

"Tell her," Will said.

"I'd feel foolish talking to her about it," Rick said. "And I can't tell Evan or Elaine."

"Too beneath them?"

"More or less, though Elaine seems to be climbing off her high horse."

"Seems to be."

"Bryan's a douchebag."

"A total douchebag," Will agreed.

"Anna is so…Anna."

"Agreed."

"And Lucy, she's…I think I could fall in love with her."

Will folded a leg, grasped his knee in what he hoped was an analytical pose. "It falls to me then, whatever this confession is."

Rick raised an eyebrow. "How do you know it's a confession?"

"You could share it with Wells."

Rick made a scoffing sound, got up, went to the window. "Have you wondered why it took so much time from the application deadline to the actual retreat?"

"Of course I have," a trifle defensively. He hadn't.

"And?" Rick asked.

"And what?"

"What do you think was happening all that time?"

Will gestured vaguely. "You know what they say. Writing is waiting. Some publishers take years to answer. Why would Wells be any different?"

"He doesn't work like that. He's impatient. He wouldn't wait longer than he has to."

Will stared at Rick's profile for a long moment, the bright lunar glow making Rick look a bit ghostly himself. "What the hell are we talking about?"

Rick leaned against the windowsill. "Wells didn't choose us for our writing abilities."

"Why did he choose us?"

"Can I trust you?"

"You don't have a choice."

"What if I told you Wells was really something else? That his face was just a mask?"

"Rick—"

"Do you believe in monsters?"

Will's guts had drawn taut. "I believe there's something... uncanny about Wells."

"What about ghosts?"

Will couldn't stand the look in Rick's eyes. He glanced at the wall clock. "Look, man, it's late. I'm sure that freakshow in the ballroom wore you out as much as it did me, so we might as well—"

"It follows me."

Will stared at him.

"I've moved nineteen times since college, and every time I do, it finds me."

Will couldn't move, couldn't breathe.

"It started when my mom remarried," Rick said. "My stepfather was a narcissistic, abusive son of a bitch."

Will pushed to his feet. "I'll listen, but I don't want to do it in here."

"Too close to where Wells is lurking?"

Will eyed him ruefully. "You meant it, didn't you? You really think Wells is something unnatural."

Rick's voice was soft and deadly serious. "I've seen him change, Will. I've seen the horror beneath the mask."

178 • JONATHAN JANZ

CHAPTER FOURTEEN

Dear Justine,

I truly didn't mean to kill you.

You probably don't believe that, but I'm telling the truth, and the truth is, after sending the text, I realized there might be a more dreadful outcome.

You lived forty minutes away, but it took me less than thirty to reach Lacona. Upscale neighborhood, two-acre lots. White three-story house with black shutters and a chartreuse door.

I parked close enough to see your window. I watched it for an hour. The blinds were down, but maybe that's how you kept them, even though at the sorority you insisted on as much sunlight as possible because you loved peering out at the snow.

There was no snow that cheerless March evening, only wet brown earth and closed blinds.

The scream came around eight o'clock, dark by then. Your dad burst out the front door and scampered across the street. The neighbor trailed your dad inside. The ambulance arrived a few minutes later – good response times in affluent neighborhoods – and the warbling sirens swept away into the night, your parents' Mercedes trundling after.

You want to know the worst part, Justine? The punch line to the world's sickest joke?

I almost died that night too.

On some level I knew I was pushing you too far. If a boy calling you a slut had 'ruined your life', how much more profound would the damage be when you learned you'd become the viral star of a coed sex tape?

I guess I got my answer.

I learned something that night. I learned that stories have incredible power. They can teach. They can transport.

But they can also bring misery. They can enslave.

Some stories can kill.

A writer can become an evil king, one who takes rather than gives. One who uses his magic to destroy love.

Justine, when I found out you were dead, I drove my MG convertible to a semi-deserted road and knocked back some tequila. I drove the convertible as fast as it would go. I had killed my best friend, marred my reputation – of *course* people would know it was me in that tape – and I couldn't imagine the fallout awaiting me at the university.

The next thing I know, my MG is veering off the road and heading for an oak tree: the ultimate karmic moment. One second I was veering toward the tree, the next I was bouncing into a sodden field, my tires sinking into the muck. I sobbed and pummeled the wheel and wished I could take back what I'd done to you.

Then I heard the *ding* from my phone, the first text message about you. It was a sorority sister.

Deanna: Did you hear about Justine??
Me: What happened?
Deanna: She OD'd on sleeping pills. Did you see the video?

It was pitch black outside, my MG was stalled in a cabbage field, and my best friend was dead because of my cruelty.

Me: What video?
Deanna: It's basically a porno. With Justine and Jake and some other woman. Is it you? Sorry but I had to ask.
Me: Justine is dead?
Deanna: Yes. Is that you in the video?

I admitted it that night to Deanna and a couple others. They all knew it was me anyway. I told them about the stolen camera and awaited their wrath. I was sure I'd be expelled, maybe prosecuted. Shunned by everyone, barred from any meaningful future, a scarlet letter tattooed on my chest.

Then something remarkable happened.

Jake and I became victims.

Our friends believed our story, that we were just a trio of drunk kids fooling around, that some sick predator took advantage of us. The video had been posted anonymously at a public computer and was never traced to the guy I hired. I feared for a while that the boy – a creep I met in Com class – would blackmail me. But I never saw him again after what happened to Justine. Maybe he killed himself too.

Jake and I were feted as survivors of a cybercrime, and perversely, we became more popular than ever.

I threw myself into my writing, now armed with legitimate emotional suffering. It must have helped because my professors commented on the rawness of my narratives.

You'll never see this on an inspirational poster, but it's the truth:

Bad girls finish first.

This contest?

This is one of those times.

There are only eight of us left. Wells likes me best.

I like my chances.

Wish me luck, Justine.

Your friend,

Anna Holloway

CHAPTER FIFTEEN

They made their way through the meadow. Out here in the night air Rick felt exposed. It was foolish, but he was glad he wasn't alone.

Will asked, "You going to talk, or are we just gonna listen to the crickets?"

"And the cicadas," Rick said. "I've always loved that revving sound."

"Not me. Puts me on edge."

"Reminds me of where I lived when I was little. By the forest." He smiled, remembering. He inclined his face, took in the multitudinous stars. "She got remarried when I was eleven. I was excited at first, thinking I finally had someone to play catch with, someone to wrestle. You know, the stuff kids do with dads."

"My dad was never the wrestling type."

"My stepdad wasn't either. He shoved me and hit me, but we never wrestled."

Will looked at him. "Sorry."

"You didn't know." He studied the sky. "Most of it was verbal. He was just so damned…controlling. He had to know exactly what my mom was doing at all times. I guess he worried she'd cheat on him, but I don't know why. She never gave him reason to think…." He stopped, shook his head. "The stuff I need to tell you about, it happened when I was twelve."

The forest loomed ahead.

"The summer before my seventh-grade year, I was really skinny and not very tall." He laughed without humor. "I tell you that so if you wonder why I didn't do more to help, you'll think, 'Well, he was only twelve.' But deep down I hate myself."

The trail before them was wide enough they could walk two abreast.

Rick nodded. "My stepdad, he was all about money, so when the break-ins began, he got scared. The prospect of losing his possessions frightened him the way most of us are frightened of losing a loved one. So he gave me an extra chore. Double-checking the locks to make sure no one would rob us."

"You had a lot of chores?"

"About three dozen. The burglaries finally spilled over into our town. There were eight or nine by that time, and one of them had turned violent. The homeowners hadn't been killed, but a man in a ski mask had threatened them at gunpoint and pistol-whipped the husband. The guy sustained a skull fracture. Brain damage. Everybody was tense, most of all Phil."

The trail narrowed, and Rick took the lead for a few paces until it widened again. "He was relentless in his belittling. He'd criticize the way Mom looked, the clothes she wore. She was never supposed to be without makeup."

"Why not?"

"How the hell should I know? Maybe he was worried about the president showing up and judging him for having a wife who wasn't wearing eyeliner."

Rick paused. The bile was boiling in the back of his throat, but he forced himself to continue. "When she mentioned divorce, his money alarm went off. He went ballistic, telling her she wouldn't get a penny. He knew lawyers, friends who'd make sure she was ruined by the time they got through with her. He even threatened to take me away." Rick hawked, spat into the underbrush. "As if he wanted me."

"What a cocksucker."

Rick stayed focused, knowing he'd lose his nerve if he stopped now. He told Will about the burglary, about Phil erupting on his mom.

"What'd the guy take?"

"Quite a few things, including this Civil War musket my stepdad was crazy about. Thing was supposedly worth twenty grand."

"What happened?"

Rick scuffed the dirt with the toe of a sneaker. "Mom crushed his skull with a hammer."

"Holy shit."

Rick told him the rest of the story. They mounted a steep rise, clawed the pebbled ground to keep from tumbling backward. When they'd crested a hill, Will bent over, hands on knees, panting. "Let's rest, okay?"

"You a smoker?"

Will shook his head, grimaced. "Nope. You're telling me this why?"

"I told you. There's a ghost."

"You're haunted by a ghost named Phil?"

"Not Phil. The thief."

Frowning, Will straightened.

"The thief was caught the next day," Rick said, "and charged for Phil's murder."

"Your mom didn't come forward?"

Rick shook his head. "Neither did I."

Will hesitated, though Rick knew what he'd ask next.

"What was the sentence?"

"Death."

After a long silence, Will said, "Jesus."

Rick swallowed. "The haunting began a month after the execution."

"You keep calling him 'the thief'. What was his—"

"Personalizing him brings it back."

"Sounds like it never went away."

Rick hung his head dispiritedly. "It didn't." At length, he said, "His name was Raymond Eddy."

"He haunts you?"

"Raymond usually shows up as a shadowy figure. Or a nightmare."

Will was staring at him. "What do you mean, a shadowy—"

"I'll tell you something else," Rick said. "The worst thing."

Rick's skin was icy with sweat. He started to pace, as though he could physically evade the memory. "They didn't make me testify in the same room with Raymond. Why would they, right? I was a kid, and I'd never even seen him. Our story was that we'd found Phil's body right after the attack. My mom, she claimed she'd been awakened by the slamming door when Raymond left."

He could sense Will running it around in his mind, the logical questions arising. Rick braced himself, but when Will spoke, it was still painful to hear the words.

"There were no witnesses? Nobody saw Raymond at your house?"

Rick shook his head, the dread cinching tighter.

"How could they—"

"The justice system sucks," Rick said, more harshly than he'd intended. But he couldn't help it, the words came tumbling out. "Raymond was poor, which was why he started stealing in the first place. He was smart, the way a jungle animal's smart, but he didn't have a pot to piss in—"

"—so he couldn't afford a good lawyer."

"His lawyer didn't give a shit, and it showed. Everyone knew Raymond was the one who'd been doing the break-ins, and when they traced him to a storage unit, they found the stuff he'd taken from us. The guy whose skull Raymond had broken – from the previous break-in? – he was pretty well-off, and they made sure the prosecution had everything it needed to crucify him."

"You feel guilty about it."

Rick glowered at him. "What the fuck do you think?"

Will held his gaze. "Raymond knew what was happening?"

Rick reached out, leaned against a tree, the scabrous bark rough on his skin. "He knew it before anybody else. He barely even protested."

"He just let them do it?"

Rick shook his head, sucked in a shuddering breath. "He knew exactly where it was heading, and it was like…like he was preparing for what came after."

He knew Will would ask the question, but that didn't make it any easier when Will said, "After the execution?"

Rick swayed a little. "They interviewed him on the local news station. After the sentence had been given. Mom…she tried to shield me from the whole thing, but it's not like I was a little kid. I was in junior high by that time. I saw the interview at a friend's."

"What did Raymond say?"

Rick looked up, tried to spot stars in the night sky, but there were only shadows.

"It was partly what he said, and partly how he said it. He kept changing the subject, speaking in this cryptic way. The reporter asked him if he was scared of dying, and instead of answering directly, he talked about an ancestor of his who fought in the Civil War, for the Confederacy. Said this great-great- uncle believed in reincarnation and wasn't afraid of death. Raymond claimed the soldier had come back in the late 1860s, just a few years after his death, to redress the wrongs of the war." Rick sighed. "Raymond said he was going to do the same thing. Get back at the people who put him in jail."

There was a silence.

"The reference to the Civil War," Will said. "Was that...."

"An allusion to the musket he stole from our house?" Rick finished. "I didn't make the connection at the time. At least, my conscious mind didn't. But later...ever since Raymond's death I've been replaying the interview, and it's like the whole thing was directed at me and Mom."

"You sure it wasn't the guilt?"

"I've told myself that, but the haunting...it's real. He follows me wherever I go. And even though it's just the outline of a man... pitch black...I see Raymond's face there." He paused. "The end of the interview, they asked Raymond if he had anything to say to the audience."

"Did he?" Will asked, not sounding like he wanted to know.

"He looked straight at the camera – straight at me – and said, 'I'll come for you.'"

Will was quiet a long moment. Then he said, "Holy shit."

"He made good on his promise," Rick said. He saw the look on Will's face. "What?"

Will was gazing down the hill. "What's that look like to you?"

Rick screwed up his eyes. "There used to be a house there."

Will was silent a long moment. Then he muttered, "Fuck."

"Wrong answer?"

"Let's head back."

They descended the hill, Will falling and cursing a couple times.

Rick said, "Because of the haunting, I've always been reluctant to settle down. One time I thought I'd broken the spell. I took her to Cancun, one of those all-inclusive vacations?"

"Love all-inclusives," Will said. "I usually gain fifteen pounds."

Rick smiled. "I'd proposed to Sarah that night. We made love.

Later, when I came out of the bathroom, she was huddled in a corner, her mouth open in a silent scream. There was a darkness enveloping her. It was…Sarah had to be admitted to a psychiatric hospital. Her family…they blamed me. Wouldn't let me see her." He shook his head. "They returned the ring by UPS."

Will didn't make a joke of it. Rick was grateful.

When the mansion came into view, Will asked, "This is why you think Wells chose you. The haunting?"

Rick gazed up at the vast structure. "Mom and I had two years to break our silence. You know…trials like that take a while. The appeals.…" He shook his head. "But we didn't. I was too afraid. Mom…she didn't want to go to jail. Raymond was a violent criminal, but.…"

"But he didn't deserve to die."

Rick stared at his shoes. "No, he didn't."

"You think Wells chose you because of your sins."

Unable to meet Will's gaze, Rick nodded.

Will said, "I agree with you."

Rick did look at him then, was surprised to see tears in Will's eyes.

"You think I'll tell you my secret," Will said.

Rick studied Will's face. No use lying. "Do you have one?"

"I let someone die too. You ever hear of Peter Bates?"

And as they stood at the edge of the forest, Will told him the story.

PART FOUR
REVENANTS

CHAPTER ONE

The rain moved in at midmorning and now, nearing noon, was still falling steadily. Unable to sleep even after he and Will had spent most of the night tromping around the wilderness, Rick had been working since dawn and had gotten nearly seven thousand words down. Yet as he chipped away at a crucial scene, one thing kept intruding.

Lucy.

She was more than just smart. She cared about people. And he respected that.

He needed to see her.

Because his tendency was to shut people out. Maybe he was that way naturally, but after what happened with Raymond Eddy and the dread that had darkened his life for more than two decades, he'd resolved to never again get close to someone.

He pushed the laptop away. Sat and listened to the rain pelting the windowpanes.

Dammit.

He left his room and knocked on Lucy's door.

"Yes?" she said from within.

"Howdy," he said. Knew it was lame but didn't care.

"Rick?"

"Can I come in?"

The pause was so long he thought she'd lowered herself out the window with a rope of bedsheets.

"It's open," she said finally. Her tone was noncommittal. Or unenthusiastic, if you were being cynical.

He was tired of being cynical.

He entered, found her on her bed, fully dressed, feet crossed, reading a vermilion cloth-bound book.

She said, "Did you know Fred Astaire had huge hands? I guess it's bad for a dancer to have hands that big, so he was always trying to hide them."

"I can't dance."

"He failed his first screen test. They thought he was unattractive, untalented. He almost flamed out before he began."

"Interesting. I need to talk to you about something non-Fred-Astaire-related. Two things, actually."

She placed the book on her bed and laced her fingers in her lap. She was wearing a red-and-black flannel shirt and blue jeans with the cuffs rolled halfway up her calves. No shoes. Cute toes, the nails painted red like her shirt.

"I'm listening," she said.

"I've been avoiding you."

"Too competitive?"

He shook his head. "Nothing to do with it."

"I've never gotten that vibe from you," she said. "Still, not much point in getting close, is there?"

"That's another problem," he said. "You've got issues too."

He saw the way her eyes narrowed, waved her off. "It's not a criticism. It's just to say…I want you to write a great book."

The annoyance left her face, in its place a world-weary look that hurt him to see.

"I don't know if I can anymore."

"I do." He moved deeper into the room. "Writing a great book is hard. It doesn't happen by accident."

She opened her mouth, but he went on. "I haven't read *The Girl Who Died* cover-to-cover, but I've read enough to know you're a hell of a writer."

Her eyes grew larger.

"You're better than I am," he said, and when she started protesting, he said, "I know we write in different areas, but I've read pretty widely, and your stuff is the best I've seen in a while."

"Sherilyn—"

"—is very good. So is Will, what little he's let me read." He shook his head. "It doesn't compare to yours."

The look in her eyes, she wanted to believe him but couldn't bring herself to.

She gestured toward the desk. "What if my work-in-progress sucks?"

"Let me read it."

He thought she'd demur, but she paused, thinking about it. "What about your story?"

"If I write any more today, my skull's going to implode."

She moved to the desk and opened the laptop.

He allowed himself to study her profile. Her brow furrowed when she was concentrating, a tendency he found endearing. There was an almost imperceptible dimple in her chin, a feature he hadn't noticed until now because the angle had to be just right to see it. Add to that the brain, the personality…it almost wasn't fair.

Papers began to feed out of the desktop printer.

"Can't believe I'm letting you see this," she said. "My rough drafts are train wrecks. Full of typos, extra words. The one time I let my agent see something raw, he acted like it was an affront to literature."

"This agent of yours…isn't he supposed to be helpful? I mean, he works for you, right?"

She propped her fists on the desk. "I should have fired him a long time ago. I get to the brink, but this panicked voice screams, 'Are you crazy? He's one of the most respected agents in New York!'"

"A guy like that," Rick said, "is he the type who could make things hard on you? If you let him go, I mean?"

Lucy didn't respond, nor did she need to.

"It's a good thing you're done with him."

She looked at him.

He pointed. "Now give me those pages. I want to be the first to read *The Fred Astaire Murders*."

A small smile. "You really like the title?"

"Fork it over."

Laughing softly, she did.

"Hey," she called when he was halfway through the door. "You said you needed to talk to me about two things. What was the other?"

"Oh," he said, "that."

He leaned in and kissed her. She was stiff for a second or two, then she moved into him, her body pressing his. She threaded her arms around his neck, her fingertips sending warm chills down his back. They stood that way a minute, breathing together, but it still ended too soon.

CHAPTER TWO

Finally, Bryan thought as Lucy exited the library. She'd been there when he'd arrived a little after one, and she'd hung around for more than an hour, leafing through books on anatomy and true crime.

He glanced right and left to make sure no one else was there, then searched for a book on botany. He scanned the titles, amazed at how much shit there was on the shelves. Horror, fantasy, even young adult. Shit genres all. His faith in Wells was diminishing by the second.

Bryan rounded the corner, located the shelf he needed. He selected two books – the Royal Horticultural Society's *Good Plant Guide* and *The North American Field Guide to Trees* – and moved to the table where he'd been pretending, for Lucy's benefit, to read a book called *The Art of War for Writers*. It was a piece of crap, like every other writing manual he'd ever skimmed.

Scooting in, he opened *The North American Field Guide to Trees*. He found what he needed right away, the confirmation that, yes, most of what he'd encountered here was indigenous to the Midwest.

Most.

Bryan glanced about the library and fished the objects out of his cargo shorts: a pinecone, a leaf, and a black nut roughly the size of a marble.

He found a match for the pinecone and chided himself for not identifying it earlier. Red pine. Larger than the kind he was used to finding in Minnesota, but in essence the same.

He examined the leaf. Frowned.

Nothing in zones three-through-seven that resembled it. He flipped to zone two.

Nothing.

Nothing in zone one either. He mentally castigated himself for looking in that section. You wouldn't find a flamingo in Alaska, would you? Then why piss away time trying to find a tree in Indiana that wouldn't survive north of Georgia?

Bryan flipped the pages of the *Good Plant Guide*, wondering why he was wasting his time. It wasn't as if—

"You won't find it in that book," a voice from behind him said.

Bryan spun in his chair, knocking things from the table, the black nut spinning like a top on the hardwood floor before disappearing under a bookshelf.

Wilson stared down at him impassively.

"Jesus – where did you come from?"

Bryan tried to push the chair from the table, but Wilson crowded him. "You mind? I'd like to pick up my things," Bryan said.

"A species of beech," Wilson said.

"What?"

"That nut specimen is only found in the Carpathian Mountains," Wilson explained.

A pause. "The Carpathians."

"Correct."

"In Romania?" Bryan turned and gazed up at Wilson. "You're joking."

Wilson didn't smile. Stared down at him with eyes like tar.

Bryan shook his head, made to slide his legs out from under the table, but a hand clamped over his shoulder, riveted him in place.

"Let go of me." Bryan bared his teeth. "Unless you want your ass kicked."

Wilson said, "I told you to be more competitive, Mr. Clayton. Can you honestly say you've done that?"

"Damn you," Bryan growled, seized Wilson's forearm with both hands. But the fingers were implacable. Bryan grunted, thrashing now, and only by slumping all the way to the floor and twisting sideways was he able to free himself.

Wilson was laughing.

Motherfucker.

Bryan squared up to him.

Wilson's expression remained serene. "These grounds go on forever. It's my job to ensure they remain fed."

"Who are you?"

"I wondered about you. After your application was pulled."

Bryan hesitated. "Who pulled it?"

"I did. It showed me things."

The library suddenly seemed too dark, the lamps failing.

Bryan worked to keep his tone neutral. "I don't know what—"

"Impressions, Mr. Clayton. Your handwriting leaves impressions." He tilted his head. "Didn't you find it strange that you were required to fill out the application by hand?"

Bryan glanced over his shoulder, realized he wasn't far from the door. Had Wilson locked it? Was the door thick enough to muffle screams?

Wilson brayed laughter. Bryan nearly soiled himself.

Bryan passed a hand over his brow. "You're telling me you chose us by reading our applications? I mean, reading them in the psychic sense?"

"We needed a…" his hands made little circles in the air, "…a hammer. A dissonant chord in the symphony. A spoiled ingredient in the soup."

Bryan's voice was toneless. "I'm the spoiled ingredient."

"We knew Elaine would push people's buttons, that Sherilyn had spunk. But we had to add someone else to the brew. It was down to you and one other."

"Why me?"

"Carlsbad."

Bryan's chest calcified into a hard, bony knot.

Wilson's grin broadened. "Did you really think I chose you because of those pitiful little yarns about hunting?"

"My readers send me letters…."

"You're the worst kind of coward, Mr. Clayton. You're afraid of everything, most of all yourself."

"Don't—"

"Don't what?" Wilson said, eyebrows rising. "Don't talk about how you fantasized about other boys? How you'd sneak glances at them in the locker room?"

Bryan shook his head.

"And when you finally got the nerve to act on your desires, the boy you fucked had the audacity to fall in love with you."

"Stop."

"He threatened to talk, didn't he?"

"No."

"He did, Mr. Clayton. So you kept on with him, and you lived in terror of being discovered."

Bryan covered his face, but Wilson continued. "You tried to break up, and he went wild with rage, said he'd tell your parents, your classmates."

Bryan began to sob.

"And you killed him for it, didn't you? You used the only thing you had, a jagged rock you found in the cave."

Bryan ground his palms into his eyes.

"You were bigger than he was, stronger, so you sat on his back and slashed at his throat with that rock. You slaughtered him like a pig—"

Bryan sobbed so hard he couldn't breathe.

"—and that night, the tide took him out. Your family moved to Minnesota a couple months later, a stroke of good fortune. But you lay awake deep into the night. You remade your image, reshaped your body and quit choir because your father said singing was for homosexuals, and began taking an interest in outdoor sports because that was what real men did."

"*Stop it,*" Bryan wailed.

"You've slept with women, but it's never really taken, has it?"

"*Please stop.*"

"You should have accepted who you are. You and some man might have lived a happy life together. But you chose to forsake your humanity, to adopt your parents' lies and prejudices."

"Why are you doing this?"

"You've murdered before."

Bryan backpedaled. "I can't hurt anyone. The last time…it really messed me up."

Wilson matched his steps. "There's no use hiding."

"Please let me go."

Wilson's teeth gleamed, the apotheosis of a smile. "Don't grovel, you unctuous little fuck. Roderick put his faith in me."

Bryan lunged for the door, but Wilson pounced on him, pinned him on his back. "You were supposed to have guts!"

"*Please—*"

"Stop that, you nasty little shit." Wilson slapped him. "You couldn't even kill Evan."

Bryan shook his head. "It wasn't right."

"I'll tell you what's not *right,*" Wilson shouted into his face. "That Roderick might replace me due to your ineptitude. *Listen,*" he commanded, his breath yeasty. "You have until tomorrow night." Another slap. "*Tomorrow. Night.* If you don't kill by then, you better take your sniveling carcass far away from this house. Because if I find you, you're worse than dead. You'll drown in a sea of anguish. Tupped by torment." Wilson's voice became guttural. "I will *flense* you, Clayton. I will don a coat of your flesh and caper through the forest like Puck."

Wilson threw open the door, planted a shoe against the side of his ass, and shoved him into the hall. "Out with you, excrement. Kill if you want to see another sunset."

CHAPTER THREE

After supper they met in the courtyard. Lucy had visited here during Corrina Bowen's visit, and at the time her impression had been similar to her impression of the rest of Wells's home: once beautiful, now fallen into disrepair.

Looking around, she realized how much the place had changed. Evidently, Wilson and the other servants had been hard at work out here, spreading mulch, trimming shrubs, rehabilitating the entire courtyard.

The space was enclosed on all sides by the brick and stone of the mansion. Though the sundown light was fading, several hanging lanterns cast a cheerful apricot glow over the courtyard. The ivy clinging to the walls had been restored to a deep green, and evergreen plantings abounded. The dead leaves had been removed, allowing the gardens to flourish. The seating area was festooned with boulders, over which crept phlox and thyme. The lilac bushes and jasmine imbued the space with a medley of fragrances, and the tall cascading fountain, now fixed and burbling constantly, provided a soothing backdrop. The air was damp from the downpour, but rather than rendering the air frigid, the humidity was just warm enough to make Lucy feel comfortable rather than oppressed.

Or maybe it was Rick who made her feel that way.

He sat beside her, frowning over his pages. Lucy's own manuscript lay in her lap, and if Rick was to be believed, it was better than she'd believed. He'd delivered his critique a few minutes earlier, and though she'd wanted him to, he hadn't kissed her again.

Maybe, she decided, that was because they'd been standing in the hallway at the time. She hoped that was the cause, instead of her being an out-of-practice kisser.

As for the manuscript, he'd been ecstatic. Her characterization, he said, was top notch, particularly her female lead. That had alleviated one of Lucy's deepest fears, that she'd made the protagonist too sarcastic. In her experience, readers were intolerant of snarkiness in women. A male lead smarted off, he was a loveable wiseass; a female did the same, she was an unlikeable bitch.

But Rick loved her. He also appreciated the way she'd painted her setting.

"I've been to New York a hundred times," she told him. "I should be able to describe it."

"Visiting and writing effectively about it," he'd pointed out, "are different things."

He'd loved her word choice, her dialogue, her voice. The voice comment was what buoyed her the most, as that was what Fred Morehouse most frequently criticized. "It's bland, Lucy Goosy. The voice here is no more distinct than what you'd find in any high school comp class."

According to Rick, her voice was mesmerizing.

He only had one criticism: she sometimes got wordy.

At that, she'd nodded. "I need to trust my audience."

"Trusting your audience," he'd answered, "is a matter of trusting yourself. Of knowing you've conveyed the information in a way that the reader will understand."

She'd given him a wan smile. "Believing in myself is hard for me."

"It's hard for anyone, but you know what helps?"

"Cocaine?"

"Can't afford it. You ever hear of Jack Ketchum?"

She frowned. "Horror writer, right?"

"Sort of. I mean, he's horror, but not of the werewolf and zombie sort. Stephen King called him 'the scariest man in America'."

"That a compliment?"

"Would you use it for a cover blurb?"

"If you changed the gender."

"I'm the biggest self-doubter on the planet. When you get rejected by everybody in publishing, you tend to lose faith."

"It's not much better when it happens in reverse," she pointed out.

"I wouldn't know."

She winced. "Sorry."

"I met Dallas – that's Ketchum's real first name—"

"Seriously?"

He nodded. "Fascinating dude. He was Henry Miller's literary agent."

"No way."

"And he's a hell of a writer. His stuff is so raw and emotional, you never recover from it."

"That good, huh?"

"Damned good." He gestured irritably. "Point is, I was talking to Dallas and telling him how I get down on myself, and he shared two words that changed my life. I still haven't gotten published, but I no longer write like I've got a gun to my head."

"I'm listening."

"Fuck fear."

She couldn't suppress a laugh.

"No, really," he said. "I know how simple it sounds, but when Dallas said it, I knew it was the truth. What has fear ever done for you? What constructive role does fear play in writing?"

Lucy thought about it. "When I edit—"

"I'm not talking about editing, I'm talking about writing without fear. About sitting in front of the keyboard, and saying, *To hell with it, I'm going to do this, and it's not gonna be perfect, and that's fine, it doesn't have to be. But I'm not going to sit here like a cowering dog.* That's a sure road to failure. Writing without fear doesn't guarantee it'll be good, but it puts you in the game."

"You're fired up."

"Damn right I'm fired up." He brandished her pages. "This is magnificent. And it's only a rough draft. Imagine how good it'll be once you sand off the rough edges."

In the courtyard, Lucy replayed the conversation in her head, focusing particularly on Ketchum's advice.

"*Fuck fear,*" she whispered to herself. "*Fuck fear.*"

Wells entered the courtyard. He wore a burgundy smoking jacket and a gold cravat. He walked with a grace that belied his age, his movements far more assured than they'd been at the outset of the retreat.

Lucy watched, mesmerized, as he approached his chair. His posture was more erect, his bearing undeniably regal. The worry lines and haggardness in his face had diminished, and within the smoking jacket his shoulders and arms appeared fuller. Far from the gaunt, aging writer that had greeted them upon their arrival, Wells now resembled a virile outdoorsman in his late fifties. She could easily imagine him taking on a leading role in an adventure movie. The battle-scarred but still-formidable hero returning for one final battle with evil.

Wells sat and beamed at them. "Are we ready to begin?"

Anna said, "Shouldn't we wait for Evan?"

Wells eyed her. "Why don't you just ask if he's left the competition?"

Anna colored. "Well, I—"

"He has. Miss Lafitte gave us word a few minutes ago."

"Was Evan hiding a cell phone too?" Sherilyn asked.

Wells permitted himself a smile. "He was not, Miss Jackson. He wrote a weak story."

"He never even read," Rick pointed out.

"This isn't a reality show, Mr. Forrester. Eliminations aren't based on oral recitation. I read Mr. Laydon's play excerpt in private."

"Makes sense," Anna said. "He knew it was unsalvageable and decided to go home."

Lucy waited for Bryan to echo Anna's theory, but he only stared morosely into his lap. Nor did Elaine comment. In fact, now that Lucy looked at Elaine, she noticed several changes. Her blond hair, normally stylish, had been contained with barrettes. Her clothes, though presentable, weren't up to her usual edgy standards. Even the tattoos on her chest and ankle appeared drab.

"At any rate," Wells went on, "Mr. Laydon is no longer in the running, which brings our number to seven. And since we have an open chair," Wells explained, "I have invited Wilson to take part in the evening's festivities."

The French doors opened at the far edge of the courtyard, and Wilson entered.

Lucy's throat tightened.

Looking more like a college professor than a groundskeeper, Wilson moved confidently into the semicircle and took Evan's seat. Like Wells, Wilson exuded vitality. He wore a navy blue sport coat over a white polo. His jeans widened at the cuffs to accommodate pale alligator-skinned cowboy boots.

No one else in the group reacted to Wilson's appearance, save Bryan, who looked even more morose.

What's happening to you? she wondered.

Wells gazed upon his servant fondly. "We're delighted you could join us, Wilson."

Wilson crossed his legs contentedly. "I look forward to the reading."

Wells watched them, steepled forefingers touching his lips. He said, "Writing is many things. It is passion. It is talent. It is love. But above all things, writing is *endurance*." Wells spread his arms, glanced about the opulent courtyard. "You are all a step closer to having all of this. But all of *this*," he said, grinning slightly, "is only attainable through sacrifice. Through endurance."

Lucy read disparate emotions on the other contestants' faces — skepticism on Rick's, boundless hunger on Anna's — but no one in the courtyard spoke.

Finally, Wells nodded and said, "Miss Still."

The words acted like a blow to her stomach. She'd suspected she'd be chosen tonight, but the suspicion didn't make the reality any less terrifying.

"Proceed," Wells said.

She willed her body to stand, but it wouldn't comply. She'd always been beset by nerves at readings, but never before had it mattered like it did tonight. They were down to seven, and if Rick were to be believed, her book had real potential.

What if Rick just wants in your pants? a voice whispered.

Let's hope so, she answered.

She glanced at Rick, who smiled encouragingly. "You can do this," he said in an undertone.

"Miss Still?" Wells said.

"Catch me if I faint," she muttered to Rick.

The walk to the fore of the group seemed to take hours. She could feel the eyes of her peers riveted on her. Wilson's presence jangled her nerves the most. The memory of their creepy encounter in the ballroom remained etched in her mind, the insinuating way he'd spoken.

Get a grip, she told herself.

She glanced at Rick, whose expression also suggested she needed to get a grip.

"Mr. Wells?" a voice asked.

It was Anna, who, unlike Bryan and Elaine, looked more vibrant than ever. Perhaps channeling Amanda Wells, Anna had chosen a black sundress, only Anna's revealed more cleavage.

Wells's expression was stern. "Unless this is urgent, Miss Holloway—"

"It is."

"Well?"

"Could you tell us what you're after during these readings?"

Wells cocked an eyebrow. "What I'm *after*, Miss Holloway?"

"What do you want from us?" she said. "When Lucy reads, for instance. Let's say it isn't good…"

Asshole, Lucy thought.

"…should we give feedback?"

Sherilyn sat forward. "Truthfully, I've wondered the same thing."

Anna tossed her scarlet hair over her shoulder. "Do our opinions have any bearing on whether someone is eliminated?"

Lucy stared at her, thinking, *Colossal asshole!*

Wells laughed silently. "Come now, Miss Holloway. You're pupils, not editors."

"Why are we here then?" Sherilyn asked.

"Why indeed." Wells leaned back. "Have you ever played a team sport, Miss Jackson?"

"Not my thing."

"You, Miss Kovalchyk?"

Elaine offered a shrug. "In seventh grade I was on the volleyball B-team. Someone spiked me in the face and broke my glasses."

"The rest of you?"

Will, Rick, and Anna nodded. Bryan frowned at his hands.

Lucy thought, *Can I sit down now?*

"A good coach differentiates his instruction because no two players learn the same way. However, embedded in his public correction will be lessons for the rest of the team, universal truths from which they can all benefit."

Anna leaned forward. "So when you tell Lucy everything that's wrong with her piece—"

"Take it easy," Rick said.

"—you'll really be addressing all of us?"

Wells narrowed his eyes at Anna. "You speak as though you want Miss Still to fail."

Anna shrugged. "I've read enough of her work."

Lucy's belly gurgled. Of all the things she needed at the moment, diarrhea was the least of them.

Wells looked at Lucy. "We're waiting."

So Lucy read, her voice dry and croaky at first, but gaining lubrication after Rick handed her a bottle of water. As she took a couple swigs, he said, under his breath, "I used to get dry as a bone when I'd give a speech." His tone went lower, so she had to strain to hear him. "The good thing is, you've got a script. Read it proudly. Taste the words. I know how dumb that sounds, but it works. Your words have texture, different flavors. Savor them. *Know* this is a great story."

Anna gave Rick a caustic look. "Knight in shining armor, huh?"

He shook his head. "Lucy doesn't need to be saved."

A warm wave spread through her belly, her innards no longer churning.

She looked down at her pages. Thought, *Fuck fear.*

And read, "'Unfortunately for Jenna Carter, the ice pick in her cerebellum didn't bring instant death.'"

CHAPTER FOUR

When Lucy finished, there was a thick silence. Amanda Wells and Miss Lafitte had entered the courtyard at some point. She must have gone on for at least fifteen minutes because the gloaming light had all but drained from the sky.

To Lucy's surprise, Elaine was the first to applaud.

Her clapping wasn't ironic, either; her accompanying smile seemed genuine. Will and Sherilyn joined in, applauding lustily. Rick did as well, though Lucy looked away from him quickly when she felt her eyes begin to burn.

Miss Lafitte headed back inside the house, but Amanda set aside her drink to join in.

Lucy became aware of muttered words. Wells and Wilson conferring.

Wells waited for the adulation to die down. "Yes, Miss Still, that was rather good." He rose. "Would you mind sitting while I share a few thoughts?"

There was no sensation in her feet as she made her way to her chair. Sitting, she glanced at Rick and exhaled powerfully. He extended his fist, and after a confused moment, she bumped it with her own.

Feeling better than she could remember feeling, she listened to Wells, who had taken her place before the group.

"I selected Miss Still tonight because the early chapters of *The Fred Astaire Murders* showed considerable promise." He favored her with a look that made her forget his past cruelties. "I'm happy to say the manuscript has only improved since then." Wells nodded at Elaine. "Miss Kovalchyk, you were the first to applaud. Why?"

"Surprising, huh?" she said and gave Lucy a mordant grin. "I have trouble admitting when I'm wrong, but...I was wrong. I still think she was given her big break because of her looks and her age—"

"Hey now," Sherilyn protested.

"—*however*," Elaine went on, "it's clear to me she's learned a lot in the years since. The characters are just terrific. Especially the protagonist."

"Thank you," Lucy said.

Anna watched her with a speculative gleam.

Wells noticed it too. "Something to add, Miss Holloway?"

Anna cleared her throat. "What I want to know is how you'll make it stand out in a saturated suspense market. The plot seems engaging enough. But…I don't know." She shrugged. "It doesn't strike me as special."

Rick gave her a look. "Then you weren't listening."

"Just because you two are sleeping together—"

"*Yikes*," Will said. "No need to get nasty."

"That's what nasty people do," Sherilyn said.

"Please, everyone," Wells said, raising his arms for order. "Let's keep our heads."

They all fell silent, but the antagonism crackled the air like an electrical charge. Rick was staring at Anna as if seeing her for the first time.

Wells said, "Miss Holloway asked how this novel will stand out in a crowded marketplace, a question I'm happy to answer, having some experience in the industry myself."

Sherilyn nodded and winked at Lucy, who found herself smiling despite her nerves.

"First of all," Wells said, "the book has a splendid premise. That is essential. Secondly, Miss Kovalchyk brought up the protagonist, and while I'd echo her sentiment, I would assert that it is your villain, Miss Still, that tips the scales in the novel's favor. He is charming, attractive, and absolutely ruthless. Writing instructors correctly point out that a villain needs to be the hero of his own story, but what they forget is that the villain also needs to be *frightening*. In fact, I'd argue that the effectiveness of a story is directly correlated to the threat posed by the antagonist." He turned to Lucy. "Your antagonist, with his slicked-back hair, his rugged good looks, and his elegant attire, is effective because of the brutality lurking beneath. I even like the Florida-shaped birthmark on his neck." He tipped his head. "Well done, Miss Still."

Lucy kept quiet, worried that if she said the wrong thing, Wells might take it all back.

Wells rose, the warm glow of the courtyard sharpening his handsome features. "Remember that your villain must be both mysterious and comprehensible. You mustn't allow the audience to know what he will do, yet his actions must always make sense in retrospect." Wells stopped, looked at Anna. "You must provide him with a motivation. A *purpose*." He continued to pace. "Revenge. A desire for power. Even self-preservation." He nodded. "Make your villains live, my friends. Through them, you shall become legend."

Rick shifted in his chair, seemed about to say something. If Wells noticed Rick's reaction, he didn't let on.

"That is all for tonight," Wells said. "You have work to do, and I'd like to have a drink with my wife."

They laughed and got to their feet.

They were migrating toward the French doors when Wells called, "Miss Still. A moment."

She told Rick she'd catch up with him, returned to where Wells stood gazing up at the nearly black sky. "I wanted to reiterate my appreciation for your pages. They were inspired."

She smiled. "I'm glad you enjoyed it."

"Inspired by what, that's the question," Wells said. "The Fred Astaire Killer is able to get close to his victims before puncturing their brains with sharp objects."

Lucy nodded.

"I wonder then," Wells continued, "if perhaps the idea of betraying someone close to you is familiar."

Lucy tightened.

"Yes," Wells said, a vicious grin curving his lips. "I suspect it is. I suspect your sister would have a *deep* appreciation of this theme."

Lucy bit down on the scream that arose in her throat.

CHAPTER FIVE

Eight the next morning, and Anna was waiting. *Come on, Lucy,* she thought. *Get your ass up.*

She imagined Lucy sleeping in, a complacent smile on her face after last night's triumph. But she wasn't fooling Anna. Anyone could take a few chapters, polish them, make them glimmer. The rest of the manuscript probably sucked.

The fact that Wells raved about it in front of everyone – the first time he'd complimented a writer publicly – had kept her up most of the night. Which meant she wouldn't be able to do her best work today. Not without gallons of coffee.

A knock next door scattered Anna's thoughts.

Rick, Anna thought. Showing up to escort his darling to breakfast.

Christ, it made her sick.

Where'd you meet your husband? someone would ask Lucy ten years from now.

Oh, it's the wildest story! We were actually part of the same competition. Yes, the Wells writing retreat? Rick was one of the other writers. He helped me win.

No! Anna thought. Lucy was *not* going to win this competition. Wells had praised her out of pity. Trying to make the retreat more competitive. The same reason he crapped on Anna's work. He was propping up the weaker writers to ensure the stronger ones didn't run away with the prize.

Footsteps next door. Anna listened as the door creaked open.

"Hey," a voice said. Not Rick. One of the women.

"What's up, Elaine?" Lucy asked.

Anna frowned. Now why....

"I know it's early," Elaine said, "but I wanted to say it before I go—"

"What?" Lucy asked, a sharpness puncturing the grogginess in her voice.

"This isn't a good fit for me," Elaine explained. "Wells is right. I have a long way to go before I'm ready for the big stage."

Anna pumped a fist. *Yes.*

"Hold on a second," Lucy said. The sound of her door closing. Both voices in the hallway now. "You need to reconsider."

What? Anna thought. *Are you crazy? Let her go! We'll be down to six!*

"I bet your story is good," Lucy said.

Anna made a fist, tapped it against her thigh.

"That's sweet of you," Elaine said, "but yours was on a different level."

They both suck, Anna thought. You *both suck*.

Lucy started to speak, but Elaine overrode her. "It isn't just the writing."

A pause.

Lucy: "What else is there?"

Elaine: "Ghosts."

Anna frowned.

Lucy: "You mean...."

Elaine: "I mean what I said. Look, I did something bad once. It was a mistake. But...I'm having nightmares about it."

Silence from Lucy. Anna couldn't breathe.

Elaine, on the edge of a sob: "I would have left last night, but I was too afraid."

Lucy: "It's okay...here, do you want me to get you—"

Elaine: "Don't." A softening. "Really, it's very sweet of you. But...before I go I wanted to tell you I was wrong. Too little, too late." A rueful laugh. "Story of my life."

Lucy: "You're only in your twenties."

Elaine: "And emotionally, I'm in my teens. God, my poor parents. I've been such a bitch."

Lucy: "I don't think you should go."

Elaine: "I'll stay with my folks while I get myself together."

After a long silence....

Lucy: "You should call me one of these days. My number—"

Elaine: "Let's not pretend we're pals, all right? What do we have in common, other than being part of this horror show?"

Lucy muttered something unintelligible.

Elaine: "I've gotta go. I just wanted you to know I was sorry."

Elaine finally left, which saved Anna the trouble of projectile vomiting from all their heartfelt words. Anna paced, working herself up to what she had to do. With four writers eliminated, there were fewer who might discover her, but that didn't ease her nerves. Being caught meant elimination, maybe even prosecution. The risk was extreme.

The alternative, however, was worse.

She refused to allow Lucy to win.

After an interminable wait, Lucy finally left.

Anna counted to twenty, and when she heard no one stirring, she emerged from her room and hurried next door.

Which Lucy hadn't locked. Funny how trusting everyone was around here. She assumed some of them had brought the means to back up their work, but her suspicion was that most of them hadn't.

She was counting on Lucy being one of those who hadn't. Even after all Lucy had been through, there was something naïve about her.

Anna snatched the laptop from the desk, as well as the printed manuscript, and hurried to Lucy's door. Listened. If someone came, she was screwed.

Silence from the hallway.

Anna slipped out the door and hustled to her room. After locking her door behind her, she opened the laptop on her bed.

Lucy's story popped up right away. Though she knew Lucy might return to her room at any moment and discover the missing laptop, her curiosity overcame her, and she found herself skimming several chapters.

The inside of Anna's mouth was bleeding before she realized she'd been biting it.

The story was good, dammit, and what was worse, the writing was confident, strong, the antithesis of the milquetoast whimper of Lucy's last two books.

Anna moved the cursor to *Edit*.

Clicked *Select All*.

She only paused a second before choosing *Delete*.

Save.

Anna closed the now empty file, debated for a moment, then dragged the file into the recycle bin.

She emptied the recycle bin.

Anna paused, chewing her lip. The taste of copper filled her mouth.

She worried the file could still be recovered. She didn't think so, but what if she was wrong?

She thought of *The Fred Astaire Murders*.

Scowled at the computer.

No. She couldn't take any chances.

The only way to be sure was to destroy the laptop and the printed copy.

Anna pushed to her feet.

She moved to her dresser, fetched a baggy gray sweatshirt. She would look absurd in it, but what could she do? She didn't have a sack to carry the laptop in, didn't bring a large enough purse. Yet it was at least seventy degrees outside. She'd be a spectacle with the suspicious bulge in her belly.

Anna paced. She couldn't smuggle it out. Too many people might see her. The other writers. Wilson. Miss Lafitte. Amanda Wells.

Roderick Wells.

Her insides shriveled at the prospect:

My, my, Miss Holloway. Balmy day for a sweatshirt.

I have a sunburn, Mr. Wells. I was just trying to protect my—

—chances of winning. Yes, I know exactly what you're protecting. And I know precisely what you have stashed under that ridiculous sweatshirt. I want you off my property within the hour, Miss Holloway, and you'll be hearing from my attorney....

Anna gazed down at the computer, not really seeing it. Seeing only the disbelieving stares of her fellow writers, knowing she'd have to live with yet another bad deed.

The main floor was crawling with people. Even if she managed to slip outside with the computer, anyone could glance out the window and catch a glimpse of—

Anna's eyes snapped open.

If everyone was downstairs or outside, that left only one option.

Anna seized the pages, shut the machine with a *clap*, and hurried to the door. Listened. Emerged from her room, found the hallway empty. If someone saw her now, she could claim the laptop and pages were her own.

Soon she was on the third floor, her mind racing. She hadn't spent much time up here, in fact had only visited one place, the ballroom, and she had terrible memories of her night there.

Still…she did remember several storage cabinets along one wall.

Anna made a beeline for the ballroom and slipped inside.

No need for lights, though it was awfully dim in here. The skylights, however, provided enough illumination for her to make out the cabinets. Heart pounding, she hurried across the dully gleaming floor, swerved toward a cabinet. Found it open and bent to slide the machine and the pages onto the bottom shelf.

The laptop bumped something before she could slide it all the way to the back of the cabinet, and when she leaned down to see what the obstruction was, a white face lunged at her and bit down on her fingers. Anna screamed, attempted to pull away, but the teeth clamped down harder, the white face pinched with hate, and she realized she was shrieking because the face was Justine's, despite the mud in her black hair and the bluish-white cast of her rotting flesh. Justine was growling, grinning, the middle three fingers of Anna's right hand tearing loose at the knuckles. Anna writhed, thrashed to be free. It was tugging at her, laughing around her spurting fingers, the blood coating Justine's cheeks in bright red splashes, and as Anna struggled harder, the fingers tearing loose now, the Justine-thing moved with her, began to lurch out of the cabinet. For a moment Anna believed she could break away from the Justine-thing, but when the dirty, broken fingernails sank into her thighs, she knew there was no escape.

But that didn't make it hurt any less when the Nachzehrer sank its teeth into her throat.

CHAPTER SIX

Elaine stood outside the library, suitcase at her heels. She knew *The Stars Have Left the Skies* had potential, but writing it – or writing it *here* – no longer seemed important.

It was time to end this. The retreat had seemed like an incredible opportunity, but with every passing day the sense of wrongness increased. She wasn't a prisoner here, for Christ's sake, she was a guest. And guests were allowed to come and go as they pleased. She'd thank him for the opportunity, but....

But what?

But I've decided I'm not ready for the big stage yet. I won't tell anyone of your location, so that shouldn't be a concern. Actually, I'm not at all certain of where I am right now....

Elaine bit her lower lip. It wasn't very good.

But it would have to do.

She entered and strode over to where Wells sat with his back to her, the wing-backed chair and the top of his slick hair limned by the fire.

"Mr. Wells," she said.

Wells didn't answer. She edged around his chair. Why was she shuddering so violently?

"I couldn't find Wilson...." Elaine tried to smile. "Actually, it's Wilson I want to talk to you about. I figure he goes to town for provisions...."

"Sit," Wells said.

She didn't like that, not one bit. With a *please* it would have been demeaning enough, but without one....

"Mr. Wells," she began.

But before she could continue, he leaned forward and looked at her. The firelight flickered in his slag-colored eyes, but his gaze wasn't cruel. His smile was open and solicitous. Distant alarms went off in her mind, but she ignored them. He gestured toward the ottoman near his knees, so she sat there with the fireplace warming her back and felt her disquiet ebb.

Maybe, she decided, she'd been wrong about Wells. He could be a demanding teacher, but hadn't his methods proved effective? Look at Corrina Bowen. A novice when she arrived, and *bam*, within a year of the contest, she had book deals, adulation, a robust readership. Wasn't that why Elaine came? Wasn't that why they'd *all* come? Was she really going to bail out so the others could....

"Mr. Wells," she said, "Corrina Bowen was your pupil?"

"Why, Ms. Kovalchyk, you know she was."

He sat back in the chair, his legs crossed, one hand resting on the other. Her dream crept up on her, the surreal, alcohol-fueled nightmare of a naked Wells and a forest of pulsing lights. Unexpectedly, her body responded to the memory, to the dream Wells. The hard, bulging islands of his chest; the abdominal muscles standing out in sharp, moonlit relief; the smooth pillars of his quadriceps; his sex, large and tumid.

His hand covered hers. "Miss Kovalchyk – may I call you Elaine?"

She swallowed. The hives were creeping up her neck, as they always did when she was embarrassed, but she scarcely noticed them. Wells's hand was strong, warm, gently stroking her bare knee. She decided she was glad she'd worn her pink shorts rather than black Capri pants. His touch on her flesh was soothing.

"This experience has been hard on you, Elaine." He searched her eyes, his eyes empathic, profound. "Hasn't it?"

"Yes," she admitted.

"Do you realize how far you've already come, Elaine?"

Unexpectedly, she felt a surge of emotion. "I...when I came here...."

"You were overconfident then, and I admit I was a demanding teacher." His fingers moved in feathery, insistent circles. Heat spread from her knee up her thigh. "But I only invest my time and talent in those with a rare gift."

Through the thickness in her throat, she said, "Really?"

He cocked his head, his eyes lowering to her chest. "Is that a butterfly, Elaine?"

She glanced down at her tattoo as if to confirm its existence. "I got it when I graduated from NYU." She smiled, gave a little shrug. "You know, to show how I was transforming, spreading my wings, that sort of thing."

"Lovely metaphor," he said, his strong, gentle fingers reaching out and tracing the design on her flesh. "Butterflies are fascinating creatures, Elaine. Not unlike yourself."

She was blushing furiously, and though she knew she should pull away, she found she wanted him to touch her, yearned for him to trace the butterfly down to the cleft of her breasts.

"In every part of the world," Wells said, his fingers caressing her, "butterfly legends abound. In some Native American cultures, the insect brings sleep. Blackfoot women used to create an image of the butterfly and twine it into their infants' hair so their children would be more restful."

A languid heat, feverish but not at all unpleasant, had taken hold of her. The warmth from the fireplace enveloped her, the aroma of the burning wood mingling with Wells's subtle, summery cologne. She stared into Wells's face, took in every detail. An older man, no doubt, but not nearly as old as she had once believed. He wore his age in experience, in knowledge. His body, as she had seen in her dream—

(*it wasn't a dream*)

—was marvelously preserved, the body of a much younger man. But a younger man endowed with the experience of many years, of

(*eons*)

a lifetime, and she allowed her gaze to crawl over his skin, his sensuous mouth, as he said, "Other legends center on rebirth. The first Christians viewed the butterfly as a symbol of metamorphosis, of renewal. In early Mexican culture and in ancient Greece, the butterfly was associated with the human soul."

She looked into his eyes and read nothing but comfort there. Nothing but wisdom and virility and infinite power. She leaned toward him, willing him to reciprocate, hungering for his mouth, his tongue.

His fingers slid away from her, the spell broken. She tried but failed to conceal her disappointment.

He smiled at her with a father's understanding. "You're seeking help, are you not, Miss Kovalchyk?"

She noted his return to formality with a pang of frustration. "I am."

He spread his arms, smiled his charming smile. "And I'm here to give you anything you need."

She rushed on, fleeing the undertow of desire. "I was asking you about Corrina Bowen."

"I remember," he said, still smiling.

"Everybody knows about Corrina, but she wasn't the only one to come here seeking your help. Was she, Mr. Wells?"

He watched her silently, his handsome face relaxed in the pumpkin-colored glow of the fireplace.

"There were others. Just like there are now."

"Yes," he said.

"But only one can win the contest," she said. "Only one of us is going to…"

Elaine noticed something about Wells she hadn't before.

"…is going to…." she started to say, but the necklace Wells wore and the object lying against his chest stole her breath.

"Is something wrong?" He shifted in his chair, the necklace shifting into full view.

Elaine shrank from him, a hand pressed to her mouth in horror.

"What is it?" Wells asked in the same pleasant voice.

Elaine couldn't breathe, couldn't think. She rose unsteadily. Somewhere beneath the strata of shock, she could hear herself moaning.

Wells only watched her, the object on his necklace small but unmistakable in the orange light. He called after her, but she didn't answer. She lurched toward the door, wrested it open, and in a nightmarish fog hastened down the hallway and out the front door.

She staggered through the meadow, still moaning, and though she fought against the memory of that awful night last summer, it recurred, unbidden and infinitely monstrous.

CHAPTER SEVEN

Three hours later, Elaine was hopelessly lost. Nettle-whipped, moaning, she stumbled through the forest and recalled the night last summer. She'd downed tequila shots until early morning, and despite everyone's urgings, she climbed into her Camry. She was cautious, for once ignoring the stereo, for once not texting or checking her phone. She made the longest stretch of the drive without issue, and maybe that's why she was so mellow by the time she made it to Brooklyn.

So mellow she caught herself nodding off at the wheel.

Elaine jerked awake and goggled at the road in disbelief. She gripped the wheel in the ten and two o'clock positions and threw a quick glance at the green digital clock on the dash.

Four-thirteen a.m. Was it any wonder she was exhausted? She considered pulling over and sleeping, but that was an invitation for trouble. If a cop discovered her asleep, wouldn't he wonder why she'd chosen a Camry over a bed? He'd ask her questions, and once he did that, he'd be sure to notice her slurred speech.

She swallowed, made a face at the fulsome taste in her mouth. She wasn't merely inebriated, she was entering the first hairy stages of a savage hangover. Her tongue felt furry, her eyes itchy and dry. There was a whanging throb in the back of her skull, and she had to go to the bathroom, numbers one and two, and where the hell was she supposed to go? There wasn't a gas station nearby and her apartment was a good ten minutes away. She imagined herself squatting in an alley, but that was not only degrading and messy, it was downright dangerous.

She was imagining herself squatting in some seedy back alley when a police cruiser drifted by in the oncoming lane.

Her stomach clenched. She shot a look in the overhead mirror, furious with herself for losing focus. She watched the cruiser as it diminished in the mirror, the red taillights glowing but not flaring brighter, the ghastly red-and-blue cherry lights remaining dormant. *Please don't turn around,* she thought. *I'll never drink and drive again.*

The cruiser described a gradual left turn, disappeared from view.

The Camry jolted as she slammed into something.

Her face swung back to the road, and the car jounced again, its suspension bellowing.

Numbly, she stomped on the brakes and rocked forward, her seatbelt biting her skin. There was a heat in her abdomen, her bladder having let go.

Cold rivulets of dread trickling down her back, Elaine peered at the road behind her to see what she'd run over.

A human body. Facedown, unmoving.

Her gorge clenched. *Jesus God no,* she thought. *Jesus God Jesus God it can't be.* She began to sob silently, her body shaking, her mouth full of bile and tequila. She knew she should do something, but she could only stare at the rumpled thing and sob.

There were streetlamps, but none were positioned to cast their luminance over the body. The car windows had begun to steam up.

She was surrounded by apartment buildings. All but a handful of their windows were blackened rectangles. As her eyes swept the mirror she caught sight of herself, her face chalky and blank.

Behind her, twin headlamps appeared.

Elaine froze. It was the cop, she was sure of it. Maybe she'd been weaving.

The headlights swelled, coming nearer.

Even if it wasn't the cop, whoever drove the car would no doubt spy the motionless hump beside the road and stop. The Good Samaritan would call for help.

Go!

She couldn't drive away. Not because of any moral obligation. She was simply incapable of moving. The twin halogen pinpricks grew into harsh orbs. The car approached, its headlamps now spotlighting the body in a fierce white corona. Elaine commanded her nerveless fingers to grip the gearshift, to get the hell out of there, but she remained frozen.

Then, amazingly, the car turned and disappeared.

Elaine stared after it, unable to accept her good fortune.

Now go. You've been blessed with a second chance. Take it and never mention this to anyone.

But her hand was betraying her, opening the door. Her legs swung out over moist asphalt. Her whole body thrumming, she stepped closer to where the unmoving heap lay. Though she did not want to, she noticed the folds of what looked like a beige overcoat.

Weeping into her hands, she circled the rumpled shape until she could see the man's face, half-buried in the crook of an arm. His eyes were closed. A smear of blood spread like a fan at the corner of his mouth.

"I'm sorry," Elaine whispered into her hands. "I'm so sorry."

The eyes opened. Elaine clapped a hand over her mouth to stifle a scream. The man, his whiskered jowls streaked with blood, pushed up on an elbow, and as he did, the necklace with its gleaming pendant slithered out of his shirt. A Star of David with some greenish stone in its center.

"*I need....*" the man croaked, but he coughed, a gout of blood splashing over his chin. He opened his mouth again, but the blood choked him, doubled him over.

Elaine had no notion of fleeing until she bumped her still-open door. Automatically, she dropped inside, didn't look back as she shifted the Camry into gear, motored away from the dying man.

In Wells Forest, Elaine remembered all this, remembered reading about the senseless death of Harry Yudkin, a distinguished professor at Touro, a Jewish grad school.

She staggered through the trees, blood and sweat slicking her skin.

It was possible the necklace Wells wore in the library had been mass produced. Maybe the world was full of sterling silver Stars of David with green opal insets. But she was pretty sure Wells wasn't Jewish, and if that were true....

"No," she whimpered.

Ahead, she glimpsed a narrow filament of dirt, not wide enough to be a trail, but a hell of a lot better than bulldozing her way through the underbrush the way she was now.

Elaine thought of her nightmare, Wells's naked form kneeling in the meadow, the pulsing lights and black liquid feeding him, revitalizing his body.

Moaning, she sprinted toward the path.

And skidded to a halt when she saw the humped shape crouching before her.

CHAPTER EIGHT

Wilson's words echoed in Bryan's brain: *Kill if you want to see another sunset.*

Bryan peered into his bathroom mirror, noticed the purple half-moons under his eyes, the accumulated stubble. He never skipped a shave, was disdainful of men like Rick and that slob Will Church, who treated shaving like an optional thing rather than a facet of good grooming.

Still....

Bryan thought he looked rather menacing with the five o'clock shadow.

His grin faded when he remembered what he'd seen just minutes earlier.

He'd decided to enlist Anna's help. After all, they'd formed an alliance, hadn't they? Maybe she'd help him eliminate one of the other writers.

He'd been on the way to Anna's room to talk things over when he glimpsed Wilson at the end of the hallway, descending the third-story stairs and carrying something on his shoulder. Bryan had hustled after Wilson, peered over the edge of the handrail, and froze.

A body. The object slung over Wilson's shoulder could only be a human body.

"Wilson!" he called down the stairwell and then regretted it when Wilson stopped.

Slowly, Wilson's head swiveled up to stare at him. "Yes?"

Bryan glanced at the body. Its face was mercifully concealed, but he didn't need to see the attractive features to know it was Anna Holloway. The red hair and shapely body gave her away.

Anna wasn't moving.

"What's..."

...*wrong with her*, he was about to ask, but decided he didn't want to know. Instead he said, "Where are you taking her?"

"She suffered an accident," Wilson said.

At his words, Bryan noticed the droplets of blood on the carpeted risers. He glanced at Anna's inert body and discovered something that made his gorge clench.

Three fingers of her right hand were missing.

Wilson's grin spread. "I suggest you follow my advice, Mr. Clayton, before you suffer a similar accident."

Bryan had fled.

Now, remembering Anna's limp body and Wilson's savage grin, Bryan stared into the bathroom mirror and told himself he had to do it. If he wanted to win – hell, if he wanted to *live* – he had to go through with it.

He was on the way to Lucy's room when Will rounded the corner. He saw Will before Will saw him, and in that instant he noted Will's gnomish belly beneath the sloppy button-down Cubs jersey. The faded khaki shorts, the scuffed sandals. Slovenly. Soft.

Okay, then, Bryan thought. *I'll kill him instead of Lucy.*

"Hey," Bryan said, mustering a smile, "just the guy I want to see."

Will scowled at him. "What do you want?"

"Someone to guide the boat while I check my trout lines."

Will looked at him like he'd lost his mind. "Trout lines?"

"Come on," Bryan said, ushering Will along. "I tried to do it earlier, but the current was too swift. It won't work unless I have another body."

"I need to write."

Dammit. Not only was Will walking away, but the longer this took, the greater the chances of someone seeing them. His idea had been to lure Lucy outside by praising her reading. Writers loved to hear praise. Plus, of the remaining competitors, she'd be the easiest to overpower.

Will was almost to his room.

"Okay," Bryan said, hustling to rejoin him. "I'll tell you the truth. It has nothing to do with trout lines." A pause. "I'm worried about Anna."

"What about her?"

Other than the fact that she's dead?

Bryan remembered her limp body, her missing fingers....

He shoved away the image and put on what he hoped was a pensive expression. He knew Will worshipped the scarlet-haired girl. If he played this right....

"She's up to something dangerous."

Will searched his face, no doubt scouring for the lie. "Like what?"

"Like I don't know. She goes into the forest every day, and when she comes back, she's...."

Will gestured impatiently. "She's *what?* Covered with burrs? Rashy?"

Bryan exhaled. "Look. You get the feeling the eliminated contestants never made it home?"

A veiled expression came over Will's face. "I have to write."

"Don't you think it's strange that no one who leaves says goodbye?"

"Maybe they're embarrassed."

"You'd leave all your stuff behind?"

Will frowned. "Wilson probably sent it to them."

Bryan shuddered at the mention of Wilson. Because Wilson wasn't really Wilson, was he? Bryan had an idea of who the groundskeeper really was, yet he refused to accept the notion. Because if it was true, this whole retreat was....

"See you at supper," Will said, reaching for the knob.

"I think she's leaving," Bryan said quickly.

Will's hand stopped six inches from the knob. "Anna?" he asked without looking up.

"Uh-huh. That's where she's been going. She gets further and further each time, trying to find her way out. I've been following her."

Will arched an eyebrow. "Stalking her?"

"*Tracking* her. Look, I'm just...worried about her."

Shit. The excuse rang hollow even to Bryan's ears.

"*Worried* about her? Hell. You'd give her a piggyback ride to the limo, man. Who do you think you're fooling?"

Bryan opened his mouth, shut it. Will could see he was full of shit. Best to let it go and find someone else. Pick Lucy after all.

If he didn't, he'd be dead by sundown. And it was already late afternoon.

He was turning to go when Will said, "Hold on, man. I think I see what's happening here."

Bryan eyed him without much hope.

"You like her," Will ventured.

"I do," he admitted. "I've…had a crush on her since the first day."

Will was watching him now.

"And maybe I have been stalking her a little," Bryan said sheepishly. When Will's frown deepened, he hastened to add, "But I'd never harm her. I just think she's, you know, fed up with things."

"She's not in her room?"

"She was heading toward the forest when I passed her. She looked really…I don't know. Melancholy?"

"That doesn't sound like her," Will said, more to himself.

"I think she's serious this time."

Will got moving. "You said she was heading toward the woods?"

"About ten minutes ago," Bryan said, hurrying to catch up with him. "I know the path she takes too."

"Hope you're wrong," Will muttered as they descended the stairs.

"We'll talk some sense into her," Bryan said. If they passed anybody on the way out of the mansion, he'd have to abort the mission. He could feel the weight of the buck knife in his ankle holder.

Three hours. He had three hours to commit murder. He'd missed his chance that day with Evan in the forest. He should have gutted the pompous bastard like a carp.

He eyed Will's white shirt with the tiny blue pinstripes, felt his pulse quicken. Imagined the bloom of red after he stabbed him.

Face grim, he followed Will out of the mansion.

CHAPTER NINE

They reached the lake in fifteen minutes. On the northern shore loomed the beech trees, Bryan's first indication that something was wrong here. It messed with his sense of order, so he faced the lake, visored his gaze from the sunglare, and thought of Wilson, that phrase Wilson had uttered: 'tupped by torment.'

Bryan hated the classics. One that especially drove him insane was by none other than Roderick Wells.

The Seer.

What distinguished it from other novels, Bryan's English 201 professor had claimed, was its use of the negative hero to illustrate man's innate savagery. Or some such bullshit.

The novel had contained a freaky protagonist, there was no arguing with that. The Seer was a handwriting specialist who received impressions from the samples he was given, and then, in cases where guilty people were acquitted, the Seer would visit them and read their sins through their handwriting. 'The echoes of their damnation' – a phrase that had jumped out at Bryan when slogging through the book. The Seer was an avenging angel of sorts, or an avenging demon, rather, since he murdered people for sins they'd committed long before.

Now that Bryan thought about it, what made him hate the book wasn't the complex language, but rather the idea that no one can ever really be forgiven for a sin that remains secret.

The notion hit too close to home.

They paused at the lake's edge. Will said, "What now, Deerslayer?"

"We need to probe the shoreline. We find her tracks, we can follow her."

"What makes you so sure she was running away?"

Bryan shrugged. "I could be wrong. But she seemed desperate. Kind of frayed around the edges."

"That doesn't sound like her."

"Exactly what I thought."

Lips pressed together, Will set off along the shoreline. Bryan moved in the opposite direction. The lake was maybe two hundred acres all told, the shape of a kidney bean. On the eastern shore the hills rose dramatically, resulting in numerous crags and inlets.

Plentiful hiding places.

Bryan would take his time, meet Will halfway around the lake. Conceal himself in the shadows. Something near the water to make it easier to wash the blood away.

He shot a look over his shoulder to see if Will was watching him, but no, Will was studying the sand like a lovesick puppy.

Bryan's upper lip curled into a sneer. *Fool.*

To imagine a goddess like Anna Holloway would ever dream of fulfilling Will's prepubescent fantasies....

He began the arduous climb up the boulders, into the encompassing veil of forest. He clambered over a massive boulder, mounted a second. Scaled that one effortlessly. Leaped over a gap of perhaps five feet, feeling good now, all thoughts of Wilson and his resemblance to the Seer shunted to the back of his mind. He paused to calculate his next move, and spotted something below that made his heart gallop.

No way, he thought.

There was someone down there.

He'd been sure it was just a trick of the shadows. Or merely an old heap of refuse. But now, screwing up his eyes to penetrate the gloom, he realized it was no trick, and it certainly wasn't a pile of trash.

It was a person.

Forgetting for a moment about Will Church, Bryan lowered himself down the curving rock face until he was low enough to jump onto the sand. He inched closer to the gap between the rock formations and realized he'd been correct: this was a human being. Before dying, the person had commandeered an old brown blanket and now lay beneath it, bare feet poking out.

He crept closer and thought of *The Seer*. Impossible as it seemed, he was convinced that Wilson was none other than the eponymous character in Roderick Wells's novel. Which unleashed a world of frightening possibilities. Had Wilson merely inspired the character, or had Wells created Wilson? And what of Wilson's age? Christ, what about that? Wilson didn't look a day over fifty. Yet *The Seer* was written more than sixty years ago....

Bryan thrust the thought away before it undid him. He was losing his edge. He was supposed to be plotting a murder now, not investigating a moldering pile of bones. He reached out, chiding himself—

—and gagged when the corpse swiveled its head toward him, the face mottled with dirt and old blood. Sprawling on his side, Bryan pleaded with the thing rising from the sand to leave him alone, yet even as he gibbered and flapped his hands to ward the thing off, he registered the corpse's eyes, so familiar, and the corpse's teeth, which were not decaying nubs after all, but straight and white.

"Elaine?" he whispered.

She closed her eyes, weeping silently, and dropped to her knees. "Help me," she begged. "Oh God, I never thought I'd see anyone again."

Bryan barely heard her. He shot looks around the shadowy embankment. Fifteen feet away a creek trickled. Beyond that, forest. Behind them, rock formations loomed.

Elaine had only been gone since morning, yet in that short time, she'd become a total mess. It disgusted him.

He blew out a pent-up breath. "Let's get you cleaned up."

He rose, brushed the sticky sand off his arms. She was crying. She'd shed the smelly brown blanket, but the sight of the snot creaming her upper lip was revolting.

"Thank you so much for helping me," she said, getting unsteadily to her feet. Her clothes, he realized, covered very little of her. Short pink shorts and a tank top that might once have been white. There were blotches on her skin; perhaps she'd contracted some disease? Thank God he hadn't touched her.

"I've been wandering all day," she explained. She sank at the edge of the creek and palmed water into her mouth.

Her slurping noises made him sick.

Remember the man you were supposed to murder? a voice reminded him. *Will's going to be circling the lake soon. How will you do it with Elaine around?*

She splashed water over her hair, which was matted with substances he didn't care to identify.

"What happened to you?" he asked.

"I can't believe how big this place is," she said. She swept her hair to the side, revealing a gash the size of an earthworm below her ear. "I tried to find my way back, but I got lost. I've been trying to find you guys…my throat's raw from screaming…."

He took in the weals on her calves. "How the hell did you get lost?"

She rocked, made pathetic humming noises.

"Don't freak out on me," he said.

"They come alive."

He couldn't keep the irritation from his voice. "I know that."

She turned, gazed up at him with wide eyes. "You do?"

"I can't believe none of us figured it out earlier. *The Seer* is one of his most famous books."

Her expression clouded. "What are you talking about?"

He looked away. There'd been snot bubbling from one of her crusted nostrils.

"Whatever Wells writes becomes reality," he said. "At least, the Seer did."

She was washing her arms now, the wounds garnished with caked blood. "You think Wells brought him to life?"

He scowled. "Isn't that what you're talking about?"

Her lips trembled, that mad glitter seeping into her eyes. "Our pasts. They followed us here."

Bryan stared at her a long time. He was dimly aware of the creek, the rustle of leaves in the late-afternoon breeze.

"Don't you *see*?" Elaine demanded, unwilling to leave it the fuck alone. "I killed him."

He made to move away, but she followed him, raving, "I didn't mean to, I swear…."

She stank like a homeless person.

"It was so dark," Elaine said, her fetid breath reeking of sewage.

"Shut up."

She was tugging his arm, babbling something about drunk driving. He tried to dance away from her, but she clung to him, her talons hooked in the front of his shirt.

"It's why they chose us," she said, half-sobbing now.

He was dragging her along the wet sand, trying to pry off her fingers, then wringing her goddamn wrists. She cried out, hit the sand mouth first, lay weeping. He stumbled sideways, his shorts splashed by the shallow water, one of his shoes going completely under. She kept coming, begging him to help her. She grabbed his wet shoe, and in desperation he kicked out at her, cracked her in the nose. Her sob was replaced with a braying wail, one loud enough to hear from half a mile away.

"*Shut up,*" he said between clenched teeth.

Her bloodshot eyes flared in anger, and she lashed out.

Bryan grabbed for his ankle, saw blood on his palm.

"Stupid...*cunt.*" He kicked at her face, missed. Despite her wretched state, she no longer looked so helpless. Her voice was a growl, and she was swatting at his kicks, her broken nails flashing.

He swung at her, but his punch went wild. She fell against his legs, spitting curses. He tumbled backward, in desperation swinging a fist straight down at her. It connected with enough force to clip her teeth together. She came with him as he fell, her talons carving up his calves. Yelping, he reached down, grabbed her temples, and twisted. It elicited a cry, but still she clawed at him.

He snapped open the ankle holder, jerked out the buck knife.

Her eyes went huge. "*Oh don't you—*"

He pumped it into her Adam's apple. A gurgle sounded in her throat, a gush of hot blood squirted over his wrist. She craned her face toward his, their eyes locking, and he slapped his other hand over her face to cover those staring eyes. He shoved sideways on the knife, unzipping her throat, and the sound grew worse, like an old man's phlegmy cough.

Will could arrive at any moment. Bryan dragged her toward the water and rolled her in. Her limbs convulsed but she wasn't dead, not yet, so he plunged her face into the water, only six inches deep, but enough to swamp her gibbering mouth. Blood billowed around her head in a crimson penumbra, but thankfully, her screams were replaced by the fat burble of air popping on the creek's surface.

There was no resistance now, but Bryan kept her pinned to the creek floor, willing her lungs to fill with water.

He stared down at her body.

Her *body*. What the hell was he to do with her body? He couldn't leave it in the creek. It would float unless he weighted it down, and he didn't have time for that.

Casting frightened glances into the forest, Bryan dragged her toward the rock wall. She left a bloody trail in the sand, not to mention heel marks. He might as well erect a flashing neon sign that said MURDER SITE. If Will appeared now, Bryan was well and truly fucked.

He looked down at her. Elaine's eyes stared sightlessly up at him. Glassy. Dead.

A voice yelled, "Bryan?"

"*No*," he whispered, the fear encircling his throat like a noose.

"Hey, man," Will called from somewhere above, "I haven't seen a thing. You?"

Bryan didn't dare breathe. *No*, he thought. *I haven't seen anything, haven't killed anyone.*

"What's wrong?" Will shouted.

His body encased in ice, Bryan peered up and saw Will staring down at him. He couldn't make out Will's expression – the slob was too high up for that – and what was more, he didn't think Will could see Elaine's body from where he leaned out on the rock formation.

"I'll catch up with you in a minute," Bryan answered.

"You sure Anna ran out this way?" Will asked.

Bryan's lips twitched, and he suppressed an insane urge to laugh. "Pretty sure."

"Well, I can't find her," Will said. "I'm heading back."

"You do that," Bryan murmured.

He stood there, his pulse beating in his ears. Another minute passed, and he realized Will had gone.

The tension bled out of his shoulders. He stepped away from Elaine's body and trotted toward the woods.

The unpleasantness was over. And he was still in the game.

His eyes widened. He realized he'd done it. He'd killed someone, and even if he hadn't plotted Elaine's murder, it counted, didn't it?

Of *course* it counted. He was safe from Wilson.

Bryan ran harder, his face splitting in a cruel grin. It hadn't been easy, but he'd done it. And something told him the more he did it, the easier it would become. He hadn't planned on killing Elaine, but it had proved necessary.

If Bryan could kill one writer, he could kill another.

His grin widening, he pounded through the forest.

CHAPTER TEN

From *Garden of Snakes*, by Rick Forrester:

"No more," Jimmy whimpered. He couldn't look at the body lying next to him on the ground. "Please, no more."

"No more?" Anderson said. "Jesus Christ, boy, we're just starting the home stretch."

"I didn't wanna…didn't wanna—"

"Didn't wanna *what*?" Anderson said, hurrying over to crouch beside him. "Didn't wanna die, so you took out this poor piece of shit instead?"

Jimmy squeezed shut his eyes and wondered how much worse death could be. Or hell, if there was such a place.

Anderson reached down, smacked his cheek. "Don't lie to yourself, kid, we're way beyond all that. You know you could've put a scare into this sorry son of a bitch instead of killing him."

Jimmy wailed.

Anderson smacked him, harder this time, Jimmy's brains banging around his skull.

"Evolve, you little shit, *evolve*," Anderson growled.

Jimmy thrashed his head, muttered that he wanted to be done.

He was lifted into the air, and when he opened his eyes, his feet dangled a foot off the ground.

Anderson held Jimmy with his mad gaze. "Look at me, you little worm."

Jimmy tried to, but evidently it wasn't good enough. Anderson shook him as though rattling a chain-link fence. When the world stopped swooping, Jimmy poured his concentration into meeting the chief's insane eyes.

"Now or never, son. It's now or never. You either get with the program or I'm gonna make you as dead as this dude beside you.

It'll be a suicide, and not one soul will doubt you ate your gun." His body suspended in the air, Jimmy was drawn nearer the chief, so close he could have kissed the psychotic bastard if he'd pooched out his lips. The smell of the enormous man enclosed him, the days-old sweat, the woodsmoke from the house they'd torched last night. Jimmy even fancied he could smell the scorched meat of their victims, the husband and wife whose only sin had been looking out their window when Anderson was killing that jogger, another poor soul who happened along at the wrong time, a night when the chief's bloodlust was roused.

It has to end, Jimmy thought. This death cycle has to end.

Like always, it was as though Anderson read his thoughts. "Fess up, Jimmy," the chief said with a terrible grin. "You like it." He scowled, shook his head. "Uh-uh, what am I saying? You *love* it. You love the power, love knowing you can snuff out a life like a votive candle."

Jimmy's chest began to hitch. "It's destroying me. I can't eat or sleep from the guilt."

"Guilt is what you *want* it to be, Jimbo. What it really is, it's the savagery in you awakening. It's what we are. At our cores. We go on as a species by killing."

Jimmy shook his head.

"*Yes*, Jimbo," Anderson went on. "We both know it. You're all balled up because you've tapped into that dark vein, and deep down, you love that gush of blood, you revel in it."

"I'm done," Jimmy said, and he shut his eyes in abnegation. If he didn't look at the chief, the chief couldn't deceive him anymore, couldn't trick him into believing he had to kill to save himself, the way he'd done with the man on the ground. When Jimmy could stand it no longer, he opened his eyes and met the chief's unblinking stare.

"The last step," Anderson said.

"What is it?" Jimmy heard himself ask.

"The greatest of all."

"I'd rather go to hell than kill again."

Anderson grinned. "Hell's a certainty, boy. This—" he gestured at the empty park around them, "—this is all there is. Once you take an innocent life…"

Jimmy felt his face begin to crumple.

"…and I need not remind you," the chief went on, "of the poor innocent bastard on the ground…."

Tears seeped from Jimmy's eyes.

The chief's voice was almost gentle. "Now that you've chosen damnation, there's only one thrill left."

And staring into Anderson's eyes, the knowledge of what the chief meant crashed down on Jimmy. He began to shake his head.

But Anderson only nodded, said in that same soothing voice, "When you kill the ones you love the most, that's freedom."

"No…."

"That's liberation. That's knowing you're safe."

Jimmy stared at Anderson, unbelieving. "Safe?"

"Well hell, son." Anderson gave a breathless laugh. "*Of course* you'll be safe. Don't you know you have to kill them before they kill you?"

CHAPTER ELEVEN

Per a note from Roderick Wells, Rick went to the library at five that afternoon. He discovered Sherilyn and Will engaged in an animated discussion. He approached them, noting as he did how brightly the bookcases gleamed, how fresh the vast room smelled. The carpet underfoot seemed cleaner, springier. Even the books appeared newer.

He reached Will and Sherilyn and said, "Why don't you two just arm wrestle?"

They stopped arguing but favored him with grim expressions.

"What?" Rick said.

"Something's up," Will said.

Rick tightened. "Where's Lucy?"

They'd spent the prior evening together, Lucy initially subdued but thawing as the night wore on. They'd spread a blanket on the lawn and talked. He'd kissed her lingeringly before saying good night at her bedroom door, and didn't realize how long they'd been together until he returned to his room and discovered it was one in the morning.

He hadn't seen her all day.

"We don't know," Sherilyn said. "That's the point."

Rick shrugged. "Where are the others?"

"Not in their rooms."

"I went to the lake with Bryan earlier," Will said.

Rick frowned. "Why would you do that?"

Will rolled his eyes. "It's not like I craved his company. He said Anna was acting weird. He was worried she might be leaving."

"Bryan doesn't worry about anyone but Bryan."

"I know that. But *I* was worried. I still am."

Sherilyn nodded. "When Will got back, we started talking. We found it peculiar we hadn't seen anyone all day. So we went around knocking on doors. No one answered."

"What about you?" Will asked.

Rick glanced at him. Was it suspicion he saw in Will's eyes? Or just nerves?

"I went exploring," he said. "I came to a plot impasse."

Will arched an eyebrow. "Thought you didn't get writer's block."

"Well, I do," he lied.

A voice behind them: "You're early."

They turned and watched Wells approach. He looked taller and broader than Rick remembered. *My God*, Rick thought. Even Wells's skin looked firmer, as though some renowned plastic surgeon had snuck into the mansion to perform a facelift in the dead of night.

What's happening to you? Rick wanted to ask. He glanced at Will and Sherilyn and discovered the same stupefaction on their faces.

Wells nodded at the bookcase by which they stood. "I see you've found my Southern Gothics."

Wells ignored their scrutiny. "May I?" Wells said. He stepped between Sherilyn and Will and selected a leatherbound edition. "*Wise Blood*, Flannery O'Connor." A glance at Sherilyn. "You've read her?"

"Twice," Sherilyn said, her tone distant.

"You, Mr. Forrester?" Wells asked.

"Not that one," Rick said, "but I've read 'A Good Man Is Hard to Find'."

"Oh man, I love that one," Will said. "So twisted."

Sherilyn gave him a dour look. "That a good thing?"

Will shrugged. "Absolutely."

"Hm," she answered, gazing at Wells. "I'm starting to wonder."

Wells replaced the book and squared up to them. To Rick, he looked like a veteran major league pitcher. Near the end of his career, perhaps, but still tough enough to win games.

"Events have accelerated," Wells said.

Sherilyn looked alarmed. "What happened?"

"Miss Kovalchyk and Miss Holloway have left the competition."

"Both of them?" Sherilyn asked.

Rick thought of Elaine on that first afternoon, her shell of arrogance. Last night she'd seemed more human.

"You make them leave, or they go on their own?" Rick asked.

"Come," Wells said, "the others can join us in the keep."

"The what?" Will asked, hurrying to keep up with the group.

"The tower," Sherilyn explained. "I assume that's where you're taking us? Your inner sanctum?"

"Correct, Miss Jackson. It's your reward for being the final five contestants." He moved toward a door inset in a gloomy alcove. "I hadn't planned on this rapid attrition, but alas...." Wells opened the door, disappeared into the shadows.

Will followed. "I'm disappointed the entryway isn't hidden. You know, pull on a book and the whole case moves?"

"That wouldn't be practical," Wells said, his voice echoing down a spiral stone staircase. Rick had studied the tower from outside, but now that he was here, he couldn't escape the sensation of time travel. The rough-hewn walls reminded him of his favorite Gothic literature, novels like *The Monk* and *The Castle of Otranto*.

"Why do you call it a keep?" Sherilyn asked. "Looks like a big tower to me."

"A tower is an architectural feature. A keep is a bastion. A structure fortified to fend off adversaries."

The staircase was broad, the ascent gradual, so that climbing to its peak took longer than Rick anticipated. He estimated the keep was roughly seven stories tall, but the climb felt more like nine or ten. In contrast, Wells advanced steadily up the stairs with the surety and grace of a man in the prime of his life.

Rick hurried to keep up.

Sherilyn asked over her shoulder, "How old did Wells say he was? Good *Lord*." She sounded out of breath too.

"Keeps were built by the nobility," Wells explained, "to fend off uprisings and guerilla attacks." A door came into view, outside which Wells paused and stared down at them. "Very few have entered this one. Permitting you inside represents an act of trust, one I don't take lightly." A pause, Wells's dark eyes searching theirs. "I hope you won't either."

They stopped just inside the arched doorway.

"Sweet Jesus, Son of Mary," Sherilyn said.

That about sums it up, Rick thought.

The walls of the keep were perfectly round, fifty feet wide at least, the conical peak soaring high into the air. Like the chapel, there were stained-glass windows beginning at floor level. Like the third-floor hallway, the keep was adorned with paintings and tapestries depicting scenes from Wells's fiction.

But the deathly images here weren't *only* from Wells's stories. He'd read all of Wells's novels and most of his short tales, yet a cursory scan of the tableaus revealed half a dozen things Wells had never written.

A macabre painting of a man garbed in black rags.

Creatures nine or ten feet tall with fish-white skin and glowing green eyes.

A large barroom with a balcony decorated with severed human heads.

A woman dousing herself with gasoline and flicking a lighter.

A satyr perched atop a castle, some vast body of water behind him.

And on the peripheries Rick spied unfinished paintings. He should have been surprised to see the grinning mountain of a policeman leering down at him. But he wasn't. He could only gaze at the half-drawn cop, his prow of a forehead and his rocklike jaw fixed in triumph, the sunglasses John Anderson wore somehow magnifying his malevolence.

"The Siren," Will murmured.

The figure Will was indicating resembled a naked, seductive woman. Supple curves, dark, flowing hair. Absent of that, the figure was pure imagination. Pupilless white eyes. Dagger-sharp teeth. Though this painting wasn't finished either, the Siren seemed to be crawling along some shoreline.

"Effective," Rick said.

"Yours too," Will answered.

"I told you this is a place of magic," Wells said, beginning to circle them. "You are joining my legacy."

Wells smiled at Sherilyn, who was squinting uncertainly up at the ceiling. "Yours is there too, Miss Jackson, though you can't see it clearly. Why don't you invest in a pair of contact lenses?"

"I'm not sure I want to see it," she answered.

"Mr. Forrester, perhaps you'll describe Miss Jackson's scene for her?"

The image from *The Magic King* was a dramatic one, the point of view behind the king as he regaled the commoners. Two details struck Rick right away. Firstly, the king's uncanny resemblance to Wells. Secondly, the faces in the crowd. They were inchoate, only the hints of faces. But Rick thought he could make out Lucy in the crowd. Tommy. Evan.

He looked away before he could discern his own face.

"Whoa," Will said.

Rick glanced at Wells. "The deeper we get into our stories, the closer these paintings get to completion?"

"Word count is only part of it. Imagination is paramount."

Will grinned. "Who painted these? Wilson? Your wife?"

"Doubt is the artist's handicap, Mr. Church. You might have noticed how clear Mr. Forrester's villain is compared to your Siren?"

Will's grin faded. Though Rick didn't comment, there was a noticeable disparity.

"So when one of us wins," Sherilyn said, "our painting gets finished, and the others will just...fade?"

Wells smiled. "I'm impressed, Miss Jackson. You might survive this contest yet."

Sherilyn frowned. "That's a weird way to put it."

Rick scanned the ceiling. "There are more images up there than contestants." He glanced at Wells. "A lot more."

Wells didn't answer.

"The Corrina Bowen contest," Rick went on. "If those images faded – the ones who didn't win – and some of these images aren't ours...or yours – where did they come from?"

Wells didn't answer.

Rick was about to press it further, but before he could, footsteps sounded from the landing. They turned in time to see Wilson step into the keep. Bryan followed.

Sherilyn eyed him sourly. "Thought you might have bowed out too."

Bryan's hair was drenched, as if he'd just showered.

Wells said to Wilson, "And Miss Still?"

"Locked in her room," Wilson explained. "She wouldn't answer."

Wilson stepped closer to Rick. Uncomfortably close. He could smell the servant's body odor. Like lightning-charged air permeating a dog kennel.

Will said, "Maybe someone should check on her."

"Yes," Wilson murmured at Rick's ear. "Maybe someone should go to her while she's still alive."

Sherilyn said, "She could just be—"

But Rick didn't hear the rest. He was already moving toward the door.

CHAPTER TWELVE

Rick knocked again; again there was no answer.

"This sounds like the creepiest statement in the world, but I'll say it anyway: I know you're in there." He winced. "It sounded even worse coming out. Like, serial killer stuff. I feel like I should be wearing clown makeup."

The door swung inward. Lucy glowered at him.

She'd been crying. Her eyes were swollen and her cheeks were an exhausted shade of pink. More troublingly, her suitcase was out, several articles of clothing heaped inside.

He mulled several comments, but none of them seemed appropriate. She was grasping the doorframe with one hand and the door with the other.

"Okay," she said, "you've seen me. Will you leave now?"

"I miss something?"

"My story's gone."

He stared at her.

"I was in the library doing research, and when I got back to my room, the laptop was sitting outside my door. Like a big fuck-you."

"Someone deleted it?"

"The whole thing. It's not in the recycle bin, not in the file directory. Gone."

"What about the printed—"

"Gone too."

"My God. I don't know what to…. Who did it?"

"Does it matter? Anna despised me. Elaine acted like we were friends before she left, but maybe that was a ruse…."

Rick gazed down the hall, thought of Bryan….

"Truth is," she said, "I don't trust anybody. I was stupid to trust you."

"Hey, I don't blame you—"

"Oh, you don't *blame* me! That's big of you. Some...*fucker* invades my room, wipes out the best thing I've ever written, and then taunts me with it?"

"It's a terrible thing, Lucy. I can't imagine—"

"Have you ever lost work?"

He shifted uneasily. "Parts of chapters...a paper I wrote—"

"Were you able to get them back?"

He hesitated. Shook his head.

"Any other brilliant suggestions?"

"Maybe Wells can bring in a computer guy."

"Maybe you can join me in reality. It's gone."

"Hey, Lucy...."

"Imagine the best thing you ever wrote. Imagine *Garden of Snakes.* You doing that?"

He nodded, knowing where this was going, but hoping it would help her blow off steam.

"Now it's gone." She snapped her fingers. "How does that feel?"

"Terrible. Catastrophic."

"Now think about someone doing it intentionally. Someone violating your space, being spiteful enough to take it all away."

"You can get it back."

She looked at him like he'd lost his mind. "There's no way to get the file—"

"In here," he said, tapping the side of his head. "It's still in here, right? You know the whole thing. You were only, what, a third of the way in?"

Her eyes shot wide. "*Only a third?* Well, holy shit, Rick. And here I thought it was a big deal! I'll just mosey over to the keyboard and reproduce the whole book!"

He hung his head. "I didn't mean to sound insensitive."

She moved to the dresser. "I know that. I know I'll feel guilty for barking at you."

"You don't have to. Anyone would be mad."

She grabbed a couple shirts. "Probably deserve this anyway."

"Wait a second."

"If you're ever in Virginia, look me up. Now let me pack."

He was about to go when he noticed something he hadn't

previously. Her bathroom door was open, the light on. On the edge of the sink, a heap of pills. Little red ones.

His pulse beat in his temples.

"You can go now," she said, "unless you want to see my bras. I promise they're not that exciting."

Stay or go, he thought. *Stay and you'll exacerbate the situation. You'll enrage her, and she'll guzzle those red pills and die before they get her to the hospital.*

Lucy dropped a shirt into the suitcase. "Maybe you enjoy watching a woman pack. Everyone has different turn-ons. Maybe yours is white cotton panties."

Or, he thought, *the pills aren't laid out for sinister reasons at all; she's only transferring them from a pill organizer to the bottle.*

"Seriously," she snapped, rounding on him, "it's getting a little weird."

He muttered, "Sorry," but didn't move from the doorway.

"Check that," she said. "A lot weird." She began pushing the door shut. "You're a great guy, Rick. I wish we could've met somewhere else. Then again, I'd have found a way to screw it up no matter where we met."

"Lucy—"

The door closed. The lock snicked.

Rick stood in the hallway, listening.

CHAPTER THIRTEEN

Lucy's fist shook, the pills within them hot on her skin. Her other hand clutched the sink, the white porcelain frigid. Her agent's merry voice repeated in her head, *It's over, Lucy Goosy! It's over!*

The red coating from the pills swirled in her sweat, patted on the white porcelain. Lucy stared down at the red spots. They weren't the red of menstrual blood, but that's what they reminded her of, the beginning of a period, and for reasons she couldn't explain, this increased her sense of desolation, her fatalistic certainty that this moment, this bathroom, was the end of the road.

Lucy thought of her manuscript. Remembered the story. How could she not? Every waking moment she hadn't spent with Rick, she'd been writing or researching. *The Fred Astaire Murders* was the best thing she'd ever done.

But it's gone, Fred reminded her. *Granted, it may have been good, but it's gone now, and it's just you again. You and your failure.*

She pounded the sink edge. It hurt, so she did it again, harder. She bludgeoned the sink with both fists, the pill juice stippling the porcelain in cherry-red splats.

Let's say, just for kicks, you earn enough to justify another advance. What then, Lucy? The same. Damned. Thing. You'll stumble your way through another atrocious follow-up – The Ginger Rogers Slayings? *The* Gene Kelly Massacre? *– and you'll be right back where you started. You don't have the guts or the heart or, let's face it, the* skill *to be an honest-to-goodness writer. You're aging, you've sabotaged the one relationship that may have gone anywhere—*

A growl welled in the back of her throat. Lucy pummeled the sink, the sides of her fingers splitting open...

—and it's time to do what you should have done years ago, Lucy Goosy—

...fists slamming, blood splashing the basin...

—no friends, no family, no husband—

...the growl becoming a scream...

—*so do everyone a favor and just TAKE THE PILLS*—

With an inarticulate cry, Lucy crammed the handful of pills in her mouth, choked them down, thinking, *Down to four contestants now!*

And she remembered something else, something infinitely worse....

The pills slid down her gullet, eager to spread their killing poison.

She remembered Molly, her little sister, and Poland, the place Molly's life ended. Where both their lives ended.

That's right, she thought, her distress fading. *The Girl Who Died* was Molly, true, but what Lucy should have called the novel was *The* Girls *Who Died*. Because Lucy died that day as surely as her sister. Lucy's death just took a little longer to play out. The successful first book, the failed second. The disastrous third. The wretched excuses for relationships. And all of it leading to this moment, the consummation of the death that began a quarter-century earlier across the Atlantic Ocean on a frozen rural creek.

She'd died then.

This was just the removal of life support.

She looked into the mirror.

Saw the red pill smear riming her mouth. Her lips were a garish, uneven red. Like an over-the-hill actress gone round the bend, too shaky even to apply her lipstick properly. There were pinkish dribbles on her chin, a trickle of red juice wending its way down her throat.

She looked ridiculous. Clown-like.

Lucy stared at her reflection, gripped the sink edge, barely aware of how her bleeding hands ached. *She'd* done this to herself. Not her agent, not Wells, not the other writers.

You, Lucy. It was you.

The clown stared back at her.

"Oh my God," she whispered.

She lurched to the toilet and plunged three fingers down her throat. Her gag reflex triggered hard, and she splashed the underside of the toilet seat with a red torrent of pills, stomach acid, and what little she'd eaten that day. She vomited long and powerfully, but she knew it wasn't enough. She jammed her fingers farther, scourged the back of her throat, the column of puke so tall and hot this time her whole face hinged open, like some horror movie character giving oral birth to a slimy alien newborn. She knew some of the poison was in her bloodstream, understood this might be a pointless measure, but she made herself gag anyway, this time shoving her fingers so far down her throat a witness would have believed she was attempting to swallow her forearm. Lucy sprayed vomit, the pain indescribable, and then the dry heaves began, clenching her core and forbidding breath. *Gonna die*, Lucy thought as her lungs seized up. *Gonna die, and it won't even be from the pills. It'll be from oxygen deprivation.*

She fought for breath, failed, then drew in a single sip. Then she gasped. It burned her windpipe. Her whole body burned. But she was alive.

Dimly, she realized she was weeping. She might be the most pitiful creature in the cosmos, but dammit, she was still here and still breathing.

Unlike your sister, a voice whispered. But it was not her agent mocking her this time: it was Wells.

You abandoned her, Wells said.

Moaning, Lucy stumbled out of the bathroom. *I didn't mean for it to happen, didn't mean—*

To kill her? Wells asked.

Lucy shook her head, but Wells's voice would not be displaced: *You deserve it all, Lucy. The heartbreak, the humiliation, the pain. You bought it all in Poland. You've been carrying it with you ever since.*

Not anymore, she thought.

It's part of you, Wells insisted.

"Not anymore," she said aloud.

She stood panting in the center of her bedroom and told herself she had moved on from the horror and the pain surrounding Molly's death.

But at a marrow-deep level she knew she had yet to face it.

CHAPTER FOURTEEN

He answered the door right away, but instead of speaking he looked down at her hands, which she'd wrapped in towels. A ragged job.

"I did something stupid," she said. "I took some pills."

He started toward her. "Let's get you to a hospital."

"I puked them up."

"How many did you take?"

"I don't know. A lot."

"The hospital...."

"I think I'm okay."

"You a doctor?"

"What I'm saying," she continued, "is that by the time we explain it to Wells, hike all the way back to the lane, hitch a ride into town...."

"You can still—"

"What I need is for you to stay with me while I shower. I need you to make sure I stay awake."

"They were sleeping pills?"

"Anti-anxiety," she said. Thought about it. "There's irony in there somewhere."

"Get in here," he said.

He proved a very respectable nurse. She knew it was stereotypical of her to be surprised, but the men she'd known – her occasional boyfriends, her agent – possessed the sensitivity of a socket wrench. Rick got the shower temperature just right, looked in the opposite direction as she climbed inside, then closed the curtain. Despite her disheveled state, she found herself watching his eyes as she stepped into the tub, hoping he'd steal a glance at her. Truth was, she'd lost weight and gotten more exercise and sun since arriving; other than the cuts on her hands and her rumpled hair, she felt good about her appearance.

But Rick didn't look, only went out, leaving the door open.

She took her time in the shower. There was no razor for her to shave her legs, but she'd done that yesterday, a part of her hoping she'd be wrapping them around Rick soon.

Which was funny, she thought as she soaped her armpits. She genuinely enjoyed talking to Rick, yet she also wanted to be ravaged by him. She couldn't recall that combination in all her years of interacting with men. When she and Rick were talking, it was like conversing with an old friend. When she went to bed, she'd imagine him bending her over a table.

Funny.

Though her hands ached, she managed to wash away the blood and the pill residue. Wincing, she twisted off the shower knob, drew the curtain aside. She wanted Rick to be standing there, wanted him to see her emerge from the shower. But only his feet were visible in the doorway, like he was manning a post. She reached out, slid a towel off the shelf, and wrapped herself up. As she did, she noticed he had a hole in his left sock where his middle toe poked through, like his foot was performing an obscene gesture.

"Ready for me?" he asked.

She bit down on a response.

"Oh," he said, popping to his feet. "You can wear this."

He handed her a gray *Stranger Things* t-shirt, his face averted. She accepted it. Whether his shyness was genuine or feigned, she liked it, thought it an interesting facet of his personality. He was highly intelligent, what she would call enlightened. Yet surprisingly old-fashioned.

He returned to the bedroom. As he sat again, she noticed him retrieving a book. Elmore Leonard's *Out of Sight*.

She let the towel fall, squirmed into the t-shirt. Considered how insane she was. A half-hour earlier, she'd been low enough to take her life.

Now she couldn't wait to talk to Rick.

Then he was moving into the bathroom, rifling through the first-aid kit in the medicine cabinet. He found gauze pads, Band-Aids, medical tape. She rested on the toilet lid while he knelt before her and set to work. It wasn't a neat job, but the effort was there, and he was gentle.

When he'd finished, he glanced at her mummified hands and asked, "Does it hurt?"

"Some. My throat's worse."

He seemed to consider. "Was it the lost book that did it?"

"My doctor said I suffer from mild depression, anxiety, some OCD tendencies. Basically, I'm a mess."

He waited.

She went on. "Everyone says depression isn't situational. That you can be in a perfectly happy place and be totally down. Empty."

"I've heard that."

"It's true, I suppose. But the idea that it's *all* chemical for all people…it doesn't account for everything."

"I wouldn't think so."

"It's not just the book."

"Want to talk about the other stuff?"

"An impromptu bathroom therapy session?"

"Other room's more comfortable."

She sat on the edge of the bed, and he pulled up a chair. Without really planning to, she told him the parts of her fourteen-year descent she hadn't previously. The wrongheaded belief that she was better than other writers, the horror she experienced as the delusion slowly came undone. She told him about her family's dysfunction, how Molly's death had been like a portcullis falling between her and her parents, barring emotional connection, keeping her forever outside their hearts.

To her ears, it sounded maudlin, but evidently Rick didn't think so. He listened intently, asked questions now and then. He sympathized with her parents for having lost a child but considered their freezing out of their remaining daughter unconscionable. She told him she'd never really had a close friend or lover. It was the truth.

"Do you shut people out?" he asked.

"When you're thirty-three and you've never been married, people think you're some sort of oddball. Like that character in *The Haunting of Hill House*."

"Eleanor," he supplied.

She nodded. "Eccentric, batty...."

He squinted at her. "You sort of remind me of Eleanor."

"Piss off."

He laughed.

"So," she said, fiddling with a bandage, "what should we do now?"

"I'd sort of like to go down on you."

She stopped fiddling with the bandage.

He took hold of her hips, lifted her backward on the bed until her head was nestled on a pillow.

The t-shirt had ridden up, and the down comforter was cool and soft against her rear end. She was aware of how odd she must look – bandaged hands, nude from the stomach down – but she only felt slightly self-conscious in his presence.

He crawled over her, kissed her. Their tongues brushed together, almost shyly, and he broke the kiss, looked at her a moment with that crooked smile. He crawled backward until his head was between her legs.

Lucy lay back, allowed herself the luxury of feeling his lips, his tongue. He wrapped his arms around her thighs, his biceps flexing against her skin. His tongue began to tease her, gently at first, then with greater insistence. Lucy closed her eyes, a heat already building. Soon she was crying out, her mouth open, the sound a rising sigh. Her body reached that sweet, fiery place, and lingered...lingered... her hips shuddering, her buttocks tightening....

And she turned to jelly. When she opened her eyes he was climbing onto her. She gladly took him inside, let him determine the rhythm. She lifted her head, kissed him, tasted herself in his mouth, and for some reason this drove her crazy, and she kissed him harder, her tongue working his, and he moaned deep in his throat. She reached down, cupped his buttocks with her fingers, and gathered him into her, driving him deeper inside, their bodies clapping together, their bellies sweaty, his movements animalistic, and he was grunting, moaning in time with their slapping bodies, and his thrusts began to jag, his control spiraling away, and she kept jerking his ass into her, thrusting her hips, and his groan was of wonderful pain.

He lay atop her, spent, sweaty, panting. When their eyes met, they were both smiling.

Later, as they lay together, he said, "I'm supposed to be the brooding one."

"I'm not brooding, I'm relaxing. Finally."

"Good."

"I was thinking about my novel," she said.

"Huh."

She glanced at him. "The sex was great and everything—"

"You want to get back at it?"

She squeezed his hand. "Let's just lie here a little longer. Then I'll get to work."

"On me or your book?"

"Sorry," she said. "*Fred Astaire* is calling."

CHAPTER FIFTEEN

Will gazed out the window and thought, *It's not possible.*

He watched the trees swaying gently in the moonlight, the ghostly clouds beginning to mass overhead.

If I go to the island, he wondered, *is she going to be there?*

He turned, looked at the computer's bluish glow.

The Siren and the Specter.

He'd never written anything approaching the quality of this story.

What if they aren't just stories? What if Rick really did unleash a homicidal maniac on the world?

Will began to sweat.

How much worse will your Siren be if she becomes real?

Do you hear yourself? his inner critic demanded. *You don't have the skill to write a decent character. You really think you can conjure one in the flesh?*

"Dammit," Will muttered and stalked over to the bed. He sat down, worked his feet into his sneakers. He had to escape this room.

To the island?

Maybe I will go to the island. All the way there this time. And if the sand is just sand, I'll know it was all my imagination. If not....

You'll die?

"That's asinine," he said. He left his room, moved down the hall. There was no doubt Wells's estate was…different. Mysterious things happened here, things he had trouble explaining. The Siren he thought he'd spied on the beach. The fact that none of the eliminated contestants spoke to anyone before they departed. And Rick's story about the cop…Raymond Eddy…

…Peter Bates.

Will closed his eyes. He made a mistake when he was a kid, but didn't everyone? What would have happened if he'd told the cops about Bates? They would have picked Bates up. Will's abandonment of the fugitive just made Bates's death quicker.

Okay, he decided as he neared the stairs, *maybe* quicker *is the wrong word. Starving to death is a hideous way to die, but wasn't it better than....*

No, it wasn't better, and Will knew it. He could pretend it wasn't his fault, but that didn't change what he'd done. Or hadn't done.

He started down the stairs.

Froze midway down.

"Ah...shit," he muttered.

It was the last thing he wanted to do, but he had to anyway. He jogged up to the third floor, noting as he did how distinct the carpet patterns had become, how vibrant the colors. Even the banister he clutched shone like new. He was thinking of the restoration of the castle at the end of *Beauty and the Beast* when he reached the third floor.

He started down the hallway, which glowed a lambent orange. He knew exactly where the tapestry was. He passed a painting featuring an apparition. A tapestry depicting a severed head. The tapestry he was looking for should be up here on the left....

Will stopped.

Hell. It was worse than he remembered, the resemblance uncanny.

His body thrumming, he stared into the woven image of the woman in the black dress. The long-stemmed glass in her hand. The knowing smile. The eyes that picked you up, turned you over, and dismissed you as unworthy. The woman from one of Will's favorite short stories.

By Roderick Wells.

Well, fuck a duck, he thought.

The woman in the tapestry was Amanda Wells.

CHAPTER SIXTEEN

Rick had never been a womanizer, but neither had he always been as considerate as he should have, particularly in his early twenties. After a one-night stand, the woman would want to sleep over, and though he'd been okay with that, it was occasionally a chore concealing his impatience for her to leave in the morning.

So when Lucy left to begin resurrecting her novel, he was surprised, and on a level he didn't like to think about, disappointed. The prospect of spending the night with her, bodies close, had been a comforting one. Though he was proud of her for reviving her story, the bed felt particularly empty without her.

He lay there remembering their lovemaking. He considered writing but knew his focus would be scattered. Same with reading.

He was finally nodding off when a voice said, "Pretty goddamned proud of yourself, aren't you?"

Rick opened his eyes in the darkness.

"You like to pretend you've got these ideals, morals." A soft chuckle. "Shit. You just wanted to screw her."

Terror clutched him with icy fingers, moored him to the bed.

"Was it worth it?" the voice asked. "I hope to hell it was. Because you know what you've sicced on her. Know what's gonna hunt her down."

Rick tried to swallow, couldn't. He was scared for Lucy, but though he despised himself for it, he was even more frightened of the individual – he dared not call it a man – in the room with him.

"What do you want?" Rick asked.

"What kind of a dumbass question's that?" the police chief asked.

"You're not real," he said, but his voice came out shaky.

The rustle of clothes, the groan of a floorboard.

Rick smelled the cop's perspiration. Gamey, stale, laced with madness. Like an abandoned kennel where a feral dog ate the others to survive.

Rick stared at the hulking figure in the dark and thought, *This is the feral dog.*

"You've been entertaining some wicked thoughts, Forrester."

No point pretending he didn't know what Anderson was talking about. "I go where the story goes—"

"You've been thinkin' about killing me off."

Rick's mouth had gone dry. "Readers want a happy ending."

"I don't give a fat fuck about your excuses, boy. I wanna *live.*"

A dozen responses auditioned in Rick's head, but he uttered none of them.

"Get your lazy ass outta bed."

Rick stood, moved as far away from the cop as he could. He kept his back to Anderson, acutely aware of his own nudity. After sleeping with Lucy, he hadn't bothered getting dressed. He'd been happy. Hopeful even.

What a fool he'd been.

He couldn't locate his clothes. He screwed up his eyes, peered at the foot of the bed—

"Jesus H. Christ, son, turn on the fucking lights! You think I want to stand here waiting for you to find your tighty-whities?"

Rick twisted on the desk lamp. And though he could now see just fine, he wished it were still dark in the bedroom.

The chief looked bigger – and scarier – than he had before.

Rick couldn't study the man for any length of time. But the glimpses he did steal as he scurried around the bed retrieving his clothes revealed a disturbing portrait:

A frame huge and muscled.

A head that swiveled wherever Rick went, the reflective sunglasses like the eyes of some mutant insect preparing to feed.

Dark stains on the beige uniform.

"Move it, soldier!"

Rick hopped into his shorts and tried not to overbalance. He couldn't corral his spinning thoughts. He felt exactly as he had when his stepfather used to bark at him.

"Downstairs," the cop ordered.

Rick started to cast about for his shoes, but the cop said, "Leave 'em."

Anderson opened the door. Rick moved through.

"The black lady thinks you're everyone's savior," Anderson said. They started down the steps. "From where I stand, you're the most deluded one of all."

Rick felt ten years old. Vulnerable in his stockinged feet. Half a foot shorter than Anderson, a hundred pounds lighter.

Anderson went on. "You knew who I was. But you let Sokolov leave with me anyway."

Rick's chest squeezed tight. They rounded the landing.

"Look at what's happened since. Tommy, Evan, Elaine, that luscious bitch Anna. All gone. And what did you do to help them? You lift a finger?" They reached the first floor. "You let 'em go. Saving yourself, Forrester. That's the only talent you have."

They entered the back hallway. Rick glanced over his shoulder, toward the kitchen, where he might arm himself. A knife or a cleaver. A corkscrew, for God's sakes.

"You run, boy," Anderson said, his tone conversational, "and I'll not only kill you, I'll chop your girlfriend's tits off."

Rick's shoulders slumped. If he really had made Anderson – he still couldn't wrap his mind around the thought – he certainly couldn't physically vanquish him. In fact, it was a major problem with his manuscript. He hadn't found a plausible way for the protagonist to defeat Anderson. Sure, someone could get lucky, aim a well-placed bullet at the chief's heart, but that was cheap. A sloppy, unsatisfying conclusion. But that's what you got when you tipped the scales too far in the antagonist's favor. He became insurmountable.

"Go," the chief ordered when they reached the basement door.

"What am I gonna find?"

"The gateway to Hades. Who gives a shit? Get your stupid ass down there."

The sensation of descending to his death was overwhelming. Anderson followed on his heels, so there was no question of attempting to escape.

Bottom of the steps. The shadows surrounded him.

"Light," Anderson said.

"I could stop writing."

A chuckle. "You think you're the one in charge, boy?"

"I made you. You can only—"

"I'm not talkin' about myself, you jackhole. I'm talking about the big man."

He was shoved headlong into the murk. Rick spun, sure Anderson would be disappearing up the stairs.

A single pallid filament dangled from the ceiling.

"Light," Anderson ordered.

Rick tugged the string. Illumination the color of overripe lemons spilled over them.

And gazing upon the giant cop, something shifted in Rick.

"How do you exist?" Rick asked.

Anderson grinned. "Why you think I brought you down here?"

"You mean this place—" Rick gestured toward the steel doors, "—has something to do with it?"

"Stop stalling, Forrester. You and me, we're closer than you and that Lucy chick. And you had your tongue halfway up her snatch."

Controlling his temper, Rick said, "Tell me."

The chief pointed. "That one."

Rick followed the chief's finger to a door. "What am I gonna find in there?"

"Move, Forrester."

"If I end my novel—"

"You're not gonna end a goddamned thing. Open the fucking door."

Rick didn't see any way around it. He stepped toward the steel door. He sensed Anderson following him, and maybe without the chief blocking the stairs Rick could scurry around him and make it out. Or maybe Anderson would shoot him in the back.

Rick stopped before the door, breath thinning.

At his ear, the chief said, "Open it."

Rick reached for the knob, the hackles on the back of his neck rising.

"What is it?" Rick asked.

"You'll never be man enough to take it. Might as well get it over with."

Rick twisted the knob, opened the door.

"Oh my Jesus Christ," he whispered, his legs buckling.

He closed his eyes as his knees hit the floor, but the afterimage of what he'd glimpsed remained, as vivid as sight:

Elaine Kovalchyk fixed diagonally in the wall of dirt, as if she'd been hurled there by a giant. Elaine was nude, but Rick hardly noted this.

Because though she was obviously dead, the wall around her was alive.

Encased in moist dirt, Elaine's corpse hung like an astronaut floating in zero gravity. Purple-brown ridges undulated against her limbs, her torso. Rick noted with horror the livid red marks where the soil probed her skin. He heard noises, the constant pulsing hum and – he clapped his hands over his ears to blot it out – the wet slurping sounds, as if a hundred newborn pigs were suckling a sow's teats.

"You're all just fuel," Anderson said.

Rick scarcely heard him above the sucking noises. Jesus, the soil was *feeding* on her. He dug the heels of his hands into his eyes to rid them of the sight. He forced himself to stand. He turned his back on Elaine, stared with bleary eyes into the chief's sunglasses.

"You won't hurt me," Rick said.

The chief grinned, seized Rick by the shirt front, hauled him closer so the cop's rancid breath washed over him, garlic and flyblown pork. "The better question is why the hell would I let you live?" The chief lifted him off his feet, began to walk with him. "Bleeding heart. Believin' you're better. You know the real man in this thing? It's the Clayton kid. At least he's got the stones to do something."

"You're done," Rick said into the chief's face. "I'm not writing another word, and you're just going to fade away."

"You think I need you?" One of the chief's hands went away, but Rick still hung suspended by a clutching fist. "I'm ready to take on the world."

The chief reached up, removed his sunglasses.

Revealing eye sockets that teemed with maggots and centipedes.

Gagging, Rick looked away in time to see another door blowing open, the wall of soil rippling restlessly within.

"They're hungry," Anderson said into his ear. "And I refuse to die."

Anderson hurled him through the doorway. Rick crashed into the moving wall of soil, jerked away, and dove for the door just as it slammed shut.

He heard the chief tug the pull string, and what scant light had been filtering under the door went away. In total darkness, Rick pummeled the steel door, scrabbled for the knob.

But there wasn't one.

Rick bellowed for help. Then he heard it.

Behind him. The sound of someone breathing.

He turned slowly, stared into the murk.

The voice that spoke in the darkness was a deep, rumbling growl.

"*Murderer,*" it said.

PART FIVE
THE MAGIC KING

CHAPTER ONE

Will had to tell somebody.

Wells called it a place of magic, and it was. But the magic was of the darkest, most demented sort.

Moving toward the dining room, Will began to perspire. When he stepped through the doorway, he found Bryan, Sherilyn, and Lucy waiting, orange juice and coffee sitting before them but no food yet. It didn't matter. Will didn't think he could swallow a bite. He noted without surprise how brilliantly the overhead chandelier shone, how unscuffed and polished the floor appeared. The crimson-and-gold wallpaper looked like it had been hung yesterday.

Like new, he thought. *The whole mansion looks new.*

He eased down beside Lucy and Sherilyn. Bryan reclined across the table from them, his smirk cranked up to maximum shitheadedness.

Ignore him. Focus on the others. Lucy will listen. Sherilyn too.

He cleared his throat. "I've been thinking—"

"There's a surprise," Bryan said.

Will shot him a look. "Last night I took a walk."

"Don't tell me you've been slacking on your word count," Sherilyn said.

"Where'd you go?" Lucy asked.

"I'll get to that. But first, I read for a while in the library."

"Goody," Bryan said, sipped his coffee. "A book report."

"A collection of Wells's short works, *Darkness and Other Dreams?*"

"I love that one," Lucy said.

"Me too," Will responded. Frowned. "There's a story that spoke to me." He shrugged. "I'm sort of a romantic."

"There are other words for that," Bryan said.

Lucy turned. "I've got a few words for you."

Will went on. "The tale is called 'Incident on a Paris Rooftop', and—"

"Is that the one – sorry for interrupting," Lucy said, putting a hand on his arm, "– but is that the one where the guy falls in love with the woman who jumps to her death?"

Sherilyn arched an eyebrow. "Spoiler alert."

"That's the one," Will said. "Ever since I came here, it's been on my mind, and last night, I figured out why."

"Women want to kill themselves when you talk to them?" Bryan asked.

Will regarded him evenly. "The woman is Amanda Wells."

There was a silence.

Sherilyn watched him. "What do you mean, 'The woman is Amanda Wells'?"

Sweat dampened his armpits. "I mean what I said."

Lucy moved in her chair. "Maybe the character was inspired by Amanda."

Sherilyn stared at Will. "When was the story written?"

"Nineteen sixty-two."

"That's impossible," Sherilyn said. "Mrs. Wells wasn't born yet."

Lucy sat forward. "It's a wonderful tale…maybe Wells saw something in Amanda that reminded him of the woman in 'Incident' and married her because of it."

Will shook his head. "I know you're trying to help, but that's not what I mean."

"Spell it out for us," Sherilyn said.

"You remember *Lust and Deceit in Jacmel*?"

"My favorite Corrina Bowen novel," she said. "What's your point?"

"Have you ever thought about the maid in that story?"

"I'm not in a patient mood," Sherilyn said.

He glanced at Lucy, whose eyes were as skeptical as Sherilyn's.

He took a steadying breath. "I know how it sounds. Just hear me out."

No give from Sherilyn. "I can't think of any earthly explanation."

"Take a step back," he said. "Really think about Bowen's novel."

"I have."

"Think about the maid...how quiet she was. All through the novel, she stayed in the background, never featured in a scene, but always around."

"I have no appetite for horseshit."

"I'm not getting it either," Lucy admitted. "Will, are you really saying—"

"He is," Sherilyn said. "And I'm getting pissed off."

He expected Bryan to join the chorus of disbelief, but he'd turned away.

"Just consider the possibility," Will said. "The other night I went to the island."

"In the dark?" Lucy asked.

"I can't get past the fictional-characters-made-flesh stuff," Sherilyn said.

"Think about *Lust and Deceit in Jacmel*. How was that character described?"

Miss Lafitte walked in.

Sherilyn nodded. "Why not ask her?"

Will blushed.

Sherilyn kept going. "If you think she's some sort of phantom—"

"That's not what he said," Bryan muttered.

"What's up your butt all of a sudden?" Sherilyn asked him.

Will watched Miss Lafitte set down a platter domed by a silver lid. She removed the lid, revealing a sizable ham, a carving knife, and a large fork. Miss Lafitte bustled out.

"Never mind," Bryan said.

"Don't 'never mind' me," Sherilyn said. "You've been shitty since the moment we got here, and the first time you agree with anyone, it's about something outrageous."

Lucy was watching Will. "What happened on the island?"

His nerves drew tighter, the hair of his forearms tingling. "Maybe we should let it go."

"Might as well get it off your chest now," Sherilyn said. "I wanna hear what you found on that island. Snow White and the Seven Dwarfs? Pennywise the Clown?"

Miss Lafitte reentered, a tray of bagels and cream cheese braced on one arm, a colorful platter of sliced fruit on the other. She set about arranging them on the serving table.

Will said, "A Siren."

Sherilyn blinked at him. "Like, a mythological Siren? The character from your book?"

Lucy was looking more and more uncomfortable. "Let's just eat."

But Sherilyn was not to be put off. "If there was a Siren there, why didn't she eat you?"

"She wasn't formed yet," he answered. The words tasted bitter in his mouth.

"So by your logic," Sherilyn said, "there should be an evil king running around the property and a peasant who's going to overthrow him."

"There is," Bryan said, finally facing them. "There are."

Sherilyn grunted laughter. "Hell, half the reason I wrote that was to piss Wells off."

"I liked *The Magic King*," Lucy said.

"Oh, I do too. Make no mistake. Whether I win this competition or not, I plan on getting it published."

Bryan chuckled. "Never happen."

"Oh no? Why not?"

"Only one of us is leaving here alive."

"That a threat?"

Bryan's smirk grew nastier. "Have you ever read *The Seer*, Sherilyn?"

"Everyone's read *The Seer*."

"Doesn't he sound familiar?"

Sherilyn's eyebrows went up. "Who? The character?"

"It's Wilson," Bryan said.

This is all wrong, Will thought. *Wrong time, wrong place.* A glance at Bryan. *Wrong ally. Just get up from the table and deal with it later.*

Sherilyn nodded. "Oh, I get it. That means Wilson is able to, what? See the future? Solve crimes for the government?"

"For Wells," Bryan corrected. "Wells created the character. Wilson does his bidding."

"If he wanted a handyman that badly, why not just hire one? He's got plenty of cash."

"Wilson is how we got here," Bryan said. "He touched our handwriting samples, figured out who had the right combination of character traits."

"This oughta be good."

"Discretion. Ambition. Some level of talent."

"Of course," Sherilyn agreed, mock serious.

"What else?" Lucy asked, though she didn't look like she wanted to know.

"We all have terrible secrets," Bryan said.

Sherilyn spiked her napkin on the table. "I've had enough of this shit. Why don't we ask Miss Lafitte here? According to you, she's a figment of Corrina Bowen's imagination." She glared at Will. "That's what you're saying, isn't it? That this little maid is a killer?"

Miss Lafitte stared at the wall.

Will put up his hands. "Let's just forget it, okay? Miss Lafitte, I apologize. I didn't think—"

"Why are you apologizing?" Sherilyn demanded. She rotated her chair to face Miss Lafitte. "You're just a make-believe person."

Lucy cringed. "Sherilyn...."

"I'm making a point," Sherilyn snapped. Turned her attention back to Miss Lafitte. "Why don't you tell us what it was like in Haiti? Did the plantation owner abuse you? Was there really all that lust and deceit?"

"I'm going upstairs," Lucy said, rising.

Sherilyn put a hand on Lucy's shoulder, kept her in her chair. Will watched the maid step over to the platter of ham, grasp the carving knife.

He said, "No, don't—"

The maid pumped the carving knife into the side of Sherilyn's throat, the foot-long blade slicing all the way through her neck. The maid wrenched the knife out, blood spraying from both sides of Sherilyn's throat. Lucy screamed, Bryan scrambled away. Will gaped in horror.

Sherilyn cupped her wounds.

The maid slashed down. Sherilyn's ear split in half, blood bubbling from the wound like crude oil. Sherilyn half rose, her eyes almost all white. The maid pumped the knife into her breastbone, jerked it out with a horrible scrape. The maid stabbed her again, the wounds spraying everyone with scarlet.

A head taller than the little maid, Sherilyn swayed on her feet.

"You should not mock me," the maid said.

And plunged the knife straight through Sherilyn's voice box.

CHAPTER TWO

The last thing Lucy saw before Will grabbed her hand was Sherilyn dropping to her knees, the tip of the carving knife poking out the back of her neck like a bloody dorsal fin.

"Run," Will said, his voice barely more than a croak.

He dragged her away from the psychotic maid. They reached the doorway and bolted through. The hallway was empty, but that meant nothing. The world had come unhinged, Sherilyn was dead, and there was a homicidal maniac loose in the mansion.

Lucy and Will broke for the foyer. She let go of his hand, cast a glance over her shoulder. She reached the front door first, fumbled with the handle, and with Will crowding her, got the door open. The day was gunmetal gray, and if it stormed, they'd be exposed out here.

But nothing would compel Lucy back inside that mansion. Not her manuscript, not the chance at literary redemption. Certainly not Roderick Wells and his spookshow of a retreat.

She and Will hurried through the meadow. Will labored for breath, even more out of shape than she was. He grabbed her arm. Lucy tried to shake loose, but Will wouldn't let go of her. Finally, she rounded on him, both of them nearly falling as they stopped.

"We have to go," she said. "Miss Lafitte—"

"Agreed. But we can't go near that island. The lake. We have to..." he licked his lips, "...we have to take the long way around."

She started to move.

He seized her again. "Wait."

"That psychopath is *coming*."

"Which one?" Will asked.

Lucy stared at him, appalled.

"What about yours?" Will asked. "You know, the guy in the tuxedo?"

Lucy hadn't thought about the Fred Astaire Killer. The notion, despite all she'd seen, was too absurd to entertain. Those were words on paper. A story. And being part of a story was different to being *spawned* by a story.

Will grasped her upper arms and spoke directly into her face. "We're past the doubting stage, Lucy. This is happening. You need to believe this, so you can help me."

She stared into his eyes. "Help you with *what*?"

"I don't know, either get out of here or—"

But Lucy didn't catch the rest because something exploded out of the forest behind him. He saw her eyes shift, had time to whirl and face whatever it was, and then someone was crashing into him, knocking Lucy aside, and as she fell she caught a glimpse of Will's head snapping back, his skull bashing the unforgiving trail. He lay without moving.

Bryan, however, rose to his feet. Grinned at her.

"All right, gorgeous," he said, the Bowie knife glinting in the overcast light. "Looks like it's down to you and me."

CHAPTER THREE

The tendrils were subtle.

The lightlessness, Rick was certain, was essential to their attack. They didn't dart at him, drag him screaming into the undulating soil.

They were treacherous because their touch was so light. You didn't even sense it until you were being drawn forward into the wall of dirt. The tendrils were gossamer thin and not unbreakable, yet they found a way onto your body, insinuating themselves like a virus, creeping, swarming, until three dozen of them had bound you up.

Their combined strength was obscene.

At first Rick's breathing had been too loud for his ears to be of any use. The tendrils had slithered over his legs, his shoulders, and it wasn't until he broke contact with the door that he realized he was being drawn forward.

After an interval of horrorstruck panic, Rick forced himself to calm down, to listen to the darkness. He'd read that when one sense was taken away, the others grew more acute. He didn't know if this was true or not, but he found it was at least easier to concentrate when the only stimuli were sounds and tactile sensations. There was a smell, sure, but that was unchanging. There was a taste in his mouth, but that stemmed from his own terror, the acrid tang of adrenaline.

There was no light at all. No vision.

But the sounds were constant. He imagined a white noise machine dialed down to its lowest volume, nearly inaudible, but detectable if you strained hard enough. Along with the white noise, which he imagined was the constant unspooling of the threadlike tendrils, there was another sound, one that reduced him to a quivering child.

He'd seen too many movies, read too many books. Images of Frodo suspended in Shelob's lair, of young tourists attacked by carnivorous plants inside an ancient ruin, of Poe's character prematurely interred inside his coffin, the cold wood pressing in, the air dwindling to fatal thinness....

But that other sound...dear God, the sound was worse than the images, a voracious chorus that swelled each time the soil believed it was about to claim him.

Rick shivered. It was an unfortunate irony that though he'd lived with insomnia for more than two decades, now, when he needed to stay awake the most, the inexorable blue tide kept rolling in, weakening his mind when he needed to remain sharp.

What, Rick wondered as he pressed against the door, did the tendrils look like? Were they colorless strands, like a spider's web? Or did they possess some pigment, the jaundiced yellow of the light bulbs or the foreskin pink of underwater plants?

The filaments wormed their way across the floor, the walls, the ceiling. Once he'd found himself nodding off only to realize the door behind his back was moving. Only it hadn't been the door, it had been a crisscrossing web of tendrils that had wrapped him up so completely that he could scarcely move his limbs. Alone, each strand was frail. Together they formed a net like steel mesh.

The tendrils seized him.

As the strands hauled him nearer, he understood he was hearing the ridges themselves, the undulating brown-purple surface moaning in expectation.

Yes, he thought wildly, his arms pinioned to his sides, there was something appallingly sexual in the noises. They didn't just long to devour him, they wanted to *mate* with him. In their high-pitched cry he heard lust, ferocity, and exultation. He recalled how the ridges had pumped and moved. He bucked against the netting. He didn't know how far he'd been dragged, but if he wasn't upon the undulating wall, he would be at any moment. It was this thought – his flesh chewed and sucked by the hungry ridges – that forced him to jerk his right shoulder down. The web didn't tear, but it did give slightly. He heard the baying of the broken filaments. Rick contorted his body, wrenched down with his left shoulder, and this time he felt a perceptible give. He tightened his abdominal muscles, jerked his shoulders down in a violent crunch, and the whole web shifted enough to allow his elbows to move. Then he was flailing against the threadlike assemblage, his hands bursting free, his fingers steamshoveling at the web entombing his legs.

His wrist brushed the wall, and at the slimy feel of it, the nodes squirming against his flesh, Rick bellowed in terror. His feet were bound up by the ravenous web, but the strands were too numerous to snap. He dug at the webwork, and again he brushed the moist, meaty wall. But this time he felt the damp surface enfold the tip of his middle finger, a rapid scratching sensation on his flesh. In the moment before he jerked his hand away, he was reminded of a cat's tongue, the tiny bones embedded in the pink tissue lapping at him, abrading his flesh. The image was enough to nudge him into a frenzy. He tore madly at the strands. Then he was clambering back, whimpering against the steel door.

He had no idea how long he'd been down here, but his internal clock told him it was midmorning.

If that were the case, no one would have raised a fuss about his absence yet. Hell, maybe no one had even noted it.

Rick thought of Elaine's undulating corpse. The slow feeding of the purple-brown ridges.

The sucking sounds.

His airway narrowed. His flesh crawled as the tendrils continued to grope for him. He tried for a very long time to suppress the scream.

But he could only hold back the terror so long.

Rick gave in.

CHAPTER FOUR

Lucy pelted down the trail, Bryan's laughter pursuing her.

"Where's your boyfriend?" he called.

Lucy pounded around a bend, bared her teeth. She remembered the playdates her parents used to set up with the other homeschooled kids. There was one family, twin boys, a snot-crusted girl who rarely spoke. Lucy figured the reason the girl never spoke was because of the way her brothers tormented her.

During playdates the twins would concoct games designed to exploit their physical advantage, normal games with macabre twists. *Tag*, they'd say, though it wasn't really tag. It was Push Tag, it was Make-Lucy-It Tag and then dance out of arm's reach because she wasn't very athletic. And the moment her fingers would brush one of their shirts, the tagged boy would shove her to the ground, and the game would start over again. When Lucy complained the boys were bullying her, their mom would say, "They're just boys, dear. Don't pay any attention to them." And Lucy's mom would nod and not say a word, and Lucy would slink back outside for more torture.

"I think he took off," Bryan called, very near now.

Lucy kept running, but as the woods grew darker, the trees denser, and the sky overhead an increasingly moody gray, she noted without humor the irony of her situation. Earlier, she'd tried to end her life. Now she'd do anything she could to prolong it.

"You may as well give up," Bryan called.

He was closing on her. She scampered down a hill, followed the trail though a thicket of pines. The boughs loomed so close they scraped her arms as she rocketed past, but Bryan's footfalls were audible now, their heavy clumping rapid and relentless. Ahead, the trail curved, the thicket of pines showing no signs of thinning. She neared a wall of deep green needles.

Without thinking, she lunged into the pine trees. The crashing sounds drowned out all else. She bulled her way into the network of pines, the needles scratching, the branches flicking her breasts and whapping her belly. Cobwebs collected in her eyelashes. Her skin crawled at the thought of spiders in her hair, their eggburst babies teeming over her ears, burrowing into her scalp.

She stumbled into a slender clearing and worked furiously to dislodge any bugs from her hair.

Then she remembered Bryan.

Eyes widening, Lucy listened. The forest was noiseless.

She was sure he'd seize her, startle her one last time. But he remained silent, hidden.

She threw glances all around, but swaddled as she was by the pine boughs, she could see nothing, hear nothing.

She had to move.

She pushed through the trees, closed her eyes as prickly needles raked her skin. She reached out, found another gap, opened her eyes.

Stared in disbelief at what lay before her.

A house. One she'd seen before.

No, she thought.

But the protest was feeble. The house was real. Lights glowing inside, a hostile ribbon of black smoke curling from the chimney.

Whether it was coincidence or another element of Wells's accursed magic, this place looked exactly like the one in Poland.

But Bryan was coming.

Lucy emerged from the pine grove and approached the house. Two stories tall, the gabled A-frame reminded her of a fairy tale.

Out here in the forest she stood no chance. Bryan was a hunter, a survivalist, a depraved asshole who'd kill her for sport. She knew it as surely as she knew this house was an exact replica of the Poland house, the one owned by her mother's uncle, or some other faceless relative. At least here she might find refuge.

As she hurried nearer, Lucy glanced at the sky, judged the storm to be imminent. Another reason to take shelter.

She mounted the stoop, raised her fist, but paused. Knocking would echo in the woods. She might as well call out to Bryan, invite him to murder her.

Just go in. If the homeowner got testy, Lucy could throw herself at the person's mercy. Maybe it would be an old woman. She'd dial the police and soon Lucy would be rescued.

Or it could be a crazed hilljack who'd blast her with a shotgun the moment she stepped through the door.

At least it would be quick.

Lucy tried the handle. Unlocked. She entered.

Her mother sat at the kitchen table.

She didn't look up as Lucy closed the door. Lucy considered saying something, but her mom's morbid silence forbade it. Outside, distant thunder rumbled.

She stopped, peered down at her mom. She half expected the woman to be the age she'd been when Molly died. But the seamed forehead, the crow's feet that no amount of Botox could erase…this was her mother as she was now. Though Lucy hadn't seen or spoken to her for years, she was certain of this.

She became aware of a persistent creak.

It was coming from upstairs.

"You in there?" a voice called.

Lucy gasped, spun.

Bryan.

He'd spoken from just outside the door, which she'd forgotten to lock.

A thudding sound. Bryan's fist.

Another.

Lucy glanced about, spotted a knife rack. She hurried over, grasped the largest handle, and drew it out. A chopping knife.

"Lucy?"

She retreated, found herself in a narrow hallway. Behind her were two bedrooms. To her right, the stairs leading up.

Lucy chose the stairs.

She was halfway up when the front door closed. She listened.

"Wilson?" Bryan called. "You here?"

Lucy frowned. Was this Wilson's house? And if it was, what of the woman at the table? Just a phantom?

The groan of floorboards below.

Bryan's voice: "If you're here, Wilson, I hope you stay out of my way. I'm doing what you told me to. If Forrester's gone, it's almost over."

Lucy grasped the handrail. Stepped onto the next riser. The next. The stairs were not carpeted, but they made little noise as she climbed. Maybe Bryan would think she'd bypassed the house. If so, she could simply wait here until nightfall, and then, under cover of darkness, attempt her escape.

"Someone up there?"

Lucy cringed. He wasn't directly below her, but he'd advanced well into the kitchen. Had he noticed her mother?

Was her mother really there?

Moving as methodically as she could, Lucy climbed the final three risers and found herself in a dark hallway.

"Lucy?"

Instinctively, she backpedaled, and before she realized where she was going, she bumped the door of the back bedroom, the one in which she and Molly had slept.

Her hand shook so wildly she could barely grip the knob. She slipped inside. She reached down, thumbed the lock, the cheap kind any kid could open with a paperclip.

She was trapped, her only hope that Bryan would ignore the upstairs and head outside to continue the hunt.

She turned and her breath clotted.

Her father dangled from the ceiling, a length of electrical cord noosed around his throat. His corpse was bloated, discolored, the way it had been when she'd found him on the fifth anniversary of Molly's death. After the accident, he'd been taciturn, a ghost flittering around the edges of their house. Then, as quietly as he'd mourned his youngest daughter, he'd hanged himself from a garage rafter.

His corpse twisted slowly toward her. Lucy covered her mouth. She saw his knobby fingers, his maroon-colored forearms. The puffy throat bisected by orange electrical cord. The body continued to revolve. It faced her.

Rick's face.

The corpse opened its eyes. Lucy screamed.

Behind her, the door rattled in its jamb.

Bryan had found her.

CHAPTER FIVE

Will opened his eyes, thought, *Where am I?*

The day was the color of undrained dishwater, the branches ribbing the sky like bones painted brown. *Funny*, he thought. *I'm in a forest, but all I can see is gray and brown.*

He blinked, smiled.

His smile faded.

Oh hell, he thought. *Bryan. Lucy. The dark game.*

The glimpse he'd caught of Bryan was fleeting. A single frame in a poorly edited film sequence. One moment Will was talking to Lucy, the next he was being waylaid with such force that he marveled his head didn't rip free of his body.

The pain flooded back and Will groaned. It was so much nicer without the pain. This was a shrieking orange hell. It was as though some mad forest ranger was tamping a tent spike into his spinal sheath.

He was dying.

At least he told himself he was. Dying meant not having to deal with Bryan.

There was a catch in Will's throat as he thought, *Lucy.*

He couldn't let her die.

Will attempted to rise, but agony unlike any he'd experienced pierced his torso. He dropped, writhed. Maybe he wasn't dying, but he was seriously injured. Severely concussed. He wasn't a doctor, but he suspected his vertebrae had been fractured. His father had chronic back issues, and Will had never been particularly sympathetic toward him.

But now, as he tried to rise, he rued every ungenerous thought he'd ever harbored toward his father. Because this pain was *monstrous*. A level of pain uncalled for. Like some dreadful gypsy curse. He imagined a knobby forefinger pointed at him, a hag's screeching declaration: *You will suffer the torment of a thousand lifetimes, wicked boy. You'll suffer for letting that poor man die in that hole.*

The memory of Peter Bates took hold.

Yes, Will thought. This was where it brought him.

Bates in the hole, starving, alone.

Will on his back. In agony.

Was it any less than he deserved?

He closed his eyes.

Opened them when something pattered on his forehead. His first thought was *blood*. But that didn't make sense. Unless the heavens were raining blood. Not that such an event would surprise him. There was something biblical about Wells's estate. The sign read A PLACE OF MAGIC.

What it really was, it was a place of judgment.

More droplets splashed Will's face. More indignity. Not only was he disabled, he was about to be soaking wet. He ground his teeth, watched the drops of rain tumble from the dishwater sky. Turned his head and noticed, through the now-shiny branches, a grimmer darkness. Storms coming.

He knew he couldn't sit up. Hell, he had trouble doing sit-ups when his back was healthy. He rocked onto his side, managed to get an elbow under him. Forced himself to sitting. The world described a delirious sideways revolution. Shit, the concussion was worse than he'd thought. Did they rate them like tornadoes and earthquakes? If so, this was a Code Red, an F7, a You're-Seriously-Fucked concussion.

Will pushed to his feet. Managed to stand there, miserable, as the rain accelerated.

Lucy and Bryan could be anywhere. Back at the mansion? Deeper in the forest? Frolicking through the meadow or building a goddamned treehouse? Who knew?

Searching for them was a fool's errand. He knew it.

He took a halting step toward Wells's mansion. As he did, he felt a pressure building behind his left eye.

That can't be good, he thought.

Then he heard it. Humming.

Glenn Miller's 'Moonlight Serenade'.

Will scuttled up an incline, and the world whipsawed violently. He staggered, threw out an arm, but this time he couldn't prevent a tumble. He fell uphill, onto his stomach, and as the tune crescendoed, the voice drenched in mockery, Will knew who he'd see if he turned. His fingers sank into mud, the rain pattering faster.

"Thought you were quits with me, didn't you, champ?" Bates said.

Will whimpered, dug his knees into the mud, but he was weak and the world was tilting.

Bates's gruff voice was very close now. "We can meet savagery with love, but do we?" A snort. "Hell no. We vent our hateful impulses. Snap at our loved ones. Shut people out. Turn our backs on friends."

Will collapsed on his belly, his face buried in the crook of his elbow. "You were a murderer."

"I needed love, champ."

"You killed your kids. You tortured them."

Footsteps squelched closer, black work boots circling his body. The legs crouched, the voice right over him. "I needed a grace note, kid. Just one kindhearted gesture in a lifetime of meanness. You ever hear about my upbringing? The kinda things I had done to me?"

Will shook his head.

"Ever had your genitals burned? Ever watch your kid sister get molested knowing you can't do anything about it?"

"Stop."

"I was a monster," Bates said, "but damned if I was born that way."

Will could barely breathe.

"I could kill you quick," Bates said, "but I won't."

He forced himself to gaze into the eyes of the man hunkering before him.

Bates looked perfectly healthy.

"You could've saved me, champ."

The ground around Will began to shift.

"See what it's like to get left behind?" Bates said, and Will realized Bates was rising. The entire forest was rising.

Will threw out his arms too late. The forest wasn't rising, he was falling.

Sinking.

"Let's see how you like it," Bates muttered.

And as the hole sucked him deeper, Will wondered, *Is this the end? Am I really going to die this way?*

He began to scream, to claw at the dirt, but his body kept sinking, and beneath his terrified voice he heard the laughter of Peter Bates.

CHAPTER SIX

When the bedroom door gave way, the top hinge tore loose and the whole thing hung askew like a baby tooth clinging to its last tendril of flesh.

Frozen, Lucy thought. Molly hadn't even lost a tooth yet. Hadn't ridden a bike or gone to kindergarten.

Yet Molly had died, and Lucy had lived.

Until now.

Rain pattered on the window.

Twenty-five years, Lucy thought. *You got twenty-five years you didn't deserve.*

Bryan's eyes glittered in the gloom, his white teeth like freshly cut tombstones. Lucy retreated, terrified she'd bump into her father's corpse, and his puffy purple hands would close around her throat. It's no more than she deserved. A gruesome death. A lonely death. No one would know what became of her.

Something brushed the back of Lucy's arm.

She flailed at the dangling corpse, but when she spun she discovered it was only a baize curtain, yellow with age.

Bryan's big arms enfolded her.

Hissing, she pushed away from him. He didn't hang on, only gusted laughter as she tumbled against the unmade bed.

His eyes flicked to something near her waist. "That's more than I would have expected from you."

She glanced down at the chopping knife in her hand.

Raised it.

"Good girl," he said. He gestured to his ankle, his knife holder. "Wanna see who's better with a blade?"

She cast a quick glance around the bedroom, confirmed what she'd suspected. There was no way out. Unless she leapt through the window, in which case he'd simply walk outside and put her already-broken body out of its suffering.

He misread her look. "You think someone is coming to save you? Your boyfriend maybe?"

"No one's coming," she said.

He stepped nearer. "Well, poor fucking Lucy. Handed everything when you were a teenager."

"Did you murder the others?"

He grinned. Invisible mice scurried over the nape of her neck.

He crept closer, his bulk seeming to fill the room. "You going to use that knife or quit and let me have my way?"

Something in his voice stopped her. She stared at him, a realization slowly dawning. From the beginning there'd been something artificial about Bryan, something forced. "You mean the way Rick did?" she said.

All mirth drained from his face. "Shut up."

Her voice was a husky purr. "The things he did to me, Bryan... the way he made me moan."

His eyes were glittering brown marbles. He'd bunched his fists and begun tapping his upper legs with them. Like a toddler cranking toward a breakdown.

"But never you, Bryan," she said, edging to her right. "Even that first afternoon, my body responded to Rick. Not you. Because he knows who he is. He's authentic. But you...you're trying to be someone else. You're running from yourself."

The corners of his mouth drew down. "You...*bitch*."

Now, she thought. *Do it* now.

She swung the chopper. Bryan's eyes flew wide. He dropped toward the bed. The chopper missed him by inches and whooshed down so hard she was thrown off balance. She stumbled forward, knowing she'd lost her chance at surprising him. Her momentum carried her toward the door. Her feet got tangled and she nearly plunged headlong – a brief image strobed through her head of her impaling herself, the blade chunking into her belly like a warrior committing hari-kari – but she righted herself before she fell, ducked under the broken door. As she thundered down the stairs she heard Bryan give chase, his footfalls like sinister tympani behind her. The kitchen table was unoccupied, the vision of her mom proving to be just that, and then she was grasping the doorknob, a surge of fear washing over her. Had Bryan locked it?

She ripped open the door and burst outside.

Lucy's only hope was to find a hiding place. She still clutched the chopper, so if Bryan discovered her she might be able to make good on the death blow she'd attempted to strike in the bedroom.

Lucy veered into the forest, sprinting wildly. She didn't even glance over her shoulder. What was the point? If Bryan had spotted her, there was nothing she could do.

Ahead the terrain dipped. The decline lent speed to her steps, and it took all her energy to match her body's inertia as she barreled down the hill.

Soon, the forest bottomed out, and she found a trail winding along a creek. If Bryan followed the same path, she'd be in a dire position. But if he didn't track her down here, the ridge would make detection unlikely.

She kept on, the strength in her legs flagging. The rain was frigid on her bare arms. It was chilly, like a freakish fit of winter. She considered crossing the creek. It was a risk, certainly, but so was remaining on Bryan's side of the water. Her teeth chattering as much from fear as the cold front sweeping through the forest, Lucy splashed into the creek at a diagonal, her eyes already scanning the opposite bank for a place to clamber up.

Her foot caught on something. Lucy pitched forward.

The water enveloped her in a freezing blast, its depth disconcertingly deeper than she'd assumed. She opened her eyes underwater to find what had felled her, and when she saw the red coat, the skeins of light brown hair waving like kelp, she began to scream...

...*because the ice under Molly's snow boots was cracking. In a fit of meanness, Lucy had dared her little sister out on the ice. It seemed a minimal risk. Their uncle had taken them fishing here two weeks prior, and because winter hadn't yet gripped the land, Lucy had been able to see the pebbly bottom of the creek. It wasn't more than three feet deep, and Molly was about that height, so even if the ice did fracture and Molly plunged through, all she'd have to do was stand up.*

But even as her sister took her first halting steps onto the ghostly white surface, Lucy knew the dare was stupid, knew she was doing this because *it was stupid. The entire trip had been stupid, her parents promising the*

Eiffel Tower, the Blarney Stone, the Coliseum, when that stuff would only happen after they'd spent an interminable month in Poland, in a boring old farmhouse. They hardly spoke English, and Lucy knew no Polish. Molly griped incessantly, cried often, and found ways to perturb her when Lucy simply wanted to be left alone. If she discovered some interesting object, a painted birdhouse or a doll made of cornhusks, Molly simply had to hold it. And when Lucy implored her parents to intervene on her behalf, the answer was always the same: Can't you let her have her way this once?

This once actually meant every danged time, and Lucy took to locking herself in the upstairs bedroom to get away.

So it was with grim anger that Lucy had exited the farmhouse that winter afternoon, her parents having ordered her to entertain her sister. She hadn't intended to put Molly in peril, but yes, there was a slight undercurrent of meanness in her dare.

Her chin held up, Molly had stepped onto the frozen creek and immediately begun to giggle. The ice was slippery, she informed Lucy, and Lucy, who'd been bored out of her skull, had followed her sister without considering their combined weight.

Soon Lucy was slipping and pinwheeling her arms as Molly brayed laughter. For once Lucy didn't mind because she was laughing too. She finally reached Molly, and in their desire to steady themselves, they grasped each other's forearms, for perhaps the first time since they'd arrived in Poland feeling happy.

The first crack appeared under Lucy's right boot. She tightened, Molly not yet noticing. Lucy didn't move for several seconds. She simply stared at the fissure, hoping it wouldn't lengthen.

Another crack formed, this one larger, directly between the two girls. Molly's laughter ceased, her eyes shooting wide, and somehow they were no longer grasping each other's arms, somehow Lucy had taken a step away. The ice was groaning and Molly was inclining her face to stare at Lucy, all the fear in the universe contained in those liquid brown eyes, her tender age showing in her still-plump cheeks and her babylike mouth.

"Lucy...." she started to say, or maybe that was Lucy's imagination, because the word was lost in the cacophony of snapping ice, a whole section giving way beneath Molly, and lightning bolts zigzagging at Lucy's boots. Her instinct was to spin away, to lurch toward the bank, and from the corner of her eye she discerned a flurry of movement, flailing red arms and gouts of *freezing creek water splashing onto the frost-kissed ice. Molly barely made a sound as the hole swallowed her. Lucy reached out, but her sister was ten feet away, and even if Lucy had been able to graze the gloveless little fingers, the ice under Lucy was a chaotic grid of crisscrossing lines, and though she knew she should be rescuing her little sister, the fear of drowning seized her, the atavistic terror compelling her backward, backward, until she was huddled on the narrow bank, knees drawn in, a quivering fetus girl, and the only sign Molly had been there at all an occasional swirl within the jagged pool of floating ice chunks.*

Lucy was too frightened to form a coherent thought. Thirty seconds passed. A minute. She huddled there, shivering, and told herself it hadn't happened. This was a bad dream, the worst nightmare of her life, and had she known how it would turn out she might have leapt into the freezing hole too, her mother hating her, her father becoming a bloodless wraith…

…and in Roderick Wells's forest the icy creek water rushed into her throat, dragged her under, the bottom of the creek bed dropping away. Below was a sable, watery tomb, and her sister's tiny body, untouched by time, rose through the darkness, the plump cheeks and the smooth brow pale in death, the red-coated arms splayed, the body rising to meet her, and Lucy screamed, but the water clogged her throat. The face of her sister rose to meet her, the eyes open, and though Lucy expected them to be white and pupilless, they were as they always were, Molly's eyes. Kind, hopeful. Molly stared at her, raised a hand, and the tiny fingers caressed Lucy's cheek.

Her dead sister's touch sent a shockwave through her body. Lucy spread her arms, pushed down on the freezing water, and incredibly, she rose a few inches. As the water rushed into her lungs, Lucy thrust her chin up, scissored her legs, and though her body felt inexpressibly heavy, she rose higher. She looked up desperately, her lungs shrinking. She threw her arms down, kicked, and this time her face breached the surface. She thrust against the water, summoned what strength she had, managed a sip of air. She remembered the shallower water, extended a leg, and there, blessedly, she felt rocks underfoot. Her legs buckled, her whole frame wobbly, but she fought against the lethargy. Both feet touched solid ground. Spluttering, gasping, Lucy fell sideways, and when she'd reached a place where it was only knee deep, she jackknifed, retched, the creek water spewing from her mouth like a pestilence. She coughed, wheezed, her throat aflame.

"Who were you talking to?"

Lucy gazed up at Bryan. "Don't make me kill you," she said.

"In the farmhouse," he said as if she hadn't spoken. "And just now. You keep talking to someone and it's only you and me. Why do you keep doing that?"

There was a weird light in Bryan's eyes, the raindrops smaller but more persistent. They stung her flesh, bit like hungry mites.

Bryan waded closer. "Are you doing that to confuse me?" His eyes lowered, came up again. "You dropped your knife. Why do you keep confusing me?"

Lucy gaped stupidly at her hands. She must've lost her grip on the chopper when she was submerged.

"All of you," Bryan muttered. "You're all so damned inscrutable. It's like you have meetings after I go to bed. You plan ways to keep me outside the group."

She looked wildly about. Nowhere to go. "We don't do that, Bryan. We—"

"—want to win the contest, just like I do." Ten feet away. Closing. "You figured you'd eliminate the toughest candidate." Five feet. "But I'm still here."

His hands shot out.

Lucy spun away, but he snagged the back of her shirt. She splashed forward onto her chest. She pushed to her knees, but Bryan smashed down on her. She fought against him, but he weighed so much. God, like a stone column crushing her.

She surged ahead, the rocks underwater goring her knees, but Bryan came with her. Lucy shot an elbow at him, caught him in the shoulder, but he only laughed at her. Lucy strained forward, half spun, and only when he was seizing her by the shoulders did she realize her error. Her face went under.

A cold shroud enveloped her. Bryan was leering down at her, great hands gripping her arms, but between them there were two feet of creek water, and Lucy was choking. But this time there was a massive body on top of her and no way to escape.

She grasped his forearms, her nails harrowing his flesh. Through the muffling barrier of water she heard him cry out. He scuttled over her. A moment too late she realized what he had planned, and then his knees were pinning her shoulders to the rocky creek bottom, his crotch in her face, no chance at all for her to buck free. She was going to die here.

Panic set in. Water rushed into her mouth. She clawed at his hips, but he seemed impervious.

She closed her eyes, a coldness seeping into her limbs. Her fingers scrabbled on Bryan's granite-hard calves, his ankles.

The Bowie knife in its case.

Her eyes shuttered wide. She pushed the snap open.

Fight! a voice in her head screamed.

She'd slid the knife most of the way out before Bryan's hand slapped down at her.

Kill or be killed!

With the last of her strength she whipped the knife up.

Then Bryan's weight was gone, and she rolled onto her knees, thrust her head up. She attempted to inhale, but her system rebelled, the water exploding out of her in a flood. While she knew she was badly exposed, her back to Bryan, she could no more prevent the expulsion of water from her body than she could go back to her childhood and make a different decision on that frozen creek.

Lucy wiped her mouth, stood with the Bowie knife clutched at her side. *End him*, she told herself. *Put him down.*

"...fucking bitch," Bryan was snarling. "I need a doctor...."

Lucy saw he indeed needed a doctor. The knife wound spanned the length of his forearm, beginning at the elbow and terminating just shy of his palm. She remembered hearing somewhere that slitting your wrists was only effective if you went north–south, like this incision. Though Bryan had peeled off his t-shirt and was attempting to tie a tourniquet at his elbow, blood was absolutely gushing out of his wound.

Bryan fumbled with the makeshift tourniquet. "Stupid...cunt..." he muttered. "I can't believe...."

Lucy rose, faced Bryan.

She strode over to him, raised the Bowie knife.

Take him down!

Bryan glanced at her, comprehension dawning, but Lucy didn't give him time to react. She swung the knife in a looping stroke, the blade parting the skin of his throat. A necklace of crimson rills streamed down his chest. He opened his mouth, issued a gargling cough. He pawed at his throat, his eyes opening and shutting.

Finish it!

She gripped the Bowie knife with both hands and plunged the blade into his chest.

His blood-slimed fingers fell on her wrists. She jerked the knife from his chest, heard a lung whistling. Just as she was about to stab him again, he sank to his knees, coughed out a splat of blood, which hit the water and separated in snot-like streamers.

His face was very pale, the wound in his throat deep. It yawned open, reminding her of fish gills, purple and raw. Unmoved, Lucy gripped the knife and waited for him to spring one last surprise. She'd been conditioned by movie villains to expect it.

Instead, he rolled sideways and went under, surfacing only when the current had taken him several yards down. She walked after him for a time, but his face remained under. Dead for sure.

Lucy turned. She had to check on Will.

And on the heels of that, she thought of Rick. Had he really left the competition without telling her?

No, she thought, wading toward the shore. He wouldn't have left without saying goodbye, especially not after last night.

She had to find him. If he was still alive.

Wiping the bloody knife on the hip of her shorts, Lucy emerged from the creek.

CHAPTER SEVEN

Will thought, *Bates was a monster.*

The cold, implacable voice of truth: *That's not why you left him there.*

Will: *He killed his kids.*

Truth: *Leaving Bates in that hole was the act of a mean little bastard. You'd been bullied by your brother and your father and damned near every kid in elementary school, and you seized your chance to spew that meanness back out.*

Will: *Did he deserve it?*

Truth: *Deserving or not, you took a* life.

Will: *Okay, yes! I took a life! I was young and stupid and full of anger. I should have called the police. I should have done it all differently, and I'm sorry.*

Truth: (silence)

Will: *But I don't deserve to die now, do I? Or is God or fate or nature or chaos or whatever is in control just as cruel as I was? Or does mercy play a role somewhere?*

"Will?"

He froze. The voice had not been in his head. It had been....

"If you can hear me, speak up."

Lucy, he thought.

He opened his lips to answer, but soil seeped into the corners of his mouth. Will spluttered, made to push it away, but his hands were buried.

At once he remembered where he was. The slow landslide had dragged him down, and at some point he'd lost consciousness. He had no idea how far underground he'd ended up, but it couldn't have been too far because he was still able to make out Lucy's words. She called to him.

With a grunt, he thrust his shoulders against the dirt. *Buried alive,* he thought, then tried to unthink the words, but as the dirt sifted over his cheeks, tiny clods of it pattering on his knuckles, they repeated an unholy refrain: *buried alive, buried alive, buried alive*—

"NO!" he bellowed.

Lucy cried out. She'd heard him! But it didn't mean a thing if she didn't see him too. He thrashed in the dirt, refusing to die this way. His chin upthrust, he worked his shoulders around, loosened the soil. He'd sinned badly in allowing Bates to starve, but dammit, this wasn't poetic justice, it wasn't karma, it was fucking overkill, and he refused to succumb to it. His injured back howled, yet the will to live was greater, the need to *breathe*....

His face emerged from the soil and he sucked in a great heave of air.

Lucy gasped, "Will! Oh my God!"

It scarcely registered. All he could think about was the rain peppering his face, the delicious oxygen, and as he wriggled his way out of the soil, he drank in all the fragrances of the forest. The spruce trees and the fecund soil and the rain, and with a groan he jerked one arm free and then the other.

"Oh God, Will," Lucy said, hands linking under his arms and hauling him up, "what happened to you? How did you...."

She never finished, or if she did Will didn't hear it. All he could hear was the full-throated chorus of raindrops showering the forest. He grimaced at the intense spinal pain but managed to extricate his shoes from the hole and flop onto his back. He was alive. Broken, maybe, but alive.

Then, a terrible thought intruded.

"Where's Bryan?"

Her face went hard. "Floating."

He took in her bedraggled appearance. Blood streaks on her face and throat. "You killed him?"

She smiled wanly. "He messed with the wrong failure."

"We're all failures." He sat up, hissed in pain. "Hell."

"You can wait here."

"And what?" he said, making it to his knees with an effort. "Sit here until the next horror arrives? Miss Lafitte or Rick's lunatic police chief—"

"Or Wells."

He glanced up at her.

"Wells is the key," she said. "It starts and ends with him."

Will planted his palms on the soil, got slowly to his feet. Even with Lucy supporting him, it took an effort. "It's a good thing I never played football. One hit and I'm like a decrepit old man."

"He was a freight train. We didn't see him coming."

Will massaged his lower back. "What's your plan?"

"Fight them. Try not to get killed."

He took in her tangled wet hair, her torn, bloodstained clothing. She'd never looked smaller to him. Or tougher.

They began to move. In Will's weakened state they made bad time, but after a while the forest began to thin, and the emerald of the meadow grass started to peek through.

"I think I have a way to beat Wells," he said, and as he spoke the words, he realized they were true. He glanced at her. "You gonna look for Rick?"

She nodded.

"What about Miss Lafitte?" he asked.

Lucy held up the Bowie knife. "Bryan kept this sharp."

"It is a wicked-looking thing."

Lucy grinned. "Am I wicked-looking?"

"You look like a drowned muskrat."

He joined her in laughter, though it hurt like hell.

They reached the edge of the forest, gazed up at the rainswept mansion.

"I'm going inside," Will said.

"To your room?"

"Uh-uh," he said, beginning the slow, painful climb. "To Sherilyn's."

CHAPTER EIGHT

They climbed the hill in silence. Drawing nearer, Lucy noted how different the exterior of the mansion now appeared. No missing slate shingles, no water stains on the stone and brick façade. The broken windows had been replaced, the shutters no longer aslant. Despite its age, the house looked like it could have been built this spring.

Restored, she thought. *Just like Wells.*

They reached the porch.

Will said, "I'll go in first."

Lucy just gave him a look.

He sighed. "Okay, you go. But what'll you do if—"

"This knife took care of Bryan."

"Yeah, but Bryan was—"

"—human? Barely." She drew in a shuddering breath. "We have to kill them before they kill us."

Will nodded at the immense doors. "Miss Lafitte could be on the other side right now. Or Wilson."

Or Wells, she thought.

"Hey, Lucy…" Will started, but she was already reaching for the door. "What are you doing?"

She opened the door.

Nothing attacked them.

She went in. "If I find Rick, we'll come get you."

"Then what?"

"We leave together. Winning the contest doesn't mean a damn thing now. We're good enough writers to make it without him."

He gave her a smile that made her wish they were anywhere but here, just sitting together and having a drink. She imagined him at a Cubs game, joking with his buddies.

"We can do this," she said. "We can beat them."

He nodded. "Be safe."

"Don't die," she said, and moved toward the back hallway.

CHAPTER NINE

As he hobbled up the stairs, Will thought of Peter Straub's *Ghost Story*. So many of his favorite books featured writers and their tales, fictional characters that came alive and tried to harm their creators.

Somehow, Roderick Wells had tapped into that potential in a way no other writer had, in a way no sane person would believe.

Will didn't know if it was Wells or his land, but the power here was real. More importantly, it was transferable.

Corrina Bowen had created the murderous maid.

Rick Forrester had coaxed Police Chief John Anderson to life.

The sensual abomination Will had glimpsed on the shore…yes, even Will had begun to create something.

But it was none of these he was interested in now.

Will started down the second-floor hallway.

The estate was vast. Maybe it was growing. Maybe it fed on their words, expanding and changing and forming new worlds.

Maybe none of them would escape.

Will reached his room, kept moving.

Maybe the others had created villains as well, but he could only focus on the ones he knew. What did they have in common?

Malice. Unpredictability.

Violence.

But what if one of their stories was coming to pass in a different way? What if one tale was playing out without any of them realizing it?

He reached Sherilyn's door.

Unlocked. Thank God. He entered the room, locked the door.

He performed a slow scan of the bedroom, thinking, *Is this the moment? Will this decide all our fates?* It sounded melodramatic, but he suspected it was near the truth.

Wells had been growing younger. And the mansion had been, what? Healing? Rejuvenating?

Insane.

But true.

He made his way to the writing table, bent to slide out the drawers.

The key, Will believed, was the stained-glass mosaic in the chapel. He thought of Wells garbed in armor, his golden sword aloft, the keen blade flashing as it commanded the serpents. Like the eyes of the fanged vipers bearing down on the villagers, Wells's eyes had shone with a perverse light, a ruthless joy that reveled in the massacre.

Had Sherilyn captured the true Roderick Wells in her fairy tale?

If so, he had to find her story. *The Magic King* was the key to everything.

The desk drawers were empty, the only items within a few pencils and a tube of magenta lipstick.

The rain tapped the windowpanes, the ticking of the grandfather clock the only other sound in the bedroom.

He swiveled his head, stared at the clock.

As he approached, he remembered something his father had once said about this type of clock. Some had full bonnets, some didn't. Some simply had faces and were flat in back, and Sherilyn was tall....

Will reached up and probed the top of the grandfather clock. His fingers rasped against the edge of a notebook. He seized it and hobbled over to the desk. Reached into the middle drawer and found a pencil. He opened to the middle of the notebook, skimmed until he got the sense of the story. He remembered the scene in which the main character met the peasant boy. The girl in the story, she could have been Sherilyn or Lucy or neither of them.

But the peasant boy...the one who would challenge the Magic King...Will had believed all along that the boy was Rick, and judging from the way Sherilyn had looked at Rick on the night of her reading, she'd felt the same way.

Will tried to control his galloping heart. He didn't think he could match Sherilyn's talent.

But he could remain true to her vision. Yes, he thought that was something he could do. Sherilyn had written a fantastic opening, but she hadn't been given time to finish it. Will didn't have much time either. He suspected Wells and his emissaries were preparing their onslaught. There was no way Will could withstand the ferocious entities Wells would unleash.

He could, however, try to vanquish Wells in *The Magic King*. It was a small chance, but in his weakened state, it was all he could do.

He finished reading the last chapter Sherilyn had written. Richard, the peasant boy, was locked in the dungeon. Will had to find a way to save the boy, to overthrow the king, to bring his reign of terror to an end.

Will sat in the dimness of the dead woman's room, let his mind drift to a magical realm where a vicious tyrant held sway.

The same way Roderick Wells ruled this estate. Could Will defeat him in these pages?

He raised his pencil, took a breath, and began to write.

CHAPTER TEN

Every molecule cried out to slow down, to exercise caution, but an even deeper layer of her psyche understood that time was short, that if Rick was in the basement, and if he was still alive, he'd be in terrible danger.

Creeping along the back hallway, her thoughts shifted to Wells. What upset her most was how childlike her fear of him was, how superstitious. After all, she hadn't seen him hurt *anyone*. Or, for that matter, perform any nefarious deed.

Yet there were reasons to fear him.

Not the least of which was the way he'd grown younger.

Yes, she thought. Wells was a psychic parasite, a demon of flesh and blood. Most of all....

He's a vampire.

Lucy froze six feet from the basement door. It was the first time the word had popped into her head, but now that it was there it would not be displaced. She couldn't think of Wells as a fanged bloodsucker with a garlic allergy. But the sort of creature who feeds on others, who through canniness and willpower can survive epochs...yes, she could imagine Wells as that sort of being.

Yet what flickered through her head as she compelled herself forward was a scene from Stephen King's *'Salem's Lot*, which featured one of the scariest scenes she'd ever read. The protagonist – *A writer! What a lovely coincidence!* – venturing into the basement of a creepy old house to kill the king vampire.

Lucy clamped down on the thought. Granted, she had every reason to be afraid; in the past hour, she'd witnessed things that weren't possible, been hunted and nearly murdered by a psychopath.

Not to mention committing murder herself.

But any reason not to descend those basement steps was a cowardly reason, a retelling of her abandonment of Molly to the hungry ice.

Lucy had to go down.

She grabbed the knob, twisted it open, and flicked the light switch.

The illumination seemed weaker than ever. Several steps down, her doubt began to grow. Why, she wondered, would Rick have chosen to descend these steps?

She decided there were two reasons:

One, he'd been drawn down here before. Curiosity, fear, and half a dozen subtler emotions had been stirred by this dank, eerie place.

Two, he might not have had a choice.

This second possibility deepened the chill in her bones, made it harder to step from the wooden risers into the pool of shadows at the base of the stairs.

The pull string was, if she remembered correctly, fifteen feet or so from the steps. She thought she could see it, but that might have been just a downhanging cobweb. Lucy waded into the murk.

Would she reach for the string only to encounter her father's dangling corpse?

She took the last few steps in a rush and groped for the string.

Found it. Yanked.

Sucked in breath as the bulb washed the basement with light.

But not *enough* light, she realized.

She heard a weak thumping from her left.

She honed in on a single steel door. And heard the sound clearly.

Someone was screaming in there.

CHAPTER ELEVEN

Rick's shrieks echoed through the door.

Lucy grabbed the handle, hauled up on it. Steel ground on steel, the sound enough to make her teeth chatter, but the door came loose. She flung it open, beheld what lay within, and felt her body go limp.

Rick was half-cocooned in a dingy white web, which issued from the wall in quivering tendrils. His body had been forced into the wall, his torso and arms fixed in place by the undulating surface, leaving only the feet to drum on the ground.

It was the sight of Rick's face that got her moving. Or rather the gossamer threads crawling over Rick's cheeks, the strands grafting themselves to his flesh, and the livid marks there, like the tendrils were feeding on Rick's body.

She went for his head, which was almost entirely encased in the horrid white webwork. The tendrils were swarming over his lips, slithering greedily toward his tongue.

Lucy raked her fingernails down the side of his head, rending the strands easily, and then she was at it with both hands, heedless of the way the wall began to shriek, unmindful of the hissing sound the tendrils made as they shot toward her. She brought out the Bowie knife, began to slash at the tendrils cocooning his torso. She was working on his arms when she realized the tendrils had closed over one of her ankles. Grunting, she kicked to sever the strands. Rick joined her in freeing himself.

They both fought, Lucy slashing at the skeins with the knife, Rick jerking his left arm loose and bucking against the hammock of tendrils.

When Rick was free, they tumbled back and landed in the open doorway. They scrambled away from the hungry ridges and didn't stop until they were directly under the yellow bulb in the main room.

She inspected his face. There were angry red splotches on his skin, but it didn't appear as though the flesh had been pierced or corroded.

Lucy cast a look around the shadowy basement. "Will's upstairs," she said. "Let's get him and go."

"The forest goes on forever."

Lucy thought of the farmhouse, her father's bloated corpse.

"Where then?" she asked.

He leaned against her. "I think those things…they siphon the energy.…"

Lucy cast a fearful glance over her shoulder. "Rick," she pleaded, "we have to—"

"Wells is in the tower," Rick said. "The keep."

"Can't we just, you know, get the hell out of here?"

"I don't think it's possible," Rick said. "I think we have to kill Wells."

"How can you.…"

But the rest died in her throat when she beheld the open doorways.

Ghostly white strands protruded from several of them, floating, yearning, creeping nearer.

The house was alive.

I've made it stronger, she thought. *In killing Bryan, I somehow fed it.*

She turned away and peered through the other doorways. They were crammed with bodies.

Marek Sokolov.

Tommy Marston.

Evan Laydon.

Anna Holloway.

Elaine Kovalchyk.

Sherilyn Jackson.

Staring at their nude, undulating corpses, Lucy could scarcely breathe. Marek's body lay imprinted in the rippling wall at a weird angle, his midsection completely sunken in, the edges of his limbs and shoulders eaten away by the house.

He was the first killed, Lucy thought. *That's why his body is so desecrated.*

By contrast, Anna's body appeared pale but preserved. Only the expression of frozen terror on her face, her missing fingers, and the livid bite marks dotting her flesh indicated she was anything but a healthy young woman.

The worst by far was Tommy. In life he'd been arrogant, too handsome for his own good.

In death he was scarcely recognizable.

Except for a few patches here and there, the bones were denuded, his fleshless musculature reminding her of those grisly renderings in biology textbooks. His exposed teeth resembled some comic book villain, his lidless eyes unnaturally large. She only recognized him because of his curly brown hair, which was matted with blood and undulating along with the rest of his carcass.

"*Look out!*" Rick gasped.

She spun in time to see him smashing away a webwork of strands, which had nearly claimed Lucy.

Her flesh crawling, she joined Rick in ripping the pale skeins.

"Let's move," he said. "This is a deathtrap."

They reached the top of the steps and burst into the hallway.

CHAPTER TWELVE

…and with a wicked grin, the king slashed down at her with his sword.

Will reread the paragraph he'd just written, took a deep breath. Anna, the protagonist, had just saved Richard from the castle's hellish dungeon. Now Anna and Richard were battling the Magic King in the tallest tower….

She felt the bite of the blade on her shoulder, dropped to her knees. The king's grin became triumphant. He surged forward, his sword poised for the killing blow.

A wave of dizziness swam over Will, his vision darkening. The pain in his back was growing more acute by the minute.

Concentrate, he told himself. *Concentrate and finish the tale.*

Blood dripping from a score of wounds, Richard lunged at the king, the sharp knife aiming for the weak point in the royal armor. The king's eyes widened as the blade darted nearer, and though his reflexes were astounding, his surprise was—

"Too slow," a voice behind Will said.

Will spun in his chair, and though the movement sent a squalling pain through his back, his shock eclipsed everything.

Wilson stood in the center of the room, a beatific smile on his face.

"Did you truly believe you could rush this?"

Think, Will told himself. *Think.*

Wilson had never looked more imposing. The man's hair had been loosed of its accustomed ponytail, and that, combined with his broad shoulders, made him appear leonine.

"This is the end, Mr. Church."

Will knew he should mount some sort of defense. But Wilson's sudden appearance, the expression of infinite wisdom on the man's face, the nasty pain ratcheting higher in Will's body…all of it conspired to undo him.

"You have failed," Wilson said.

"Go to hell."

"Say it with *feeling*, Mr. Church!" Wilson commanded. "You returned to the mansion to fight, did you not? Why tremble as your end draws near?"

Will glanced at his pages.

"The notion was a sound one," Wilson said. "Take the story based on this retreat and use it to assassinate your host." Wilson stepped nearer. "The truth is, I don't know what would've happen had you killed Roderick in this fairy tale. No one's attempted it before. And that, though I'm loath to admit it, is a credit to you, Mr. Church."

Will stared at the pages, his vision blurring.

Wilson stepped nearer. "Though you lasted longer than I ever would have believed, I'm sorry to say that your tragic flaw will be your undoing."

Will frowned.

Wilson uttered a breathless laugh. "You still don't know, do you? My dear boy, it's the misuse of *time*. Don't you know that all stress, all anxiety, can be traced to a lack of time?"

Wilson towered over him. "You've never appreciated it. Your mind has always stewed in the past or fretted about the future. Which is precisely why you squander the present." Wilson bent at the waist, hands clutching his knees. "Did you really believe you could finish a novel in a few minutes? It took Miss Jackson days to reach this point. How did you think you'd finish it?"

Will opened his mouth, but Wilson interrupted, "By *cheating*. You thought you'd skulk up here like some treacherous jackal and undo Mr. Wells with your woeful scribblings."

A thought dawned in Will's head, one so obvious he couldn't believe he hadn't arrived at it earlier. "You had to stop me," he said. "Why else would you be here?"

"Mr. Wells deemed it necessary."

"He knew I'd figured out—"

"Nothing, Mr. Church. You've figured out nothing, learned nothing."

Will gripped the pencil tighter.

"And now," Wilson said, reaching for him, "you're out of time."

Will swung the pencil at Wilson's face, but Wilson snagged his wrist, squeezed.

Above the cracking sounds, he heard Wilson growl at his ear. "Have you forgotten, Mr. Church? I *see*. I *know*."

Will twisted in his seat. "Let go of me."

"Let go of you?" A wintry smile. "You're like an idiot in a Faulkner novel, spouting revelatory dialogue without realizing it."

"Fuck you," Will moaned, sinking to his knees.

"More profundity!" Wilson crowed.

Will glanced about for the pencil, but it had rolled under the bed.

Wilson drove him to the floor, his mad face drifting nearer. "'Let me go,' you say. Don't you realize how selfish you are? Everyone considered you a good person, but at heart, you're an abandoner."

"*Didn't…abandon…my friends.*"

"Have you saved anyone?" A rough shake of Will's wrist. "Good intentions mean nothing."

"Why did you stop me then?"

A pause, Wilson's face tightening. "What?"

Will glared up at the man. "Why did you stop me? I was at the climactic moment—"

"Ungainly drivel."

"—and the peasant was getting ready to strike the king down—"

"'Smite', you dolt. It should have read 'smite'."

"—but you weren't writing it," he said. And as he stared into Wilson's bitter face, the thought revealed itself to Will, as lucid and brilliant as a spotlighted marquee. "You're jealous of me."

Wilson snorted. "Of all the writers Mr. Wells has entertained—"

"You can't write," Will said. "You can't create."

"—to believe I would envy you, the indolent, passive—"

"*The Siren and the Specter*," Will said. "You know it's a good book, maybe even a great one."

"I know no such—"

"And you know you could never create something like it because you're only what Wells allows you to be."

Wilson's upper lip twisted in a snarl. "Silence."

"An errand boy. A lapdog."

"Silence!"

"You'll never do anything worthwhile because Wells holds you prisoner."

Wilson clutched the front of Will's shirt. "I am in every college in the world! I am better known—"

"Paper," Will answered. "You're only known on paper. Even when they discuss you, they do it in the abstract, studying you like a rock, reading you through different lenses—"

"I'll kill you," Wilson spat.

"Marxist, feminist, postmodernist—"

Wilson shook him.

"—at the whim of undergrads—"

Wilson slapped him.

"—but you'll never be real."

Wilson's hands closed over Will's throat.

"*WILSON!*" a woman shouted.

Wilson's grip loosened. Will gazed up into the man's outraged face, the eyes darting in impotent rage.

"Roderick needs you to bring Mr. Church now," Amanda Wells said.

Will looked up at her, remembered the tapestry on the third floor. If she really was the woman in 'Incident on a Paris Rooftop', she'd never sanction this sort of depravity. Will mentally implored her to look at him, but her gaze remained fixed on Wilson.

"Bring him to the keep," she said.

The snarl still fixed on his face, Wilson released him and stood up shakily. "Get up," he muttered. "I'm going to enjoy your death."

CHAPTER THIRTEEN

When they entered Sherilyn's room and found the overturned chair, Rick didn't hesitate. "We have to go to the keep."

Lucy raised her eyebrows in question.

"Come on," Rick said, leading Lucy toward the staircase. "Everything points toward the keep. Wells writes in the tower, the ceiling is covered with paintings...I think it's the psychic center of the house."

They moved down the hallway. Rick's body throbbed from the welts and lacerations. He attempted to block out the pain, not because of its intensity, but because of its associations. His skin still crawled from the sucking, gnawing ridges. He had no idea what sort of creature had been feeding on him in that lightless pit, and every time his thoughts tended in that direction, he mentally fled.

How large was the creature?

How far did it go on?

What in the holy fuck was it?

"You sure this is the way?" Lucy asked.

"This is how Wells took us last night. There's a door tucked in the back corner of the library."

Lucy watched him. "You all right?"

"Considering I just got the full body treatment from the world's largest leech."

She shivered. Rick didn't blame her. He couldn't stop shivering either.

They paused outside the library door.

"Have you noticed how dark it is?" Lucy glanced over her shoulder. "It's the middle of the day, but it's like there's an eclipse on."

"How—"

"The house is stronger now," she said. "I think it wants us dead."

"Let's go in. I stand still too long, I start to feel those ridges on my skin. Like a toothless old witch chewing on me with whiskery gums."

"*God.*" Her face crumpled in a look of terror and disgust.

He twisted the knob, pushed it open.

Even at a distance of more than thirty feet, the heat plowing out of the sooty stone fireplace was blistering. Yet the library had never appeared darker. The bookcases, lamps, and chairs were mere shadows in the gloom.

They advanced into the room, by tacit agreement keeping as far away from the shadow-steeped bookcases as possible. Rick had begun to sweat.

"You ever think," Lucy said, her voice hushed, "we might be playing into Wells's plan?"

"If his plan is to dehydrate me."

"Should we—"

He didn't see the cleaver until it swept down.

Lucy reacted first. She thrust him out of the way. The cleaver whistled past and severed the tip of her middle finger.

Stumbling forward, Rick watched Miss Lafitte follow through with her swing, heard Lucy yelp and grasp one hand with the other. The firelight was strong enough he could glimpse the damaged finger, the blood spurting out of it.

The crazed maid had been hiding in the shadows and was already gathering for another attack. The maid raised the cleaver and flew at Lucy again.

Lucy retreated, and though Rick saw the handle of the Bowie knife still protruding from Lucy's hip pocket, he could see she was too focused on stemming the blood flow from her injured finger to fight back.

His eyes had adjusted to the firelight. He seized the back of a wooden chair, rushed toward the maid, chair raised high. He'd brain the maniacal bitch with it.

But Miss Lafitte was too sly. She ducked just as the chair whooshed toward her. Rick was thrown off balance and ended up on his knees. She swung the cleaver in a deadly arc. Rick dodged it. The blade chunked into the wooden seat of the chair.

The maid shrieked in fury.

Her body arched over Rick, she made to extricate the cleaver. Rick jacked an elbow into her gut. The maid *oomph*ed and doubled over; Rick was calculating his next move when she roared in pain and wheeled around.

Lucy had remembered the Bowie knife. Blood sluiced from Miss Lafitte's flayed shoulder.

The maid lunged at Lucy, swiped at her with sharp fingernails. Lucy sucked in breath, twin stripes of blood forming at the top of her chest.

Goddammit, Rick thought. He strode toward Miss Lafitte and gripped her waist from behind. Miss Lafitte began to twist in his grip, but before she could carve him up with those wicked nails, he pivoted and hurled her into the hearth, the blaze lighting up the whole room and throwing out a cough of heat so intense Rick suspected his eyebrows had been singed. Judging from her lack of a scream, the maid had been knocked unconscious before burning alive. Better for her, probably, but Rick didn't give a shit. He had to make sure Lucy didn't lose more blood.

He glanced around in confusion.

No sign of Lucy.

She'd been beside him a moment ago, and now....

He heard the sounds of a struggle. Traced them to the farthest reaches of the library. Saw the shadows roiling back there, someone dragging someone else, a hand clamped over the person's face.

Wells and Lucy.

"No!" Rick yelled and started to run.

The door to the tower clanged shut. Rick charged into the shadows, found the door, but it wouldn't give. He banged on it, bellowed at Wells to let him in.

But Lucy was gone.

CHAPTER FOURTEEN

She's dead, he thought. *You'll never get her back.*

Rick stood before the unyielding door to the keep, breath heaving, a salty, acrid odor tingling his nostrils. After a moment he realized what it was.

Miss Lafitte's burning flesh.

He turned, hurried back through the library. On the way past the fireplace, he spotted Lafitte's fire-wrapped corpse, glimpsed the bacon smoke skirling out of the hearth. Though the maid's death was gruesome, it did imbue him with a species of hope.

If Lafitte could be killed, Wilson could too.

And Wells?

Rick jerked open the library door, hustled through the foyer, and was moving toward the workshop when a scream from above froze him where he stood.

Will.

He paused, mind racing. Just because Wells had never shown them an alternate entrance into the tower, didn't mean there wasn't one.

Go for the axe now, chop down the library door.

Another scream, this one belonging to Lucy.

Rick charged up the steps. Wells had taken Lucy and Will to the tower. If Rick played this right, he might be able to save both of them.

He reached the third floor and skidded to a halt. He heard Will's and Lucy's voices again, but they weren't coming from his left, from where he knew the tower to be. They echoed from his right.

Rick sprinted that way. He didn't know how or why Wells had smuggled Lucy down this hallway, but he could hear her now, crying softly for help.

Wells is tricking you!

He ignored the thought, hastened down the corridor. He neared the source of the sounds, realized they were issuing from a room Lucy had shown him on one of their walks.

The chapel.

He stopped outside the door, listened.

Heard a woman weeping softly.

He ripped open the door and rushed inside. Spotted the figure in the front pew. The hanging lamps cast a spectral orange glow, spotlighted the stained-glass mosaic of the medieval Wells.

Rick moved deeper into the chapel. It wasn't until he rounded the pew and gazed down at the stooped figure that he realized it was his mother. Her sobbing shoulders froze. She removed her hands from her face and peered up at him.

Her features were emaciated. Purple crescent moons cupped her eyes. Yet her anguished expression was far more lucid than it had been the last time he'd seen her.

"Why did you leave me, Ricky?"

The tide of grief was instantaneous. It choked him. He opened his mouth to answer but couldn't.

"They were mean to me, Ricky. They snapped at me when I'd ask about you. They told me you didn't care anymore."

He swallowed. "It's not true."

"That's why people take their loved ones to Memory Walk," she said. "To forget about them."

"I visited you."

"Almost never, Ricky. You figured I was too far gone to notice." She leaned forward, the drooping eyelids terrible, accusing. "But I did."

"Mom, I...." A tear slipped down his cheek. "I had to make a life."

"I *gave* you life."

His chest hitched. "You know I loved you. I still do."

"You love *yourself*. After what happened with Phil—"

"Please don't."

"And that awful man who followed me..."

Rick's pulse began to race, a bright blade of fear scything through his grief.

"...staring at me from the shadows," she said, her voice frantic.

"I begged them to turn on the lights, but they said no one sleeps with the lights on." She clamped down on his wrist with appalling strength. "I begged them, Ricky, but they just laughed at me. The crazy woman at the end of the hallway." The gnarled fingers squeezed. "I *needed* you."

"Mom," Rick pleaded.

"I was relieved when he went away," she said, "but deep down I knew he was going after you. But *then*," she said, a nasty smile twisting her mouth, "I realized you were just doing what you'd learned."

Rick yanked his arm away.

"It's what we do, Ricky!" she said, laughing. "We save our own hides, don't we? We killed your stepfather, we let Raymond Eddy die."

Rick buried his fingers in his hair.

"You were carrying on the family tradition."

"Mom, please—"

"'*Mom, please*,'" she mimicked. "If we'd only told the truth, maybe we would've gotten off. Maybe we wouldn't have lost our souls."

Rick was moving away when a voice sounded from the altar. "Blind are the wicked, for their sins grow scales over their eyes."

All the strength left Rick's body. He turned and regarded Police Chief John Anderson, who leaned on the lectern, a mountain made flesh, his sunglasses glinting in the orange light.

"That's not scripture, by the way," Anderson said. "Just a fact you never learned."

"Where is she?" Rick asked.

"Your mama? I thought you didn't give a damn—"

"Lucy."

"Ah," Anderson said, grinning. "Your new piece of tail."

Rick took a step forward. "I control you."

"Control me? Boy, you can barely control your own bladder." The chief moved around the lectern. "I see how scared you are."

Anderson approached, his massive body moving with a sinuous fluidity.

Why couldn't you have made him smaller? a sardonic voice asked. Or given him some sort of handicap?

Because, Rick thought, *that would have cheated the story*. He had to be dangerous. Otherwise, it wouldn't be scary.

Mission accomplished, the sardonic voice said. *You couldn't be more overmatched. Have to go back to David and Goliath to find a disparity this severe.*

"You writers," Anderson said, "you're all so danged perceptive about other people. But when it comes to yourselves, you're as clueless as the rest of us. You're so busy looking at the world that you never bother to look inside yourself."

"I'm going to get Lucy."

"Just what I'd expect you to say." The chief advanced, and with a jolt Rick realized his mother was no longer sitting in the church pew.

Anderson nodded. "Frightened little babe. Don't you know you can't run from me?"

"I need you to help me get Lucy back."

"The fuck you think I am, boy? A genie?"

"You're in my story," Rick said. "You're part of that world."

"I'm in *every* world."

The chief was drawing nearer, only fifteen feet away. Rick glanced toward the altar, scouring the area for something with which to defend himself.

"We don't have much time, so I'm gonna lay it out for you." Anderson stepped closer. "There's power in stories. Even though you writers are a bunch of self-important pussies, I gotta admit, the imagination is an awesome, terrible force. But like any power, it carries the potential to spin out of control."

"Don't come any closer," Rick warned.

Anderson kept coming.

"Last warning," Rick said, but even to his own ears his voice lacked conviction.

"Tell me this," Anderson said, almost upon him now. "That night Raymond attacked your fiancée, why didn't you help her?"

The old hollowness spread through him, the unbearable self-loathing.

"I'll tell you why. You were happy it wasn't you."

"That's not true...."

"Come on, boy. You're about to die. Why not admit what you are?"

Heat licked the base of Rick's neck. "No."

"Raymond Eddy, your mama...."

"Fuck you."

"Your fiancé...the other writers...."

Rick's fists squeezed white.

"...most of all that little quim Lucy."

"You son of a bitch."

"Can't write for shit yourself," Anderson said. "At least you got the chance to bang a real author."

Rick raised his fists.

Anderson grinned. "Do it, boy. Show me what you got."

Rick did.

CHAPTER FIFTEEN

Lucy thrashed in Wells's grip all the way up the winding stone staircase, but no matter how she elbowed his shoulders or kicked his shins, he wouldn't relinquish his hold. She took to lashing at him with her fingernails, but he was too powerful. When they reached the main tower room, he heaved her through the air, and Lucy crashed down painfully on her side.

She peered up at him from where she lay.

He smiled. "I concede that I'm vain. The latter stages of the cycle are always disagreeable for me. My bones aching, my joints sore. Even rising from a chair is difficult. But now—" he executed a quick tap dance and a spin, "—I am nimble again. Whole. The ravages of age have fallen away."

He strolled over to a stone pedestal, rolled down the cuffs of his white shirt and splashed water over his face. She'd sliced his left cheek with her fingernails. "I do have to admit you're a fighter," he said.

"Where's Rick?"

Wells eyed her speculatively. "Did you suspect? The reverse aging, I mean?"

"Yes."

"But you told yourself it was ludicrous."

Lucy didn't answer.

"What do you think?" he asked. He gestured toward his body, which not only moved with a sinuous vitality, but was tight with muscle. Several buttons of his white shirt were undone, revealing upper pectoral muscles that were chiseled and tan. His forearms were striated, the muscles there writhing each time he moved. "Do you find me attractive, Miss Still?"

"Where is he?"

"Your Mr. Forrester rather pales in comparison."

"Where is Rick?" she demanded.

Wells eyed her a moment longer. "Bring him, Wilson."

Wilson emerged from the shadows dragging a bound figure.

Lucy experienced a leap of hope. Was Rick still alive?

Then she discerned the curly hair, the protuberant belly.

Will.

He wasn't a small man, but Wilson hurled him forward like a sack of laundry. Wilson reached down, tore away a strip of duct tape from Will's mouth. Will yelped in pain and covered his mouth with hands bound at the wrists. Lucy suspected a portion of Will's goatee had been removed when the tape came off, and judging from the way he was uttering obscenities, perhaps a goodly bit of skin had too.

Wells was smiling down at Will. "I don't believe the duct tape was necessary, Mr. Church, but you seem to have incurred Wilson's ire. Things seldom go well for people who do that."

"He wants out from under you," Will said.

"Divide and conquer, Mr. Church?"

"I'll divide his skull," Wilson snarled.

Wells stilled his servant with an upraised palm. "No need, Wilson. Assault is beneath you."

Judging from his expression, Wilson didn't look as though torturing and vivisecting Will was beneath him.

Wells turned to Lucy. "Mr. Forrester is in the chapel."

"Is he—"

"He's in the process of dying."

She felt like she'd been slugged in the gut.

Wells began to pace. He moved with the confidence and power of a professional athlete. "That leaves the two of you, Miss Still. And since your narrative has developed to a greater extent, the choice will be yours."

"What do you mean, 'to a greater extent'?"

Wells only looked at her with eyebrows raised. "You've created something marvelous, Miss Still. Something…electrifying."

Lucy began to tremble. "He's not real."

"Yes he is," Will said quietly. When Lucy looked at him, he said, "I haven't seen your character. But I did see my Siren."

"Half-formed," Wilson put in, "like the rest of your novel."

Wells said, "Be charitable, Wilson. Mr. Church has created something interesting. Only time will tell whether or not the Siren will wreak havoc upon the world."

Lucy leaned forward, a horrific thought dawning.

Wells nodded. "Yes, Miss Still. The Fred Astaire Killer has already gone forth. Has perhaps claimed a victim already."

Lucy's voice was barely a whisper. "It's impossible."

Wells raised his chin. "Your creation is as skillful as he is amoral. He will kill with the precision of a surgeon."

Will's voice was hollow. "You're saying we've created murderers?"

"Not all of you, Mr. Church. Only the ones with vivid imaginations."

"Marek failed to create anything of substance," Wilson said.

"Quite true," Wells said, pacing again. "The same for Ms. Kovalchyk."

"Sherilyn—" Lucy began.

"—was the most interesting case," Wells said. "Some writers forged small worlds. Lucy with her farmhouse—"

"It's madness," Will said.

"The estate is malleable, Mr. Church. Your memories and stories are bound to swirl together."

Lucy couldn't help but remember her father's corpse, her sister's frozen stare.

Wells went on. "Whether Miss Jackson's fairy tale informed Mr. Forrester's behavior, merely influenced it, or was a fair prediction based on what she'd observed, we'll never know."

"But it started to come true," Lucy said.

Wells gave her a frank stare. "I didn't know what would happen. I'd never seen a writer try to allegorize the retreat before."

Lucy imagined the Fred Astaire Killer stalking his victims. "I can still change the story," she said. "He doesn't have to—"

"He does, Miss Still. Once begun, the cycle cannot stop. Your villain has been unleashed."

Will looked like he might be sick. "I thought only one could win."

Wells smiled. "There can be hundreds of characters hatched from a writer's psyche." His expression darkened, a hardness taking hold. "But in each cycle there can be only one winner."

"Let us go," Lucy said. "Let Rick go."

"It's too late for that, Miss Still, and much too late for Mr. Forrester." He grinned. "The champion will emerge from this room."

CHAPTER SIXTEEN

Rick landed a few punches before Anderson's fist pounded him in the gut. The breath whooshed out of him, replaced by a nauseating pain. This was the first time Anderson's ham-sized fist had connected, but what rage had been fueling Rick's attack was beginning to wane.

Extreme pain, he supposed, had a way of stealing your stamina.

To give himself time, Rick sidestepped toward the seating area.

The chief followed, a savage grin on his face. "See, this is what amazes me about people. So many know the theory of something, but when you get down to it, very few people are *doers*."

Rick slipped between pews, shuffled toward the section opposite.

Anderson nodded. "You can scurry around like a fucking mouse if you want, but sooner or later, you're gonna have to face me."

Rick's wind returned by degrees, though the pain from the hammer blow to his belly persisted. It felt as though Anderson had ruptured his liver.

"Where'd you come from?" Rick asked.

Anderson lumbered after him. "Gonna talk about me now, huh?"

Rick reached the far side of the chapel, where the shadows were thickest.

Anderson barked out a mirthless laugh. "'Course, you're thinking you can get me distracted. I'll be so flattered you're takin' an interest in me, I won't notice you tryin' to escape."

"I'm not running," Rick said, noticing that Anderson had begun to cut off the exit.

"Suit yourself, Forrester. But don't forget: you might think you're my Dr. Frankenstein, but I can read your sorry ass like a motherfucking billboard."

I hope to hell that's not true, Rick thought, but kept his expression neutral.

Rick gestured to the mosaic. "The stained glass. Is that from life?"

Anderson moved apace with him. "Your other question was better."

Rick retreated toward the raised altar area. "Did you come from the basement? From the walls?"

"Those look like birth canals to you, boy? The feeding soil only goes one way."

Feeding soil, Rick thought. *Jesus.*

Anderson glanced up at him, and Rick felt his stomach give a little lurch. He could swear that....

He brushed away the thought.

"You leak out of my ears one night while I slept?" Rick asked.

"I awakened in the meadow."

He remembered the shock of seeing Anderson for the first time, but beneath the memory was another thought, a more important one. Something about Anderson's wording....

"If you kill me," Rick said, "what becomes of you? You gonna be Wells's slave?"

The chief grinned. "I reckon he'll let me out of here, go where the action is. It'll be a lot like your story. I'll convince everyone I'm a good guy, and when I can, I'll have some fun."

Rick frowned, something ill-defined trawling through the depths of his brain.

Without warning, Anderson reached up, yanked a glass sconce off the wall, and hurled it at Rick, who'd been so transfixed he was barely able to dive out of the way. The sconce shattered on the altar, spitting shards of glass all over the hardwood floor.

Recklessness, Rick thought as he pushed to his feet. He remembered the night he'd begun *Garden of Snakes*. The sound of the chainsaw. The image of the maniacal cop heaving the buzzing machine into the air, plunging his recruit into a deranged form of Russian roulette.

Yes. Recklessness was Anderson's defining characteristic.

His flaw.

"You know," Anderson said, patting the gun on his hip, "I could just shoot your sorry ass."

Rick stepped onto the altar, making sure his stockinged feet didn't tread on any shards. "You'd never do that. There'd be no sport in it."

Anderson nodded. "I suppose you're right. No point in taking the easy way."

Anderson darted at him. So abrupt was the huge man's charge that Rick froze. When the chief was almost upon him, he ducked, felt the huge man's tailwind sweep over him. Anderson crashed into the lectern, the solid wood fracturing into a dozen pieces. Rick glanced about, spotted a promising shard of glass, and retrieved it. Anderson was pushing to his feet when Rick rushed at him. The chief looked up in time to see Rick pumping the shard at his face. Anderson jerked his head aside, but not swiftly enough. The razor-sharp glass sheared off his earlobe and carved an inch-deep trough in his neck.

Anderson roared, clamped a hand over his spraying ear. Rick reared back to slash Anderson again, but the chief struck him a bone-crunching blow to the ribs. The punch lifted him off his feet, but the sight of the chief's blood had given him hope.

He tore at the chief with a vicious backhand, the jagged glass ripping open his shirt at the chest, a dark tide of blood darkening the beige material. Anderson bared his teeth, a growl sounding deep in his throat, and thrust a lightning uppercut at Rick's jaw.

The blow sent him a foot in the air, and when he landed he felt the bite of glass and splintered wood.

Rick lay on his back, his consciousness flickering. He'd constructed Anderson too well. The chief was relentless. Bent on inflicting violence.

And now Rick realized what his subconscious had been trying to tell him. Without a gun, without an army behind him, he couldn't mount an effective attack.

But that didn't mean he couldn't win.

"You did good with that glass, boy," Anderson said. He fingered his mangled ear, inspected the bright red blood. "Good thing I'm not the piercing type, huh?"

"You're a waste," Rick said.

"That's not very civil, Ricky." The chief stalked toward him. "Why would you say such a thing?"

"You're like my stepdad," Rick said, pushing onto his knees. "You can't create anything. You can only—" he winced at the shooting pain in his side, "—can only tear down."

Anderson tilted his head, ten feet away now. "You think I'm like that cocksucker? You haven't got a clue."

"I'd be angry too if I were like you," Rick said, casting a quick glance to his left. What he needed was within reach.

"Like me?"

"Someone's stooge," Rick explained. "Unable to think on his own."

Anderson's lips drew back. "You...little...fucker."

Now, Rick thought. *Now.*

Anderson leapt at him. Rick's fingers closed on the lectern fragment, the tapered spike eighteen inches long. Anderson descended just as Rick thrust the spike up, plunged it into Anderson's chest. As the chief came down, Rick shifted just enough to avoid being impaled by the opposite end.

He scrambled around, saw the chief flop onto his back and gape down at the wooden spike protruding from his chest. Though Rick yearned to leave now, to save Lucy, his rational side told him to damn well not leave Anderson's fate to chance. After all, a creature like this.... Who knew if he could really be killed? He had to be sure.

Rick cast about, discovered another fragment from the shattered lectern, this piece not as long as the first, but every bit as sharp. He crawled closer to Anderson, raised the spike, and that's when the chief started laughing.

Rick's hand froze a foot above Anderson's face.

Because the chief's face was changing.

Gone was the oversized jaw and the prowlike forehead. Gone was the enlarged lump of nose and the salt-and-pepper hair.

In their place were Rick's features.

Rick stared down at himself.

"Now he sees!" the being who was no longer Anderson crowed. "It took him a while, but now, by God, he understands!"

It can't be, Rick thought.

The bleeding figure reached up, seized him by the shirtfront. "I'm *part* of you, Forrester. You really think you can kill me off without harming your own sorry ass?"

And now Rick sensed the ache in his torso, the pulse in his left ear. He glanced down at his chest, expecting to see spreading blood, but thus far there was only the pain. And the dread that the chief had defeated him after all.

"You're not me," Rick said, knocking the hand away. He leaned over. "You're not me!"

The figure grew still, the voice dwindling to a whisper. "You're right, Ricky. Look."

Fingers trembling, Rick reached down, removed the figure's sunglasses.

Opened his mouth in a voiceless scream.

The figure's eyes were swirling darknesses. As Rick watched in horror, the figure reached up, hooked the bottoms of its eyelids, and pulled them down, revealing more darkness, a face that wasn't a face, a shadowy, swirling mass of onyx that began to glimmer, and then to form into something hideous, a visage too fiendish to be called human.

"*I claimed your mother,*" the creature rasped. "*She screamed and screamed.*"

Rick tried to pull away, but the creature caught him by the throat with one hand, peeled off its skin with the other, the head entirely black now, the darkness continuing at the throat and torso. "*I'll claim you after I take your bitch.*"

Rick took hold of the hand that gripped his throat, but the fingers only tightened, the black vulpine face leering at him. "*You're going to hell,*" the figure growled. "*We'll all burn together.*"

Rick's fingers closed on a shard of glass, but before he could slash at the creature's satanic face, the dark form thrust out its arms, slamming Rick backward. He pushed onto his elbows in time to see Raymond Eddy rise, turn.

Raymond grinned. "*I told you I'd come for you.*"

Rick watched in numb shock as Raymond darted away, his body blurring, and disappeared into the wall.

Straight toward the tower.

CHAPTER SEVENTEEN

"Down to the end!" Wilson called, his eyes gleaming in the lurid candle glow.

"I leave it to you, Miss Still," Wells said. "Everything you've ever wanted is now within reach. You can be famous, can have more money than you've ever dreamed. What will you decide?"

Lucy looked into Wells's black eyes. "How long have you lived?" she whispered.

"You've *killed* for this moment, Lucy," Wells reminded her. "All you have to do now is choose."

She glanced at Will, read the terror in his face. Looked back at Wells. "I won't let you hurt him."

Wells opened his mouth. "*Let* me? My dear, the only question is which one of you will condemn the other first."

"We won't do that," she said. "Right, Will?"

"Hell no," he answered.

But something in his tone gave her pause. Had he lacked conviction, or was it the turmoil of the moment that had rendered his voice so listless? She gazed into his eyes and wondered, *Will you sell me out, Will? Will you let me die so you can win?*

"You're right to doubt, Miss Still. Poets talk of love, loyalty. But self-preservation is the most basic human urge."

Her lips thinned. "For the heartless, maybe."

"An eight-year-old girl," Wells mused. "Unblemished, untainted. Possessed of an unconditional regard for her baby sister."

"I *was* jealous of her," Lucy said. "I wanted the attention. But that doesn't mean I wanted Molly to die."

"Lies," Wilson said.

Tears filled her eyes. "Part of me died that day too."

Wells nodded. "The part of you that shared your parents' attention. The part of you that had to compete for their love."

"*No.*"

"Leave her alone," Will said.

Wells ignored him. "The creek wasn't deep, my dear. You could have easily saved her."

"I would've died too," Lucy said, but her words were half-lost in a sob.

"A risk you weren't willing to take," Wells agreed. "Then or now."

She smeared the tears away. "I won't let Will die."

Wells said, "You are about to behold something incredible, Miss Still. Something my champion storytellers have witnessed through the ages. A century ago in a Boston mansion. Half a millennium ago, within a remote Scottish castle. In ancient—"

"You're a parasite," she whispered.

"I'm *alive*," he corrected. "I am rich and famous and possessed of a power beyond comprehension. I am *eternal*, Miss Still."

"No," she said.

"Hold her, Wilson."

Wilson swung her around, pinned her arms to her sides.

Wells stalked toward Will.

"I don't want to die," Will said.

Wells smiled. "You've decided Miss Still will die in your place?"

Will stared up at Wells, breath heaving. Then, his face seemed to clear. "You lose, Mr. Wells."

Wells's smile vanished. "You think I need a winner to survive, Mr. Church? It's merely my sporting nature that honors the agreement."

Will rolled sideways in an attempt to gain his feet, but the bonds around his wrists and ankles foiled him.

Wells straddled him, pinned him to the floor. "*Look at me, Mr. Church.*"

Lucy began to thrash against Wilson.

Wells reached out, covered Will's mouth and nose. Will whimpered against Wells's hand. Lucy watched in sick horror as Will's legs began to scissor.

Behind her, Wilson let out a pleased sigh. Lucy bucked against him to free herself.

The tower began to pulse with strands of light. They started in the walls, the domed tower, and snaked their way across the floor toward Wells and his victim. From her vantage point she could just glimpse Will's face, but it was more than enough. The bulging eyes, the reddened skin. The muffled cries.

She became aware of the noise then, a deep, metronomic throb that accompanied the light pulses, the sound so deep and powerful the floor underfoot vibrated.

The pulsing light crept nearer to Wells with each beat, until the incandescence reached his shoes, throbbed up his legs, swam over his torso, and his entire body was flashing in time with the keep.

Will's eyelids began to flutter, his body gripped in a paroxysm of anguish.

"Let him go!" Lucy shouted. She jerked against Wilson, clawed at his arms, but he would not relinquish his grip.

Will's cries weakened, and then his spasms ceased altogether.

Soon, the lights and the sound were gone, and Wells was rising from Will's dead body.

Wells now looked no more than twenty-five years old. His body was corded with muscle.

He strode toward her, a Greek god made flesh. Within his white shirt, his muscles bulged. "Transcendence is a myth, Lucy. You believe your actions are noble. But all you've done is select a different manner of suicide."

She glanced at Will, hoping he would rise again.

But his body was motionless.

She was alone.

No! she thought. *You're not dead yet.*

She strained against Wilson, but he refused to let go.

Wells smiled at Wilson. "Ten victims this time." He laughed softly. "I wonder how Amanda will enjoy making love to my teenage self."

"Where is she?" Lucy asked.

"Doesn't matter," Wilson muttered, but something had caught in Lucy's mind. Some important scrap of memory....

"She disapproves of this," Lucy said.

Wells shrugged. "She's inexperienced. In time, she'll appreciate my renewal."

Lucy probed her mind for recollections of the tale. Imagined the woman in 'Incident on a Paris Rooftop'. She said, "The character in your story.... Amanda would never have sanctioned this sort of ritual."

Wells made a scoffing sound. "Ritual? My dear, this is the glorious culmination of scrupulous planning. The game has never gone this swimmingly before. In the past, mistakes were made, the unfolding of events far too messy."

"Not this time," Wilson said.

Wells smiled warmly, reached over Lucy to grasp Wilson's shoulder. "But not this time. *The Seer* was not only one of my greatest novels. He's proven an invaluable resource."

"But your wife...does she approve of this?"

Wells rolled his eyes. "What do I care of her approval? I made her. I gave her life."

"You enslaved her," Lucy said. "In the story, Amanda yearns to be free."

Wilson's voice was tight. "Mr. Wells, don't listen to this—"

"I know what Miss Still is trying to do." Wells glanced at Lucy, a crafty gleam in his eyes. "You want to see where Amanda's loyalties reside. Will she choose her husband, or will she side with a stranger?" Wells nodded. "Come, Amanda."

Out of the darkness stepped Amanda Wells, and to Lucy she'd never appeared more lovely or fanatical.

"I'll never betray Roderick," Amanda said.

"You're brainwashed," Lucy answered.

"I *love*. Passionately, unselfishly. I wouldn't expect you to understand."

"The woman in the story would never allow herself to be subjugated."

Amanda uttered a breathless laugh. "My dear. How many of us remain the people we were?"

Lucy glanced at Will's lifeless body. Remembered his wiseass grin. His self-deprecating humor. "I'm not."

Amanda lowered her nose at Lucy. "You're not what?"

"The same," Lucy said. She turned to Wells, nodded toward Amanda. "You can manipulate this poor creature—" a nod at Wilson, "—or this mindless automaton."

Wilson took a step toward her.

"But you can't control everyone," she said. "Will...me...Rick."

As if in answer, a muffled boom sounded from below.

"Ah," Wells said. "Your prince."

He's alive! she thought. She'd wanted to believe it, but after Will's death, any hope she'd clung to had faded.

"He's supposed to be dead," Wilson murmured, his eyes darting about.

Lucy studied the servant's perplexed face. "You didn't foresee this, did you? That's why you're angry. You can't see the future."

"He's supposed to be dead!" Wilson shouted.

But Wells only smiled. "We come to it," he said. "The end of the fairy tale."

Another boom. Rick attempting to stave in the entrance to the tower?

"You'll have to kill us both," Lucy said. "Rick won't sacrifice me any more than I'll sacrifice him."

The booming sounded again.

Wells grinned. "My dear, you don't remember Miss Jackson's story. It wasn't the king that the peasant girl most feared, but rather the king's chief executioner."

Wilson started forward.

"Wait," Wells said. "I hate to deprive you of the pleasure, Wilson, but I must."

Wilson stopped, a look of exquisite frustration twisting his face.

A cracking sound from below. Rick breaking through?

"It is time, Miss Still." Wells turned toward the darkest region of the tower and nodded. "I command not only my characters, but the ghosts that haunt my writers as well."

The shadow hurtled at Lucy.

CHAPTER EIGHTEEN

Rick swung the axe again, and this time the steel head broke through. Shards of wood clattered on the floor beyond, and Rick shoved his hand through the hole he'd made, the jagged splinters harrowing his wrist. He ground his teeth, his fingers probing for the lock. He found it, twisted it. He shouldered open the door, rushed up the steps, wishing he hadn't needed the detour to the workshop, but without the axe, he'd never have broken through the heavy door.

How long had Raymond been in the tower? Had Wells killed Lucy even before Raymond arrived?

Rick didn't know, but he raced up the steps, ignoring the sharp pain in his ribs, the mystifying aches in his chest and his ear. Had he truly injured himself when he attacked John Anderson? Was the character that much a part of him?

He hustled around the steps, rose higher and higher, and when he reached the keep he was stunned to find the door standing open.

Rick burst into the tower and beheld a scene that made his blood freeze.

Raymond Eddy stood clutching Lucy, who thrashed in his arms. A rumbling bass throb accompanied a continual pulse of light, which began at Raymond's face and spread outward along the floor, the walls, illuminating the entire keep. Most of the light, however, seemed to flow toward Wells, who stood near the stained-glass windows, his black eyes gleaming, an expression of sexual hunger on his face.

He looked a decade younger than Rick.

Open-throated shirt fluttering as the light galvanized his muscles, Wells spread his arms, relishing the malignant energy Raymond was sending out.

It all leads to Wells, Rick thought. *Anderson, Raymond Eddy, the ghosts of our pasts. Everything depends on Wells.*

As if to confirm this thought, figures had surrounded Lucy and Raymond Eddy, and though Rick didn't recognize all of them, he could identify enough to understand what was happening.

The female lead from *Birds of Monte Rey*.

The villain from *Lightning Aria*.

A memorable old man from a novella called *The Last Day at the Park*.

Like a carnival of oddities, characters from Wells's stories surrounded Lucy and her captor and watched with solemn approval as she was drained of energy.

Rick approached.

Wilson stalked forward to meet him. "You won't interrupt the rite."

Rick raised the axe. The only thing he saw was Wilson, just outside the circle of onlookers, guarding the unholy ceremony with an expression of ruthless glee. The keep was silent, save the deep throb and someone murmuring words in a weak voice.

Rick swung the axe. Wilson's hands shot up to intercept it, and Rick aimed a vicious kick at Wilson's knee. Wilson let out a surprised grunt. The knee didn't buckle, but Wilson's arms dropped. Rick mustered as much strength as he could and wrenched the axe downward.

It was enough.

The axe bit into Wilson's shoulder, the clavicle crunching. Wilson hissed, clutched at the axe head, but Rick was already ripping it free. Wilson's face was a rictus of surprise as he stumbled forward, groped toward Rick, perhaps thinking to fend off another blow.

Rick sidestepped Wilson, braced his back foot, and swung the axe as though unloading on a fastball.

The blade sliced through Wilson's neck like a scythe through winter wheat. Wilson's head tumbled off, came to rest just outside the circle. The headless body canted sideways, the jetting stump spitting blood on the backs of the onlookers' legs.

The silent figures finally noticed Rick. Wells had too.

The newer, more virile version of Wells strode forward, fists clenched and eyes wide with outrage. "How...*dare* you attack Wilson? Do you have any idea how important he is?"

"Was," Rick corrected. He repositioned the axe for a better grip. "Important enough to imprison him like the rest of these poor souls?"

Wells waded into the circle, the onlookers stepping aside to let him pass. "*Poor souls?* I sired them, Mr. Forrester. I gave them purpose."

"Slaves."

"A writer—"

"—lets his characters be themselves," Rick interrupted.

Wells smiled incredulously. "Do you dare tell me what a storyteller does? You have no—"

Rick darted at Raymond Eddy. He was raising the axe to strike the shadow figure when Wells sprang.

Rick almost made it. He'd thought Wells was distracted enough – furious enough – to allow Rick to deal Raymond a killing blow.

But Wells was quicker. Three feet from Raymond, who still clutched Lucy's slumped body, Wells crashed into Rick, sent the axe clattering. The impact lifted Rick off his feet, Wells driving him upward and down in a merciless arc. Rick's head smacked the floor, sending starbursts of pain through his vision.

Wells seized Rick by the shirtfront, pivoted, and heaved him across the circle. Even as he tumbled through the air, he marveled at Wells's power. Rick crashed to the floor and skidded toward the outer wall.

The light was stronger here. Rick pushed onto his elbows, unsure whether it had been the head trauma or a break in the clouds beyond the stained glass that had brightened his vision. Regardless, Wells was coming; Rick heard determined footfalls from behind.

Fight the bastard, he told himself. *Your life depends on it. Lucy's life depends on it.*

Rick compressed his lips. For all he knew, Lucy was already dead. Raymond was draining her, sucking the life from her marrow. Rick glanced at the pair, saw the brilliant light throbbing out of them in all directions, but most of all to Wells.

Rick peered into that face and saw Wells as he'd seen him that first night, the monster behind the mask. Wells's handsome features morphed, became vulpine, hideous. His teeth elongated, his eyes fathomless, and in his head Rick heard Wells's triumph: *The end, Mr. Forrester! This is the end!*

Wells wore a dreadful goblin's leer as his fingers closed over Rick's shoulders, drew him up. The eyes glowed an infernal orange.

Rick swung his head as hard as he could into Wells's nose.

Wells bellowed in pain and stumbled back. Rick scrambled to his feet and swung. The blow caught Wells in the jaw. Rick yearned to free Lucy from Raymond Eddy, but if Wells controlled Raymond, wasn't defeating him the surest method of saving Lucy?

God, he hoped so.

Rick cocked his fist, swung, but Wells parried the blow. Rick tried to jerk his head aside, but it was too late, Wells's fist crashed into his temple. Rick spun backward, the left side of his face aflame.

He went down, and in his periphery, he saw Wells surging toward him. Desperately, he pushed upright, whipped an elbow at Wells's face, but Wells merely dodged the attack and unleashed a savage blow to Rick's jaw.

Rick flew backward, toward the stained-glass windows. The evening light had intensified so much that even with his eyes closed, the afterglow brightened his vision.

Fight! he told himself. Blood dripped from his lips as he staggered to his feet, aimed a looping roundhouse at Wells, who evaded it easily.

Wells smashed him in the mouth again, this time with a brutal backhand; Rick went tumbling backward. He sprawled on the unforgiving stone, his thoughts veering in all directions. Toward Lucy, dying at the hands of a ghost. Toward Will, his body like a broken mannequin. Toward Rick's own novel.

As Wells strode forward, a pitiless grin upturning the corners of his mouth, Rick thought of his favorite books. Of the problem of an unstoppable antagonist. Sometimes things grew so bleak that only a pyrrhic victory was possible. In those situations, a single, unpleasant route remained. In those situations....

Wells reached down, seized him by the throat. Lifted him to standing.

Snarled into his face. "You cheated the game. I brought you here in good faith, and look at the misery you've wrought. Your friend, dead. Your true love, dead. And now you." Wells shook him. "You thought you could mingle with gods? Believed your paltry gift could measure with mine?" Wells drew closer, his nose touching Rick's. "I keep my promises. Otherwise, I'd drain you myself."

Rick stared back uncomprehendingly, then deciphered Wells's meaning. His vision blurring, his mind foggy, Rick swiveled his head toward the circle, noticed how limp Lucy's body had become, how brilliantly the pulsing lights strobed through the keep.

You've failed her, a voice declared. *You failed to protect her, just as you failed to protect your mom. You're a coward, Rick. A failure.*

The throb continued, through the floor and walls of the tower. Into Wells's bones and sinew, through Wells's fingers...

...into Rick's body.

Rick's vision cleared. Light surrounded him. And colors he hadn't noticed before. He beheld the stained-glass windows, the evening sunlight now blazing in concert with the spangled glow in the keep. Wells's attention had shifted to Lucy, and because of this he didn't notice what Rick could now see, a new stained-glass image, one that depicted a man in tattered clothes and what could only be a king in a brilliant purple robe. The glass design featured a peasant tackling a king, driving him toward a window situated at a fearsome height, and with a bone-deep shock, Rick realized the scene in the stained glass was occurring in a tower.

In a keep.

At that moment, as the energy pulsed through Wells and into Rick's rejuvenating body, he realized where the voice was coming from, why Lucy's lips kept moving despite her imminent death.

She was finishing Sherilyn's story.

Which crystalized now in the stained glass. As Rick watched, the panes of colored glass were clarifying, swimming into focus.

And as Rick beheld the glorious new image, he remembered how the old stories had ended, how the protagonists vanquished evil, even if it meant doing so at the ultimate cost.

A sacrifice.

With one last glance at Lucy, whose lips scarcely twitched now and whose body lolled lifelessly in Raymond's hands, Rick reached up, clutched Wells by the shoulders. Wells turned toward him, a mixture of bemusement and mockery in his face, and Rick swung him around, turning Wells's back toward the stained glass.

Wells's expression shifted to astonishment.

Rick cinched his fingers tighter into Wells's flesh, drove the man backward.

All humor fled Wells's face. "What do you think you're—"

"Winning," Rick growled.

Wells fought against him, but the pulsing light had surcharged Rick's body, transforming it into a crackling mass of energy, and as they neared the stained-glass window, Rick thought he heard Lucy call out faintly. Then Wells's body crashed through the multicolored panes, which shattered and sliced Rick's fingers, his arms. Blinding sunlight embraced him, and as he prepared himself for the vertiginous drop toward the courtyard below, he felt his body jerk, something arresting his motion.

Rick looked down and watched Wells's groping arms, his hateful face. For a moment the beast beneath the mask surfaced: tapered teeth, elongated chin, protuberant cheekbones, satanic eyes. Then it was gone, and only the man remained.

Wells's body plummeted rapidly until, with a dull crunch, the base of his skull met stone and the top of his head erupted in a gout of skull fragments and brain matter. Wells's shattered body, spread-eagled, lay motionless in a growing lake of blood.

But Rick teetered on the edge of the keep, shards of colored glass glittering around his feet.

Someone had caught him by the back of the shirt, was even now supporting him in the jagged aperture. He turned, expecting Lucy to have somehow broken away from Raymond Eddy and prevented Rick's fall.

But it wasn't Lucy who grasped his shirt.

It was Amanda Wells.

Wordlessly, she gazed back at him. If she relinquished her grip, he'd plummet to his death.

Maybe that was her plan. She made no move to haul him backward from the brink of the drop, nor could he distinguish the emotion in her face.

After an endless moment, she drew him back inside the keep.

His stockinged feet crunched on broken glass. He winced, faced Amanda Wells.

"Why?" he asked.

"In my story," she said, "I turned my back on the man I loved."

He glanced sideways, though from where he stood, a few feet from the shattered window, he couldn't make out Wells's broken body. "That's why you let him fall?"

She shook her head. "It's why I saved you." She looked around, something wistful in her expression. "Living here, you don't get many opportunities to atone for your mistakes."

Rick tightened.

His gaze shifted to Lucy's motionless body.

He froze as he remembered that hideous, soul-shattering word, that necessary measure for evil to be vanquished.

He stared at Lucy's shut eyelids, her splayed arms, and thought, *Sacrifice.*

He began to shudder, the word repeating in his mind like a dirge.

Sacrifice.

Sacrifice.

Rick opened his mouth and screamed.

CHAPTER NINETEEN

He rushed across the room, muttering, "No no no no," under his breath. The silent figures moved aside to let him pass. Though he was focused on Lucy, several details did register:

None of the figures attacked him.

Raymond Eddy had disappeared. Forever, he hoped.

Wilson's headless body was still headless.

He fell at Lucy's side, gathered her into his arms. If not for the boneless way she lolled, he might have assumed she was sleeping.

But she wasn't. Her skin was warm. Feverish, even. But her chest no longer rose and fell, and when he kissed her, no breath issued from her lips.

"Don't fucking quit on me," he said. He stroked her forehead, brushed the sweaty hair from her temples. "Come on," he said through clenched teeth. "We can't come this far only to have you…." He shook his head. "Come *on*, Lucy. Fight it."

He glanced about, but there was no help from the watching faces. They stared at him with what might have been curiosity. But none of them, including Amanda Wells, moved to intervene.

"Dammit," he growled. He laid Lucy down, careful not to bump her head on the hard stone. He put his ear to her chest, listened.

His eyes widened.

Though faint, he detected a heartbeat.

Okay, he told himself. *Apply CPR, mouth-to-mouth, chest compressions, something. Don't just sit here!*

He set to work, straining to remember the course he'd taken in college. He checked her airway, found it unobstructed. Rick laid his palms over her chest and pushed. He knew it wasn't perfect, but he felt like he was reasonably close. He'd shove down on her chest, wait, blow into her mouth, listen to her heartbeat.

Still faint, but growing stronger.

He continued. A primal region in his brain told him her recovery was not a matter of medical precision, but of contact, of love.

"Rick," a voice said from behind him.

He glanced at Amanda Wells, who nodded toward Lucy.

Lucy was staring up at him.

"Oh Jesus," he whispered, and kissed her full on the lips. He slid an arm under her, cradled her in his lap.

In a weak voice, she asked, "Why'd you stop?"

Laughing, he kissed her again, wrapped her up in a powerful hug. He rocked her and relished her warmth, the feel of her smiling face against his neck.

"I thought you were gone," he said.

"I was."

When he pulled away to meet her gaze, she said, "That…thing. It fed on me…."

Rick's throat tightened. "It followed me here. I'm so—"

"Shut up," she said. "It's gone now." Her eyes shifted to Amanda Wells. "Is your husband gone too?"

Something steely came into Amanda's face. "He was never my husband."

Rick didn't need to ask her what she meant. Her saving his life was explanation enough.

He held Lucy for a long time. She seemed content that way. None of the onlookers spoke.

The blazing sunlight began to soften.

Lucy said, "Can we leave now?"

CHAPTER TWENTY

Amanda stood with them in the meadow, the westering sun sinking below the tree line, the sky above it a series of colorful ridges, purple and pink, orange and blue. The rain had left the land cool, the wet grass dappled by the sundown glow. The others who'd been with them in the tower had dispersed throughout the mansion.

Lucy nodded that way. "Where will they go?"

Amanda shook her head. "Some will probably die purposeless, others will start anew." She smiled. "Speaking of new starts, here you are."

She held out a manila envelope to Lucy.

"Take it," Amanda said. "You've won."

Lucy shook her head. "My book isn't complete."

"You finished Sherilyn's story. And your manuscript demonstrates the most potential." A small smile at Rick. "Sorry."

He chuckled. "Hell, I agree with you."

Amanda went on. "This envelope contains the key for a safe deposit box in New York. In the box you'll find three million dollars."

Lucy didn't speak.

"Additionally," Amanda continued, "the envelope contains letters to several senior editors. Roderick thought it best for the nature of the deal to be left to the winning author, or her agent."

Lucy's temple began to twitch.

"You'll not tell anyone what went on here, nor will you discuss my husband's demise. The publicity surrounding his death will only augment the notoriety of *The Fred Astaire Murders*. A bestseller is virtually guaranteed."

Lucy didn't reach for the envelope.

"Is something wrong?" Amanda asked.

"Other than eight people dying?" Lucy said.

Rick cocked an eyebrow. "Why does something tell me you aren't going to accept your winnings?"

"Oh, I'm going to take the money. I'm not a fool."

He exhaled. "Thank God."

"But I'm not going to use my association with Wells to make this book successful." Lucy took the envelope, tore open the top, reached in and found the key. "Where's the box?"

Amanda told them the address.

Lucy looked at Rick. "You get that? I'm bad with numbers."

He nodded. "I got it."

Lucy handed the envelope back to Amanda. "I trust you're not going to carry on your husband's tradition?"

Amanda's lips thinned. "That's not a very nice thing to say."

"You've been complicit in his schemes. I appreciate your saving Rick's life – truly, I do – but I can't pretend to like you."

A wintry smile. "Then we have something in common."

At length, Rick said, "Well, hell. I've had enough conflict for one day. You mind if we head out?"

"You talk like a cowboy sometimes," Amanda said. "You sort of look like one too."

He glanced at his shoes and said, "It's funny. I've loved Westerns forever. Read a ton of them." He glanced at the horizon. "When I finish *Garden of Snakes*, I think I'll try a Western."

Lucy took Rick's hand. "Let's go."

They'd taken a few steps down the hillside when a thought occurred to her. She looked back at Amanda. "Will we have to walk all the way to town?"

"I've arranged a driver for you. He'll be there by the time you reach the clearing."

Rick scratched the back of his neck. "It's not some crazed murderer, is it?"

"Just a local farmer. One who delivers our mail once a month."

Lucy studied Amanda's face. "I thought no one knew Wells lived here."

Over her shoulder, Amanda said, "We all keep our secrets. Don't we?"

AFTER

Helen Marshall, her new agent, sold *The Fred Astaire Murders* for seven figures. Helen also agreed to represent Rick, though she worried his subject matter was too edgy for mainstream readers.

Not only had the publisher acquired Lucy's novel, they'd allocated an ungodly sum toward the book's success. By the time Lucy and Rick arrived at the Ritz-Carlton for the launch party, *The Fred Astaire Murders* had become what the *New York Times* called 'an event book'. The publicity embarrassed Lucy, but Helen assured her it was all deserved. The advance reviews bore this out, though Lucy was still dreading that first vicious pan.

"I thought I was supposed to be the silent, brooding one."

She jarred, glanced over at Rick, who lounged next to her in the limousine. She shook her head. "I wish we could've done something under the radar."

He grinned at her, looking irresistible in his dark brown sport coat, white button-down shirt, and blue jeans. She'd tried to talk him into slacks, but he informed her the sport coat was his one concession to formality. Eyeing him now, she decided the blue jeans were just fine.

"Your days of flying under the radar are over," he said.

She made a face. "Please don't—"

"I'm kidding. You can have as much or as little of the spotlight as you like. If you want, you can buy a hundred acres in the country, become a weird cat lady."

"You probably don't like cats."

"I love them," he said. At her expression, he added, "No, really. I always had cats growing up. We had a dog or two, but we always had a cat."

"Which was your favorite?"

"This scrawny one named Cuddles. She had long hair and a broken tail."

"Cuddles?" she asked, trying not to laugh.

"Lay off. I was five years old."

"Thanks for coming tonight," she said, taking his hand. His grip was firm but gentle. He was always careful not to bump the place where she'd lost the end of a finger. It was still tender.

He glanced at her. "Think the portions will be big enough? I'm starving."

"That why your palms are sweaty?"

"I'm nervous as hell," he admitted. "I'm not used to this kind of soiree."

"They're not here for you."

He grinned. "Well listen to you. Already acting like a pampered starlet."

"I'm too old to be a starlet."

"Sexy enough. In fact...." He leaned over, nuzzled her neck.

"*Rick*, the driver."

"Give him something to tell his wife about. The famous author and her salacious fiancé."

Smiling, she pushed him away. "We're here."

They went inside.

On the way past the concierge, Lucy glanced at a painting of a Southern landscape, a river bordered by oak trees that were festooned with Spanish moss. It reminded her of the article Rick had shown her last week.

They'd followed the stories of the missing writers closely over the past year. There'd been little in the Alabama newspapers about Sherilyn's disappearance. After all, she'd been divorced several years, and she'd moved away to live with Alicia before the competition.

But the murder of David Zendejas, a prominent Baptist preacher, had dominated the news since his body was found by the two prostitutes he'd brought back to his upscale Montgomery home.

The murder had occurred in the master bathroom. He'd been killed when a sharp object punctured his right ear and entered his brain. Neither prostitute – their names withheld because they were both underage – had seen the killer. The theory was that Zendejas's murderer had waited for him in the bathroom and then escaped through the window after the deed was finished.

As they approached the banquet hall, a chill coursed through her. "Feeling all right?" Rick asked.

Lucy nodded but knew she looked unpersuasive. She could no more fool Rick than she could fool herself.

When they came through the door and beheld the crowd, Lucy's heart performed a violent lurch. She'd hoped there would only be fifteen or twenty people, but the number was closer to a hundred. She spotted her editor, Janice Roth, along with Janice's husband, but if Helen was here, Lucy hadn't seen her yet.

Lucy paused in the entryway and surveyed the room. She'd worried there would be wall-sized banners of her face strung up everywhere but was heartened to find only a few glossy foam board book covers, none of them wall-size.

"Sure you're okay?" Rick asked.

"I might faint."

"At least you don't have to give a speech."

"A reading is just as bad. Maybe worse. What if I—"

"Kick ass?" He squeezed her hand. "Seriously, you rock at readings. It's like you're making love to the words."

"Do you think of anything other than sex?"

He considered. "Books. Movies. Baseball. Sometimes food."

"Nice."

"What else matters?"

She punched him on the arm. "You're trying to distract me."

"It working?"

"Not really."

"Worth a try. Let's go."

They entered the banquet hall, the sounds of smooth jazz reaching Lucy's ears. The aroma of perfume mingled with what might have been roasted chicken.

"Still jealous of that cover," Rick murmured as they neared the milling crowd. Lucy glanced at the nearest foam board version of *The Fred Astaire Murders*. She had to admit to loving the cover too. The composition was simple but elegant: a man in a black tuxedo and top hat, head bowed to obscure his face, a black cane clutched at his side. The end of the cane tapered into a sharp silver blade, one of the killer's weapons. The title was lettered across the bottom in simple white; Lucy's name was positioned at the top in a slightly larger version of the title font.

A voice behind them: "I can't believe they let this guy in."

Helen Marshall.

Smiling, their agent leaned in and gave Rick a hug. For such a short woman – five-one, tops – she carried an aura of intelligence and power. Fiftyish, her graying hair and glasses gave her the aspect of a barn owl. But whenever she spoke about publishing, she made Lucy feel good about the present and hopeful about the future.

In other words, the opposite of how Fred Morehouse made her feel.

Lucy had fired Fred, via a phone call, shortly after arriving back in Williamsburg. As expected, it hadn't gone well.

"I've got good news," Helen said.

"Quentin Tarantino decided to option *Garden of Snakes*?" Rick asked.

"Sorry, it's for Lucy. Janice wants to buy the series we've been talking about. Three books at least."

"Good money?"

"Assuredly."

Lucy glanced at Rick. "What do you think?"

Rick nodded at Helen. "Don't ask me, I'm over here wallowing in blood."

Helen smiled. "Just dial it down a little. One decapitation per book."

"What if they're all important?"

Helen gave Lucy a look. "Can you rein him in?"

"You think it'll do any good?"

"Good point," Helen said. She winked at Rick, who smiled back at her proudly. Lucy resisted an urge to kiss him.

Lucy gave her reading before dinner, mainly because she'd begged Helen to schedule it that way. If she didn't have anything in her stomach, she reasoned, she'd reduce her chances of vomiting all over the microphone. When she finished, she sensed it had gone well. Either that, or the crowd was trying to save her feelings.

The only mistake she made was when she misspoke on the word 'cop', so the line she read was, "It got ugly when the cock showed up."

When she sat down, Rick murmured, "Everything's good until the cock shows up."

"Shut up," she said, but her mouth began to twitch.

He wouldn't let it go. "You know, I think there are too many people in this room. Fire-code violation. Better call the cocks."

Chest rocking with laughter, she swatted him on the shoulder. "Are you really that juvenile?"

"Part of my charm."

She was on her way to the bathroom when a voice said, "I could've gotten you more money."

Fred Morehouse.

She turned and there he was. Tailored gray suit, cashmere-silk necktie, blue with yellow pinstripes. Stylish as always, skin as tan as ever.

"Helen wouldn't return my calls," he said. "I had to pull some strings just to get a seat."

Lucy's mind swirled. She didn't want to speak to him, but there was little choice. Walking away would admit defeat. Shouting would cause a scene, and she'd end up looking bad: *Suspense Author Unleashes Incoherent Tirade on Agent Who Discovered Her.*

She licked her lips. "Did you hear the reading?"

He shook his head. "No need. I know you well enough."

Damn you, she thought.

He favored her with an assessing look. "You seem healthier, Lucy Goosy. Your new man must be treating you nicely."

She refused to take the bait. "Rick's my best friend."

"Where'd you meet him?"

Lucy paused, wondering for the thousandth time if anyone knew what had gone on at Wells's estate. The passing of Roderick Wells, of course, had caused a media firestorm, but none of the eight writers' disappearances had been connected to the retreat.

Still…something in Fred's tone bothered her.

Then again, Fred's tone always bothered her.

She repeated the story she and Rick had rehearsed. "I went

to a charity event in Williamsburg called Scares That Care." She shrugged. "We met in the hotel bar and hit it off."

Fred appeared to lose interest. "Never heard of it."

"You never were the charitable type."

That got his attention. "I never figured you for a snake, Lucy Goosy. The type to turn your back on someone."

"Helen treats me with respect."

"Helen's a mollycoddler."

Lucy suppressed an urge to rake his eyes out.

"I do have to give her credit though," he said. "She found an editor good enough to prop you up."

Lucy clasped her hands so they wouldn't shake. "Janice does a marvelous job."

"I'm sure she does. Or maybe your new man is doing the work. The story doesn't sound like you at all."

"How would you know what I sound like?"

"How would I *know*? I'm the one pulled you out of the slush pile and taught you how to write."

"'It's gotta be a sequel.' That's what you said."

Fred looked annoyed. "What the hell are you talking about?"

"After *The Girl Who Died*," she explained. "I wanted to write a standalone. You insisted I do a sequel."

"A good sequel, yeah."

"A writer can't create a story that isn't in her. That she isn't passionate about."

He rolled his eyes. "Ah, Christ, Lucy. That's writer-speak for 'I fucked up and decided to blame my agent.'"

She nodded. "It was my fault."

He raised his hands, shouted hysterically, "Hallelujah! She finally sees the light."

"I should've listened to my gut rather than you."

"Gotta have guts to listen to them."

"Typical Morehouse ugliness," she said. "I used to let it bother me."

"I see. You're above my ugliness now."

"Far above," she agreed.

"You made a serious mistake, Lucy Goosy." He stepped closer, all charm bled from his face. He was in his late sixties, and despite the plastic surgeries and the perpetual tan, his age was beginning to show. The loose skin at his neck gave him a vaguely reptilian look.

He nodded. "Everybody knows everybody in this business. You think this is a new start for you? It's a repetition, only you're older this time. Big advance, great reviews…then reality sets in. Your next book will be shit, and it'll all crash down again."

She detected shades of Roderick Wells in his gaze. The malice. The need for control.

His grin was sharklike. "Nothing to say, Lucy Goosy?"

"I was just wondering what it's like to expend so much energy wishing failure on others."

His grin disappeared.

Lucy pushed past him and strode toward the restroom.

When she returned to the banquet hall, she noticed that Fred was sitting at a table by the entrance. His charming grin was back, and he appeared to be regaling a pair of couples with one of his patented Morehouse anecdotes, presumably one in which he played the hero.

Taking her place beside Rick, she said, "My former agent is here."

He'd gotten a beer while she was gone. He sipped from it. "I saw. Want me to kick his ass?"

"We already spoke."

"You look like you won."

She returned his smile. "I did."

For the moment, they were alone at the table. The Marshalls and the Roths had joined a group of partygoers near the lectern where Lucy had read. The sight of the lectern reminded her of Rick's story about the chapel, his battle with John Anderson.

She barely noticed when their entrees were placed before them.

Roasted chicken, asparagus tips, and seasoned mashed potatoes. It was typical banquet-hall food, but nevertheless, Lucy's stomach growled.

Rick dug in.

Lucy watched him. "You shouldn't skip lunch."

"I was too nervous to eat," he said through a mouthful of food. "I mean, I knew you'd bring the house down, but still…."

"You wanted me to succeed."

He stopped chewing, frowned at her. "Of course I did."

She kissed him lingeringly on the cheek.

At that moment, someone in the rear of the banquet hall screamed. Lucy jolted, craned her head in that direction, and caught a glimpse of one of the servers jerking something away from the base of Fred Morehouse's skull.

A split second later, Lucy realized the server grasped a bloody knife.

Blood drenched Fred's shoulders, his eyes goggling in dismay. Several people stood and obstructed Lucy's view, but between them she saw the killer staring at her.

Handsome. Slicked-back hair. Florida-shaped birthmark on his neck.

He winked at her, then strode briskly through the exit.

The banquet hall, which had been eerily quiet after the attack, erupted with shrieks and the clatter of overturned chairs.

His eyes huge, Fred toppled onto the table and didn't move. He was blotted out by scurrying partygoers.

Lucy turned away, heart pounding.

Rick said, "Poor Fred."

People were scrambling behind them and shouting for someone to call the police.

"What do we do?" she asked.

"Wait," he said.

Voices shouting, hotel security.

Her hand shaking, Lucy took a sip of water. She nodded across the room, where whey-faced partygoers were gaping at Fred's corpse. "Was that who I think it was?"

Rick took a swig from his beer bottle, set it down. "I expect."

They were silent for a time.

Her breathing thin, she kept her palms on the table so her dizziness would pass. Finally, she looked up at Rick. "Should I feel responsible?"

"For what?" he asked. "Stopping assholes like Fred Morehouse from being abusive?"

She glanced at the shocked onlookers, heard a siren in the distance. "He *was* an asshole."

"Indisputably."

"But that doesn't mean he deserved to die."

"I never said he did."

Helen returned to their table, visibly shaken. "Isn't it awful?"

Lucy swallowed. "I'm in shock."

Rick took a bite of chicken. "Shock always gives me an appetite."

Lucy kicked him under the table.

Helen didn't seem to notice. Looking toward the cluster of people around Fred's table, she said, "I suppose this will cut the launch party short."

"We could schedule another one," Lucy said.

Rick looked at her, eyebrows raised.

Helen nodded. "That's a fantastic idea." She lowered her voice. "Not to sound like a ghoul, but the publicity will be even greater for the second event."

Rick swigged his beer. "Makes sense."

Helen looked at her. "Lucy?"

"I'm up for it if you are."

"I am," Helen said, smiling. Then, she coughed into her fist. "I suppose I should make an announcement."

"Do us a favor, though," Rick said.

"Yes?"

"Let us get out of here first."

Helen nodded. "Of course."

Rick finished his beer, indicated a red Exit sign in the corner. "We head out that way, we won't have to pass Fred."

"Good plan," Lucy said.

He scooted away from the table. "Let's pick up Chinese on the way to the hotel."

She twined her fingers around his. "Only if we get two orders of crab Rangoon."

"Why—"

"Because you always eat a whole order yourself."

He winced. "I thought you didn't like them."

"How can I? You inhale them the moment we get home."

He grinned at her. "You're feisty tonight."

"Wait till the hotel," she said.

They exited the banquet hall hand in hand.

FLAME TREE PRESS
FICTION WITHOUT FRONTIERS
Award-Winning Authors & Original Voices

Flame Tree Press is the trade fiction imprint of Flame Tree Publishing, focusing on excellent writing in horror and the supernatural, crime and mystery, science fiction and fantasy. Our aim is to explore beyond the boundaries of the everyday, with tales from both award-winning authors and original voices.

•

•

Join our mailing list for free short stories, new release details, news about our authors and special promotions:

flametreepress.com